DEATH
IN
BAYSWATER

A FRANCES DOUGHTY MYSTERY

DEATH
IN
BAYSWATER

LINDA STRATMANN

The
Mystery
Press

To
Tim and MEG

First published 2016

The Mystery Press, an imprint of The History Press
The Mill, Brimscombe Port
Stroud, Gloucestershire, GL5 2QG
www.thehistorypress.co.uk

British Library Cataloguing in Publication Data.
A catalogue record for this book is available from the British Library.

ISBN 978 0 7509 6362 6

Typesetting and origination by The History Press
Printed and bound by CPI Group (UK) Ltd

CHAPTER ONE

G uilty!' said the foreman of the jury. The word thundered in the packed and shadowy court like a blast from the trumpet of doom. It echoed from the throats of eager spectators, and as the doors were pushed open to release the scampering jostling crowds, the word preceded them, and flowed unrestrained through the corridors. Out it went, into the open air of the walled bail-dock, where prisoners waiting to be tried that day shivered as they reflected gloomily on their chances of meeting a similar fate. It sprang into the thoroughfare of the Old Bailey, where those unable to gain entry to the court had clustered in the autumnal drizzle, kept warm by expectation. 'Guilty!' they exalted, and hurried away to drink to the death of the prisoner, for there could be no doubt even before the judge had donned his black cap that Jim Price was going to swing for the cruel murder of his sweetheart Martha Miller.

'Guilty!' said the newsmen to the chattering telegraph, 'Guilty!' exclaimed the presses as they inked the good news into the morning papers, 'Guilty!' wrote the sketch artists for the illustrated editions under pencilled likenesses of the condemned man and his victim. Only one person was silent, and that was the unfortunate prisoner's mother, who, her initial cry of anguish muffled by the loud approval of the onlookers had sunk into a dead faint, from which it appeared she might never recover.

Cool rain was rattling the windows, but in his comfortable parlour, Inspector Bill Sharrock of the Paddington police was cosy and content. He had just eaten a good dinner and was sitting in his favourite armchair, warming his toes by the fireside, enjoying a pipe and a bottle of beer. The children had all been put to bed, the house was quiet and his wife Bessie was knitting him a new muffler. ·

Earlier that day Jim Price had been rightfully condemned for a murder that had shocked all of Bayswater. Sharrock had seen the body of his victim, a pretty young thing, who had trustingly and innocently loved the man who had killed her. Martha Miller had been stabbed in the chest and stomach more than twenty times in a frenzy of jealous rage following a rumour that she had been seen in the company of another man, a rumour that had since been proved false. Sharrock found it hard to understand how anyone could expend such savagery on a defenceless girl, and mused that had any man dared to show more than a polite interest in Mrs Sharrock, it was the man he would have sorted out, and enjoyed doing it, too.

Murder, he reflected, was thankfully rare in Bayswater, although that prying detective woman Miss Doughty had an annoying habit of uncovering old murders that no one had ever thought were murders in the first place. There was only one unsolved case at present, a nasty one, where the victim, a shop girl called Annie Faydon, had been killed while walking home from her work in the dim of the evening, her throat cut right back to the spine, and great disfiguring gashes made on her face. Sharrock felt sure, however, that the culprit would not kill again. Marios Agathedes was a young confectioner who, having come to England entrusted with the investment of his family's fortune, had recklessly lost every penny. He had recently been committed to the public asylum after being found wandering the streets in a state of hysteria. Agathedes, who had had some slight acquaintance with the murdered girl, was not fit to be interviewed, but the police, convinced that the perpetrator of such a gruesome crime had to be either mad or a foreigner, and preferably both, had decided not to look any further.

Other than that Sharrock had the usual assaults and burglaries and forged cheques to deal with, and a recent spate of window breaking, but the cold and damp were keeping most of the idlers indoors, and that suited him very well.

An urgent tapping at the front door disturbed the peaceful scene, and Bessie started anxiously, lest the children should hear. Once one of them was awake the other five would join in the unrest and then it would take time and careful soothing to get them to settle again. She knew better than to ask who might be calling at that time of night. As a policeman's wife, she already knew the answer.

Sharrock grunted and went to open the door. He was unsurprised to see young Constable Mayberry on his front step, the lad's pale face blanched by the shine of the gas lamps, rain spotting his pimpled cheeks like teardrops. Mayberry was often a close shadow to the Inspector in his work, and despite his inexperience, could show commendable reserves of courage and common sense. 'I'm sorry, sir,' said Mayberry, but there was a strange wild look in his eyes that needed no further explanation.

'All right, I'll get my coat,' growled Sharrock, and turned to see that Bessie had already brought it, his stout warm wool that repelled the rain if it was not beating down too hard. There was a touching little domestic scene as she buttoned the coat and saw to it that his old worn muffler was properly wound about his neck.

'Young woman dead, sir,' said Mayberry, as they trudged along the damp street, its paving stones slick with mud. 'Norfolk Square. Not sure who she is, yet, but looks like a respectable type, servant class. Clothes all wet, so she's been lying there an hour or more.'

'Drunk or killed?' asked Sharrock. Public drunkenness was not unknown in Paddington, and sometimes people staggered out of beerhouses, lay down in the street to sleep it off and were found dead next morning. Norfolk Square, however, was another matter, quiet and select. When its residents were mentioned in the newspapers it was usually in the births, marriages and deaths columns of the quality publications and not in the doings of the coroner's or police courts.

'Killed sir. No doubt about it. I whistled up Constable Cross and sent for Dr Neill. They won't move her until you say so.'

'Good.'

'It was a horrible sight, sir. I've never seen anything as bad.'

'Early days yet, lad, early days,' said Sharrock, reflecting that Mayberry would not have said what he did had he seen what Marios Agathedes had done to Annie Faydon.

That thought provoked a question that started eating busily away at Sharrock's brain, but he said nothing to Mayberry. It was a worry and he pushed it aside. No need to jump in too quickly and make the wrong assumptions. One murderer about to hang, another one locked away where he could do no more harm, that was nice and neat, just the way he liked it, but a third one, and in a fashionable square, that was bad. Most murders were simple; man strangles wife, wife poisons husband, man gets drunk and stabs his best friend; you didn't need to look far for the culprit. If a servant was dead in Norfolk Square, then, Sharrock reassured himself, most likely her killer was another of her class, and someone she knew well – probably rather too well. The guilty man would be in the cells before the week was out.

They turned on to Edgware Road, a broad busy thoroughfare that never truly slept. Nothing seemed out of place; carts and cabs rattled by, candles glowed from apartment windows, and if the people who clustered in shop doorways were up to no good then they did not, as the two policemen passed by with a searching glance, have the guilty look of murderers. The more peaceful residential streets they traversed on their way to the boundary of Norfolk Square appeared similarly untroubled by serious crime.

Norfolk Square was oddly named because it was not a square at all, but an elongated rectangle, where two rows of town houses faced each other, roughly north and south, across some pleasant enclosed gardens. To the west was London Road, leading directly up to Paddington railway and Praed Street underground stations, while the east was dominated by the Gothic spires of All Saints church.

'She's lying in the gardens under some bushes,' said Mayberry. 'They lock it after dark, so I had to climb over the railings. I only saw her because the lantern light shone off her – her lower limbs, sir.'

Sharrock did not know how much experience Mayberry had of female lower limbs, although from the young policeman's hesitation, he suspected not a great deal.

'There wasn't any – I mean her skirts weren't pushed up far, not as if there'd been any interference. It was just the way she fell, like she'd been struggling.'

Sharrock nodded. That was useful information. There was too much business with well-meaning people messing about with a body so the police never found it as the killer had left it and what were they to make of it then?

As they entered the square they saw a disgruntled-looking man, evidently the keeper of the keys, shivering in a doorway clad in a heavy greatcoat he had thrown quickly over his nightclothes. The gate was open and through it they saw the light of Constable

Cross's bullseye lantern shining on something that lay huddled on the ground, while the figure of Dr Neill crouched beside it. The glow polished the dark leaves of evergreen shrubs that grew hard against the railings giving privacy and shelter to the gardens, and a fine mist of raindrops sparkled in the air. Neill stood up and stretched his back as they approached. 'Ah Sharrock, you'll want to see this one before we take her to the mortuary. Nasty business. Dead about one to three hours I'd say, can't make it any closer than that. Her throat's been cut, so it was quick, which is more than you can say about what followed.'

Sharrock took it all in; the victim's youth, no more than twenty-five, the costume of a servant from a good household, the skirts rippled up to the calves, legs flexed in a last effort to escape before she died, boot heels pushing into the damp earth, hands resting on her breast, fingers clenched. The throat was laid open in a single wide wound, and bloody rain had pooled about the neck and shoulders, but it was the face that it was impossible to forget. One cut had not been enough; the killer had wanted not just to kill the woman but blot her out. He had carved at her, and what was most alarming, he had done so in a way that both Sharrock and Neill had seen before and very recently.

'Judging by this I'd say your Mr Agathedes is innocent,' said Dr Neill, 'and somewhere out there is a homicidal maniac on the loose who has done this twice and will probably try and do it again.'

CHAPTER TWO

rances Doughty, Bayswater's youngest and only lady detective, her morning newspaper unread, letters unopened, tea untasted, a breakfast egg congealing on its plate, was studying a marriage certificate. Her burly assistant Sarah Smith, not liking to say anything to interrupt such earnest thought, gave her a worried look, added a piece of bread and butter to the egg and pushed it closer. Frances ate them absent-mindedly.

It was only recently that Frances had learned that her mother Rosetta had not, as she had always been told, died in 1863, when Frances was three years old and her brother Frederick eight, but had, to the family's great shame, run away with a man. In the following January her mother had been living with that man in a Chelsea lodging house where she gave birth to twins, a girl who had died in infancy and a son who still lived. Frances had confronted her mother's brother, Cornelius Martin, with this discovery, and he had, after much soul-searching, revealed his suspicion that it was Rosetta's mysterious paramour, and not her husband William Doughty, who was Frances' natural father. Frances had long ago forgiven her uncle for hiding the unpalatable truth, something she knew he had done out of kindness, but her lost family were often in her thoughts, and sometimes she ached to find them. She did not even know if the younger brother she had never met, named Cornelius after her uncle, knew she existed. He had once been seen boarding a train at Paddington Station, and she could only hope that his destination was some good school where he was even now distinguishing himself.

It should have seemed obvious for Frances to use the skill and persistence that she brought to her detective work to try and locate her mother, but she had hesitated for a long time, afraid of what she might find. Every so often, overwhelmed by curiosity, she had dug a little further into the mystery, but had applied no concerted dedication to it. For most of the years of her mother's absence, Rosetta Doughty had known exactly where Frances was to be found, helping William at his chemists shop on Westbourne Grove, and yet she had not so much as sent a message. If she had ever entered the shop to glimpse her daughter she had done so under a veil of anonymity. William had passed away in 1880 in circumstances that would have engaged the attention of anyone who perused the newspapers, and had his presence in the shop been the only factor that had kept Rosetta from visiting her daughter she would surely have contacted Frances after his death, yet she did not. The business was now under new management, and had been advertised as such in the newspapers, but had her mother truly wanted to find her, she would easily have been able to do so. The new proprietor, Mr Jacobs, knew where Frances lived, and often directed potential clients to her address. The only conclusion Frances could draw was that her mother did not wish to see her, the prospect of a meeting being more painful than not seeing her daughter at all. Perhaps she thought that Frances would reject her as a dishonest woman, and revile her for abandoning both her and Frederick at such tender years. The inevitable distress Frances had felt on learning that she had been deserted had, however, been tempered by later thought. She had seen a letter written by her mother after the desertion in which Rosetta had begged her husband to be allowed to see her children one last time before their lives were finally severed. It was obvious that she loved them dearly, and perhaps she was more to be pitied than censured. Frederick had died in 1879 and Frances often wondered if her mother had ever visited his grave.

All this time Frances had imagined, indeed hoped, that Rosetta and her unknown lover, a man enigmatically referred to in the letter as 'V', were still together, living quietly, perhaps raising a family, and giving every outward appearance of respectability. They might even have married after William's death. This recently discovered document proved otherwise.

Frances had been trying to locate Louise Salter, an old schoolfellow of Rosetta's who had been a witness at her wedding to William Doughty in 1855. The Salter family had left Bayswater many years ago following a business reversal but Frances hoped that Louise might have corresponded with Rosetta and know where she was to be found. The registers in Somerset House held no record of either Louise's marriage or death, but an old Bayswater directory listed a Bernard Salter, silversmith, and the *Bayswater Chronicle* confirmed that he had gone bankrupt in 1858. An examination of records held at Somerset House revealed that Bernard Salter, silver finisher, had died in Tower Hamlets in 1864, leaving property valued at less than £30 and probate had been granted to his son, Vernon Horatio Salter.

A terrible thrill of excitement had pervaded Frances' body when she saw this name, the name perhaps of the man who was her natural father. Eagerly, she scoured the registers and found no record of the death of Vernon Salter, only his birth in 1837, which made him five years younger than her mother. If he and Rosetta had married after the death of William, it was too soon to know, as the most recent registers were not yet available for public examination. Frances had previously searched for a bigamous marriage under her mother's maiden and married surnames, and found nothing, but her new searches had uncovered a marriage record in 1865 for a Vernon H. Salter, in the fashionable district of St George Hanover Square. She purchased the certificate, and it was this horrible document that she was now examining.

Vernon Horatio Salter, son of Bernard Salter, silversmith (deceased), had on 3 April 1865 married Alicia Dobree, daughter of Lancelot Dobree, gentleman, with an address in Kensington. Louise Salter had been a witness to the wedding, the other being a Miss Edith White. For a moment Frances wondered if she had been led astray by a series of coincidences, but then she saw that the certificate gave Vernon's address as the same lodging house in Chelsea where Rosetta had given birth to the twins. The conclusion was inevitable. Less than two years after stealing Rosetta away from her family, her lover had deserted her for another woman.

Frances, feeling suddenly chilled to her soul, said nothing. She could have tried to discover more, but heart-heavy, the will to do so had drained out of her. She replaced the certificate in its envelope and put it in her desk drawer with the other family papers. By the time she returned to the table to sit there in silence, Sarah was clearing away the breakfast things. She gave Frances a wary glance, but did nothing to disturb her reverie, and took the dishes down to the kitchen. So this, thought Frances, was the bitter reward for her curiosity. She was the daughter of a woman who had abandoned her husband and children and a man who had left his mistress and child to marry money. She had always feared that by prying into her own history she might uncover something that it was better not to know, and now she had. What this might mean about herself and her character she dared not imagine.

Sarah returned with a fresh pot of tea and this had barely been finished when there was a knock at the front door. They exchanged glances of surprise, since no clients were expected that morning and Sarah crossed to the window and peered out. Frances and Sarah occupied the first-floor apartment in what had once been the family home of a man of substance. The other residents were elderly ladies of the most impeccable respectability, whose rare visitors were usually antiquated clergymen, or quiet females devoted to charity work. 'Two women,' said Sarah, 'one young one not so young, mother and daughter I'd say. Daughter holding up the mother who looks like fainting away any minute.'

'For us, I am sure.' Frances welcomed the distraction, reflecting that hard as her situation might be there were many others who had worse trials to endure. Perhaps, she thought, the reason that being a detective suited her so well was that she could make wrong things right, and thus avoid the tendency to transgression that she was now very afraid must lurk in her nature. There was just enough time to tidy the little table across which she interviewed all of her clients, make sure that the carafe of water was filled, and bring clean napkins for the wiping of moisture from foreheads and eyes.

All was in place when the maid announced that a Mrs and Miss Price had called asking most urgently to see Miss Doughty. Frances had, like every inhabitant of Bayswater, studied the reports of the trial of Jim Price although she had probably given the details of the case more careful attention than most. Although the clients who came to her door were more likely to be concerned about a lost dog or faithless spouse than presenting her with a case of murder, she thought it best to know all she could about Bayswater crimes, since in that small bustling part of London everything seemed to be connected with everything else, like the strands of a spider's web. She knew that the mother and sister of the condemned man had, despite the pain it must have caused them, attended every day of the trial, hoping that some miracle would occur to provide the vital piece of evidence that would prove his innocence. Even after the verdict was announced they had not according to the newspapers wavered in their belief that Jim Price had not murdered his sweetheart, a belief that, as far as Frances knew, they shared with no one else.

Frances asked the maid to show the visitors upstairs, and Sarah took up some knitting and settled into an armchair by the parlour fire. Her solid reliable presence was always a source of immense comfort. Sarah had once been a maid of all work when the Doughtys had lived above the chemists shop, but in her new occupation as assistant detective, she had become as indispensable to Frances as her ability to think. Sarah's strong arms had saved Frances' life on more than one occasion, ensured her health when sometimes she had been so absorbed in a problem she had almost forgotten to eat, and the former servant's stout common sense was an antidote to many a wild theory.

If Frances had entertained even a moment's doubt that the two women who had begged to see her were any other than the mother and sister of the convicted murderer Jim Price, that doubt vanished as soon as they entered the room. Mrs Price was a short round woman in her forties, though much aged with grief, her face, grey with misery, folded into deep lines. It was clear that she cared nothing about her appearance or comfort, but that her daughter had been making gallant efforts to tidy the wisps of faded hair that fluttered about her face, and ensure that she was well-wrapped against the autumn chill in a long coarse woollen shawl that constantly threatened to slip to the floor. Mrs Price, oblivious to heat or cold or anything but the pain within, clung tightly to her daughter's arm. The girl, who could not yet be eighteen, was a slender shadow of her mother, and looked almost too frail to support her parent, something she was achieving only through courage and necessity. Sarah rose at once to assist the struggling girl, and guided Mrs Price not to the straight-backed chair that faced Frances across the table, but a more comfortable seat by the fire. Mrs Price whispered her gratitude, and panted softly, the dry sobbing of a woman who had no tears left inside her.

'It is very kind of you to see us, Miss Doughty,' said the girl, looking relieved at seeing her mother so well looked after and almost falling into a chair with exhaustion. 'You must be so very busy, and I was afraid, as we had no appointment …'

'Think nothing of it,' said Frances quickly. 'May I offer you some refreshment? You both appear very fatigued.' As a rule Frances only offered her clients a drink of water but in this case she did not want either of them to faint or, in the case of Mrs Price, actually expire before the interview was over.

'It is very hard to think of food at a time like this,' the girl admitted. 'I do not believe mother has eaten these two days.'

Frances glanced at Sarah who nodded, and went down to the kitchen. It would not be long before a jug of nourishing hot cocoa and a plate piled high with bread and butter appeared. 'How may I help you?' Frances asked her guest.

Miss Price cast her gaze to the floor. 'I expect you have read in the newspapers about my brother, Jim.'

'I have.'

'We were allowed to see him yesterday. He is bearing up well, trying to maintain hope of a reprieve. But I fear that unless something new is discovered …' She sighed, a sigh that seemed to have been torn up from the depths of her thin body. 'We have met with Mr Rawsthorne the solicitor. He is writing a letter to the Home Secretary on our behalf. He mentioned you, Miss Doughty; he thought you might be able to help us. He said that you had often succeeded where others had failed. But there is so little time, eighteen days before the …' Her eyes filled with tears. The effort of saying the last word 'execution' was beyond her.

Mrs Price uttered a gulping sob. Sarah returned with the refreshments so swiftly that Frances felt sure she had found some cocoa ready-boiled and begged it from their landlady, Mrs Embleton, a kindly soul who had suffered far worse inconvenience with very little complaint since Frances had taken up residence.

'This is what you need,' Sarah told Mrs Price, in a tone that anticipated only compliance. 'Drink it all up!' As she poured the thick liquid into a cup a faint whiff of warm brandy enhanced the atmosphere.

'What is it you would like me to do?' Frances asked, as Sarah brought the jug to the table, poured cocoa for the daughter, and began to distribute thickly buttered bread.

Miss Price held the warm cup as one would have cradled a gift. Her fingers were pale and slim as bone, the tips abraded from long hours spent plying a needle. 'We want you to prove him innocent,' she said, earnestly. 'Jim has sworn to us on all that he holds most holy that he did not commit this dreadful crime. But it looked so bad for him when the police found blood on his hands and clothes. He has always said, and still says that the blood was not Martha's but that of a man he found lying in the street, a drunken man who had fallen, and whose face was bleeding. Jim helped him up and set him on his way, and that was how he was stained with blood.' She sniffed the aroma of the cocoa cautiously, then sipped.

'But the man was never found, he never came forward,' Frances observed.

'No, and it is possible, of course, that since he was the worse for drink he does not even remember the incident. Or perhaps he was doing something he ought not to have been doing, and dare not admit where he was. But supposing he could be found, and even if he is unable or unwilling to speak up, then some person who knows him might recall that he came home that night with blood on his face.'

Frances had undertaken and triumphed in harder tasks than this one, but not, she knew, in so short a time. 'I will see what can be done, but even if this man is found, and can tell his story, it may not ensure that your brother is exonerated.'

'I know that,' said Miss Price with a little quiver of her lower lip, 'but Mr Rawsthorne said that where doubt is raised in a case then a respite is possible. If Jim's life can be spared, if the — his fate —' at this, Mrs Price uttered a wail of misery, 'if it can be delayed by a few weeks while new witnesses are examined then there will be time for the police to find the real murderer.'

At least, thought Frances, with some relief, she was not being asked to solve the murder. Sarah disapproved of Frances getting involved in cases of murder, which seemed to happen quite often, and Frances, without even needing to look, knew that her assistant was frowning hard. 'Let us approach our task one step at a time,' she said gently. 'The first thing to do, I agree, is to find this witness. I can guarantee nothing, but I promise I will do my best.'

'Anyone who knew Jim would never have believed he could have hurt Martha,' pleaded Miss Price, 'why they were sweethearts since they were children, and we always knew they would marry one day. Martha was such a dear good soul, she would not have been untrue.'

The unhappy client was undoubtedly sincere, but Frances judged her to be a girl who would always think the best of others. She had not, as Frances had, come into contact with the worst elements of Bayswater – the liars, the cheats, the thieves and the cold-hearted murderers. 'I must interview your brother as soon as possible, it is essential that I hear the whole story from his own lips.'

'You'll need to write to the justices to get an order to let you in to see him,' advised Sarah, returning to her knitting. Frances could not help wondering how Sarah was familiar with the protocols of visiting a condemned felon in a death cell at Newgate, and decided it was best not to enquire, at least not until they were alone.

'There won't be any trouble about that,' Miss Price reassured them. 'Mr Rawsthorne told me that if you call on him he will let you have the paper you need. Mother and I have promised to go and see Jim once we had spoken to you. If you could come with us and tell him you were helping him it would give him new heart, I know!'

'Then we will go at once,' said Frances.

Miss Price turned to her mother with a brave smile. 'There, mother, what did I say! Miss Doughty will put it all right!'

Frances was not so confident, but she knew that there was no time to waste. Both she and Sarah would have to concentrate all their energies on the task. She examined her appointment book. 'Sarah, while I am out I would like you to send a note to Ratty to say that I want to see him later today. Then could you study the newspaper account of Mr Price's trial and make a list of all the witnesses and most especially anyone who was mentioned in court but did not appear. I will need to see them all. I have one client calling this afternoon, it's Mr Candy again; if I am not back in time, see him and find out what he needs.'

Sarah nodded. Ratty was one of a band of messenger boys who knew the streets of Bayswater and the comings and goings of its inhabitants better than anyone. Sarah's young relative Tom Smith had organised what might have been a ragged rabble into a flourishing concern that fetched and delivered anything and everything all over west London with speed and reliability, and counted Ratty as one of his best 'men'. Ratty, a bright and industrious youth, harboured ambitions of becoming a detective and now commanded his own group of agents who were dedicated exclusively to carrying out searches for Frances. If anyone could find the man with the injured face it was he.

Frances and Miss Price helped the older woman down the stairs, Mrs Price murmuring grateful blessings on Frances with every step, and a cab was secured to take them to the office of Mr Rawsthorne. That gentleman had been the Doughty family solicitor for many years, and he and Frances' father William had counted themselves as friends. It was a matter of some embarrassment to Frances that one of her earlier investigations had inadvertently resulted in the failure of the Bayswater Bank which had very nearly ruined Mr Rawsthorne's business, but he had recovered from this setback and bore her no ill-will. Many of her clients came from his personal recommendation and she in turn was happy to direct those in need of a solicitor to him. She rather hoped that he would be available to speak to her that morning and she would not have to deal with his confidential clerk, Mr Wheelock, a scrawny young man with ink-stained teeth and an insolent manner, a hoarder of secret and sometimes damaging documents. Mr Rawsthorne's office occupied the ground floor of his handsome villa in Porchester Terrace, which ran north from Bayswater Road. There were no means by which the Price family could afford his services, but Frances knew that some solicitors took on important cases such as this with little or no fee, as success could be just as lucrative in terms of fame. She had not yet discussed her fee with her visitors and felt that a similar arrangement must have been expected and could hardly be refused.

The early morning fogs that had recently been such an unwelcome feature of the season had thankfully cleared, to be replaced by an unfriendly breeze, making a cool day into one that excited wintry shivers. Frances looked anxiously at her companions, but they appeared to be not so much impervious to cold, as accustomed to it. She was just boarding the cab when a voice called out and she turned to see a slight but energetic figure, Mr George Ibbitson of the *Bayswater Chronicle*, running up waving his hand. Ibbitson was a seventeen-year-old clerk, who having displayed both promise and enthusiasm, was currently being instructed by his superiors in the ways of a newspaperman, and was always to be seen where there was information to be gleaned. He often called on Frances for the exchange of intelligence. 'Miss Doughty, have you heard the latest?' he exclaimed.

'No, I have had urgent matters to attend to this morning,' Frances admitted, a little shamefacedly as perusing the newspapers and her correspondence was usually the first thing she did.

'I'll call on you this afternoon,' said Ibbitson, and hurried away.

Miss Price's expression was suddenly alight with interest. 'I think I know that young man. He was at the inquest on Martha, and the police court and trial. He –' she paused, and a little glow appeared on her cheeks, 'he was very kind to mother and gave up his seat to her when she felt faint.' Her face fell and she sighed. 'I suppose he might not have been so kind if he had known who we were.'

'He is a good young person,' Frances assured her, 'a junior correspondent with the *Chronicle* with excellent prospects. And I think he is kind by nature.'

Miss Price said nothing, but she appeared pleased, and a little wistful. She had obviously, thought Frances, been impressed by young Mr Ibbitson, but felt that she had little prospect of a better acquaintance. As the cab moved away, Frances studied her two clients more closely. Their gowns were poor and thin, yet neatly patched, Miss Price's reticule looked as if it had been made by cutting up a scrap of faded black velvet and adding a twisted cord, while holes in Mrs Price's shawl had been artfully concealed with darning that resembled rosebuds. There was care and love and a quiet fortitude in every stitch, demonstrating the family's constant struggle to make an honest living and appear tidy and respectable, but their rank in society was far lower even than that of a humble junior clerk with or without prospects.

'I read about your brother's trial in the newspapers, of course,' said Frances. 'Am I correct in that he claimed to have been drinking in the Cooper's Arms at the time of Miss Miller's murder?'

'Yes, but no one remembered seeing him there,' sighed the girl. 'It wasn't where he usually went, so his face wasn't known, and he knew no one there to speak to. Jim often liked a glass of beer at the Shakespeare on his way home from work, and poor Martha called there that night to speak to him, but he wasn't there.'

'I recall that the landlord at the Shakespeare said he remembered her coming in briefly at about ten o'clock to ask after your brother, and it was hardly more than five minutes later when her body was found in a shop doorway nearby. So we do have an accurate time for the murder. The prosecution case was that your brother's alibi was a lie, and he went to the Shakespeare, but didn't go in, as he encountered Martha in the street as she was leaving, then they quarrelled and he murdered her.' Frances reflected that even if Price had gone to the Cooper's Arms, which was just a few minutes' walk from the Shakespeare, after committing the murder, it was an establishment where bloodstained clothing did not excite comment. According to Price, however, he had not acquired the bloodstains until after leaving the Cooper's Arms.

'But he didn't do it, Miss Doughty! You do believe that, don't you?' pleaded Miss Price.

'I believe in uncovering the truth.' Frances was already sketching out in her mind a diary in which she would enter the events of the fatal night, moment by moment. She would have to establish the location of every possible witness throughout the evening, and since many of them were probably either too inebriated to remember, or unwilling for a variety of disreputable reasons to give an account of their movements, it would be a difficult task.

As the cab proceeded, Frances encouraged Miss Price to talk about her family and that of Martha Miller. The two households lived within a few doors of each other, not far from Richmond Road, which was a busy thoroughfare just off the main shopping parade of Westbourne Grove. A little to the north of the Grove was the uninviting entrance to Bott's Mews where the Cooper's Arms beerhouse was to be found, for those who really wished to find it. Just a few steps further on was the turning into Victoria Place, a narrow alleyway where two rows of small rented cottages faced each other across a cobbled track. Widowed Mrs Price, her son and daughter occupied the lower part of a cottage, the outside amenities being shared with another family consisting of a labourer, his wife who made paper bags, and two small children, who lived in the rooms above. Mrs Price had always been on good terms with Mrs Miller although the continued absence of Mr Miller, on what had once been referred to as 'a long voyage', was never discussed. It was generally suspected that the voyage had not gone very much further than Pentonville Prison, but Mrs Miller was an honest, brave, industrious woman who took in washing, sought no pity and never made a complaint. Martha was her youngest daughter, the two elder both being married and raising families of their own, and there was a son, Stanley, a carpenter who worked with Jim.

Alighting at the office of her solicitor, Frances went inside. She was shown into a waiting room and very soon a man who was a stranger to her entered and approached her with an envelope in his hand. A scrupulously groomed fellow in his thirties, he greeted Frances with a deferential bow and a confiding smile which was meant to be friendly but served only to arouse her distrust.

'Miss Doughty, it is my very great honour to make your acquaintance,' he began in a smooth, high and rather nasal tone. 'Allow me to introduce myself. I am Carter Freke, Mr Rawsthorne's confidential clerk.'

'A recent appointment I presume?' Frances wondered what had become of Mr Wheelock, who had dug himself deeply into the body of the firm like a burrowing parasite, so much so that she would have thought him impossible to remove without killing the whole.

'Indeed. Mr Wheelock, who you would no doubt have encountered previously, is no longer with us. He has gone on to …' There was a pause and an airy wave of the hand, 'higher things.'

'Deceased?' exclaimed Frances before she could stop herself.

Mr Freke tittered. It was not an attractive sound. 'No. Married.'

'Well, that is a surprise!' Frances struggled to imagine who in the world might want to marry the horrid Mr Wheelock and could come up with no possibilities.

'As it was to very many persons, so I believe. I have not met the gentleman but have heard nothing good of him. Mr Rawsthorne is with a client at present, but he told me that he was expecting you to call, and you would require some documents, which I have here. If you wish to make an appointment to see him he will be available this afternoon at five o'clock, if that is convenient.'

'Yes, it is,' said Frances, taking the envelope. She wondered as she returned to the cab whether she would have preferred to deal with Mr Wheelock after all. He was unremittingly unpleasant but at least she knew where she stood with him.

CHAPTER THREE

Frances had never before visited Newgate Gaol although she had read a great deal about that grim institution in the newspapers and history books. She was, however, rather too familiar with the Central Criminal Court in the Old Bailey, which lay adjacent to the prison, where she had sometimes been called upon to give evidence, and had seen men condemned to hang. Newgate Street was a busy thoroughfare with a characteristic stench, since it was much used by butchers and carriers, whose carts churned up straw, mud and ordure beneath their wheels as they passed, the debris being cleared away too rarely for any visit to be comfortable. It was not a place to take a pleasurable stroll, rather it was to be hastened along and left as soon as possible, or better still, avoided altogether. There were other far worse streets in the capital, but few so deeply shadowed with memories of the hangman's noose.

Necessary business still brought Londoners there, however, and as the cab turned into Newgate, Frances drew aside the window blind just enough to peer out in curiosity. Sour-faced men hurried by clutching dirty parcels, youths slouched past without a sideways look, hands thrust deeply into their pockets, and ragged children ran after them watching for opportunities to thieve, but there were also the idlers, drinkers and beggars who did not mind the aroma because they probably formed a part of it, or the history, which they relished in the telling, and they were not inclined to go anywhere.

If the dark granite gaol was meant by its appearance to inspire a dread of entering its gates in those who saw it then the architect had succeeded, but the worst of its days were behind it, and there had been talk of pulling it down. The time was mercifully past when felons were hanged outside its walls for anyone to see; that awful duty was no longer carried out in front of a filthy jeering mob who welcomed executions as free entertainment, but privately within, attended by only a very few approved observers. Gone also was the time when the cells were crowded with long-term prisoners of every description, and were breeding grounds for disease from which few hoped to emerge. Today the prison, although still lacking adequate sanitation or ventilation, housed only those who had been committed to take their trials and the condemned awaiting execution. One of those condemned was Frances' new client.

The cab brought them to a stout iron-studded door housed in a granite arch, and Miss Price stepped down, her mother leaning heavily on her arm, while Frances rang the bell. A servant answered and looked at their papers. He gave Frances a curious look before he ushered the visitors inside. Currently there were no prisoners awaiting execution who were there because of her handiwork, but the servant might not have known that, and Frances hoped he did not imagine that she had come to gloat. They were conducted to a small office where an ancient clerk in rusty clothes perched on a stool in front of a desk piled with ledgers, and were asked to wait. There was nothing to while away their time other than the requirement to enter their names and addresses in a record of visitors, and Frances brought forward a chair so that Mrs Price did not need to stand. Miss Price delved into her reticule, and produced a small green glass bottle with a pinch of salts at the bottom, and offered it to her mother, who waved the pungent item under her nose and pronounced herself better for it although she scarcely looked any different.

Frances' presence did, however, seem to comfort the unhappy mother, who reached out and took her hand and pressed it, wordlessly. Whatever the rights and wrongs, Frances felt determined to do all she could. Even if it should transpire that the trust of the mother and sister was misplaced and Jim Price had indeed murdered his sweetheart she wanted to know that he suffered for a crime of which he was guilty.

A uniformed officer arrived and gave the visitors a sympathetic look. 'Come along ladies, I'll take you to the consulting room, that will be more comfortable for you.'

'That is the room where the prisoners see their legal men,' explained Miss Price, with an expression of great relief. 'I am glad we are to go there because the cell where he is kept is such a terrible place. Mother finds it almost too much to bear.'

Mrs Price was helped to her feet, and the little party was conducted along a chill stone passageway. It must have been an illusion but to Frances she seemed to be travelling downhill as if she was being taken to a dark place from whence no one, neither the living nor the dead, could ever return to see the light of day. On the way they passed a door from which hot savoury fumes billowed, advertising the fact that the prisoners' dinner – some sort of greasy meat soup judging by the smell – was on the boil.

The corridor opened out into a large hall with a vaulted ceiling like old cloisters, where there were uniformed warders standing in attendance. In the centre of the hall, bulky square stone columns and low walls enclosed a room whose arched windows and door were glazed in thick plate glass. The room was furnished after the fashion of a counting house, with a desk and chairs. A young man wearing the coarse grey garb of a prisoner, his hair cropped close to his skull, was seated there, looking about him expectantly. Seeing the visitors approach, he sprang up with hope bringing a warm new light to his expression.

Their guide paused outside the entrance. 'We leave this door open when family are here so the warders can hear all that is said. You may converse, but you cannot touch the prisoner or pass anything to him. You will be watched, and he will be searched before you go.'

'Might I beg a cup of water for mother?' asked Miss Price. 'She is so very weak.'

'I'll see that one is brought,' said the officer, and withdrew.

As the women entered the prisoner exclaimed, 'Mother, Effie, and this must be …'

'Miss Doughty, yes,' said his sister, with an encouraging smile. 'She has agreed to look into your case.'

Frances had expected that the prisoner would be in irons, as she was sure she had read somewhere that this was the custom for those condemned to die, but he was not, and she felt thankful that this was another barbaric practice that had been given up.

'I am so grateful to you,' he said earnestly, sinking back into his chair. 'It gives me hope that someone like yourself believes me innocent!' Frances looked into his face, pale but unblemished, although thin lines of care and pain had drawn themselves about his eyes. His hands, which were loosely clasped and resting on the table before him, were those of an artisan. Frances wondered what it must be like to stare into one's own death, not after a long life lived well, but as a young man, seeing only a vanished future. She could not imagine how that must feel – like a bad dream, perhaps, from which it was impossible to awaken.

Frances had often looked into the bright open faces of men and women who had assured her they were innocent of any wrongdoing, and she knew all too well that words and appearances could hide the basest deceivers, and the most charming manners conceal a propensity to murder in cold blood. Despite this, she could not help but like the look of young Jim Price, his haunted brown eyes, broad shoulders and hands that did honest work.

'Mr Price,' said Frances, taking a seat opposite the prisoner and placing her notebook and a pencil on the desk, 'you may be sure that I will do my best for you. I have a great many agents who will today receive instructions to search for the man whose blood was found on your hands. But first of all you must make me a promise. You must tell me all the truth of your circumstances, and omit nothing, including most particularly anything that you might feel would place you in a bad light. If you lie to me, or leave out something of importance, and I find it out later, then you will not have dealt honestly with me, and I will not be able to trust you or act on your behalf.'

He nodded solemnly. 'I have heard of you, Miss Doughty; I know it is said that you seek out and expose all the secrets that people thought were long hidden, and I am sure I wouldn't dare try to hide anything from you, not that I think I have anything to hide.'

'Well then tell me your story.' She opened her notebook at a fresh page and took up the pencil. 'First of all, what is your occupation?'

'I am a cabinet maker, like my father was before. Apprenticed from the age of fourteen.'

'And Martha?'

'Martha was a shirt maker, and she helped her mother with the washing. We knew each other from children.' There was a brief silence as his hands tightened about each other, and he ground the palms together as if moulding clay. Frances wondered what words he was forming out of this hesitation. He took a deep breath. 'I'm not going to say that we never had a cross word, because all folk do from time to time, but there was never a bad quarrel between us. I always hoped we would be wed and I do admit that I sometimes worried about other men admiring her, but if they did it was all on their side. There was never any thought in her head that when she married it would be anyone but me.'

'At your trial it was said that you had quarrelled because you believed that Martha had been walking out with another man,' Frances pointed out.

He shook his head. 'That was all nothing, but it was blown up to look like something the way lawyers do. A friend of mine – Jonas Strong – one Sunday he came to take a cup of tea with us, and while we were just talking about this and that I could see that there was something on his mind. I thought at first that he was sweet on Effie, and had come to ask if he could court her. But then, when mother and Effie were out of the parlour, he told me that the night before he had seen a woman who looked very like Martha, with a bonnet on just like hers, and she was all cuddled up to another man. He said he hoped for my sake it wasn't her, but he thought it was. So the next time I saw Martha I said to her "What a nice story Jonas has told me" and she pretended to be angry saying I didn't trust her; that was the way we talked sometimes, teasing like, just pretending to have cross words, so then we could make it up and she would kiss me.'

'So are you saying that there wasn't a quarrel at all?'

'Yes, I am. We didn't know we were being overheard, and if it had been Mother or Effie who had heard us they would have known how we spoke, and took no notice, but the rent man had called and he heard us and misunderstood.'

'This was the man who gave evidence at the trial?'

'Yes. If I'd been allowed to speak I would have put him right. My counsel did his best to shake him, but he was so sure of himself, and that was what carried the jury.'

'But this story that Jonas told you – did it weigh on your mind? Did you give any credence to it?'

A warder called with a cup of water for Mrs Price, and her daughter helped her sip it. 'I know it troubled you,' said Effie quietly, 'but it was only a little bit.'

Price bowed his head briefly then looked up again. 'Well, I know I am to be honest with you, Miss Doughty, and I have to say that yes, it did eat at me a bit. I started to wonder if it was true or not and I thought the best thing to do was to go out and look about me to see if there was another woman with the same bonnet as Martha, so then I would know that Jonas had made a mistake. So that was what I did, then when I didn't find her, I thought I would go and see Jonas and ask him about it again. Jonas is an apprentice to a stationer's on Richmond Road. I went to see him at the shop but it had just closed for the day, and I thought he might be at the Cooper's Arms. I don't suppose you would know the place, Miss, it's on Bott's Mews. Not a place for ladies; I usually have my glass of beer at the Shakespeare; but Jonas says Cooper's is warm and the beer is cheap.'

Frances simply nodded. Due to a previous investigation she was better acquainted with the Cooper's Arms than she was prepared to admit.

'So I went in and looked about, but Jonas wasn't there. I thought he might come in later, so I had a glass of beer and waited for him, just sitting in a corner with my thoughts, but he didn't come.'

'Who sold you the beer?'

'A man. The landlord I suppose.'

'Did you see anyone you knew there?'

'No.'

'The landlord doesn't remember you. In fact there are no witnesses at all to your being there. Why do you think that is?'

'They can't have noticed me, sat where I was.'

'Where were you sitting?'

'As you go in there is a place to the right of the door where there are benches and tables, partitioned off. I sat there so I could watch for who came in. No one took any heed of me. There was a man and a woman sat opposite, but they were very close to each other, familiar, if you know what I mean, and talking their own business and never looked up at me.'

'Would you know them again?'

'I might, but I'm not sure they would want to know me. I guessed what they were up to so I made sure not to take any notice. After a bit I thought Jonas wouldn't be there that night,

so I finished up my beer and left. And it was while I was on my
way home that I saw the man in the street.'

Frances started a fresh page in her notebook. 'Where exactly
did you see him?'

'On the corner of Richmond Road and Victoria Place.'

'Describe him.'

Jim gave a wry humourless laugh. 'You never really think do you;
you see a man fallen over in the street and you go to help him on
his way and you don't imagine that one day you might have to find
him again and whether you do or not will decide if you live or die.
No fortune teller comes along and says "Make a note of that man
because you'll need him", you just help him up and go.'

'Anything at all,' urged Frances, 'any little clue. Try and picture
him to yourself. How old was he?'

Price was silent for a while as he explored his memory.

'Do try,' said Effie piteously, and Mrs Price gulped her
encouragement.

'Well,' said the prisoner at last, 'he was quite a bit older than me,
I'd say around Father's age if he had lived. Fifty perhaps. Short grey
whiskers, I think, but I wouldn't swear to it.'

'His height and build?'

'About my height, I think, middling. Fatter, but not very fat.'

'How was he dressed?'

'Respectable. Clerkish-looking. Not a labouring man.'

'Had he been drinking in the Cooper's Arms?'

'No, or at least I don't remember seeing him in there. But he
was very drunk – staggering drunk. Mumbling to himself. Then
his legs just seemed to go from under him, and he fell forward on
to his face. Cut his mouth. So I went and helped him up.'

'He cut his mouth?' queried Frances.

'Yes. There was a lot of blood running down his chin. He might
have lost a tooth.'

'He must have been very drunk indeed to fall on his face and
not protect himself with his hands as he fell.' Frances recalled her
days as an assistant in her father's chemists shop, and the walking wounded being brought in, usually elderly shoppers who had
taken a tumble on the Grove. The most common injuries were
grazed hands and fractured wrists.

'Oh, he went down very sudden, it was like a tree being felled.'

'Did you have any conversation with him?'

'I asked if he wanted helping home, but he didn't seem to under-stand me; he said something but I couldn't make out what it was.'

Frances tapped her pencil on the page, trying to think of what other clues might be extracted from the encounter. 'Were you able to determine what he had been drinking? Beer or spirits? It must have been on his breath. Or could it have been something else? A narcotic? Laudanum, perhaps?'

Price frowned and there was another long pause for thought. Frances had the impression that this was a question he had not been asked before. 'I don't remember a smell of alcohol, or lauda-num. I know the smell of laudanum all too well, Father was given it in his last illness.'

'When Father went drinking and he didn't want Mother to know, he came home smelling of peppermint,' Effie volunteered.

'Did this man smell of peppermint?'

Price shook his head.

'Was there any odour about him at all? I am trying to find some detail that might reveal his profession or habits.'

Price leaned forward, his chin on his hands, deep in thought. Frances found herself imagining what would happen to him in just eighteen days time, the coarse hemp rope, the pinions, the white hood, the sudden fall through the trapdoor, the violent jerk snap-ping his neck, all of this would happen if she could not prevent it.

'Orange peel,' he said, sitting up suddenly. 'I didn't think of it before, but yes, there was a smell of orange peel.'

Frances' busy pencil raced across the page. 'After you helped him up, what direction did he go in?'

'Up Richmond Road.'

'What did you do then?'

'I went home and went to bed.'

'Did you go to the Shakespeare that evening?'

'No. I never went down the Grove at all.'

'Is there a witness to when you came home?'

He shook his head. 'Mother and Effie were in bed asleep.'

'We were in our beds by half past nine,' said Effie. 'We didn't hear Jim come in.'

Mrs Price sniffed and sighed, as if she wished she could say something to help.

'Did you go straight to sleep?'

He rubbed his eyes. 'No. I lay there awake for a while, first, thinking about things, but at last, I did sleep. Then the police came in the morning and said that Martha had been found dead, and arrested me.'

'Do you own a knife?'

'Any number. I use them in my work. I don't carry one about with me.'

'I don't think the weapon was ever found,' said Effie, 'and the police looked at Jim's knives and there were none missing and none with blood on them. They said he must have had another one and thrown it away, but they couldn't prove it.' She gazed at her brother, and pushed her hand across the table, clearly aching to touch him, and comfort him.

Frances read over her notes. 'Is there anything else you can remember that has not already been presented at your trial?'

After a minute's thought he shook his head. 'No, but if I think of something I'll be sure to let you know.'

'We are allowed to come every day,' Effie told Frances. 'I'll let you know the moment Jim thinks of anything new that can help you.' She gave her brother an encouraging smile, and despite his situation he smiled back bravely.

Frances nodded, and drew aside to allow the little family group to sit more privately together. She was already planning how to start her enquiries, and an idea had occurred to her, one that might help discover the man who was Jim Price's alibi.

CHAPTER FOUR

Wh en Frances finally arrived home, having taken Mrs and Miss Price back to their cottage, and received their grateful thanks, she found young Mr Ibbitson of the *Chronicle* and Sarah sitting at the parlour table on which a number of newspapers were laid open. Both were bent over the pages studying the tiny print with great concentration. A teapot and cups were nearby and there was much evidence of biscuit crumbs but no evidence of biscuits.

Sarah looked up, grave-faced. 'There's been another murder. Body of a young woman found in Norfolk Square.'

'When did this happen?'

'Last night,' said Ibbitson, with all the enthusiasm of a newsman, and Frances had to remind herself that what was bad for the public was good for the newspaper trade. 'The inquest opened this morning. I've just sent my account in to the paper.'

'What are we coming to?' Frances exclaimed in dismay. 'That is the third murder in just a few weeks.' She peered into the teapot, and found it disappointingly empty.

'I'll freshen the pot,' said Sarah. She gave Frances a hard look before she left for the kitchen as if to warn her that she was not to agree to go running about looking for murderers while her back was turned.

Mr Ibbitson was a pink-cheeked youth who had not yet acquired the skill of growing whiskers. Frances had first encountered him during her researches at the *Chronicle* offices when he had been in awe of her and so eager to please that onlookers had insinuated he had developed romantic feelings. Whether or not this was true Frances had never sought to discover, although she thought it unlikely. His efforts to assist her were, however, speedy, effective and much appreciated. Frances suspected that just as she had a number of friends who advised her during her enquiries, so she in turn was being cultivated by Mr Ibbitson to become one of his friends who would be useful to him during his future career. He had a thoroughly disarming and very likeable manner, however, and she thought that he would go far.

'The deceased was a parlourmaid at one of the houses in the square, and her name was Eliza Kearney,' said Ibbitson. 'That was all I learned at the inquest which was adjourned for the post-mortem report, but —' here he made a significant pause, and looked very pleased with himself, 'I found out more later on.'

'From her friends? Surely not from the police?'

He grinned. 'Well, of course, as you know, the police must never give away anything to pressmen, and I dare not say who it was.'

'The police, then,' Frances concluded and he didn't contradict her.

'He couldn't tell me much, because they are being very secretive and my informant said it would be more than his job was worth to give any more away, but what I can say is that the victim's face was cut with a knife and it was in exactly the same way as Annie Faydon.'

He pushed a newspaper towards her, which was open at the report of the inquest on Miss Faydon. Frances was familiar with the case, although not with the progress of the investigation, and no one had sought to consult her on the matter, which was a relief. She reread the account to refresh her memory. 'Cause of death, a single cut to the throat, face mutilated after death. There has, as far as I am aware, been no arrest in that case.'

'No, and that's because the police thought they knew the guilty man, a Greek called Agathedes who went mad and was locked up only a few days later. But now they aren't so sure. In fact, I have been told that the police surgeon intends to report that in his opinion whoever killed Miss Kearney killed Miss Faydon as well.'

Sarah arrived with the teapot and slices of pound cake, and there was a pause for refreshment and thought.

'Sometimes,' Frances observed, cautiously, 'criminals will copy a crime that they have read about in the newspapers. Of course I don't suggest for a moment that someone who is not already a criminal will be turned into one just by reading about crimes. Many people do believe this, but I think they are mistaken.'

'There's folks wanting to ban the *Illustrated Police News*,' said Sarah. 'Pictures of men with knives and dead folk lying in their own gore,' she added with relish.

'We both read it and I don't believe either of us has been cor-
rupted by it,' Frances pointed out.

'That's true,' Sarah agreed. 'There's people I'd like to hurt if
I got half a chance but I wanted to hurt them long before I ever
read the *Illustrated Police News.*'

'And just think how many crimes there are in the Bible,' added
Frances. 'Everybody reads that.'

'It's not just that it's two stabbings,' said Ibbitson. 'It's the cutting of the faces afterwards, and the way they were cut. The papers
didn't print the exact details of what was done to Miss Faydon
because we were never told, so the only people who know are the
killer and the surgeon and a few police.'

'So there must be something similar about the two cases that
cannot be put down to mere chance,' Frances concluded, 'which
means that Mr Agathedes is innocent. I am sure his family will be
pleased to know it, but the police now have a very bad situation on
their hands. Logically, of course, it is far more probable that there
have been only two knife murderers in Bayswater and not three.'

Sarah nodded. 'Jim Price and the face-slasher.'

Mr Ibbitson's eyebrows darted up so high they almost disappeared into his hair, and he scribbled rapidly in a notebook, his
lips mouthing the words 'Face … slasher.'

'Of course,' Frances emphasised, 'you must understand that such
serious crimes are a police matter and not something I can be
concerned in.'

Sarah gave a snort that might have been a laugh, and Frances
recalled how many times she had said just that in the past and how
many times she had willy-nilly been plunged into the dark world
of murder.

'Oh, you could solve them quick as a blink,' teased Ibbitson,
'only I would never ask you to, of course.'

'But you are here for some purpose,' said Frances, with a smile.

'I am, yes. I know that you have a little army of boys who go
everywhere and are the eyes and ears of west London. Could you
ask them to keep a lookout for anything they think might be connected to the murders? The killer might think himself very safe,
and be careless and give himself away. Of course they shouldn't
put themselves in any danger – they could just make a note of

what they see and report to you. The police think the man will kill again, and the sooner he is caught the more lives will be saved.'

'I can see the argument for that. Very well, I will be seeing Ratty later on another case, and will instruct him.'

'And what case might that be?' asked Ibbitson eagerly, pencil poised.

'The case of Jim Price. You were in court for the trial, I believe.'

He looked puzzled. 'I was, but I don't see what can be done for him other than praying for his repentance before he hangs.'

'He claims to be innocent.' Frances saw that even at his young age, Ibbitson, from his reaction to this statement, had developed a mature cynicism. 'Oh, I know most condemned men and women do so in the hope of receiving a last-minute reprieve,' she added quickly, 'but there is a witness to his movements that night who has never come forward. I have been engaged to find that man.'

'Do you think you can do it?'

'I know; there is so little time, but I must try, and the *Chronicle* could assist me. I am looking for a respectably dressed man of middle height, perhaps a little plump, about fifty with short grey whiskers, who fell and cut his mouth in Richmond Road on the night of the murder and smells of orange peel. Can you publish that? All enquiries to me.' Ibbitson nodded and noted the description. Frances, observing his diligence and energy with approval, paused for thought. 'Miss Price was very grateful to you for assisting her mother when she felt faint in court.'

The youth looked a little pinker about the cheeks, and it was not from the warmth of the tea. 'I am sure the family are blameless.'

'Miss Price is a kind and dutiful daughter, and a loving sister. She could tell an affecting tale which if it was printed in the newspapers would move your readers to sympathy.'

'The family won't speak to the *Chronicle*,' said Ibbitson, with a regretful shake of the head.

'I'm not so sure about that. I think they would speak to you. Why don't I write to them and ask on your behalf?'

He brightened. 'Would you? That is very kind!'

Sarah had been perusing the newspapers again. 'I suppose there's no chance that whoever killed Miss Faydon and Miss Kearney also killed Martha Miller?' she said suddenly. 'I mean if two killers are more likely than three then surely one is more likely than two.'

'That is true as far as likelihood goes,' Frances agreed, 'but there
is a world of difference between a man who cuts throats and faces
and a man who stabs in the body.'

'Is there? They both use knives.'

The room was suddenly very quiet, and then there was a fierce
rustling as everyone picked up the newspapers and reread the
inquests on Martha Miller and Annie Faydon and the trial of Jim
Price. At last Frances put the papers back on the table with some
regret. 'Based on what I have read here I don't think Miss Miller
was killed by the same man who killed Miss Faydon.'

'Nor I,' said Ibbitson. 'Which is a great pity because it would
make a good story.'

'And save a man's life,' Frances reminded him. 'I am sure that
the police are taking another look at the murder of Miss Faydon
in the light of recent events, but I doubt very much that it will
prompt them to reconsider the murder of Miss Miller.'

'No, well that would mean admitting that they and the judge
and the jury and all the lawmen were wrong, and an innocent
man is in Newgate about to be hanged,' said Sarah, dryly. 'No one
likes putting his hand up to a mistake like that.'

There was a reflective silence, and Frances, recalling something
Miss Price had said, drank deeply of her tea. 'Supposing,' she began
thoughtfully, 'supposing I was to suggest to the police that they
ought to re-examine the death of Miss Miller in the light of the
two later murders. I could put the same idea to Mr Rawsthorne,
as well. I have an appointment with him later today.'

'Then you *do* think the same man did all three?' asked Ibbitson
in surprise.

'No, I don't, but it doesn't matter what I think, or even what
I can prove. What I need is time, time to find the missing witness,
or anyone else who might have information that could exonerate
Jim Price. It would be a miracle if I could prove him innocent in
the little time we have, but what I might be able to achieve is to
cast doubt on the verdict, enough to have the execution delayed,
or even commuted to life in prison.'

Ibbitson nodded, and there was a little gleam of anticipation in
his eyes. 'What a story that would be! The only thing our readers like better than demanding the blood of a villain is being

champions of the innocent. It gets them very excited. If there
was a public call for a respite it might carry some weight. Miss
Doughty, if you could write to Miss Price then I will go and see
her and promise to write something to be published that could
help save her brother. I know I am very green in these things,
and the *Chronicle* wouldn't let me write my own piece, but I do
have more experienced men to advise me.'

Frances smiled. No doubt the paper's senior correspondent
Mr Max Gillan would take all the credit. He was encouraging
Ibbitson in his ambitions, and must be enjoying the luxury of
having younger legs at his beck and call to do all the rushing about.

Frances penned the letter to Miss Price, and Ibbitson took it
away to the post. When on the scent of a story he always seemed
to move at a scamper. She appreciated his enthusiasm but felt it
sometimes needed tempering with better sensibility, something
she hoped would improve with maturity and experience. For a
brief moment she wondered if he was the mysterious 'W. Grove',
the author under this obvious nom de plume of a series of illustrated adventures featuring a lady detective, Miss Dauntless, which
had been proving very popular. This heroine, who was, Frances
thought, a fantastical and ridiculous version of herself, feared
nothing, and dared anything, and spent her days exploring the
most dangerous byways of Bayswater, pursuing and arresting hardened criminals. Some of Frances' clients thought she was similarly
reckless, and were disappointed when they found that she was not.
She had resolutely avoided trying to discover the true identity of
Mr Grove, although she liked to think that she could do so if she
wished, and then, she promised herself, she would have some firm
words to say to him.

There was a second letter for Frances to write. In the last year
her skills as a detective had brought her to the notice of the gentlemen of Her Majesty's government, who had realised that there
were some spheres in which a woman might move with more
ease than a man. She occasionally carried messages of a highly
secret and sensitive nature, and was well rewarded for her discretion. She knew therefore that any letter addressed by her to the
Prime Minister, Mr Gladstone, would be looked upon with favour,
and it was to him that she now appealed directly on behalf of

Jim Price. She had no great hope of success but felt that every avenue must be explored.

Sarah had been busy while Frances was visiting Newgate. Ratty was expected to arrive shortly to receive his instructions, and there was a paper on the table in the assistant's firm round hand listing all persons of interest in the Miller murder. Frances examined the list and saw that they fell into several distinct categories.

There were witnesses in the vicinity of the Cooper's Arms where Jim Price said he had been at the time of the murder. The landlord had testified at the trial that he could not recall having seen Jim Price that evening. Police Constable Stuckey, who had had the unenviable task of passing the establishment on his beat at closing time, said that he had not seen Jim or noticed any incident of a man falling in the street. Sarah had added her own observation that the pot man, the landlord's wife, and the customers of the Cooper's Arms had not been asked to testify, or any passer-by other than the constable.

The Shakespeare and that part of Westbourne Grove where the body had been found was the second location. The landlord recalled Martha coming in and asking if Jim was there. He had told her that he had not seen Jim that evening and she left almost at once. John Mackie, a bookbinder, had been drinking there and some five or ten minutes after Martha left he downed his glass of beer and departed. He had seen Martha's body in a shop doorway barely a few yards away, shouted 'Murder!' and ran straight back to the Shakespeare to give the alarm. The nearest policeman to the scene, Constable Cross, had heard the cries and come running.

Then there were the witnesses to the events leading up to the murder. Jonas Strong, who had imagined he saw Martha betraying Jim, lived above the stationery shop where he worked, sharing a room with another apprentice. Both were in their beds by ten o'clock. Jonas had wept as he gave evidence at the trial. He admitted that he had told Jim he had seen Martha with another man, but a few days after the murder he had seen the woman again and realised that he had made a mistake. Martha's mother and brother had testified as to the affectionate relationship of the young couple, but both thought that Jim was sometimes jealous if another man paid attention to her. They were adamant that Martha was true to Jim. Then there was Mr Seaton, the rent collector who had overheard Martha and Jim quarrelling only the day before the murder. For the defence there were a number of individuals who worked with Jim and were witnesses only as to his character, but they knew nothing at all about the events of the fatal night.

There was just time for Frances to see Ratty and also her client Mr Candy, before she departed for her appointment with Mr Rawsthorne. It was agreed that while she was so occupied, Sarah would speak to the landlord of the Cooper's Arms and discover if there were any other witnesses to be had from that quarter. She would also make enquiries at the Shakespeare to find an address for John Mackie and seek out any other possible witnesses.

'Sarah, I hardly like to ask, but I couldn't help wondering how it was that you knew about the rules of gaining admission to see a condemned prisoner at Newgate. It is only my curiosity, and you need not answer if you prefer not to.'

Sarah sniffed. 'Uncle of mine,' she said at last.

'And you went to visit him?'

'No, my Ma did. I wanted to go and see him hang but they wouldn't let me. Ma always thought he didn't kill that little girl but I knew better.'

Frances decided never to raise the subject again.

CHAPTER FIVE

No one, least of all Ratty, knew exactly how old Ratty was, or even his real name. He had been brought to Frances one day, a dirty child bundled in ill-fitting rags, the unwilling witness of an event that had proved crucial to exonerating an innocent man suspected of murder. That man, Professor Pounder, a noted pugilist and proprietor of a sporting club, was a tall, strong, handsome fellow, and the quietest, most peaceable individual imaginable. He and Sarah had been walking out ever since, and Sarah was employing her natural hardiness and vigour to conduct special ladies classes in callisthenics at the club.

In the last year Ratty had increased substantially both in height and confidence, grown out of two new suits of clothes, learned to read and become acquainted with the occasional use of soap and water. The only thing that discomfited him was the police, which since he looked to be a promising policeman in the making was a shame. A recent brief experience of being arrested and questioned at Paddington Green had not helped matters, although Inspector Sharrock had treated him more kindly than Frances had feared.

Ratty arrived at Frances' apartment with the jaunty air of a boy who, while probably about fourteen, was beginning to think of himself as a young man. There was a rolled up copy of a penny story paper in his pocket. Frances recognised the publication with some regret, but decided not to comment on it.

Having learnt his letters, Ratty, like most of Bayswater, enjoyed reading about the exploits of Miss Dauntless. The most recent edition was entitled *Miss Dauntless Rides to Victory!* The front page was engraved with a portrait of the heroine, clad in a thin, form-fitting chemise and bloomers, who, careless of all danger and the risk of indecency, not to mention pneumonia, was bowling along a busy road on a bicycle, her hair flying in the wind, in pursuit of a jewel thief. Sarah read all the stories too, and this one had made her chortle more than most.

''Orrible case of murder in Norfolk Square las' night,' said Ratty. 'Place is stinkin' wiv coppers lookin' f' clues.' He threw himself into a chair with such ease that for one alarming moment Frances thought he might put his feet on the table. Instead he stretched his legs out and admired his boots, which were nearly new and already much muddied. He took off his hat and scratched his head, then smoothed back his hair, which looked as though it had been greased, as it lay almost flat on his skull.

'This is the third such murder in Bayswater this month. So far all the victims have been young women, but anyone might be in danger, and you and your men must take care. The killer works in the dark and by stealth, and is able to make his escape without being seen. Ask your men to keep their eyes and ears open for anything suspicious, but if they should discover something they are to do no more than take note of what they see or hear, and inform the nearest policeman, then report back to me. They must never follow anyone to a place where they might be unable to get help, or approach any individual. Do you have sufficient agents for them to go about in pairs?'

'Fink so. I c'n always get 'em, that's fer sure, but it's gettin' the good 'uns, that's the 'ard bit. Bein' a 'tective is not fer anyone, Miss, you know that better'n most. So, what c'n I do fer you in that line?'

'You know, of course, that Jim Price has been found guilty of murdering his sweetheart Martha Miller, and condemned to death. He continues to maintain his innocence, and his one hope of an alibi is a man he says he helped up in the street outside the Cooper's Arms. I want you to try and find him.'

Ratty nodded sagely as Frances gave him the man's description. He never made notes, as he was still unused to the art of writing, but was easily able to carry all the information he needed in his head.

'I know there is only a very slight chance that he can be found and even if he is, it is doubtful that he will remember the incident, or be able to identify Jim Price as the person who helped him. But please do your best; there is very little time. It is also possible that the man who committed the most recent murders is also the murderer of Miss Miller, so any information on those cases that could help identify the culprit could also exonerate Mr Price.'

'You workin' on those cases?'

'I have not been asked to do so, and if asked I would refuse,' said Frances, as firmly as possible, not daring to glance at Sarah. 'All I ask is that your men add their eyes and ears to the efforts already being made by the police.'

'Solvin' them murders, that'd be a feather in yer cap 'n no mistake!' Ratty grinned.

'Yes, well, we are not the police,' said Sarah severely.

'W'd be better if y' were. I fink wimmin coppers'd be better'n the men. I bet they wouldn't punch the witnesses.'

Sarah sniffed as if to say that if the case required it she might do just that.

'Now then, Ratty, Inspector Sharrock might have shouted a great deal but he didn't punch you,' said Frances gently.

Ratty scowled. 'No, but I bet 'e were finkin' about doin' it.' He stood up. 'I'll get goin' then.'

'There is one other thing, and this is very important. This drunken man, the man who was so staggering drunk that he fell forward on to his face, and was unable to talk coherently – he did not, according to Jim Price, smell of any drink.'

'If he was that drunk he ought to have been reeking of it,' said Sarah.

'The other explanation is that he might have taken laudanum, but there was no odour of that, either. To someone familiar with it, it is quite unmistakable. I have been wondering about this. Perhaps the man wasn't drunk or drugged at all, but had been taken ill, and the reason he hasn't been found is that any attempts to discover him have been misguided. So Ratty, I suggest you direct your enquiries to finding not a man who was drunk, but one taken very ill in the Richmond Road area on the night of the murder. We may find him yet.'

Mr Candy, who had an appointment to see Frances that afternoon, was a regular client. He was a serious young gentleman of an unusual type, enjoying independent means and therefore with every excuse to be idle, who nevertheless liked to make himself useful to society and so gave generously of his time, devoting it to the good of others. He acted as secretary to a number of charities, a free dispensary for the poor, assistance to the families of injured work-men, and a hospital for incurable children. He often asked Frances to check on the bona fides of claims on behalf of the workmen, some of whom had proved to be capable of going out and doing a full day's labour while supposedly confined to bed with a broken leg, or had recovered from near-fatal falls with surprising rapid-ity. Frances sometimes wondered if Mr Candy's charitable works were undertaken not so much out of a selfless desire to assist the needy, or even to give him a respectable occupation and an inter-est to pursue, but to court the approval of society, since he was in himself rather a bland person.

He had first approached Frances as a personal client earlier in the year, fearing that his betrothed, a Miss Digby, had asked to be released from their engagement because he had been slandered by a rival for her hand. Frances was not acquainted with Miss Digby, but sensed that from Mr Candy's point of view, she was not so much an object of affection than a suitable wife for a man in his position. While agreeing to end the betrothal in true gen-tlemanly fashion, Mr Candy's main concern was his reputation, and he wanted to know what had prompted the lady's change of heart. Frances had interviewed Miss Digby's father, and was informed that there had been no slander, although there was a rival. The fickle maiden had recently met a handsome youth called Pargeter, with attractive manners and connections to a minor title, and had fallen in love. More importantly, her feel-ings had been ardently returned. Pargeter was best known for his devotion to gambling, at which he was persistently unsuccessful, and Mr Digby confessed to Frances that he far preferred dull, sensible, plain Mr Candy to the spendthrift interloper, but had nevertheless bowed to his daughter's wishes. Her engagement to the new admirer, which depended on the lordling both set-tling his debts and not incurring any new ones, had not yet been announced. Not wanting to hurt Mr Candy's feelings, Mr Digby had asked Frances to inform her client that his daughter wished him well, but had decided that she was too young and uncertain of herself to take such an important step as marriage. Mr Candy, relieved that his reputation stood unimpeached, had accepted his disappointment with equilibrium, remained hopeful that his addresses might be received with more warmth in future, and buried any lingering impatience in his charity work.

Mr Candy usually arrived to see Frances with a businesslike air, and a neat bundle of documents. On this occasion, however, he looked unusually troubled. 'It is really too bad,' he said as he took a seat. 'I am very worried indeed. You know that the charities are run from a small office – we have a room on the corner of Kensington Gardens Square that suits us very well and there are two clerks who attend to most of the work under my direction. We are busy all the time – collecting and distributing funds, writing to our patrons, organising suppers and concerts, preparing advertisements, cards and leaflets. I do not spend a great deal of time in the office as I am usually visiting patrons and the families of injured workmen, and consulting the managers of the hospital and the dispensary about their requirements. I recently had a conversation with a patron, a Mr Hullbridge, who is a very well-respected man in Bayswater and who mentioned that he had sent us an envelope enclosing a twenty pound note for the children's hospital. It was delivered to the office by a servant who has been with him for fully twenty-five years and is entirely above suspicion.'

Frances thought that no one could ever be above suspicion, but said nothing and let him continue.

'As you have probably guessed, the records of the charity show that no such donation was received. I have not questioned my clerks, as I fear that one of them is a thief and I do not want to either accuse the innocent or induce the guilty to run away. What am I to do? How much has already been lost without my knowing it? How much more might be stolen before the culprit is unmasked?'

'Do you receive a great many donations in the form of bank-notes and coins?'

'Yes, but usually in small sums.'

'So a twenty pound banknote is unusual?'

'I would say so, yes. Most patrons will provide a cheque for such an amount.'

'Have either of your clerks suffered financial difficulties? Has either of them asked for an increase in salary?'

He shook his head. 'I know nothing of their personal circumstances. Both are paid according to the usual rates and neither has complained.'

Frances picked up her pencil. 'I would like the names and addresses of the two clerks, also the address of Mr Hullbridge and the name of the servant who delivered the envelope.'

Mr Candy looked concerned at this last request. 'I would rather not trouble Mr Hullbridge. He has already assured me that his servant cannot be to blame, and I do not want him to think there has been any mismanagement in the charity.'

'I promise not to trouble Mr Hullbridge unless it is necessary,' Frances assured him. 'And I know how to be discreet.'

'Yes, yes of course,' sighed her client. He provided the information and Frances wrote it down.

When Mr Candy had paid his most recent account and left, Sarah took a look at the names Frances had recorded and smirked.

Do you know any of these people?' asked Frances, hopefully.

'No, but I think I can guess who is lying.'

Frances removed the page and handed it to her. 'Mr Candy is very anxious that the reputation of the charity does not suffer.'

'It won't,' said Sarah, and there was something in her tone suggesting that others might.

CHAPTER SIX

I n what was proving to be an eventful day, Frances prepared to attend her appointment with Mr Rawsthorne, while Sarah's tasks were to interview the landlords of the Cooper's Arms and the Shakespeare. It was all a desperate rush, thought Frances as she boarded her cab, but no less than the case required, and after that morning's revelation concerning her own family she was more than ready to embrace any task that kept her mind fully occupied.

A visit to her solicitor, while usually a matter of business, was made more pleasurable by the nature of the man himself. Mr Rawsthorne was a gentleman of middle years with an assured manner and a friendly smile, and one of the few professional men Frances knew who did not underestimate her abilities, or feel that as a woman she ought not to intrude into any occupation that society had dictated was reserved for the male sex. Mr Carter Freke, whose efforts at being courteous and helpful continued to overstep the bounds of what might be thought strictly necessary, conducted her to the solicitor's private office.

Mr Rawsthorne greeted her with genuine warmth and she thanked him for his assistance in authorising her visit to Jim Price. 'I felt quite sure the case would engage your sympathies, as it did mine. I need hardly say that I asked no fee for my work but I could not turn them away. Whatever Price has done, I do feel for the family, who are undergoing an ordeal little short of torture. Their belief in him was very touching.' He gave a sad little shake of the head. 'How did you find him?'

'He was bearing up well, although I think he shows courage only so as not to distress his mother and sister. I am sorry to say he looked on me as his only hope. I feel it as a terrible responsibility. I will, of course, do everything in my power to help him, but there is so little time. I assume that you have already tried to find this witness, the man who fell in the street?'

'I have, if he even exists, which to be perfectly frank with you I am not at all sure about. But yes, I did employ an agent to make some enquiries and he found nothing. It is unfortunate that no one at the beerhouse seems to recall either this person or Mr Price being there, but then the Cooper's Arms does not attract the most law-abiding men in Bayswater, and those females who frequent it are not there for an innocent purpose. The result is that few of those who were there that night, even when they were not engaged in criminality, are prepared to admit it.'

'Even to save a man's life?' asked Frances despairingly, yet even as she spoke the words, she recalled how little it took for a certain type of man to kill. Such a man would not trouble himself to save another if it meant a brush with the law. 'Can the police not promise witnesses that they will not be prosecuted for any small offence they might reveal if they come forward? Has no one offered a reward for information?'

'The family has no means to offer a reward, and no private benefactor has come forward.'

'In the circumstances, it was very good of you to act for them.'

He smiled. 'I cannot claim entirely altruistic motives. Having one's name attached to an Old Bailey trial is payment of a sort.'

'Saving an innocent man from the gallows is payment enough for me.' Frances gave the matter some thought. 'Perhaps I might offer a reward? Or start a public subscription?'

'The public believes the man guilty, so I doubt you would attract many subscribers, although they might be prepared to send funds to the distressed family after Price is hanged. But my advice to you is: keep hold of your money. A reward would produce a dozen witnesses all with a different story. And to be honest with you, Miss Doughty, I think that finding both the drunken man and a witness in the beerhouse would not help our client. The Shakespeare and the Cooper's Arms are barely five minutes walk from each other, and we know the time the murder took place almost exactly. There was more than ample opportunity for Price to murder Miss Miller, leave the scene, have a drink at the Cooper's Arms to steady his nerves and then help this unknown man.'

'I had already come to that conclusion, which suggests to me that he is telling the truth. Had be been lying he would have invented a better alibi, or perhaps drawn attention to himself at the Cooper's Arms so that someone would remember him. But if I can find the man he helped, it will suggest that the blood found on him was not Miss Miller's.'

Rawsthorne held up a warning finger. 'Ah, yes, you say "suggest" which shows that you see, as I do, the flaw in that evidence. Even supposing Mr Price's story is true, and he did help this injured man, then the blood on his clothes could still have been that of two people, the drunken man and Miss Miller – how can one tell the difference? The two incidents, if there were two, were so close together, that both sets of stains were about the same age.'

Frances, with some regret, was forced to accept what the solicitor said. Her case was weak, and it seemed probable that nothing she could achieve would strengthen it sufficiently to save her client. 'At least if I can prove that the man exists it would demonstrate that Mr Price is a truthful man,' she said, knowing that it was a poor hope at best, and uttering a despondent sigh as soon as the words were said.

Rawsthorne leaned back in his chair and Frances thought that his sympathetic expression was more for her evident unhappiness than the fate of his client. 'I fear that will not advance us. He has been honest and truthful until now, there has been no argument about that.'

'There is no prospect of a higher intervention? Miss Price told me you have written to the Home Secretary asking for clemency.'

'I have, although it was more as a favour to the family than with any hope of success. It is usual in such cases to provide convincing arguments showing why the prisoner should be granted a commutation of the ultimate sentence, and I did all I could for him. I pleaded his youth, his formerly blameless life, his honest but poor family. I described the murder as an action committed in a moment of near insanity and then regretted as soon as done. He has not helped himself by refusing to confess, or I could have added his sincere repentance before God.'

'You did not suggest that he was innocent of the crime?'

Rawsthorne looked slightly surprised at this suggestion. 'No. I had no grounds on which to do so. The evidence was not in doubt, there were no other suspects, and the judge's summing up was very fair to the prisoner.'

Frances was thankful that her own letters had addressed this possibility. 'You will let me know as soon as you receive a reply?'

'Of course.' In the moments that followed Rawsthorne regarded her carefully. He could obviously see that she remained deep in thought and made no effort to end an interview which from her manner he could see was far from over.

Frances took a deep breath. 'Another possible argument in Mr Price's favour has occurred to me. One that has not previously been advanced.'

'Oh? I must say Miss Doughty, that a visit from you always produces something of interest. Please share your thoughts with me.'

'Did you know that the body of a young woman was found in Norfolk Square last night?'

'I had heard rumours of a new tragedy, yes.'

'I have been told that the police are of the opinion that she was killed by the same person who murdered Annie Faydon.'

'Well that is very interesting, especially to the family of the unfortunate Mr Agathedes, who was thought to have been responsible. Poor fellow. Mad he may be, but not it seems, a murderer after all.'

'Both of those murders occurred while Jim Price was in custody.'

'Yes,' he agreed, with a puzzled expression, 'but I still don't see …'

'It might be argued that the man responsible for those crimes is also the man who murdered Martha Miller.'

Rawsthorne opened his eyes very wide in astonishment. 'Do you really think so?'

Frances could not in all truth say that she did. 'I have not yet come to a firm conclusion, but I would like to make others think so, or at least entertain the possibility. Will you help me?'

He gave her request some thought, but she could see he was sceptical. 'I don't see that there is a great deal I can do. I can put your theory forward in the right quarters, of course. It will certainly do no harm.'

'Then that is all I can hope for. There is one more thing I must ask of you. I do not wish to intrude on a family's mourning but would you be able to discover if the Millers might permit me to speak to them? I am not sure if there is anything for me to learn from them, but I must be thorough.'

'I expect nothing less of you. I will write to them on your behalf and I am sure they will agree to a meeting. For what it is worth I can tell you that they, like yourself, are far from convinced that Mr Price committed the crime, although they cannot suggest who might have done so. They believe it was a passing stranger, a maniac, and Miss Miller was just unfortunate to be there.' His tone suggested that he believed this to be no more than a wild theory born of a blind refusal to admit the truth.

Rawsthorne's expression suddenly mellowed into a broad smile, and he gazed on Frances as a proud parent might. 'I don't know what your poor father would have thought of your progress and position in society but if I might be permitted I would like to take this opportunity to say how much I admire what you have achieved. "Thorough" yes, that is the word for you, also clever and determined. I wish I knew a dozen men with your dedication and energy in pursuit of what is right.'

'You flatter me, but I thank you for your sentiments. My father, I am sorry to say, would not have approved of my current course of life, although he was in a way responsible for it.'

An expression of pain and regret passed across the solicitor's face. 'My poor foolish friend,' he sighed. Nothing more needed to be said. When her father died, Frances had expected to inherit his business and savings and go on to study pharmacy, but discovered to her distress that bad investments had taken all his liquid resources and plunged him into debt. She had been obliged to sell the remaining assets and had only narrowly avoided bankruptcy. Her uncle Cornelius had offered her a home, and a more sensible young woman placed in such an insecure position would have gratefully accepted his charity, but Frances had instead dared to remain independent and launch herself on an amazed Bayswater as a detective.

Frances took the sad interlude as her cue to depart, and rose to her feet. She was just about to take her leave and Rawsthorne had risen to say his farewells, when her natural curiosity asserted itself and she sat down again.

'I have just heard that Mr Wheelock was married recently.'

Mr Rawsthorne's expression darkened abruptly, and he took his seat, grasping the padded arms with unnecessary firmness.

He was not merely concerned but, and this was very plain, actually angry. 'That is so.'

Frances caught the scent of something very interesting, and pressed on. 'It was strange that I read nothing of it in the newspapers. If there had been an announcement I would surely have seen it.'

'You would, but he took very great care not to have it announced. In fact I know neither the place nor the date when this wedding occurred. Clearly it was very recent but as to the location all I have been able to discover so far is that it was not in London. The whole affair was kept very quiet indeed – I would say secret – for fear that the lady's family would find out and try to prevent the wedding taking place. But I have my spies, of course, and they told me the news.'

'Who is the lady?'

'I am not sure if you know her other than by repute. She is a widow of some means. Her name is Mrs Outram.'

The name was immediately familiar to Frances, and the news was shocking indeed.

'Surely not?' she gasped. 'There must be some mistake!'

'I wish it was, but I am very much afraid it is true.'

Frances gathered her thoughts, 'But Mr Wheelock is a young man in his twenties, and Mrs Outram, if she is the lady I am thinking of, must be …'

'She has just turned seventy-two,' said Rawsthorne, heavily. 'Of course such marriages are not unknown, indeed we have had the recent example of Lady Burdett-Coutts, but her husband is a highly respected and well-connected gentleman, and I am sure,' he added generously, 'that despite the thirty-seven years that lie between them they have much in common, as well as great mutual esteem.'

Frances had seen Mrs Outram only once in passing and had noticed then that she was susceptible to the flattery of a younger man, but even so, there had to be limits, and the pasty-faced ink-smeared scarecrow of a clerk was surely beyond any woman's limit. 'Mrs Outram is mistress of a very substantial fortune. Has Mr Wheelock secured it all?'

'I am afraid he has. It was open to her, had she wished to do so, to place a legal protection on some part of her fortune to preserve it for the use of her heirs but it appears that she chose not to do so.'

'Were there children of her first marriage?'

'A son, who died very young. But,' and here Rawsthorne permitted himself a brief smile of triumph, 'Mr Wheelock does not know everything. I have my methods, too. Shortly after Mr Outram passed away leaving his widow a very rich woman, she made a will. After providing substantial bequests to a number of excellent charities, the residue of her fortune she left to be divided equally between the surviving descendants of her late sister, who died in India some years ago. There was a time when finding those descendants might have been a very difficult and lengthy proposition, but now that London and Calcutta may speak to each other by electric telegraph, our task is much simpler. As soon as I heard of the planned wedding I set my agents to work, and they discovered that there is just one descendant alive, in fact most probably her only living relative, a great-nephew, Mr James Chandler, who holds a minor government post. As soon as he was apprised of the situation he prepared to travel to London. Just before setting out he telegraphed his aunt, telling her to delay the wedding at least until his return, but this instruction she chose to ignore. He undoubtedly anticipated this, since he also engaged me to try and convince his aunt not to marry, and should she do so, to set in motion an action to invalidate the marriage on the basis that the lady was either coerced or not in her right mind. He then took the first steamer out of Calcutta. He is expected in Southampton within the week.'

'I think the lady is foolish, and easily flattered, but I would not say she has lost her mind.'

'I have spoken to her, and I must agree. I did consider engaging a doctor to judge whether or not she was compos mentis, but I found her remarkably sharp and sure of herself. Short of abducting her, which Mr Chandler had not authorised, there was little I could do. Foolishness is not the same thing as insanity or the asylums would be full to bursting. She can hardly be unaware of Wheelock's low origins, but many a woman of sense will cast that consideration aside if the husband is young enough. I feel sure, however, that he has not told her all his story.' There was a significant pause.

'His origins?' prompted Frances. 'His story? You deliberately incite my curiosity. You know you cannot hint at information without my enquiring further.'

He gave her a knowing look, not untrammelled with embar-rassment. 'It is only rumour, of course, and you must exercise due caution with what I am about to tell you, but his mother is said to be the mistress of a – house. A house of a certain kind, you understand. It is a profession for which she is said to be well suited having lived in such a house before. I have never met her or any member of Wheelock's family, but I strongly suspect that they are coarse individuals with little regard for the law. The one thing I would like to know is how Wheelock succeeded in this mercenary enterprise. He must have some hold over the lady, but I cannot imagine what it might be, as she always seems to have led such a virtuous life.'

'Ah,' said Frances, 'I might be able to assist you there.'

'Oh?' There was a twitch at the corner of his mouth, and then he leaned back in his chair with an air of comfortable anticipation and laced his fingers. 'Do please tell.'

'Mrs Outram's first husband was, as I am sure you know, a dedicated vegetarian. She, on the other hand, was not of that persuasion. Shortly after Mr Outram's death I was approached by Mr Lathwal, the secretary of the Bayswater Vegetarian Society, who was very upset. He informed me that Mr Outram had intended to make a new will leaving a substantial property to the society, and had even showed him a copy of the proposed will, which he had drafted in his own writing. When Mr Outram died, however, the only will that could be discovered was an old one in which he had left all his property to his wife. Mr Lathwal was hoping that I could discover what had happened to the new will but there was no evidence that it had even been drawn up, let alone signed, and Mr Outram's advisor, Mr Thomas Whibley, was recently deceased. Mr Lathwal believed that Mrs Outram must have found and destroyed the new will, but of course it would have been highly dangerous for him to say so without proof.'

Rawsthorne looked thoughtful. 'Do you think Wheelock had some knowledge of this?'

'Mr Wheelock, as you know, is a collector of information which can be damaging to others and therefore profitable to himself. He does not necessarily use what he has at once but is content to conceal it until the right moment presents itself.'

Rawsthorne gave a grunt of displeasure. 'What an abominable scoundrel.'

Frances could not help but give him a keen look. 'I am sure he has proved very useful to you over the years.'

'Oh, he has, I admit it, but in truth, I am relieved to be rid of him. If he has employed blackmail on Mrs Outram then he would be well housed in prison and I shall make it my object to see that he goes there. I am sure he must have a great many enemies who will share my view.'

Frances suspected that Wheelock was more dangerous than anyone, including even Rawsthorne, knew. Wheelock was no mere collector of curiosities and was far from being a crusader against wrongdoing. He had no moral sense and cared nothing as to whom he damaged, but did so for his own gain, or sometimes merely for the pleasure of it.

At the end of a long day, Sarah reported to Frances on her visits to the two public houses. She had also commenced enquiries regarding Mr Candy's missing twenty pound note and was confident of success, although for the time being was remaining smugly silent as to her suspicions. Her other news was that she had traced Mr Seaton, the rent collector who had seen the quarrel between Jim Price and Martha, and he was willing to spare a few minutes of his valuable time to answer questions.

The landlord of the Cooper's Arms had told Sarah that nothing would please him more than to assist both the police and detectives concerning the comings and goings of his customers on the night of Martha Miller's death, but regretted that he was unable to do so. He had his regulars, of course, but he wasn't able to identify any of them owing to the unfortunate fact that he had a terrible memory for names and faces. He had a similar difficulty regarding days of the week. One night was to him very much like any other and even if he could remember selling someone a glass of beer, which was not an unusual occurrence given the nature of his trade, he could not say exactly when this event had taken place or to whom he had sold it. His wife and potman, by a curious coincidence, suffered from precisely the same affliction. All was not lost, however, since he intimated that certain sounds, like the chink of gold or the rustle of banknotes were often very helpful in improving both vision and memory.

Sarah came away with the certainty that dear as the cost of the landlord's evidence was, it would, if purchased, prove to be worthless. The Cooper's Arms was a place where a man might go either to be seen or not to be seen as his business might require and the landlord, whose memory probably rivalled that of the proverbial elephant, made it his concern to know which of his customers demanded which level of attention.

Mr Bonsall, landlord of the more salubrious Shakespeare on Westbourne Grove, was both pleasant and helpful, and charged nothing for his information. He confirmed that Jim Price, whom he characterised as a quiet and well-behaved young man, moderate in his consumption of beer, and who never gave any trouble, was a regular customer but he had not seen him at all on the night of Martha's murder. He remembered Martha coming in looking very concerned, to see if she could find Jim, and he had told her that Jim had not been there that night. As she left, Bonsall had glanced at his watch, so that if Jim was to come in later he would be able to tell him when Martha had been in looking for him. It was then almost exactly ten o'clock. John Mackie had been drinking there at the time and they had had some conversation to the effect that Martha had some worry on her mind, but neither knew what it might be. The house was busy and no one heard any screams or cries from outside, but if there had been, he felt sure that they would have been heard. About five minutes later Mackie finished his beer and said goodnight. It was no more than a few minutes after that, that Bonsall heard shouts of 'Murder!', and Mackie had come hurrying back very upset and out of breath to say that he had found the body of a woman collapsed in a shop doorway and thought she was dead. Bonsall and some of the other customers had rushed out to see if they could help, and by then a policeman was running up with his lamp. He had recognised Martha straightaway.

Mackie lived in Redan Place, and Sarah had had no trouble locating him there. He was a seventy-four-year-old retired bookbinder, who was mainly supported by his son, but earned a few coppers doing small repairs. Sarah did not think him robust enough to commit violent murder, but had suggested he come and see Frances to tell his story. He took some persuading, but eventually agreed to do so if he received some compensation for his trouble.

'I may well end up keeping half of Bayswater in beer money,' said Frances, and Sarah did not disagree.

The interview she had planned for the next morning would, however, be a far harder prospect than Mr Mackie. The only way Frances could obtain any information about the recent murders in time to save Jim Price was from the police, and she already knew what Inspector Sharrock would think about that.

CHAPTER SEVEN

As Frances alighted from the cab just outside Paddington Green police station she heard a loud roaring from inside which was followed by Inspector Sharrock charging out of the front doors like an angry bull, holding a young man firmly by the collar and shaking him as a terrier might have shaken a rat. 'And don't come back or I'll have you in the cells!' he bellowed. The youth, a slender individual who seemed to be the least aggressive of persons, gave no resistance, but as he was released, stumbled, tripped and rolled down the front steps to land in a tangle of arms and legs at Frances' feet. Sharrock was holding a document case and unrepentantly flung it down after him. It burst open and sheets of paper soared up into the air and showered down like giant snowflakes. Sharrock shook his fist and on seeing Frances gave a double-handed gesture of despair and irritation, turned, and stamped back indoors. It was not a promising start to her endeavours.

'I hope you are not hurt,' said Frances to the young man who was sitting up and rubbing his shoulder.

'The main injury is to my dignity,' he said, cheerfully, pushing a drift of auburn hair from his forehead, 'which means no damage at all.' He jumped up and started picking up his papers, which Frances saw were pencil sketches. One, she recognised from the distinctive Gothic elevation of All Saints church, was a drawing of Norfolk Square, in which a policeman was shining his lantern on a body lying in the gardens.

'Is this your work?'

'It is indeed,' he said, brightly. 'Allow me to introduce myself.' He pulled a card from his pocket. 'Christopher Loveridge. I am a student of art, a future portrait painter to the wealthy and fashionable, but currently obliged to earn a humble crust by providing sketches for the penny illustrated papers.'

Frances supplied her own card and he read it with astonishment. 'Miss Doughty the famous detective? What an honour this is! How fortunate I am to make your acquaintance! You must permit me to sketch you.' He pulled a pencil from his pocket and searched through his papers for a fresh sheet.

'That is very flattering,' said Frances, 'but I am afraid I cannot permit it. I think it would be unwise to have my portrait printed in the newspapers. Sometimes my work requires that I should not be recognised.'

He had been about to commence the drawing, but stopped at once. 'Oh – oh yes, I do understand. Why, how very exciting!'

'I assume that you were visiting the police station in your capacity as a newspaper artist?'

'Yes. I have been sent to obtain pictures concerning the recent murder in Norfolk Square.' He selected a paper from his portfolio and showed it to Frances. It was a sketch of a young woman, a portrait study showing an oval face with too long a chin and too sharp a nose to be called pretty, but interesting nevertheless. 'This is the victim in life.'

'Miss Kearney? Is this taken from a photograph?'

'No, I was unable to obtain one, but I spoke to her friends and they described her to me. I showed them this result and they all say that it is a good likeness. My intention here was to obtain permission to visit the mortuary and portray the body, not a task I would relish, but the editor was eager for me to do so if at all possible. But as you saw the Inspector was most insistent that I should not. However, I will not leave without something of interest.' He began to draw swiftly.

Frances could not help but watch enthralled as the picture took shape as if by magic, and laughed as she saw Inspector Sharrock's angry features and raised fist appear.

'There are those who say that the camera will replace the artist, but I disagree,' said Loveridge. 'My eyes are a camera, but one that can take a portrait in an instant, without any machinery or preparation, capturing a scene that is there for a moment and then is gone forever. Where is the camera that can do that? Then my pencil acts as a darkroom and develops and prints the picture on the page. No chemicals required. I can draw the discovery of a body, something no camera was ever there to see. I can picture an accused in court where no camera is allowed. Only an artist can do this.'

'You have caught the Inspector's likeness very well. Not just his appearance but his character.'

'It is all in the face,' he assured her. 'The face is more appealing to me than any landscape. Sometimes I just stand in the street and watch passers-by and draw those whose features interest me. I have placed an advertisement in the newspapers offering to produce sketches of subjects gratis hoping that it might lead to a commission, but so far, I am sorry to say, without success.'

'I would be happy to recommend you. May I have some of your cards?'

'But of course!' He supplied them with a smile. 'And I really would like to sketch you. If I might be so bold, and speak as an artist, your face is very striking and characterful. It would make a wonderful study.'

Frances didn't like to mention it, but she thought that the young man had a pleasant face; not handsome by most standards, but engaging; although not being an artist she could not say if she might like to draw it. 'I will consider it,' she conceded, 'as long as you do not send it to the newspapers.'

His portfolio case had been re-stuffed with sketches, and he clasped it to his chest in a gesture of great earnestness. 'I promise faithfully I will not. It would be yours to do with as you wish. Oh, but I am delaying you! You must be busy on one of your enquiries. Are you looking for the murderer of poor Miss Kearney?'

'No, I hope very much that the police will catch him. I am acting for Mr Jim Price, who was recently convicted of the murder of his sweetheart and is currently in Newgate awaiting execution. He declares that he is innocent and I am looking for a witness who might be able to prove it.'

He stared at her in awe. 'I admire anyone who would take on such a task. I wish you good luck in all your endeavours.'

'And I wish the same to you.'

'I must take up no more of your time, every moment of which must be of great importance. I bid you good day and hope that we may meet again.'

'I am sure we will.'

Somehow neither of them really wanted to end the conversation, but at last he raised his hat, bowed, and they took their leave of each other.

When Frances entered the police station it was to find Inspector Sharrock standing glaring at her with folded arms, and the desk sergeant sniggering behind his hand.

'All right,' snarled Sharrock, 'since I know I can't make you go away, I can speak to you for five minutes but no more. But —' he waggled an angry finger at her — 'if you tell me you are trying to solve the murder of Miss Kearney I will have you handcuffed and taken away and locked up as a lunatic.'

The sergeant went red in the face and almost choked.

'There is no danger of that,' replied Frances, calmly.

'We shall see!' Sharrock jerked his head at his office door and she followed him in.

Inspector Sharrock had always had the untidiest office Frances had ever seen, but recent events had placed even further strain on the amenities. The shelves on the wall behind his desk were stuffed with folders and boxes, piled so high that they threatened to cascade on to the floor at any moment; the desk itself was invisible under disorganised heaps of paper, and a small side table for which there was barely space had been brought in to better accommodate further material. Frances looked about her in dismay.

'Yes, well if people stopped murdering each other round here I'd have more room, wouldn't I?' snapped Sharrock. He threw himself into his battered chair and rubbed a hand over his eyes. 'Well, what is it now?' He looked very tired and strained, and Frances felt quite sorry for him. All the weight of the murders that she had decided were not her province was falling on to his shoulders.

Frances took a stack of folders from the only available chair other than the Inspector's and finding nowhere to put them, sat down and rested them on her lap. 'I have been asked by the family of Jim Price to try and locate the man he helped on the night of Martha Miller's murder.'

'Oh yes?' said Sharrock with a distinct lack of enthusiasm. 'Well we haven't found him, and neither have we found the man in the moon. Perhaps they're off having a drink together.'

Frances knew far better than to be put off by this for even a moment. 'I was hoping that with your permission I might speak to Constable Stuckey whose beat led him past the Cooper's Arms that night.'

Sharrock's glance encompassed a world of weary skepticism. 'I don't know what you hope to learn from him, seeing as how he said all he had to say at the trial, and you must have read that in the papers.'

'But you don't object?'

He puffed out his cheeks. 'Would it make any difference if I did? I very much doubt it. I suppose I ought to be pleased you asked permission. Is that all?' he added hopefully, starting to rise from his chair.

'No,' said Frances and he groaned and flopped back into his seat again. 'I wanted to ask you if in the light of the two most recent murders the police are re-examining the Miller case.'

Sharrock was visibly startled by this question, and sat up straight. At least, thought Frances, she now had his full attention. 'Why on earth would we do that? We've got the man who did it. Found guilty in a court of law by twelve Englishmen and ordered by the judge to go and explain himself to his maker.'

'Is it not possible,' Frances ventured, 'that the person who murdered Miss Faydon and Miss Kearney was also responsible for killing Miss Miller, and that Mr Price is innocent?'

The Inspector gave a short bark of a laugh. 'I don't know where you get your ideas from, I really don't. The answer, Miss Doughty, is no, for the very good reason that the murder of Miss Miller and the other cases are clearly the work of two different criminals.'

Frances pounced on the revelation. 'Then you do believe that Miss Faydon and Miss Kearney were killed by the same person?'

He made a sour grimace. 'I'd rather not think so, but it looks that way, yes.'

'Would you care to elaborate on that opinion? Is it to do with the way they were killed?'

Sharrock growled, stood up, and pummelled at a pain in the small of his back. 'Did you know, that there are some things it isn't right that I should talk about with properly brought up young ladies? And you were properly brought up, weren't you? All these stabbings and cuttings – do you really want to hear about that?'

'Inspector,' said Frances very calmly and firmly, 'this is not about me, or what I want to hear, or ought to hear, this is about saving a man's life. I am fully prepared to risk being shocked and upset for that. Was it you who questioned Jim Price when he was arrested? Did he strike you as a man who might be guilty of such a horrible murder? I have questioned him and I believe that there is a good chance he is innocent and about to suffer for the crime of another.'

Sharrock pushed his hands into his pockets and walked up and down, his face furrowed with indecision. 'Martha Miller was killed by someone she knew,' he said at last, 'someone she trusted. She let him come right up close to her and she can't have been alarmed until the last moment because she was never heard to scream. The killer put his hand over her mouth –' he suddenly pulled a hand from his pocket and thrust it towards Frances, palm first and shaped like a claw, 'there are bruises on her face, the marks of his fingers where he dug them in hard –' the fingers clenched '– and he pushed her into the corner of the shop doorway; and then he started stabbing her. It was quick. I don't think she could have known what was happening.' His other hand came from its pocket, the fist bunched as if holding a knife, and he made a series of sharp thrusts. 'Stab stab stab, in the chest and the stomach. Twenty times and more. By the time she knew she was being killed she was too weak with fright to cry out.' His hands suddenly opened. 'Then he let her fall to the ground. I don't think it took more than a half minute, if that.'

Frances made an effort to look at him steadily despite the horror he had just enacted. 'Are you sure it was a man? She might have trusted a woman to come up to her.'

'A man or a strong woman. But I've never seen a woman stab over and over like that. Women put one through the ribs and then they're done.'

'Was there a lot of blood?'

He looked at her carefully, and judging that she was equal to hearing the rest of the story he went on. 'Less than you'd think. No arteries slashed, no spraying. A lot of it was soaked up by her clothes. I doubt that the killer would have been covered in it, and of course Mr Price wasn't. There was blood smeared on his hands and the front of his shirt. About what I would have expected.'

'And you have never found the murder weapon?'

'No. But the surgeon thought it was a very common kind of knife.'

'Constable Cross was the first policeman at the murder scene?'

'He was, and did what he had to well enough. But he didn't see anyone running away. I wish he had, that would have made all our lives easier.'

'Regarding the other two murders – you say that they were similar to each other but different from Miss Miller's?'

'Exactly. Miss Faydon lived in Douglas Place and we think she must have been followed there on her way home from the confectioner's shop where she worked. It looks like the attacker approached her from behind, pulled her head back,' he mimed the action with his left arm, 'and cut her throat.' A swift movement of his right hand. 'She could never have cried out with an injury like that, and would have been dead in about a minute. Then he dragged the body into the shadows, and used the knife on her face.'

'So it was also a very quick murder.'

'Yes, but Miss Miller was killed in the heat of passion; the man who stabbed her was angry. Miss Faydon's murder was a cold-blooded disposal, like slaughtering an animal.'

'Except for the cuts on her face. That was not the work of a slaughterer, surely. Can you describe them?'

Sharrock folded his arms with an air of great determination. 'I can, Miss Doughty, but I will not do so. I have said too much already and no further will I go. No point in having every criminal in Paddington carving up their enemies in the same style. I don't want to put ideas in people's heads – they've got enough there without it.'

'It seems as if the killer is signing his name to the murders. I can understand that you would want to keep those details confidential.'

He looked relieved that she didn't press him further. 'I see you understand me, which is more than the press do.'

'And Miss Kearney?'

'Out late visiting family, coming back to Norfolk Square where she worked. Must have been crossing the gardens before the gates closed, and the attacker came out of the bushes and surprised her. Same method as Miss Faydon, attacked from behind, cut throat, then the face.' This time he spared her the mime.

'Do you know what time she was killed?'

'The gates are locked at nine, so it was before then. The body was wet above from the rain but dry underneath, and it started to rain at eight. Judging by when she left her family and how long it took her to walk there, we think just before eight o'clock.'

'If the murderer attacked her from behind then there would have been very little blood on his person.'

'I think so. Maybe none at all. On the hands of course, but easily washed off at the nearest horse trough. And seeing as both attacks were after dark, it mightn't have been noticed even if there had been some on the clothes.'

'What kind of knife was used? The same common sort as was used to kill Martha Miller? Or something different?'

Sharrock was obviously feeling easier about discussing the finer points of knife murder with Frances, because he answered readily. 'The surgeon thinks it was long and thin and very sharp. Something like a filleting knife.'

'Oh,' said Frances, and the word came from her lips like a little gasp.

The Inspector frowned, obviously regretting his openness. 'Are you feeling faint, Miss Doughty? I wouldn't be at all surprised if you were.'

'I am quite well, thank you,' said Frances, quickly, trying to cover the sudden sense of alarm that must have been apparent in her voice and expression. She almost told Sharrock what she was thinking, but decided that she needed to have an urgent conversation elsewhere first. Before she departed, however, there was another idea she wished to explore. 'Tell me, have there been any reports in west London from women who have been attacked by someone with a knife and managed to escape or have been followed by a suspicious-looking man who did not confront them? Are there any descriptions to be had?'

'There are always reports of shady characters and some of them might even exist, but it's hard to get a good description, especially of someone who lurks in the dark. We're looking into all of that, with the vast armies of manpower at our disposal.'

'What you need is an artist,' Frances advised him. 'The kind of artist who works for the *Illustrated Police News*. It is a part of their skill to draw life portraits of people from witness descriptions.

If you had pictures like that then you could have copies made and sent to all the police stations in the area.'

'That's not a bad idea,' Sharrock admitted. 'Where would I –' his eyes narrowed suddenly, 'hold on a moment!'

'Where would you find a suitable artist?' Frances finished the sentence for him. 'Well as it so happens you have just thrown one down the front steps of the police station.'

'Only because he had the cheek to ask to draw the body in the morgue!' Sharrock protested. 'I'm not having anything to do with him!'

'He was only doing what his employers asked, and he may be very useful to you.' Frances handed Sharrock one of Mr Loveridge's cards. 'I have seen his work and it is excellent. Likenesses are his speciality.'

'Alright, I'll think about it.' Sharrock looked at the card and was about to toss it on to the heaped papers on his desk, then caught Frances' look and put it in his pocket instead. 'Not that the Paddington police will be in charge of enquiries after tomorrow.'

'Why ever not?'

'Because it's too big for us apparently. So Scotland Yard are sending us two of their best, Inspector Swanson – he's the same man who arrested the Brighton railway murderer last July – and a sergeant.' Sharrock smirked. 'You might know the sergeant. Name of Brown, used to be a constable here.'

Frances said nothing. She was only glad that the desk sergeant was not in the room to see her blush. Wilfred Brown was an active young policeman with a sympathetic nature and a handsome nut-brown moustache who had been very helpful when her late father had been suspected of poisoning a customer. He was also the first man who had ever made her heart flutter with anticipation at the thought that he might call to see her. Any hope of a closer acquaintance had quickly vanished when she had discovered that he was happily and comfortably married, his wife busy raising a brood of children. His good work on the poisoning case had led to promotion and a transfer to the detective division of Scotland Yard.

Since then, whatever yearnings Frances might have had for romance or marriage she had tried to put from her mind, not always successfully. She had no fortune to attract the greedy, and lacked beauty to invite shallow admiration. Any man who sought her hand would view her only as a useful wife and not a woman to be loved. If her role in life was to work hard and be useful, as would seem to be the case, then, she thought, she could do so just as well or even better on her own behalf. She had already had more than sufficient experience of unpaid servitude in her father's shop.

'Right, well if I'm to beat Scotland Yard to the prize I had better get on,' said Sharrock. 'I'll ask Constable Stuckey to call and see you, though I shouldn't think he has anything new to say. Oh, and Miss Doughty —?'

'Yes, Inspector?'

'No chasing murderers if you please, can you leave that to the men?'

CHAPTER EIGHT

Frances did not know how many knife-wielding criminals there were in Bayswater but she was unpleasantly aware of one specific individual known only as the Filleter because of the thin sharp blade he carried, and whose occupation appeared to be the collection of debts, at which he was reputed to be highly successful. Blood smears would never have been noticeable on his clothes, which were dark and very dirty. No honest woman would allow him to approach her because of his repellent appearance and rank smell, but he was more than capable of a swift attack under cover of night.

Two of Frances' friends, Charles Knight and Sebastian Taylor, or Chas and Barstie as they called each other, business partners and directors of the Bayswater Display and Advertising Co. Ltd, had in less fortunate days been so afraid of the Filleter that they had bolted for some considerable distance at the mere mention of his name. She had first met them when they had rushed into her father's shop to hide from him. Their differences with the Filleter appeared to have been settled without bloodshed, however, and in recent months they had even been known to employ him for his very special services. Now successful, prosperous and anxious to appear respectable, the partners were often approached by the police for advice in cases of company fraud, a subject in which they had considerable expertise. Frances decided that before she mentioned her suspicions to Inspector Sharrock she ought to at least discover if the Filleter might have an alibi for the murders, and if not, warn her friends that police enquiries might well lead to their door.

Chas and Barstie had recently opened a handsome office on the Grove, where the ground floor boasted a small reception area guarded by a youthful clerk, an office for the directors where they could argue and throw buns at each other in comfort, and a shared bachelor apartment. On the first floor a suite of offices was being let out to another business, and on the second floor a small space was occupied by the flourishing firm of 'Tom Smith's Men', the firm that employed Ratty. Tom, a careful and frugal businessman, paid a nominal rent to Chas and Barstie in return for undertaking errands and deliveries on their behalf. Unlike so many masters, Tom cared about the health of his 'men' and would not allow any of them to live on the street. An attic room, mainly used for the storage of stationery and therefore quite warm in winter, allowed those boys who otherwise had no homes to sleep indoors.

Frances was pleased to see that the office of the Bayswater Display and Advertising Co. Ltd had been made into a pleasant place for visitors, in that there were comfortable chairs, a side table with a carafe of water and glasses, and a number of framed prints on the walls depicting scenes of Bayswater's past. Most of the waste paper had reached the basket where it had been thrown, and the splashes of dried tea on the desktop were quite recent. Barstie was poring over some ledgers, following lines of small neat figures with a probing finger, and Chas was reading a financial newspaper while refreshing himself from a plate piled high with cakes. Both seemed pleased to see Frances as she often brought them lucrative business, and Chas leapt to his feet and announced that she had come at a most convenient moment as it was time for tea. The clerk was sent into the apartment behind the office to provide their requirements, and Frances was ushered to a seat from where she eyed the cakes, which looked very tempting, with anticipation.

Chas flung himself back into his chair. 'What may we do for you now, Miss Doughty? What frauds and cheats and embezzlers are poisoning the respectable businesses of Bayswater? Have no fear – we will find them out!'

'I am afraid it is a more serious matter. I am currently acting for Jim Price who is awaiting execution for the murder of his sweetheart Martha Miller. I expect you must have read about the case in the newspaper. I have been engaged by his family to locate a witness who might give him an alibi.'

The two partners looked suitably solemn. 'A bad business that, but not our line of work,' said Barstie, dubiously. 'If we could have given any evidence we would have done so already.'

'Following the murder of Miss Miller there have been two other murders in Bayswater,' Frances continued. 'In both cases the victims were young women, and like Miss Miller they were killed with a knife.'

Both Chas and Barstie were by now looking alarmed. 'I hope you are not getting involved with that,' warned Chas. 'I would be very unhappy if I thought for a moment that you were placing yourself in danger.'

'No, please be reassured that I am not directly concerning myself with those cases. But I am considering the possibility that the same man might be responsible for all three murders, which would, of course, exonerate my client, who was in custody when the latter two were committed. I have just come from speaking to Inspector Sharrock, and he has advised me that, judging by the injuries, the murder weapon was a long, thin, very sharp knife. Something like a filleting knife.'

The two men looked at each other and Frances allowed them to consider the implications of this news. Chas jumped up again, clasped his arms across his plump body, and walked up and down as far as the accommodation would allow, while Barstie rose abruptly and went into the apartment. A minute or two later he emerged ushering in the clerk with the tea tray, then once the tray was laid on the desk the clerk was quickly dispatched to his place in the reception area and the intervening door locked.

'I knew we should have had nothing to do with that creature!' exclaimed Barstie, accusingly.

Frances had already made her displeasure on that subject very apparent to them, and decided it would be of no value to say any more. 'If he is to be suspected of murder then I am duty bound to inform the police of everything I know about him, and their enquiry could lead to you. But it may be that you can provide him with an alibi, in which case I need not report him. Do you have any future appointments with him?'

'He's a bit of a law unto himself that one,' said Chas uncomfortably. 'We don't arrange meetings. He just arrives.'

'Do you have a record of when he was here?'

Chas gave a questioning glance at Barstie, who nodded. 'I just put "debt collection officer" in the appointment book since he won't give his name.'

'If I tell you the dates of the murders, you may be able to help,' said Frances.

'I'll see what I can do.' Barstie opened an impressively large leather-bound book. 'I read about the murders in the newspaper. Two of them that is. When was the third one?'

'Last night, quite late.'

'We usually shut up shop at eight and have dinner,' said Chas. 'That's what we did last night and we didn't have guests.' They both looked worried as if they might be considered suspects, although Frances had never thought of that.

She provided them with the dates of the murders of Martha Miller and Annie Faydon, and while they could not recall in whose company they had been on the first occasion, the second was the night of a banquet for Bayswater businessmen, when they had dined in a company of twenty-five others. Barstie's notes of the Filleter's visits showed that there had been two in recent months, neither of which provided him with an alibi for murder.

'I don't suppose you know where he is to be found?' asked Frances without any great hope that there was a convenient business card to hand.

'No, he's very careful about that,' said Chas. 'You don't find him, he finds you.'

'We will, of course, help the police in any way we can,' said Barstie, who was looking more assured now that he knew the business dinner provided them both with an alibi. 'As far as I am concerned the sooner this fellow is in custody the better. Then we may all sleep safer.'

'I suggest that you notify your clerk that should this man come here again then he is to slip out quietly unobserved, and find a policeman or a boy who can send a message to one – or better still several – to come here at once. I will advise the police of my suspicions, and your offer of assistance to them, and also alert my own agents to keep a careful watch and inform the police if they should see him. Even if he has not committed these murders, I feel sure that there are other crimes that could be laid at his door, and it would be to all our benefit if he could be apprehended.'

'Should the police ask us about this fellow what should we say is our connection with him?' mused Barstie.

'We can hardly say that we have employed him,' added Chas uncomfortably. 'Barstie, if there are any papers mentioning him, we had better burn them now.'

'You may determine whatever story suits you best,' said Frances. 'I believe in truthfulness, of course, but if a lie may save a life then so be it.' This scheme being approved to the satisfaction of all, Frances was about to take her leave when she glanced at the prints on the office walls and had an idea. 'These prints are very good in their own way, but would it not be even better to have portraits of yourselves? If you are considering it, there is an artist I can recommend.' She handed them one of Mr Loveridge's cards. 'He is due to become quite fashionable and his work would make a sound investment.'

When Frances returned home Sarah was still about her own business, taking a ladies class at Professor Pounder's academy and following her own suspicions regarding Mr Candy's missing twenty pounds. Frances was about to send for Ratty, but there was no need as he arrived of his own accord and was clearly very pleased with himself.

Ratty's enquiries up and down the Richmond Road had borne fruit. He had discovered a Mr and Mrs Gundry, a respectable tailor's cutter and his wife who lodged not far from Bott's Mews and the Cooper's Arms. Mr Gundry was a sober, slightly portly and grey whiskered man of fifty-four. He had not taken alcohol in twenty years, and most certainly had not done so on the night of Martha Miller's murder. That evening he had been visiting his sister, who lived in nearby Hereford Road, and who was, so Mrs Gundry said, 'in bed with her leg'. Mr Gundry's sister was very fond of oranges and he had taken her some as a gift. He had not been expected home late so when he was not back in their first-floor apartment by a quarter past ten, his wife had gone to look for him and found him collapsed at the bottom of the stairs, with blood coming from his mouth. Assuming that he had fallen down the stairs she helped him up to bed then fetched a doctor who said her husband needed rest and quiet. The next morning Gundry was very much worse, unable to walk or speak or do anything for himself, and when the doctor called again he suggested that the patient might have burst a blood vessel in his head. Only time would tell whether or not he would recover, and if he did, how much progress he might make. Mrs Gundry had read in the newspaper about Jim Price and his encounter with the drunken man, but told Ratty that she had not associated this event with her abstemious husband. Ratty had asked to speak to Mr Gundry but he was asleep and his wife did not want him disturbed, although she thought he might be able to receive a visitor next morning.

A quick glance at a map told Frances that Mr Gundry's journey from his sister's home to his own would have taken him past the corner of Victoria Place where Jim Price said he had encountered the man he had helped up. While this was very suggestive, as was the gift of oranges, she still needed to positively connect Mr Gundry with Jim Price, to establish that the two were in the same place at the same time, and that Gundry recalled the incident. 'I will write to Mrs Gundry,' said Frances, 'and ask if I might visit her first thing tomorrow and speak to her husband. Even if he is unable to talk to me, I might still be able to find out what I require. I will take a copy of the *Illustrated Police News*, the one with the drawing of Jim Price at his trial, which is a very good likeness. I am hoping that Mr Gundry can point him out, or at least nod his head and identify him as the man who helped him. If he can I will summon the police at once to act as witnesses to the identification. I will also go to see the sister who should be able to confirm what time he left her. She will recall the gift of oranges. Perhaps he peeled one for her, which would account for the scent. If I can only prove that Jim Price was telling the truth it might create enough doubt to save his life.' As she composed the letter to Mrs Gundry and the note to Inspector Sharrock concerning her suspicions about the Filleter, Frances had to admit to herself that her chances of saving Jim Price remained slender.

There was a knock at the front door and after a few minutes the maid, with a very unhappy look, announced that a man calling himself Mackie had come to see Frances but if she wanted him turned away she would do so. Frances said that Mr Mackie could be admitted, and the maid, with an unreadable expression, went about her duties.

Shortly afterwards, a great deal of wheezing and grumbling up the staircase heralded the arrival of John Mackie, the man who had found the body of Martha Miller. Frances had initially placed him on her list of possible suspects but once he appeared at her door, with bowed legs, watery eyes and gnarled hands, gasping for breath and reeking of stale tobacco and cheap beer, she realised that he could only have been a witness and a poor one at that.

The first few minutes of her interview were taken up by Frances attempting to convince him that their transaction was not to involve any large sums of money and she had no fixed schedule of rewards in which the more colourful the information he provided the more she would pay for it.

He grunted in disappointment, and muttered something about it being hardly worth his while to come. Frances was annoyed and spoke to him severely. 'Might I remind you, that Jim Price is an honest young man who will die in just over two weeks for a crime he did not commit unless I can help him. Of course I will pay for your time but your information must be the truth or it is worth nothing at all, and I will pay nothing for it.'

'All right, but there's not that much to tell. I want tobacco money at least.'

'You shall have tobacco money. Now, in your own words, what do you recall of the night Martha Miller was killed? Start with when you arrived for a drink at the Shakespeare.'

It was a rambling tale, full of inconsequential detail about his health and want of money and people he disliked, although he did remember those he had spoken to at the Shakespeare and who had stayed behind after he left, thus supplying a number of local men with alibis. 'Then Martha came in, all of a bother, saying she wanted to speak to Jim, her intended.'

'Did she say what it was about?'

'No, but she was upset about something. I thought he was wanted at home, perhaps there'd been someone took ill. Anyhow, landlord said he hadn't seen Jim that night, and he thought if he was going to be there he would have come by then. He said if Jim did come in he would say she'd been in looking for him. So she went out.'

'She arrived alone?'

'Yes.'

'Was she there long?'

'No more'n a minute or so. One or two offered to buy her a beer but she said no.'

'When she left, she was alone?'

'She was.'

'Did you ever see Martha with a man other than Jim? I mean a sweetheart, not just a friend.'

He shook his head. 'No nothing like that. She liked Jim, and only Jim.'

'Were there other men sweet on her?'

'Oh, well, she was a good-looking lass, and nice tempered, not like some, so there would have been a few, all right.'

'Do you know who they were?'

'No.'

'That night – did you notice when she left the Shakespeare if anyone followed her or left very soon after she did?'

Mackie looked about him and licked his lips as if he wanted a drink. The carafe of water on the table seemed not to meet his requirements. 'Not that I saw or would swear to.'

'The men who offered to buy her a drink – they didn't attempt any familiarities?'

He shook his head. 'Landlord won't stand for that, and they know it.'

'Did any of them leave after Martha did?'

'No, I know 'em and they were still there drinking when I went.'

'You don't know where was she going?'

'Back home I suppose but she didn't say.'

'Was she carrying anything with her? A reticule? A parcel? An envelope?'

'No, nothing.'

'How soon after she left did you leave?'

He held out a dirt-grained finger and thumb as if measuring the depth of beer in a glass. 'That soon. Not long.'

'When you left, how busy was the Grove?'

'It was quiet. Most of the shops had shut up by then. Not that many folk about. I didn't see anyone sneaking away if that's what you want to know. Not Jim nor anyone else; the police already asked me all that.'

'Was there much traffic on the road?'

'Might have been. A cab, a carrier's cart.'

Frances wondered if the murderer, seeing Mackie emerge from the Shakespeare, could have escaped unseen by leaping on to the back of a cart without the driver's knowledge and so been borne quickly away, but that might have applied to anyone, including her client.

She regarded her visitor carefully, wondering how good a witness he was. 'What is your eyesight like, Mr Mackie?'

'Used to be good when I was young. Not so good now.'

'How did you find Miss Miller? She was in a shop doorway. It was dark.'

'I didn't see her at first. I heard her groan, only it wasn't a groan, more like the last breath leaving her body. Do you know what that sounds like? I've heard it more than once and it isn't something you forget. I knew someone was dying there and I went to see.' He made an odd little movement of the fingers, the kind of anticipatory rubbing as if thinking of getting something and Frances realised that he had not gone to help, but to see if there was anything he could steal. 'I couldn't see nothing, as she was all in the shadows, so I lit a match and had the shock of my life. I knew it was her straightaway, she had a blue shawl, only there was all blood on it.'

'Did you touch the body?'

'What, and get blood on my hands?' He pawed at his neck, seamed with dirt under a grubby collar. 'No, or it'd be me in Newgate now and not Jim. No, I let well alone and went back to the Shakespeare for another beer.'

The last visitor of the day was the rent collector, Mr Seaton. He was a portly man of indeterminate age whose large unshaven jowls flowed over the collar of a long coat, which boasted many pockets, all so heavily stuffed with bundles of paper that the garment was several inches in depth. The coat, Frances realised, was effectively a travelling office, containing everything he required for his business, and he walked about in it as a snail travelled in its shell. He sat down and looked at his watch. 'You get five minutes of my time for nothing, and after that we talk terms,' he said abruptly, snapping the timepiece shut.

Frances had already studied Mr Seaton's testimony at the trial in which he had been adamant that Jim and Martha had quarrelled bitterly the day before she was murdered so decided not to revisit the facts, but test them.

'Then we will get to business without delay. Do you think that it is possible that the quarrel you overheard was not a serious disagreement but something more in the nature of joking or teasing?'

His glance was hard and unfriendly. 'I know what I heard! He asked her right out; demanded to know if she had been untrue with another man; and she said she had not. Then he said that she had been seen with this man, and she said it was a lie and then she cried. Real tears. Nothing joking or teasing about that!' he added sarcastically thrusting out his lower lip.

'Had you heard them quarrel before?'

'No.'

'So you have no way of knowing if that was the usual manner in which they had a disagreement?'

'No. I don't see that matters. I heard enough to know what was going on. I've heard people argue before,' he added with a sneer. 'If that was how they usually went on, then I'm not surprised how it turned out.'

'But according to your testimony you weren't in the same room as Jim and Martha. So you couldn't see the expressions on their faces, their gestures.'

'Didn't need to.'

'Where were you?'

'I was in the parlour waiting for Mrs Miller to fetch the rent money.'

'And where were they?'

'They must have been in the back, in the wash house.'

'My point is that if you didn't see them you can't know if Martha cried real tears or just pretended to. You don't know if Jim was really angry.'

'Well, I heard them,' he said obstinately.

'Was there washing being done? I know Mrs Miller takes in washing.'

He hesitated. 'Yes.'

'So was water boiling in the copper? And were clothes being plunged and rinsed? That would have made some noise.'

'I suppose so. I was in the next room, I didn't see all that.'

'And are you saying that with all that noise of boiling and washing you could tell that Martha was genuinely crying, and could tell just from their voices that it was a real quarrel and not a pretend one? Because Jim Price told me they used to have pretend quarrels because they enjoyed the making up.'

He made no reply but looked at his watch again.

'You have three minutes to satisfy me that I ought to believe your testimony at the trial.'

'Well I can see I won't do that!' he said scornfully. 'I know what I heard and I know it was a real quarrel and I stand by what I said.'

'I must remind you that your words, your assumptions, based on a conversation you may not have fully heard, will hang Jim Price.'

'Yes, and good riddance, too.' He looked at his watch again.

'You think he murdered her?'

'Of course I do. Everyone does except his own family. Who else could it be?'

Frances was concerned, although she could hardly say so to his face, that Seaton's memory and therefore his testimony had been coloured by his belief in Jim Price's guilt. 'Would you be prepared to re-think what you heard that day, and consider whether or not you might have been mistaken in your interpretation?'

'No, I wouldn't, and I won't. I'm not going back on my word.'

'I assume that you didn't discuss what you heard with anyone else until after you learned of Martha's murder?'

'Well that's where you're wrong,' he said with a triumphant grin. 'Because when I came home I said to the wife how there was an unhappy couple in the making round at the Millers and how Jim Price's jealousy could be the death of that girl. And when I said that she was still alive.'

CHAPTER NINE

Next morning, as early as was reasonable given the urgency of her mission, Frances went to the lodging house in Richmond Road to see what she could learn from Mr Gundry. The morning fogs were just dispersing and there was a fine damp mist in the air that swirled about her in the sharp and changeable breeze. As she drew near she saw something that she felt sure Ratty would have mentioned had it been there on the occasion of his visit the previous day. From the door knocker there hung a wreath of black crape. Frances touched the wreath and it was barely speckled with moisture. It had not been there long. She hesitated, but reminding herself that since the house was divided into apartments, there was more than one individual to whom this recent addition might apply, decided to give a firm knock at the door. After about a minute it was opened by a diminutive maid in a faded dress and greying cap.

Frances produced her card. 'Miss Doughty. I am sorry to intrude, since I see this is a house of mourning, but I have an appointment to see Mr and Mrs Gundry.'

The maid nodded with a doleful look. 'Missus is expecting you, but Mr Gundry died last night. You're to come in.'

Frances' heart sank, but she entered and followed the maid up the stairs to a door. A black ribbon was tied about the doorknob. The maid knocked, and the door was opened by a lady of some fifty years, clothed in widows' weeds. 'Miss Doughty,' said the maid, in a grim monotone, and Mrs Gundry nodded and ushered Frances in.

There was a small parlour, very tidily arranged, where a gentleman sat at a table with documents before him, his sombre suit and hat trimmed with black ribbon pronouncing him to be an undertaker. He stood and bowed very formally as Frances entered. 'I will take my leave of you, now, Mrs Gundry. I can assure you that all the necessary arrangements will be made without delay.'

He gathered up his papers, and Mrs Gundry, touching her fingertips to the mourning brooch at her throat, saw him to the door and gestured Frances to sit. 'May I offer you any refreshment?' she asked, with the air of one who expected all visitors to require this politeness.

Frances, reflecting that even an expected death can be shocking when it actually occurs, would have liked a cup of tea, but did not wish to put the new widow to any further trouble. 'Thank you, that will not be necessary. I am so terribly sorry to learn of your husband's passing. It must have been very sudden.'

Mrs Gundry sat at the table, with her new grief sitting beside her. 'He was never right after that fall,' she reflected. 'I don't really know what happened. The doctor said it was blood in his brain, but it was his mouth he hurt. When I found him on the floor his lip was cut open and one of his teeth was gone.' She took a small black-bordered handkerchief from her sleeve but did not use it; she just stared at it, waiting for the tears to come. 'What was it you wanted to ask him?'

Frances showed Mrs Gundry her copy of the *Illustrated Police News*, and pointed to the portrait of Jim Price. It was a good likeness and she wondered if it was the work of Mr Loveridge. 'I was hoping to show this to your husband to see if he could recognise the man in this picture. After his fall, was he able to tell you what had happened to him?'

Mrs Gundry shook her head. 'Never a word did he utter about that night. I'm sure that he knew me and he knew where he was, but he couldn't remember falling. I asked what had happened and he just shook his head. I told him that if I asked a question he was to squeeze my hand once if it was yes or twice if it was no.' That was when the tears started to flow, as it dawned on her that her husband would never squeeze her hand again.

If Frances' errand had not meant life or death for her client, she would have left her questions for another day, but instead she went into the small kitchen and made tea for them both, and they drank it until Mrs Gundry was able to talk again. For a while she spoke only of how they had been married almost thirty years without a cross word, and how devoted her husband had been to his sister who was his only family.

'Did you notice,' asked Frances gently, 'when he came home that night after visiting his sister, was there a scent of oranges about him?'

'I suppose so. He'd taken some to her; he didn't eat them himself, but she was very fond of them. They were hard for her to peel along of her arthritis so he had to peel them for her.'

'Did he often take her oranges or was it just that evening?'

'He'd taken her some before, but not recently.'

'What time were you expecting him home?'

'No later than ten o'clock. He never liked to be out after that. When the clock struck the quarter past I started to worry and I went down to look for him. That was when I found him at the bottom of the stairs.' Her black-bordered handkerchief was by now bunched into a damp knot, and she wiped her eyes with it.

'Do you know what time he left his sister's house that night?'

'No. I went to see Liza this morning to tell her about poor Bob, and she was that upset, I didn't think to ask her. Is it important?'

'It could be. Your husband could still provide an alibi for a man suspected of murder.'

'This man?' said Mrs Gundry pointing to the picture of Jim Price. 'I thought he was guilty.'

'Why is that?'

'Well he was found guilty at the Old Bailey wasn't he?' she said reasonably.

'True, but courts have been known to make a mistake, or sometimes new evidence comes to light later on that was never presented at the trial.'

Mrs Gundry did not look convinced.

'Was your husband perfectly well when he left his sister's house that night?'

'Now you mention it, she told me he said he thought he had a headache coming.'

'Do you know if anyone saw him on his way home on the night he was taken ill? Has anyone mentioned seeing him talking to someone?'

'No, but there are some round here who are up to no good and wouldn't want to say where they were.'

Frances reflected that if Mr Gundry had left his sister's house in order to reach his home no later than ten and had been found collapsed there at fifteen minutes past the hour, then his encounter with Jim Price must have taken place at a time which fitted her client's memory of events. The available time for Jim Price to have killed Martha and then arrive at Richmond Road was still there but it was shrinking.

'I would like to speak to your sister-in-law.'

'Well you can go round and see her if you like. She knows you were coming to see me this morning. She likes visitors.' Mrs Gundry gave Frances the address and she wrote it down.

Frances thanked Mrs Gundry and took her leave. The walk from the Gundrys' home in Richmond Road to the lodgings of Mr Gundry's sister in Hereford Road took Frances barely five minutes. Unfortunately she did not know how long the walk would have taken Mr Gundry. He had been taken ill on the way, but where and how much it had delayed him could only be guessed at.

Mr Gundry's sister, a lady of about sixty, was bedridden with arthritis and being attended by a nursemaid who looked to be no more than thirteen. Miss Gundry confirmed that on the night of Martha Miller's death her brother had brought oranges and peeled one for her, and that he had complained of a pain in his head before he went home. She was sure that he had left at about his usual time, between five and ten minutes to ten. If that was the case, thought Frances, then Jim Price's encounter with Mr Gundry had taken place very close indeed to ten o'clock, which was, as near as could be guessed, the time of Martha Miller's murder.

There was one piece of information which Frances thought the most powerful argument that Jim Price had been telling the truth. He had mentioned the scent of orange peel before Mr Gundry had even been traced. It was a very strong indication that the two had indeed encountered each other.

Once home, Frances wrote a full description of what she had discovered and had it sent by hand to Mr Rawsthorne, trusting to his skill to convert the facts into enough evidence for a reprieve. She also wrote to the Price family to advise them of her progress, and sent a note with the details of her findings and actions to Inspector Sharrock.

The rest of her day was occupied in interviews. It was, when she thought about it, a crowded and exhausting time, in which a

great deal of work had to be packed into a few days, but then she
pushed the idea away and drove herself on.

Stanley Miller, Martha's brother, had agreed to speak to Frances
on behalf of the family. He was short, square, and about twenty-
five, clean and tidy, with hands that looked as though they did
hard work. Frances, having spoken to the recently bereaved
Mrs Gundry, still shocked but keeping busy with the necessary
arrangements, was now faced with someone who had been consumed by the fire of grief and in whom it still burned. There was
a dark bleak look in his eyes, which were an open window to the
pain within.

'I am very grateful that you have agreed to speak to me,' Frances
began. 'I assume that Mr Rawsthorne has told you of the reason
for my enquiries?'

'He has, yes. Not that hanging Jim will bring Martha back.
If it did I would gladly let him swing. She was a kind, gentle
girl, the very best. She deserved a good man and a good home,
and every happiness in life.'

'I understand that your family is of the opinion that Jim is innocent of the charge?'

He stared at the table. 'We've all got our opinions,' he muttered.

'Please, share them with me.' Frances poured a glass of water
and he took it and gulped at it thirstily.

'Well, I thought he might have done it. At the trial, all that stuff
the lawyer said made me sure of it. Who else could it have been?
Jim can get jealous sometimes, I know that. It was only afterwards,
what with the other killings, that I thought maybe there was some
madman doing all of this.'

'Did you see Jim on the day your sister was killed?'

'Yes, I work with him so I saw him that day. He asked me
if Martha was sweet on another man. I said I didn't know, but
I didn't think so. I haven't ever seen her with anyone else. He said
Jonas had told him he had, but he hoped it was a mistake.'

'So when you gave evidence at the trial you thought Jim was
guilty?'

'Yes. The thing about Jim is that he was always very quiet. I know Martha liked that but it sometimes seemed to me that there was more going on in his head than he was letting on. That's not right, is it?' He didn't appear to expect a reply to that question.

'Was there anything you might have said at the trial but didn't; or anything that has come to your mind since then that you would like to tell me?'

He shook his head.

'Did your sister know Annie Faydon or Eliza Kearney?'

He looked puzzled. 'I don't think so. Are those the two women killed in the last weeks? I never heard of them before their names were in the papers.'

'Did she ever say that she had been followed by anyone? Or seen something suspicious or that made her afraid?'

'No. She would have said if she had.'

'Was there anything at all happening in Martha's life that might have led to her death? Was she in debt? Had she quarrelled with anyone? Was anyone jealous of her? Was there another admirer who she had spurned in favour of Jim Price?'

'We all loved her. No one would think of harming her unless he was mad or wicked.' He looked hurt and lost. 'I want the person who did this to suffer. If it was Jim, then let him hang. If not, then you find out who it was, and let me alone with him for five minutes.' He clenched his fists.

Constable Stuckey was about thirty and therefore something of a veteran of the beat. He had the solid look of a man who knew his job and knew Bayswater and would be a very dependable and valuable sergeant one day but probably no more than that.

'The Cooper's Arms?' he said, as Frances opened the questioning. 'If you don't mind my being blunt, it's all thieves and tarts in there.'

'Be as blunt as you please,' Frances told him. 'You were on duty on the day of Martha Miller's murder, were you not? The day that Jim Price said he was in the Cooper's Arms.'

'I was, though I had no reason to go in.'

'Did you go down Bott's Mews?'

'I did.'

'What time was that?'

'About half past nine. Saw a man and a woman there up to no good if you know what I mean, and told them to clear off.'

'Did you see Jim Price or Martha Miller that evening?'

'No.'

'Do you know a Mr Gundry who lived nearby in Richmond Road? He died last night after suffering a fall.'

'Yes, I remember him well. Little man, about fifty. Liked to complain about things. Noisy drunks on the street at night. Boys upsetting ash bins. I didn't know he had died.'

'Did you see him that night?'

Stuckey gave this some thought. 'I think I did. Must have been about nine. Not in Bott's Mews. He walked past me as I was heading up Richmond Road and thanked me for chasing the street boys away.'

'Was he sober?'

'He was always sober.'

'Was he carrying anything?'

'Now you mention it, yes. A basket of oranges. Don't know where he took them.'

'Did you see him again that night?'

'No, I don't think I did.'

'Where were you at about ten o'clock? Were you near Bott's Mews?'

He thumbed through his notebook, and shook his head.

Frances was now sure that with the evidence of the constable and Mrs and Miss Gundry she could piece together the events of that night, but whether it would be enough to save Jim Price she didn't know.

Jonas Strong was a short, thin, dark-haired youth with a narrow face, blotchy skin and a haunted expression. 'I know everyone thinks Jim had a reason to do it, but I won't ever believe it.'

'How well did you know them both?' asked Frances.

'Martha used to do my mending for me after mother died a year ago. That was how I met Jim, when I took my shirts round to her.'

'Did you ever see them quarrel?'

'Not as such, no. I mean, all sweethearts have a falling out sometimes, don't they?'

'Did they?'

'I know he wasn't happy if another man looked at her. But there was never anything in it.'

'And this story you told him, that you had seen her with another man, what can you tell me about that?'

He looked uncomfortable. 'It was a mistake. I said so at the trial.'

'But you must have been sure about it at the time, or you would never have said anything. You knew Jim could be jealous. Why say such a thing, something you knew could start a quarrel, if you weren't sure of it?'

He was silent.

'If you really did see Martha with another man you should tell the police and give them a description. Perhaps he is her killer. You wouldn't want to see Jim hanged for another man's crime.'

'I said, it was a mistake,' he insisted stubbornly.

'But you saw the woman afterwards? The one who looked like Martha? Who was she? Who was she with?'

'Why do you want to know?'

'I want to know everything. And I am beginning to find something very strange about this story you told Jim, as you are so reluctant to talk about it. I understand that you feel guilty about it, because it makes it seem that Jim murdered Martha out of jealousy. If there was another man, then you have no reason to protect him and every reason to try and save your friend.'

He shook his head. 'I can't save him! No one can! I wish I'd never said it now. All along of a silly story and now Martha is dead and Jim about to die, and it's all my fault!' There were tears in his eyes and he wiped a sleeve across his face.

'What do you mean by a silly story?' asked Frances, with a sudden suspicion of where the truth lay.

He sniffled. 'There weren't no other man. There never was!'

'You never saw Martha with a man?'

'No!' he wailed.

'In fact you never even saw a woman who looked like her with a man?'

'No.'

'You made it all up?'

Jonas heaved a ragged sigh and nodded.

'Why?'

'I don't know. I just said it for a joke,' he mumbled.

'Then it wasn't a very amusing one. Why would you joke about something like that?'

He gave an uncomfortable wriggle. 'It just came into my head.'

'I have spoken to Jim and I cannot believe he laughed.'

'I thought he would know I didn't mean it serious. Martha would never go with another man. She was true to him, she always was,' he added wistfully, and his lips trembled.

And now Frances saw the whole story. 'Would you have liked it if she had been untrue?'

Fresh tears began to roll down his cheeks, and he made no attempt to blot them. 'I didn't mean it to happen like this! Honest, I didn't!'

'Only you wanted Martha for yourself and she wouldn't have anything to do with you? And you knew she wouldn't believe anything you said against Jim so you invented a story about her in the hope that he would stop seeing her?'

Jonas blubbed.

'Did you kill Martha? I have a very short list of suspects and your name is at the top.'

'No! I was working late that night. Special order. I got three witnesses to prove it. Ask the police, they know. Didn't even get out for a beer.' He wiped his eyes. 'I'd do anything to take it all back.'

Effie Price called on Frances in response to her note and eagerly wrung from her every detail of her interview with Mrs Gundry. Her mother, she reported, was feeling a little better now that Frances was helping them, and had gone to see Mrs Miller. 'So you see, they don't blame Jim, either,' she said, plaintively.

Frances decided not to mention Stanley Miller's views, but reassured Effie that she would continue to press for her brother's innocence to be established. Although she had found the missing witness, the case was not, in her mind, over, and would not be until she had secured the release of her client. Even if she failed, and he went before the higher judge, the one who saw everything and knew the ultimate truth, Frances felt sure that she would always be looking for the evidence that would give his family peace.

Effie departed with new hope in her tired eyes, and said that she would tell everyone she knew what a clever and kind lady Miss Doughty was. She took one of Frances' business cards, promising to show it to anyone who needed a good detective.

At the end of a long day Frances and Sarah were discussing progress over mugs of hot cocoa when the maid came to the door. 'A gentleman asking to see you, Miss,' she said, cautiously.

'Did he say what it was about?' Frances was disinclined to see anyone else that day unless it was urgent.

'No, Miss. He gave his name as Mr Loveridge.' She proffered a card.

'Ah,' said Frances.

Sarah tilted an eyebrow.

'Please show him up.'

Sarah's eyebrow tilted a little more.

'I have met the gentleman,' Frances explained. 'He is an artist who works for the newspapers. I am hoping he may be able to assist the police with sketches of suspects in the recent murders.'

Sarah nodded but made no comment.

Mr Loveridge arrived and Frances introduced him to Sarah, who gave him her usual suspicious glance, but his manners were so pleasant and open, that even her distrust began to mellow a little. 'It is an extraordinary thing,' he said 'but the Paddington police, who were on the verge of arresting me before, have now asked me to create drawings for them of a man suspected in those dreadful murders. I have just called on two gentlemen, directors of the Bayswater Design and Advertising Company, who reported seeing a suspicious-looking man with a knife lurking about the Grove. I understand that they are friends of yours and they said that you also might have seen him. Not only that, but they have commissioned me to draw likenesses of them to hang in their office!

This has been a very successful day, and,' he paused and gave a shy smile, 'I believe I know whom I have to thank.'

'No recommendation would succeed unless the work was skilled,' said Frances. She beckoned Sarah to fetch another mug and pour cocoa for their visitor. They sat around the table and Loveridge produced some pages from his portfolio case. Frances studied the drawings. The face that was before her could hardly be seen without a shudder, with its intense dark eyes and malevolent scowl. 'Yes, that is he almost exactly, and you might also add rotting teeth. The hair is somewhat longer than in the drawing, unwashed and quite matted.'

Loveridge produced a pencil and darkened the teeth exposed by the sneering lips, then smeared in a curtain of hair. 'What an unpleasant-looking person.'

'And there is a foul stench about him,' Frances added. 'One might almost imagine he rolls in dirt and other still worse things in order to keep people at a distance.'

'That is a little harder to show in a portrait, however I will indicate it by giving him a more dishevelled appearance.' He made a few more swift strokes of the pencil, and Frances had to admit that he had the likeness so well it could not be improved upon.

He selected a clean sheet and began to draw again. Both Frances and Sarah could not resist a glance and as they watched, the parlour took shape on the paper; the comfortable glow of the fire, the easy chairs, and the little round table with its carafe of water and glasses and the silver case that held her business cards, a gift from her friend and near neighbour Cedric Garton on the occasion of her twenty-first birthday only a few weeks before. 'There, I have abided by my promise not to sketch you, but I do hope you will permit me to do so one day.' He handed the drawing to her. 'A present.'

Frances thanked him. 'I shall have it framed and put on display.'

'If you enjoy viewing art, some of my fellow students and I are preparing for an exhibition of our work next month. Would you like to come and see it?'

'Yes, I would like that very much,' she replied, but her expression must have revealed her inner anxiety, and thoughts about what that passage of time might bring.

'Does that prospect make you sorrowful?' he enquired, mystified.

'No, it isn't that, not at all, only every time I think even a few weeks ahead, all I can think of is the condemned man I am trying to help, and how little time he has. I wish I could do more for him.'

Sarah grunted. 'You're doing more than anyone else is. Everyone but his family and you have given up.'

'I wish you every success,' said Loveridge. 'From all I have heard, he is fortunate to have you working so hard for him.' He gazed at Frances admiringly, and then suddenly remembered the reason for his visit, and rose to his feet. 'I must take my leave of you now, as this sketch is required by the police. They will have it copied and circulated to all their constables and other stations too and I trust we will see this unpleasant fellow behind bars very soon.'

When he had departed, Frances looked at Sarah, who was clearing away the mugs and the cocoa jug.

'I know you would like to say something. So please say it. What do you think of Mr Loveridge?'

Sarah gave the question careful thought, then she shrugged. 'I don't mind him.' Frances was pleasantly surprised as, apart from Professor Pounder, who was a special case, it was the most praise Sarah had given any man.

CHAPTER TEN

Sarah enjoyed reading about famous murder trials from history, an activity she always carried out with the kind of comfortable smile usually associated with the consumption of cake. She had recently taken to entertaining Frances with stories from a book entitled *Tales of Old Newgate*, a compilation of blood-curdling adventures, which proved if nothing else that the current criminals of Bayswater had achieved levels of refinement in their methods, if not their ambitions, which were previously unthought of. There was a time, not so very long in the past, Frances had learned, when convicted murderers were executed within days of their trial. John Bellingham, for example, had assassinated the prime minister in 1812 and, following a trial only four days after the crime, was hanged three days later. Frances thought it a breathlessly hasty proceeding, which had no doubt emerged from a need for swift revenge and also to discourage other disgruntled citizens from repeating the process until they got a prime minister they liked. Bellingham, however, was undoubtedly guilty, as he had been seen committing the act, and then remained at the scene waiting to be arrested. Granting him more time for a defence would not have assisted his case or changed the outcome.

Judges of that era saw little point in delaying the inevitable. A criminal, they believed, required just a few days to repent and make his or her peace with God, and after that should be allowed to meet the Almighty without further unnecessary ado. But what, argued some reformers, if more evidence could be found to mitigate the case? What if granting more time enabled new witnesses to come forward and exonerate the condemned person? Was it not more humane to allow the prisoner's representatives to exert themselves to that end, and the chaplain to perform his duties, or was it less so, promoting false hope and doing little more than give additional gloomy hours for the guilty to dwell upon the approach of a violent death? In recent years three Sundays had been allowed to elapse between sentence and execution and, for Jim Price – as Frances was very well aware, as she prayed for him in St Stephen's church – this Sunday was the first one.

Sunday afternoon was a time for reading and reflection. Frances reread all her notes, and the newspaper coverage of the trial, hoping to find something that could give another direction to her efforts, but without success. Meanwhile there were letters to write and papers to tidy. Sarah had made progress in the case of Mr Candy's missing twenty pounds and needed only to trace one individual to question, although she felt sure she knew what the answers would be, and then she would unmask the culprit.

Next morning Frances was scarcely out of bed and dressed when there was a loud and very insistent knocking at her front door accompanied by a commotion in the street. Fearing some dire emergency, she looked out of the window and saw a crowd of people, many of them waving newspapers, all of them very agitated, and a few of whom she recognised. They included Mr Candy, and Miss Gilbert and Miss John, leaders of the Bayswater Ladies Suffrage Society. A police constable approached the gathering and tried to calm them, but they only pressed around him in a circle, chattering with great vigour, so that it was impossible to make out what any one of them was saying.

Frances' landlady Mrs Embleton came to her door and gazed at her reproachfully. 'I suppose these people wish to see you, Miss Doughty. I am not at all sure I want to allow them all in at once.'

'I don't think you should. I am not expecting to see them and do not have any appointments this morning. Perhaps if you were to admit only Miss Gilbert and Miss John, and tell the others to return later.'

'What if they all rush in at once?' objected Mrs Embleton. 'I cannot have such a disturbance in the house upsetting my other ladies.'

Sarah rolled back her cuffs as if she was about to pound a particularly stiff piece of pastry. 'They won't,' she snarled.

Frances decided to join Sarah and their landlady as they descended the stairs, finding the housemaid cowering uncertainly in the hallway. Mrs Embleton kindly sent the maid away and Sarah flung open the front door. She stood on the top step, hands on hips, shoulders squared, looking like something that was usually to be seen on the prow of a battleship.

'Now then, what's all the excitement?' she demanded.

Everyone turned towards her, and unsurprisingly no one dared to try and rush past her into the house. 'It is the early edition of the *Chronicle*,' exclaimed Miss Gilbert, breathlessly, pushing her way to the front of the surging crowd, her formidable bosom heaving with emotion, 'it says that we are all about to be killed!'

'I am afraid that is too true,' piped up Mr Candy from the midst of the sea of faces. 'The ladies of Bayswater are in great danger and I am here to offer them my assistance.'

'Is this to do with the Norfolk Square murder?' asked Frances.

'Oh but it is far worse than that,' said Miss John mildly, patting her cloud of grey curls into place. 'There is a terrible beast of a man who lives amongst us and kills for pleasure in the dark with a great knife and wallows in our blood. And then –' she paused for dramatic effect, 'he takes our faces away.' She elbowed her way deftly to the head of the throng like a surgeon making his first incision, and handed Frances her copy of the *Chronicle*.

It was open at the page of Bayswater news, where heavy black type had been used to create a heading that occupied almost half the length of a column.

FACE SLASHER
TERROR IN
BAYSWATER
FIEND KILLS
THREE WOMEN
POLICE HAVE
NO CLUES.

The article that followed described the three recent murders as the work of a homicidal maniac who had left the formerly safe and peaceful streets of Bayswater swimming in the blood of mutilated women. Nothing was known about the killer except that he was easily able to overcome and silence his victims, and wielded a sharp knife which he either plunged repeatedly into the bodies of his defenceless prey or cut their throats so deeply as to almost sever their heads. The killer then piled horror upon horror by disfiguring the corpses, carving great gashes in their faces so as to render them almost unrecognisable before disappearing into the night like a phantom.

There followed a heartbreaking account of the unfortunate Jim Price, who was languishing miserably in the cold dark of the condemned cell, doomed to be executed for another's crime, and the pathetic plight of his poor but honest family. The description of Mrs Price's suffering was extremely affecting and the writer confessed to having been moved to tears of pity at their interview. Her daughter, a beautiful, virtuous and modest girl of seventeen, was nobly bearing all the burdens of her family on her frail shoulders. There was, the article went on to reveal, a vital witness who could save Jim Price's life by giving him an alibi for the time of the murder. A description was provided, with a demand that he come forward at once.

The piece ended with three strident appeals; to the police, calling upon them to arrest the real murderer before any more outrages were committed; to the Home Secretary, urging him to release Jim Price at once, and to all the inhabitants of Bayswater, to be on the alert for the diabolical madman in their midst.

This was all alarming enough but the article appended an unconfirmed rumour that the clever Miss Doughty, who was known to solve the most baffling cases, had been engaged as a special advisor to the police, and it was hoped that she would soon be able to unmask the killer.

'Is it true that you are working for the police?' shouted a young man whose notebook and pencil pronounced him to be from the press.

'Do you know who the killer is?' cried another.

There was a sudden violent push towards Frances and the hapless constable tried to hold back the surge. Mr Candy darted forward and tried to help him, but not being of an especially robust build, he was not a great deal of help.

'Please, everyone, be calm,' Frances entreated, but her voice went unheard. The constable blew his whistle for assistance, and Sarah descended the steps and added her broad shoulders to the struggle. Miss John, as was usual in such circumstances, became quite excited, and produced a sharp bodkin from her reticule, preparing to defend herself from any assailant. Fortunately another constable ran up before she could do any damage, and the pressmen, scenting that they might be in trouble if they remained, took to their heels, and were pursued down the street by the policemen. With most of the crowd scattered, Frances was left with an exhausted and disheveled-looking Mr Candy, Miss John with a cheerful gleam in her eyes and Miss Gilbert adjusting her bonnet.

'This is Mr Ibbitson's work!' fumed Frances. 'I shall go straight up to the *Chronicle* and give him a piece of my mind! How dare he write such a thing and alarm everyone! And what he has said about me is quite untrue. Sarah, get a cab!'

'I wouldn't advise it,' gasped Mr Candy. 'There is great excitement in the Grove with a large assembly of people outside the *Chronicle* offices all demanding newspapers. If they saw you arrive it would only add to the disturbance.'

'He's right,' warned Sarah.

Frances tried to compose herself. 'Very well,' she said at last. Her visitors looked up at her appealingly. 'Please, everyone, come in.'

'I'll get the parlour ready,' said Sarah and hurried up ahead of them. Mrs Embleton gave a little sigh and a shake of her head and, much to the relief of Frances, who had anticipated being given a stern warning, or even notice to quit her lodgings, retreated to her rooms.

'But you *ought* to be advising the police,' urged Miss Gilbert as the visitors all followed Frances into the hallway. 'It would be a very splendid thing if you did. You are so much cleverer than they are.'

'I am not concerning myself with the two recent murders at all,' Frances told her firmly, 'I am acting only for Mr Price, who has been convicted of the murder of his sweetheart, and all I have been doing in that case is looking for a witness who can provide an alibi for him.'

Mr Candy looked doubtful. 'Do you think you will succeed? I read the report of his trial and there seemed to be a good case against him.'

'I have found some information that I hope will assist him, but I fear it may not be enough. Sadly, the witness, though found, has recently passed away, which is a great blow. I am sorry to say that if I am unsuccessful in convincing the authorities to quash the verdict, then two weeks today an innocent man will hang.'

'Is there such a thing as an innocent man?' wondered Miss John, in a tone that suggested that she rather thought not.

'I have interviewed Mr Price and he struck me as honest and respectable. And, of course, he will not be the only one to suffer. His poor mother is likely to die from grief and the plight of his sister is pitiful.'

Candy frowned. 'I wish there was something I could do to help the unhappy family, at least.'

Sarah appeared on the landing and gave a nod to say that the parlour was ready and Frances ushered her visitors up the stairs ahead of her. 'I have suggested to the police that the perpetrator of the two recent murders might also be guilty of the murder of Miss Miller, although I am not at all sure of that myself. I was hoping they might re-examine Mr Price's conviction, but I doubt that they will. Unfortunately the theory was discussed in the presence of Mr Ibbitson of the *Chronicle*, who has chosen to concoct a melodrama that has terrified all of Bayswater.'

'But we are right to be afraid if such a nasty creature is on the loose,' insisted Miss Gilbert. 'We women are not allowed to police the streets, more is the pity, but we can do something to protect ourselves.'

The parlour was very neatly arranged and Sarah had taken care to put out two ornate and heavily embroidered cushions, gifts that were the products of Miss John's busy needle and were not usually on display as they were not especially to Frances' taste. If Mr Candy noticed those additions to the decor, which had been absent on his previous visits, he did not comment.

'Some people say that the killer hates women because we dare to demand the same rights as men,' continued Miss Gilbert. 'There are many such horrid men, and they abuse us with their words and beat their wives and insult them by flaunting their mistresses.' She shuddered. 'But they have never before stooped to wholesale murder.'

'Not that we know of,' observed Miss John, quietly.

Miss Gilbert patted a cushion and plumped into a chair. 'You will be happy to hear, however, that we have come to make some practical suggestions. Even if Miss Doughty is not advising the police, although I feel sure that that situation will come to pass very soon if they have any sense at all, there is still much that can be done. Miss Smith's wonderful classes at Professor Pounder's academy are attended by many of our friends and add greatly to the ability of us women to protect ourselves against men. I wonder,' she continued breathlessly before anyone else in the company could comment, 'could more classes be arranged? I am sure that they will be even more in demand than before. Also Miss Smith, I would beg you to speak at one of our meetings on the subject. I am sure we would all benefit from your advice.'

'I'm not much for standing up and speaking,' said Sarah.

'Perhaps you and the Professor could give a demonstration? He could pretend to attack you and then you could knock him down. Our ladies would like to see that. Then you could show us how it is done.'

'*I* think we should all carry guns,' offered Miss John. 'I would quite like to have a gun.'

'I have had an idea which I think you would approve of,' Mr Candy ventured, timidly. 'I am in full agreement that it is scandalous that respectable females cannot go about their lawful business without fear of violence. And Bayswater is such a very busy and crowded place where many young women are obliged to walk home from their occupations or go out on necessary errands. Not all of them have a male relative who can accompany them, or have money for a cab. I propose enlisting citizens of irreproachable reputation as volunteers to escort our Bayswater ladies after dark. Through my charity work I already know many gentlemen who would, I am sure, be pleased to assist. Any volunteers who are unknown to me would have to be vouched for of course – I could ask for a letter from a clergyman or a doctor or a magistrate. This is where you ladies may help me. If there are any such gentlemen who you know and would recommend, I would be happy to approach them.'

Frances reflected that women who were not respectable and did not have lawful business were still entitled to walk about

Bayswater without having their throats cut, but decided not to mention this. It was unlikely that any gentleman who Mr Candy might recruit would want to be seen with such women in the open, even if they might resort to them privately. Those poor creatures would have to do their best to assemble in groups and protect each other.

'I shall call my new organisation the Guardians of Virtue,' announced Mr Candy proudly, 'and I would be honoured, Miss Doughty, if you were to become the first patron of this endeavour. I am sure that your name would inspire confidence. I intend to place an advertisement in the *Chronicle* and all who wish to volunteer as guardians or use the service may write to me at my office. There is no time to waste. I will hold a public meeting very soon and I do so hope that you will be able to attend. In fact I am hoping that you would be willing to take a seat on the platform and address the meeting. These charming ladies would be very welcome also.'

Miss Gilbert and Miss John favoured Mr Candy with the glance they reserved for any gentleman who dared to insult them with a compliment.

Frances was not entirely comfortable with speaking in public, as she always thought she had nothing at all to say, but she usually found that once she began, her natural interest and enthusiasm asserted themselves, and then she had a great deal to say, although she could never really remember afterwards what it was. She had, however, once spoken to the Bayswater Women's Suffrage Society on the question of vigilance, and thought that would be an appropriate subject, so she consented.

There was a gentle knock at the door and the maid peered in. 'Excuse me Miss, but Mr Ibbitson is here asking to see you. Shall I tell him to wait?'

Frances narrowed her eyes, coldly. 'No. Show him in. I want to speak to him.'

'Well you have been saved a journey,' said Miss Gilbert, with a smile.

Sarah cracked her knuckles as if to say that their new visitor had not been saved a drubbing.

That impulse was abandoned, however, when Mr Ibbitson arrived, with a livid swollen bruise surrounding an area of broken skin on his cheek. 'Good morning Miss Doughty!' he greeted her cheerfully. 'Have you seen the paper? What do you think? That should do the trick!'

'Why, whatever has happened to your face?' asked Frances.

He laughed. 'Oh, this, it's nothing! There was a big crowd around the *Chronicle* offices this morning all wanting copies of the paper, and some gent got overexcited and waved a walking stick a bit too enthusiastically.'

'You'll need something on that. Sarah, can you see to it?'

'Oh, I don't think –' he began, airily.

'I insist,' said Frances, her tone rejecting the possibility of any denial.

'But –' his protests became a yelp when Sarah grabbed him by the collar.

'I'll use that stuff that stings,' she said with grim satisfaction and hauled him away. The fact that it did sting was evidenced by a series of loud exclamations that emerged from the dressing room during the next few minutes, sounds that the gathering in the parlour decided to politely ignore.

Eventually Sarah brought her unwilling patient back, with the wound cleaned, and his face much reddened. The bruise was adopting a curious pattern, which suggested that the walking stick that had inflicted it was topped with a filigree design. 'Thank you Miss Smith,' squeaked Ibbitson, rubbing his eyes, which were watering a little. 'I'm sure I am very grateful.'

'Literary criticism can be painful,' Frances observed. 'We have read your article, and you should be pleased that this is all you have suffered.'

He seemed surprised. 'Don't you like it? The editor was very happy with it. We've doubled our sales.'

Frances was incredulous. 'Is that all that matters?'

'Well that's what Mr Gillan says. And you'll be famous now!' he added brightly.

'When I wish to be famous I will let you know!' Frances' annoyance, which had subsided a little, was now rekindled by the discovery that, far from being repentant, he was proud of what he had done. 'What were you thinking of? You have had the whole of Bayswater in a panic.'

'I was thinking of Miss – I mean, Mr Price. Going to be hanged for something he didn't do. I thought that if I could get people roused up to proper indignation, then the police might look into it. I thought you'd be pleased.'

'I am *not* advising the police. What made you write such a thing? That is quite untrue.'

'Well, it's almost true, isn't it? Because even if they don't ask for your advice you always give it to them. I put that in because I thought it would frighten the murderer into giving himself up.'

Miss Gilbert laughed. 'Maybe it will at that!'

Frances was not amused. 'Mr Ibbitson, please promise me that you will not write anything in the newspapers about me unless it is true. Is that too much to ask?'

He said nothing but looked suitably crestfallen.

'Apparently so.' Frances said, frowning, 'I thought newspapers prided themselves on informing and educating the public. It is not part of their duty to delude and frighten them.' Another thought struck her, and she spoke to him sharply. 'And both you and Mr Gillan must also promise me that on no account will you write letters to the paper supposedly from members of the public or even purporting to be from the murderer himself, just to provide sensational copy for the *Chronicle*.'

The disappointment on Mr Ibbitson's face showed that he had been thinking of doing just that.

'Well, however much we may disapprove of the article it has had a good effect,' interposed Mr Candy, soothingly. 'This very day I am launching a new venture which will ensure the safety of Bayswater females.'

The young reporter cheered up at once, sat down facing Mr Candy, and took out a notebook and pencil. 'That is wonderful news! I know our readers will want to hear of it.'

There was an interlude during which Mr Candy expounded on his new project with enthusiasm. Mr Ibbitson made admiring noises and wrote very rapidly, then jumped up with a grin. 'Back to the office now. I shall go and see Mrs and Miss Price later on.'

'Another interview?' Frances enquired.

'Not exactly. They've invited me to tea.' Even under the bruise he blushed a little.

When Ibbitson had left, there was much excited talk from Miss Gilbert about how the ladies of Bayswater should take matters into their own hands, and show that they would not be frightened. If nervous men did not dare subscribe to Mr Candy's Guardians of Virtue then she knew of many fearless women who would. Mr Candy looked somewhat alarmed at the prospect and protested that he had not envisaged ladies risking themselves, but Miss Gilbert chattered on regardless, and Miss John's eyes glittered with mischief.

There was another knock at the door and Frances, hoping it was not the press again, looked out of the window and was pleased to see that her caller was Mr Loveridge. He had been hurrying, and arrived a little breathless.

'I came to tell you Miss Doughty, that there was a great crush outside the offices of the *Chronicle*. Unfortunately I arrived there too late to see a great deal of what was occurring as the police had been called out to clear away the crowds who were blocking traffic on the Grove. I was able to make only a very rough sketch. But someone mentioned your name, and that you were intending to solve the murders. Is that true?' To his credit he was anxious rather than excited.

'It is not true,' Frances reassured him. 'It is all an alarm produced by an unwise announcement in the press.'

Loveridge sat down with an expression of profound relief, then glancing about him with an artist's eye said, 'Oh what remarkable cushions! They must be new.'

'They were being cleaned when you were last here,' said Frances, quickly. 'But if you are looking for a subject for the newspapers might I suggest you make a drawing of Mr Candy? He is promoting a new enterprise to protect the ladies of Bayswater from the creature that menaces us.'

Mr Candy readily assented and made much of determining which his best side might be for the portrait, although from what anyone else could see he did not seem to have one.

Frances had had another idea to assist Mr Loveridge in his career. Once Mr Candy and the lady suffragists had departed about their business she produced her copy of the Bayswater directory and together they studied the lists of notable residents, while Frances, from her personal knowledge, was able to advise of any individuals who might recently have announced a betrothal or an addition to the family circle, and might therefore be persuaded to have such an important event recorded in a drawing. One name did stand out, that of the Outrams. With some hesitation Frances mentioned the recent wedding and her concerns and he saw at once how his observations might prove useful to her and promised he would seek an interview. Frances thought with some pleasure that her little band of helpers, friends and associates – who could multiply her efforts and go to places where she would not be admitted – was growing, and Mr Loveridge would make a very welcome addition.

CHAPTER ELEVEN

rances decided to carefully assemble all the information in her possession concerning the three recent murders, reminding herself as she did so that her purpose was not to identify the murderer but to compare the three crimes to see whether it was really possible that the same person could have perpetrated all three. Her client was Jim Price, and she did not, could not and must not act for the families of Annie Faydon and Eliza Kearney. Somewhere in the maze of information there was an answer, and her best guide was Sarah, who, when Frances felt overwhelmed by facts, often saw the clearest way.

Assembling a platter of bread, cheese and pickles for a simple luncheon, Frances and Sarah sat at the table, on which they placed all the newspapers and notebooks relating to the murders, and with a large clean sheet of paper and a set of pencils, wrote down what they knew. All three victims were respectable and good-looking females of similar age, between twenty and twenty-five. But was that merely chance or the murderer's choice? After much cogitation a large question mark was added to the paper. The women had all been killed with a knife after dark, on a weekday and within a few minutes' walk of their homes. None had enemies that anyone knew of. That was where the resemblance ended.

The face-to-face attack and the many stab wounds that had pierced the chest and abdomen of Martha Miller suggested a personal motive, a frenzy of anger that had evaporated once her lifeless body had slid to the ground. The killer of the other two victims had not, as far as was known, faced them at all, but had simply come up quietly from behind and dispatched them in one stroke with swift cold deliberation. Frances would not in the normal way have wanted to see the wounds that were then made to the faces of the dead girls, but thought that if she did, she might learn something about the man who had inflicted them. Had he been angry or calm as he carried out his evil work? Was there an order to the cuts – a pattern even – had he carved letters that could give a clue to his identity or motives – or had they been simply random slashes? Frustratingly, no one would say.

The locations of the crimes were also very different in nature. Martha's murder, even though shielded by night and the shadows of a shop doorway, was in a place fraught with the danger of discovery since it was on a main thoroughfare. The other two girls had been killed in secluded and quiet areas. This inevitably led to the conclusion that Martha had been killed for some reason that was peculiar to her, and the place itself was unimportant. The other two girls had been slain because they had been somewhere quiet where the killer was unlikely to be disturbed and from where he could make a swift escape. This suggested that any other young woman, had she been there instead, would have fallen victim to the knife.

Thus far, everyone who had considered the three murders was certain that the second two were perpetrated by the same person, and that that person had not killed Martha Miller. Frances, who was also of that opinion even after going through the facts again, wondered if it was possible to look at the killings in a different way.

'Let us start by supposing it *was* the same man who killed all three women. Can the facts support this idea?'

'Might do,' observed Sarah after some thought. 'The man who killed the last two had done it before. The man who stabbed Martha – that might have been his first. Doesn't mean it was different men, though.'

'That is very true.' Frances tried to envisage a man who was simply looking for a victim to satisfy his blood lust. Inexperienced in murder, he would have made some mistakes when he killed Martha, mistakes that he did not want to repeat. When he approached her from the front, Martha might have panicked and struggled, and he would have had difficulty in preventing her from crying out. The marks of his fingers on her face were proof of that. Perhaps he had intended to cut her face but was disturbed by the sound of approaching footsteps or a carriage. Although no one had seen the murderer leave the scene of the crime, he might well have had a narrow escape. Had he learned from this experience and chosen places for his next murders where he was less likely to be interrupted? Did he determine that when the passion came on him again, he would choose another approach, this time taking the victim from behind, making it easier to kill in silence?

Sarah left Frances to ruminate on their discussion and went to tackle one of her own cases. A lady in the twilight of her life, who deserved after many years of honest labour to enjoy a measure of comfort in the care of her loving family, had been complaining that some of her property was disappearing. Her son and his wife, who shared her home, had tried to persuade her that it was the failing memory of old age that was responsible and that she must have lost or sold the items herself long ago. Sarah was about to interview the lady and her family, but with the apprehension that it would end unhappily for them all.

Despite her earlier scepticism, Frances now found herself entertaining the real possibility that the three murders were all the work of one person. Although she was still far from convinced, the new theory gave her fresh confidence with which to promote Jim Price's case. She was just committing her thoughts to paper when the maid announced two visitors. To Frances' great surprise they were Inspector Swanson and Sergeant Brown.

Inspector Swanson was a hearty-looking man in his thirties, with eyes that stared keenly from under hooded lids, and a prominent brush of a moustache overhung by a long thrusting nose. He arrived with the bold stride of an active and busy investigator. Frances had not seen Wilfred Brown in almost two years. Life on a police constable's beat was a hard one, with long hours spent walking in all weathers, and despite his youth, Wilfred had often looked worn and tired. As Detective Sergeant Brown, although with the air of man who had much to do, he was obviously content and confident in his new position, his complexion fresh and healthy, his moustache glossy and well groomed. He was nicely suited as a plain-clothes detective, and the watch chain that hung from his waistcoat pocket was draped over a stomach that had become generously rounded.

The two men shook hands with Frances, who asked after Mrs Brown and the family, to be told that she was in the pink of health and anticipating another addition to her domestic happiness.

'It is an honour to meet you Miss Doughty!' said Swanson, in a light lilting Scottish accent. 'Your fame has reached Scotland Yard and further, too. It seems you have the mind of a detective! The stories I have heard of you are so remarkable that I wouldn't have credited them as true unless I had heard all about you from Sergeant Brown.'

'All of it is true, and more, according to Inspector Sharrock!' said Wilfred with a grin. Frances invited them to sit, and offered refreshments, which they politely declined. 'Thank you, but we have been making enquiries all over Bayswater and have drunk more tea in two days than I would have thought possible.'

Swanson, with an expression of regret, pulled a copy of the *Chronicle* from his pocket and held it up to Frances. 'I am sorry to say that I am obliged to speak to you about this. Have you really been asked to advise the police? If so, neither we nor Inspector Sharrock know anything about it. There have been people coming to Paddington Green police station asking to see you, and expecting to find that you have an office there.'

'That is none of my doing, I assure you,' said Frances, making it very plain from her voice and expression that she did not approve of Mr Ibbitson's efforts. She was only thankful that Swanson had not got hold of the Miss Dauntless stories. 'It is the work of an enthusiastic but misguided young newsman hoping to increase sales, nothing more, and there is not a word of truth in it. Please take no notice. If clients wish to consult me they know where to come.'

'This whole article has set Bayswater on its heels, that's for sure,' said Wilfred. 'All this talk of knife-wielding maniacs. Come this evening it will be in *The Standard*, and tomorrow *The Times*, *The Telegraph* and *The Post*. Only add the *Illustrated Police News* and the *Pall Mall Gazette* and your name will be on the lips of every Londoner.'

Frances spoke calmly and with great dignity. 'And a week later every one of those papers will be kindling. The sooner the better. I know that people should take care of their own safety and need to be warned of danger, but it doesn't do to frighten them with stories of monsters. I have had a very strong word with the young man concerned and I trust he will be more careful in future.'

Swanson pushed the newspaper back into his pocket. 'I real-ise that Inspector Sharrock has already said this to you, but you must be advised that certain work is necessarily reserved for men. Irrespective of what stories the newspapers might like to make up, I hope you are not thinking of going about trying to catch murderers on your own, that is far too dangerous, especially in such a case as this.'

'I have no intention of doing so. My only commission has been to discover the witness who could provide an alibi for Mr Price, and this I have done. The man is deceased but I have uncovered enough information about his movements to show that Jim Price was in Richmond Road at the time of the murder of Martha Miller. All the facts are in the hands of Inspector Sharrock and Mr Rawsthorne the Price family's solicitor.' Frances expressed more confidence than she felt, since the times were not exact and the two locations very close. 'Is there any news about this?'

'Nothing,' said Swanson, 'and I doubt that there will be. As far as I am aware Mr Price is due to hang next Monday week.'

Frances glanced at Sergeant Brown but he was nodding in agreement. Both, she thought, in common with all the police, assumed that Jim Price was guilty and did not give any serious consideration to the possibility of saving him. 'I am very sorry to hear it, since I believe him to be innocent. I have been looking at the facts, which I may easily do from the safety of my own parlour, and it is my opinion that the murderer of Martha Miller is the same person responsible for the murders of Annie Faydon and Eliza Kearney.' Her assured tone was designed to get the attention of the two policemen and in this she undoubtedly succeeded.

Swanson and Brown looked at each other. 'Miss Doughty,' began Swanson, awkwardly, 'I don't know how much you know about these murders, and I wouldn't want to go into the details with you, but I can assure you that from what is known of the last two they cannot have been committed by the murderer of Martha Miller.'

She faced him boldly. 'I probably know more than you think. Inspector Sharrock has been very open with me.'

They glanced at each other again, and Wilfred could not resist another grin.

Before either man could say more, Frances explained her theory that after the first murder the killer had realised that his mistakes had almost led to him being caught, and he had then changed his methods, giving rise to the false impression that there were two murderers involved instead of one. Her visitors listened politely, but looked sceptical. 'He probably intended to leave his calling card – I refer to the pattern of wounds on the faces – on the first occasion, but he just didn't have the opportunity.'

'But these injuries to the girls' faces, they –' began Wilfred.

'Are not something we discuss with members of the public, however well informed, even if they happen to be celebrated detectives,' interrupted Swanson sternly.

Frances tried not to look disappointed and Wilfred, realising that he had very nearly been duped into giving away a secret, shook his head. 'You nearly had me there, Miss Doughty! What did I say, Inspector? This lady can get information out of a bank vault.'

'I understand that you must do what you can for your client, however hopeless his case,' said Swanson, 'nevertheless Jim Price is not the reason we are here. We would like to be informed at once if you or any of your agents should see the man who is our main suspect in the Faydon and Kearney murders.' He showed Frances the picture of the Filleter created by Mr Loveridge. 'There have been other men whose names have been put forward, but so far all have been cleared of suspicion. This man is known to carry a sharp knife and to exist almost wholly on the wrong side of the law. If you or any of Tom Smith's boys should chance to see him, do not approach, but make a note of the time and the place, what he is doing and who he is with, then tell the nearest policeman.'

'We have decided not to post a notice to the public with his picture since he is at present only someone we wish to interview, and if he sees he is wanted he will take flight,' added Wilfred. 'Also we don't want members of the public trying to arrest him or we will have more murders done.'

'I will do whatever I can,' Frances promised. 'Whether or not he has committed those murders I think the world will be a safer place when he is in custody.'

With this settled the policemen left to continue their enquiries, but not before Swanson had emphasised that Frances was to take very great care, and Wilfred had complimented her on her recent successes.

Frances was completing her memorandum when a note arrived asking her to attend Paddington Green police station at once, and she took a cab. It was rare for her to receive such a summons and it usually involved identifying a suspect. All the way there she hoped that Inspector Sharrock had got the Filleter in the cells at last.

Sharrock met her with a scowl. 'I have a gentleman here being questioned who says you can supply him with an alibi for the night of Annie Faydon's murder. I have met him once before, and if he is a close friend of yours I suggest you choose them better in future. His name is Cedric Garton. Very suspicious type if you ask me.'

Frances was astonished. 'Mr Garton is a friend of mine, and I am not ashamed to say so. He may be a little unorthodox in some of his ways but he is a true gentleman who enjoys my complete trust, and would never even think of injuring a woman.' She examined her pocket diary. 'Yes, on the night of Annie Faydon's murder Miss Smith, Professor Pounder and I were enjoying a light supper and poetry reading at Mr Garton's apartment. The supper was served by his manservant, Joseph. Some friends of his were there, too, notably a Mr Wilde, a most respectable young gentleman and I am sure he would be happy to confirm what I have told you.'

Sharrock was disappointed but it was the reaction of a man who had been clutching at a particularly slender straw and was not, therefore, surprised to see it break. 'Humph! No that won't be necessary, I'll take your word for it.'

'I cannot imagine why you would suspect Mr Garton of committing murder,' said Frances severely.

'No? Well someone is killing women, and Mr Garton has been pointed out to me as a man who dislikes women.'

'Nothing could be further from the truth. He has many lady friends, who are all very fond of him. He is good company and courteous to a fault.'

Sharrock signalled to a constable who went to fetch Cedric from the interview room. Moments later Cedric appeared, elegant as ever in a fur-collared coat with a fresh hothouse flower in his buttonhole, carrying a walking cane and calfskin gloves. 'My dear Inspector, I am happy to find that sanity has prevailed at last. Miss Doughty you are an angel come to my rescue,' he took her fingers and placed a kiss a mere whisper away from the back of her hand. 'I am so sorry to have given you this trouble, but when the Inspector arrived to conduct me here he would not take my man's word, although Joseph would have been of little use in any case, as he has been in a perfect state over a poached trout all morning.'

'You can go,' said Sharrock, brusquely, 'but don't give me cause to see you again. I don't want you getting up to any – any –' he waved his arms about vaguely, 'anything.'

'As if I would,' exclaimed Cedric looking very shocked.

'Please leave now before I think of another reason to arrest you,' said Sharrock gruffly.

Frances and Cedric lost no time in leaving the station and boarded the cab that was waiting for them outside. 'How foolish of the Inspector to even consider you as a suspect,' said Frances.

'He is prejudiced against me I fear, because I am of the aesthetic persuasion.' Cedric brushed a mote of dust from his otherwise immaculate cuffs. 'I am probably the only aesthete in Bayswater.'

'It is very shortsighted of him. He imagines just because you are a bachelor that you dislike women.'

'It is a common fallacy, I find. There are many reasons why a man might decide never to marry and yet still be perfectly sane and a great admirer of the female sex. In fact a devoted admiration for ladies is surely the greatest test of sanity that can be devised.'

'Do you think the murderer is insane, rather than wicked?' For all Cedric's pretence at idleness and a preoccupation with the trivial, Frances knew he was an intelligent and perceptive man, something he made great efforts to conceal, and she valued his opinions.

'Without a doubt. That is why it is useless to look for a motive. Such a maniac kills for the love of killing.'

'But if that was the case, surely he would kill without any consideration for age or sex or rank. The three victims have all been young, respectable women.'

'Then that is his mania. Three, you say? I had understood there were two. Has there been another since Norfolk Square?'

'No, thank heavens and I hope there will never be. I am refer-ring to the murder of Martha Miller for which Jim Price has been sentenced to hang.'

'You believe him innocent?'

'I do, yes.'

'Can you prove it?'

'I don't think anyone can. The one witness who might have done so is dead.' Saying it in that way only brought home to Frances the hopelessness of her task.

'If I recall rightly a dead witness has never stopped you from solving a mystery in the past. But if you wish to call upon me for any assistance, please do so.' His normally light tone dropped to one of great earnestness. 'A moment's notice will be sufficient.'

Frances had a meeting with Ratty that afternoon to ensure that all the boys under his command were detailed to scour Bayswater for the Filleter. There was nothing further she could do to assist the police. Much as she would have liked to catch the horrid killer herself, she knew that it was beyond what she ought to attempt.

Later that day Sarah arrived home with an expression of great satisfaction making her broad plain face glow as if it had been buffed to a shine. 'Very nice old lady,' she said, as she bustled about getting supper. 'I got her talking and she told me the whole story. I said as how we all had to be careful nowadays with our property and she said she had some very clever ways of outwitting thieves. Then all of a sudden she remembered her hiding place under the floorboards and there it all was.' Sarah chuckled. 'She was that happy I didn't ask for payment, but she gave me one of her best recipes.' She took a scrap of paper from her pocket and studied it. 'Oh, and I made another call, and now I know where Mr Candy's twenty pound note went.' She chuckled again.

CHAPTER TWELVE

Uncomfortably aware that only thirteen days remained before Jim Price was to be hanged, Frances studied the morning papers, and was interested to see that even *The Times* had given half a column to the Bayswater murders although their correspondent, unlike those of *The Standard* and the *Morning Post*, had been careful to couch his article in less colourful terms than the *Bayswater Chronicle*. Since it was the habit of so many newspapers to simply reprint verbatim articles already published by others, she had no doubt that Mr Ibbitson's lurid words were already being inked on to newsprint all over the country. What the popular weeklies would do with the story she dreaded to think.

Frances gave strict orders to the maid that she was not prepared to see any representatives of the press, apart from Mr Gillan and Mr Ibbitson of the *Chronicle*, and if there was any suggestion of a disturbance then she should send for Sarah at once, and the police if necessary. This precaution proved to be a wise one, since when Frances peered out of the window she saw a small group of pressmen assembling outside her door. They appeared to be acting in collusion since two of them were clearly acting as lookouts in case the police should arrive. They looked more like a band of pickpockets than newsmen. After some animated discussion, one of them, who appeared to be the youngest, was deputed by the others to ring the doorbell. Frances found herself wishing for the convenience of a telegraphic office within her own parlour so that she might summon assistance immediately, or even one of the new electronic telephones she had read about. She did not feel, however, that Inspector Sharrock would approve of a device that rang a bell in the police station every time someone needed his help.

The front door opened, and there was a conversation between the young gentleman, who presented a card, and the maid, who would, according to instructions, be explaining that the detective he sought to interview was not at home to the press. Despite this the youth made no move to leave, and his associates merely shouted out encouragement. The girl withdrew indoors, closing the door firmly to prevent unwanted intrusion and as Frances heard her footsteps on the stairs she glanced at Sarah, who was rising to her feet and flexing her fingers. 'It would be best if you did not strike anyone,' she advised. 'They are only doing what their masters tell them, and I need your help more than ever now, so it would not do at all if you had to spend any time explaining your actions to the police.'

Sarah wrinkled her nose, and looked out of the window. 'You're right. Too many witnesses.'

Sarah tramped downstairs with the maid, who looked almost too excited to be nervous. Frances looked out of the window again, and after a minute or two the front door opened and Sarah appeared on the top step holding a large bucket. She said nothing, but tipped the contents over the man on the steps, and went indoors again. The soaked youth uttered howls of dismay, and his comrades showed no sympathy for his plight but roared with laughter. Frances was sure that had they been soaked they would not have found the situation so amusing. The youth, resorting to dancing wetly on the pavement and shaking his arms, remonstrated with the others, who made a great show of holding their noses, and waving him away. None of them dared go near the house, but neither did they decide to leave.

Frances was expecting Sarah to return but she did not. Another few minutes passed and then the front door opened again and Sarah descended the steps and walked towards the newsmen. This time she was holding two buckets. When the men saw her, their amusement stopped abruptly, and they hurried away. Muffled laughter from the hallway suggested that the maid had been watching the spectacle.

'That will make an interesting item in the *Chronicle*,' said Frances, as Sarah returned to the parlour. The rest of the morning was peaceful, and devoted to correspondence, then after luncheon Sarah departed to take one of her classes at Professor Pounder's academy. She carried a parcel carefully wrapped in brown paper, almost certainly some fragrant item recently emerged from the oven, a gift for the Professor. Frances, knowing how much the gentleman appreciated Sarah's skills in the kitchen, had once sought to enquire teasingly if Mr Barkis was willing, to receive only a snort from Sarah. She had not raised the subject again.

Frances had by now received replies to most of the letters she had written appealing for clemency for Jim Price, expressing her doubts concerning his guilt. Officialdom did not share her view, however, and the responses were polite, promising only to give her words due consideration. That consideration, she was certain, extended only as far as reading her letters and placing them in a file. The gentlemen were well meaning, but they rarely considered that justice might have erred. She had heard nothing from Mr Rawsthorne following her report on Mr Gundry and determined that if there was no note by that afternoon she would write to him again.

Mr Candy arrived and Frances had some good news for him.

'I am happy to inform you that neither of your clerks is a thief. In fact there does not appear to have been a thief at all. The banknote did not reach your office because of a mistake and Mr Hullbridge has kindly agreed to send you a cheque forthwith.'

'I am considerably relieved to hear it. Both my clerks are highly efficient and it would have pained me to discover anything to their detriment, not to mention my concern that other monies might have been taken. But what a curious error to occur.'

'Indeed.' Frances did not elaborate. Sarah, who kept well informed on the comings and goings of Bayswater servants, had managed to trace the banknote to the hands of Mr Hullbridge's former parlourmaid, who, on discovering that she was in an interesting condition, had been quickly paid off by her master with the first thing that came to hand, and told to leave. Given his position in the community he had considered twenty pounds a cheap price to pay to avoid scandal. His wife, however, who had set the note aside to meet a bill, had discovered that it was missing before he could replace it, and he had been obliged to invent the story of the charity donation which his manservant had loyally supported. So distraught was Mr Hullbridge when Sarah had uncovered his ruse that he had offered to bribe her into silence. Her price had been twenty pounds paid to the charity, and she had watched him write the cheque and a covering letter and posted them herself. Sarah was especially scathing as the Hullbridges' youngest child had died during the severe chills of last January, and the loss remained a tangible presence in the house. Hullbridge, rather than comforting his wife, had betrayed her.

'But to more interesting business,' Mr Candy went on. 'I can now supply you with further information regarding the Guardians of Virtue. An advertisement has been placed in all the newspapers of quality, and distributed to gentlemen's clubs, but,' he added meaningfully, '*only* those of the highest possible standing. I do not approve of gamblers and sporting men who associate with actresses and the like. I must be quite certain of the noble sentiments and most perfect and pure reputations of all those who volunteer. I have also approached churchmen for their support and approbation and have been most encouraged by their response. There will be a meeting at Westbourne Hall on Friday night, to commence at eight o'clock, immediately after the ballad concert. Inspector Swanson has promised to appear and make a speech; he will be a very great attraction; also Mr Pollaky the famous detective. I very much hope that you will attend, and your – er – remarkable assistant.' He glanced about him as if Sarah might suddenly loom into view.

'Sarah is doing her part for Bayswater ladies by teaching them callisthenics.'

'Ah, of course, so they might be athletic enough to run away if they encounter danger,' said Candy, nodding understandingly.

Frances happened to know that Sarah's version of the dainty art involved dexterity with large wooden clubs, but declined to mention this in case Mr Candy thought it not quite respectable.

In the last few months Mr Candy had busied himself with his work and made no allusion to his disappointment over Miss Digby, but as he sat before Frances his head and body suddenly drooped like a wilting plant, and a mournful look passed over his features. It was an unusual display from him since he was one of those gentlemen who prided themselves on not making an outward show of emotions, whatever the unhappiness within. He recovered his dignity very quickly, however, and sat up again. 'I called upon

Mr Digby recently. He is a good and generous man and was kind enough to receive me with great civility.'

Frances wondered what might have prompted the visit. 'Was this in connection with the charities?'

'Yes, I have been soliciting support from all the prominent gentlemen and ladies in Bayswater to add further comforts to the dispensary for the poor. I did make it very clear when I saw Mr Digby that this alone was the reason for my call, and I had no intention of discussing our previous association. Nevertheless, Mr Digby did reveal to me that Enid – I suppose I must not think of her in that way now – his daughter is being courted by some frivolous fellow called Pargeter who is quite unworthy of her. They are not yet betrothed but it may well come to that. It is very clear that her father does not approve of the connection and would much prefer me as a son-in-law.' He shook his head. 'It is a very hard thing indeed, when a man strives to be upright and honourable, only to find that the lady whose hand he seeks has turned up her nose at him in favour of another who is all polish and no substance. What am I to do? Is there a way in which you might assist me?'

Frances felt obliged to reply with caution. When she had spoken to Mr Digby on the subject some months ago, he had advised her of the new suitor's penchant for the gaming table and the racecourse, and his habit, which amounted to a passion, of turning every item of money that came his way into a debt. Since Mr Digby had stipulated to his daughter that he would not condone the betrothal until his prospective son-in-law had paid his creditors, an event that seemed far less likely than his imminent ruin, Frances seriously doubted that the match would ever take place. She thought it unwise, however, to mention the rival's manifest shortcomings to Mr Candy, in case he was tempted to denigrate the other's character to Miss Digby, which was more likely to hurt than assist his case. 'I cannot believe that Mr Digby will permit the match. If they were to ask for his blessing I suspect that he would require them to wait some considerable time in the hope that his daughter's eyes would finally be opened to the gentleman's faults, and then she might think of you more kindly. My counsel is patience.'

'I accept your advice, but if you were perhaps to hear anything that might give me some hope that Miss Digby would agree to receive me again, I would like to know it.'

As he rose to leave, he had another thought. 'Miss Doughty, you are very knowledgeable about everything that happens here in Bayswater. I have recently heard an unpleasant rumour, and you may be able to tell me whether or not it is true. I have been told that Mrs Outram, a charitable lady who is one of the principal patrons of the hospital for incurable children, has in the last few weeks made a very unwise marriage to a scoundrel who has taken total possession of her fortune. Is it true? There has been no announcement in the newspapers, but I fear it may be so, since the donation she makes every month and was expected recently has not arrived.'

'I am sorry to say that your information is correct. The husband is a former solicitor's clerk, Mr Timothy Wheelock, who is very much her junior. He is a clever and unprincipled young man who has managed to secure his wife's whole fortune to his use.'

'That is a terrible disappointment. Hardly a month ago she wrote to me saying that she intended to place a large sum at the charity's disposal to build a new hospital that was to be named after the late Mr Outram. I don't suppose Mr Wheelock might be persuaded to allow it?' he added hopefully.

'I very much doubt it. He is not of a charitable nature.'

'She has also made a will leaving an annuity to provide supplies for the hospital. I know this as a fact since she showed me the document. It was a very generous bequest.'

'All void now, I imagine. But there is some hope as her family wish to contest the validity of the marriage.'

'Then I wish them every success.'

In such a dispute Frances knew that Mr Candy could testify to Mrs Outram's intention to dispose of some of her fortune to charity, but that, she thought, would work against any attempt of her family to try and prove that the lady was not competent to manage her affairs.

The afternoon post brought nothing from Mr Rawsthorne. Instead there were several letters asking her to investigate the suspicious behaviour of certain individuals, not for any stated reason but for reasons that were obvious to Frances. She replied offering appointments. She also sent a note to Mr Rawsthorne asking if there was any news and received a response signed by Mr Carter Freke on behalf of his employer saying that there was nothing further to report. Time was running out.

CHAPTER THIRTEEN

The sensational newspaper reports had taken effect, and by the following morning it seemed that the whole of Bayswater was in a ferment over the murders. Frances found her early delivery of letters three or four times what it had been before. Some of the correspondents wanted to ask her advice about personal safety, including where one might go to hire a bodyguard, others asked if she was investigating the murders, and some demanded to know if she knew who the killer was, which was a foolish question since if she had known she would already have told the police and the man would be under arrest. Most of the letters, however, were suggesting who the murderer might be, for a variety of reasons, usually because the individual carried a knife, or had a peculiar facial expression, or beat his wife, or was a foreigner. A letter from businessman Mr Wren denouncing his partner Mr Cork arrived in the same post as one from Mr Cork denouncing Mr Wren, from which Frances surmised that the two incorrigible quarrellers had had another falling-out. Then there were the letters that did not name anyone but offered a vague theory suggesting that the culprit was a butcher, a leather-worker, a sailor on leave, a doctor or a policeman. Some wanted to know if the murdered women had been in a delicate condition, and thus proposed that their killer might be a female, perhaps a midwife, or even someone plying quite another trade, whom they had trusted to approach them. Some asked if the murdered women had been subdued with chloroform. Frances thought this highly unlikely since she knew that such attempts did not have the success that the public liked to believe. Frances tied all the letters into a bundle and sent them to the police, who she felt sure were already sifting through a similar pile of useless paper.

There was another little gathering of pressmen about Frances' door, although they now hovered at a respectful distance, and made no attempt to seek admission, since they were anxious not to cause a disturbance or indeed exhibit any behaviour that might provoke Frances into summoning a constable, or worse still, Sarah. From time to time Frances peered out of her window, and found them still there, looking increasingly cold and miserable. As they were not troublesome either to her or the other occupants of the house, Frances decided to tolerate them, and after a while she began to feel sorry for the huddled pack misted about with damp autumn fogs, lingering in the hope that she might suddenly emerge and reveal the identity of the man who was terrorising Bayswater. Eventually she sent the servant out to take them mugs of hot tea and bread and butter, and a note to inform them that she had nothing to impart. How they or anyone else imagined she might be able to solve the mystery she could not tell.

Visitors who dared to come to the front door and ask to see Frances were not invited in unless they had an appointment or were known to the maid, but were made to wait on the doorstep. Any cases of doubt were carefully scrutinised by Sarah before being admitted, and all those without legitimate business were firmly sent away.

There were two new clients for Frances to see. The first was a Mrs Underwood, who wished her husband to be followed during his regular weekly walks which he had told her were necessary for the preservation of his health. Frances had many such clients, ladies who feared that their husbands had mistresses or were calling on women of a less refined character. These wives did not, as a rule, fear desertion. They feared that their husbands were draining household finances on selfish pleasure, and carrying back a hideous disease with which he was infecting them, a disease that they felt unable to discuss with a medical man. Frances always thought that the sooner there were more medical women the better for these nervous souls who had been brought up to believe that there were some things that should never be a subject of conversation between the sexes, even at the risk of one's health or life. Some of the wives who consulted Frances were more sanguine about their husband's activities. They were quite sure that their husbands had mistresses, and did not mind that, as the men were consequently better tempered when at home, and less troublesome.

All the wives wished to know was where their husbands might be reached in the event of a domestic emergency. They could simply have asked, of course, but they knew that they were unlikely to receive a truthful reply. In any case, the men enjoyed the supposed secrecy and deception; it added seasoning to their activities. Frances wondered about such marriages, which she assumed had not been contracted out of mutual affection. She could not imagine herself paired with a husband whose absence she preferred to his presence or one who liked another woman better than his own wife.

With Mrs Underwood, however, there was another train of thought occupying her mind, one that she dared not even hint at to Frances. Still, Frances felt sure she knew what it was, and was able, by consulting the dates in her notebook, to reassure her client that Mr Underwood, whatever his numerous faults, was not the Bayswater Face-slasher.

Her next client was the worried father of a youth who was neglecting his studies, and he wanted to discover what occupation it was that so demanded his son's attention that he was in danger of failing to qualify as a surgeon. Before supplying the details that Frances required in order to undertake the commission he tried to extract a promise from her. Should she discover that his son was committing a criminal offence then she was to communicate this to him in preference to the police, and he would deal with it privately. Frances told him that if she obtained actual proof of serious criminal activity as distinct from mere suspicion – a commodity, she thought although she did not say it, with which Bayswater was currently full to capacity – and then did not report it, then she herself might be deemed to have committed an offence, one which he would be inciting her, indeed paying her to commit. The prospective client paled a little. She allowed him some time to consider his options, which were to depart and find a less honest detective, or employ Frances on her own terms. At length, he agreed to the latter course of action. 'I just hope he isn't – I mean – it would be terrible for our family if he turned out to be – well –'

'I understand. But if he is, you will want to know as soon as possible.'

Frances was now feeling frustrated and impatient at having received no note from Mr Rawsthorne since her visit six days before. She did not count the brief missive from Mr Carter Freke as a useful communication. This could, of course, mean that there was no news to be sent, however she hoped that the excitement produced by the press reports had resulted in the receipt of fresh information and she decided to pay the solicitor a visit. This time she would wait until he was available to see her no matter how long it would take.

While Sarah went to see Ratty about the new clients, Frances took a cab to Rawsthorne's office. The weather had turned very cold indeed, and the air was biting and blustery, the sky overcast with grey clouds, which shed short and frequent rain showers. The streets were slippery with thin mud and piles of rotting leaves, as well as all the usual fallen trash, an accumulation that the sweepers were having some trouble keeping at bay. It was the kind of weather the newspapers termed 'unsettled' which, thought Frances, meant that their forecasts would always be correct.

At Mr Rawsthorne's office, Frances took a seat in the waiting room and looked about her. Mr Rawsthorne had a great many clients in Bayswater and those she had observed waiting to see him always appeared as calm as anyone might do who was about to consult a solicitor. The two people with whom she shared the waiting room were anything but calm. One was a respectable-looking woman in late mourning weeds showing that she had been widowed at least a year before. Her face was fallen with grief, and she was trying her best to restrain tears. Frances could not help wondering what her story was. The other was a man of middle years, a shopkeeper she guessed, who was unable to remain still, but constantly shifted his position in an agitated manner, and every minute or two, took a large kerchief from his pocket and blew his nose very noisily.

After a wait of about ten minutes, Mr Carter Freke glided in with his usual smile. The impatient man rose to his feet expectantly but Freke simply shook his head. 'I am sorry, but Mr Rawsthorne did make it very plain at your last interview, you must wait another two weeks.

'But I can't wait any longer!' the man exclaimed. 'Where is Rawsthorne? I want to see him!

Freke made a gesture of regret, an expression that was wholly in his hands and did not reach his eyes. 'I am very sorry. Two weeks.'

'Then I am ruined!' bellowed the man, jamming his hat on his head and stamping out.

Freke sighed and shook his head, then he approached the weeping lady and took her by the hand. 'I am sorry, but there is no further news. Believe me, everything possible is being done.' The lady said nothing, but nodded regretfully, rose and took her leave.

Mr Freke turned to Frances. 'Miss Doughty? This is an unexpected pleasure, I am sure that you do not have an appointment for today. Is there some way I can be of assistance? I do hope you received my recent message.'

'I did receive it, for which I thank you. But I would like to see Mr Rawsthorne. Is he available? I am content to wait here until he is.'

'Oh, I am afraid he is not in the office at all. He has a very serious matter on his hands which has taken him out of town.'

'When do you expect him back?' asked Frances anxiously. 'Will he be here tomorrow?'

'Not as soon as that. In fact he gave me no firm date, but I would say that he is unlikely to be here again until at least a week today.'

Her anxiety escalated into alarm. 'A week today? Surely not! That is only a few days before the date set for Jim Price's execution.'

'Is it? Yes, I suppose it is,' said Freke as if the date was of no consequence to him.

Frances stared at him in astonishment and dismay. She might almost imagine that Mr Freke had somehow done away with Mr Rawsthorne in order to take over the business, and the delay was providing him with the time he required to dispose of the corpse. She pushed the thought aside. 'Has anything been heard from the Home Office?'

'No, nothing at all, but as Mr Rawsthorne advised you when you last saw him, I would not entertain any hope in that area.'

'While the man still lives there is hope,' Frances retorted, unable to prevent a justifiable annoyance creeping into her tone. 'I will not give up my efforts.'

'I would expect as much from you,' said Freke, soothingly.

Frances, seeing that any further interview would be a waste of her time, rose to her feet. 'You will inform me at once if you should receive any news.'

'Oh, I will, of course. I do, however, have one fragment of information for you on another matter. Before Mr Rawsthorne went away he received a message to confirm that Mr James Chandler, the nephew of Mrs Wheelock, has arrived in London and has taken lodgings in Bayswater. Mr Rawsthorne has advised Mr Chandler that you are acting in the case and he will no doubt call on you very shortly.'

Frances left the office with considerable feelings of disquiet. If Mr Rawsthorne, who she was quite sure had not been murdered by his clerk, was absent on some urgent matter then he had left the Price family to the mercies of Mr Freke, who obviously cared nothing at all about the fate of the condemned man, and had effectively consigned him to his doom. She wondered what work he was actually doing on Jim Price's behalf and suspected little or nothing. Neither did she think that she could rely upon him to keep her properly informed. It was only twelve days to the execution, little enough time for information to move through official channels. She could only hope that the urgent business that had taken her solicitor away from his office was connected with her efforts to save her client. There was, however, one more thing she could do.

Frances hastened to Westbourne Grove and the office of Tom Smith's Men, where Tom, Sarah's young relative, ran his own business, organising a small army of boy messengers, whose bailiwick covered all of Bayswater and extended out over most of west London. Tom, who was intelligent, active and alert to every chance of making money, employed only those boys who were prepared to work hard, and in return he treated them well, and made sure that none of them ever had to live on the streets but always had somewhere warm to rest their heads at night, and as much tea and bread and cheese as they could consume. They were the eyes and ears of the district, and often provided Frances with valuable information as soon as it came to light. Tom, who had once been the delivery boy for her father's business while running an additional enterprise carrying notes and parcels for anyone else, had long ceased to think in terms of pennies or even sixpences, but nowadays had his eyes on guineas. From time to time he would pass a bag of coins to Sarah to place in some safe investment for him. Sarah had once revealed that Tom's ambition was to accumulate enough funds so that one day he might buy a property. His plan was to let the property and make enough money to buy another one and so on. 'He'll end up owning half Bayswater,' she had mused, with a shake of her head. 'I don't know where he gets his ideas from.'

Frances found Tom at his desk, poring over a sheaf of papers, a mug of tea and a half-eaten meat pasty by his elbow. His usually spiky hair was flattened down with something that smelt very like pomade. He had grown out of the smart blue suit with shiny brass buttons that Mr Jacobs the chemist had had made for him when he had first started working for that business, and now wore a more manly attire in grey with a striped waistcoat, and a clean collar. Despite this he still looked no more than his age, which was probably about thirteen.

Tom smiled the smile he always gave when he saw Frances, as he saw the prospect of earning a good commission.

'What c'n I do fer you today Miss Doughty?'

'Tom, I expect you do a lot of business for the local solicitors.'

'Oh yes, messages out, messages in, things that won't wait for the post, things they don't want to go in the post.' He winked.

'Can your men keep a lookout for anything arriving at Mr Rawsthorne's from the Home Office? Or if they should see something or overhear anything about Jim Price, would you let me know at once? The thing is, Mr Rawsthorne has had to go away on some urgent business and has left a great deal of his work with his new clerk Mr Carter Freke, who I do not feel I can trust.'

'Right you are. Jim Price – that's the man going to swing at Newgate, isn't it?'

'I am hoping for a reprieve.'

Tom shrugged. 'Best've luck with that.'

Frances was comforted to know that even though Tom cared nothing for the fate of Jim Price, he would not neglect his commission.

❧

Next morning, Frances was pleased to see that the *Illustrated Police News* had utilised some of Mr Loveridge's elegant sketches for its new edition, although it had also devoted a significant part of its front page to an impression of a simian-looking murderer with pointed fangs carrying a knife dripping gore, who, it stated, was at loose on the streets of Bayswater. She only wished that the killer did look like the creature in the picture as it would have made him so much easier to apprehend.

In the meantime, even though the fate of Jim Price occupied most of her thoughts, Frances could not neglect the other cases that were her daily bread. Accordingly she paid a visit to the Bayswater Ladies' Reading Room, a place of peace and refinement, except that one of the members was defacing the material. The manageress, a dignified bespectacled lady of about forty with a troubled expression, apologised profusely before showing Frances some newspapers and pamphlets which had been marked in blue pencil with messages of a profoundly irreligious and almost blasphemous nature. 'If it was not for the fact that membership is only open to ladies, I might have suspected a man of trying to hinder what we do. There are men who cannot abide the mere idea of ladies educating themselves and taking an interest in the world. They think we should all be at home sewing buttons on their shirts.'

Frances studied the defacements, which were in an educated feminine hand, but one that betrayed the distraction of the author. 'When did you first notice this?'

'One of the members drew my attention to it a few days ago. I did hope it was a simple aberration, perhaps brought about by a moment of distress, but when I looked through some of the other material here I found that several items were similarly defaced. It is all in the same hand. I do, of course, oversee the room, but I cannot keep a watch on all the ladies. I have other duties, too.'

'Of course. I can spend some time watching here and I also have a lady assistant. Between the three of us, we will find the culprit. I am sorry to say that the nature of the messages suggests a disturbed brain. This is not genuine devoutness passionately expressed. To suggest that the recent murders are a punishment from God for the transgressions of dishonest women is far too extreme, and of course the deceased were all beyond reproach in their behaviour. And there are words here that no lady ought to use. Have any of your members attempted to distribute pamphlets or accosted other members with religious messages?'

'Nothing of that nature has been reported. I could make discreet enquiries, of course, but I don't wish to upset anyone, or spread the impression that something is amiss.'

'I understand. Discretion is best in matters of this kind. You do not know on which day or days the defacement occurred?'

'I am afraid not. In any case we do not keep a note of which members are here on which dates.'

Frances examined the damaged newspapers and periodicals. None was more than a week old. 'Are these all of them?'

'Yes, I thought it best to retain them.'

'And you do not recognise the handwriting? Do the members not make a written application?'

'All I have is a list prepared by the previous secretary.'

'The writer has been very cunning not to be observed or draw attention to herself. So she has some restraint. But something might have happened in her life to bring this about. She may need help and sympathy, not punishment.'

'That is my thought,' said the manageress with some relief, 'which is why I would like it resolved with as little fuss as possible.'

'May I see the list of members, please? And I would like to borrow one of these periodicals.'

Frances spent the next hour in the reading room, carefully watching all that went on. There were desks where ladies might sit and read, and these were in full view, but there were also some stands designed to take newspapers, which, tilted away from the eyes of any observers, offered an opportunity to carry out defacements unobserved. The list of members included many ladies who were known to her, or were known by reputation, many of whom, including Miss Gilbert and Miss John, were members of the Bayswater Women's Suffrage Society.

Frances decided to call on Miss Gilbert and Miss John, and found them busy preparing pamphlets to distribute at the forthcoming meeting of the Bayswater Vigilance Committee. There were bundles of publications being parcelled up and tied with string, works with titles such as 'Give Women Votes' and

'Women Cast Off Your Chains' while a more recent publication on the alarm in Bayswater was called 'Save Our Women'. Miss Gilbert, as usual, was in a great flurry of energy, dashing about like a young girl, while Miss John followed mildly in her wake like a small vessel nudging along in the rear of a mighty ship, tidying and arranging everything that was disturbed by the great craft.

There was a new product of Miss John's busy needle, whose creations were growing ever larger and more imposing – a sturdy banner in purple with gold fringes for the lady suffragists to carry on their marches. It depended from two stout poles with gold painted finials, which could serve either as supports or weapons of war, and was draped across the parlour in fine style. The room, a small burgundy-coloured, be-fringed, cushioned and tas-selled palace of embroidery, was nevertheless well arranged and supremely comfortable. As Frances looked about her she began to feel a little ashamed that she usually placed Miss John's gift cush-ions with their magnificent portrayals of Britannia and Boadicea out of sight unless the ladies were due to call. The articles were not to her taste but then, she thought, who was to say that her taste was superior? She decided to leave them on display.

Miss Gilbert greeted her with her customary warmth and thrust a pile of pamphlets into Frances' hands. 'Please do take some of our new works. I know you will find them interesting reading. If women only had the vote then there would be more attention paid to matters that affect them. There are men who believe that if a woman is killed in the street than it is her fault for being there at all, but why should we not be able to walk about in our lawful occupations without fear?'

Miss John appeared at Frances' side. 'I am sure we could almost do without men altogether. One would need to retain a few, of course, for the necessary purpose, but apart from that the world would be a better place without them.'

Frances preferred not to think about the purpose to which Miss John was referring, and believed that if Sarah's strong arm was not there to protect her then a man's would do just as well. Not all the men of her acquaintance were monsters of anti-female prejudice; indeed many of them were kindly and amusing com-pany, and pleasing to the eye. She was obliged to pull her thoughts quickly away from that reverie. 'My present concern in this atmosphere of terror, which is an unfortunate product of the press, is that there are ladies who might be tempted to do foolish things from fear.' She had been carrying the despoiled periodical rolled up and wrapped in plain paper, and now revealed it to view. 'This item was found in the ladies reading room, of which I believe you are members. I am sorry for showing you such an unpleasant object, but it was written by a lady who is clearly in some distress of mind. I know no one who might be tempted to write words of this nature, but I thought that if she was a member of the Suffrage Society she might have corresponded with you and you would know her handwriting. Or she might have spoken to you and uttered similar sentiments.'

The two ladies studied the writing and shook their heads.

'Not every lady who supports us is a member of the Society,' said Miss Gilbert. 'There are many who are wholeheartedly in favour of our cause but are afraid to say so because of their cruel husbands or fathers, and they dare not come to our meetings.'

'This is not everyday language,' observed Miss John. 'But if the lady has a great passion then perhaps she will come to Mr Candy's meeting and say something there and show herself up.'

It was a chance, of course, but Miss John's comment gave Frances an idea which she decided to pursue, and once home she wrote a letter to Mr Candy, suggesting that a petition should be presented to the police and the Paddington Vestry from the denizens of Bayswater calling for greater vigilance. Every individual attending his meeting should be asked to sign it and append an address. If he thought this a good idea she said she would like to see the completed petition before it was presented, as it might provide her with some names she could recommend to him. Later she received a note saying that he heartily approved of her idea and would have the appropriate papers drawn up.

Mr Candy had been hard at work. Leaflets were being distributed all over Bayswater advertising the meeting that would take place in Westbourne Hall on the following day. Frances found one delivered to her home, announcing her appearance, together with other notables who she felt sure would be a far greater attraction. She sent a copy to Mr Loveridge with a note suggesting that he might find something of interest to sketch. Sarah commented that it was very thoughtful of Frances to do this, as it would ensure the young artist had some business and Frances agreed, then Sarah added that this would also ensure that they saw him again very soon, an observation that seemed to cause her some amusement.

CHAPTER FOURTEEN

rances was not anticipating with any pleasure the prospect of having to make a public address at Westbourne Hall but realised that she could take the opportunity offered by the meeting to put Jim Price's case before the notables of Bayswater. She would start her speech with some words on vigilance, but then quickly move on to the murder of Martha Miller. Perhaps she might jog a memory of something seen or heard, and not thought to be important at the time, but which could suddenly blaze into significance and save her client from the noose. Inspector Swanson and Sergeant Brown would also be there and Ignatius Pollaky, who would surely have some valuable insights. Such an array of prominent persons would undoubtedly attract an audience. She knew nothing about Mr Pollaky's work, which was rumoured to be very important. He often put advertisements in the newspapers in foreign languages of which he was said to speak several, and some were even in secret code. She wondered how many murderers he had caught: a great many for certain.

As she composed her speech, frowning with concentration and refreshing herself with a constant supply of tea, a note arrived from Mr Loveridge thanking her for the leaflet and saying that he would attend the meeting to make sketches of the event. Frances found that she was looking forward very much to seeing Mr Loveridge again. He was good company and he made her smile. She realised, however, that she knew very little about him other than his profession. She estimated his age to be just a year or two greater than her own, but he had told her nothing of his family. He described himself as a student of art, but she had sometimes seen art students, sketching the elegant frontage of Westbourne Hall, or painting in one of the public gardens, and they had always looked slightly down at heel, even hungry, as if they spent on colours and paper what they ought to have spent on food. Mr Loveridge was well turned out by comparison, and she thought him not as poor as he liked to suggest.

That evening, the supper things were just about to be cleared when there was a knock at the door. The maid brought up a little card, very tasteful and discreet with a delicate edging of gold leaf, and printed with the name James Chandler BA (Calcutta). Frances went to the window and peered out. A smartly dressed young man waited outside, flexing the fingers on his gloved hands to exercise them in the cold. 'Foreign gentleman,' said the maid. 'What I meant was, not like your French or German foreign what's almost English – very foreign indeed. He asked if he might make an appointment to see you, or if it is convenient, he is not presently engaged.'

'This is Mrs Outram's great-nephew – or I suppose I ought to say Mrs Wheelock's. Show him up, I will see him at once.' Frances always relished the prospect of a visitor from far away. Her world was a very small one, and by and large she liked it that way, since she knew where everything was, but sometimes she felt a thrill of excitement at the prospect of the exotic. The only gentleman from India she had ever met was the young student of law, Mr Lathwal, and he was as polite and intelligent a person as she could ever have desired to meet, only so quiet and respectful that she had not found him altogether interesting. As they awaited their visitor, Frances and Sarah hurried to arrange the parlour to look as neat and businesslike as possible, which involved quickly putting a plate of currant buns into a drawer out of sight.

The gentleman who was ushered in was under thirty, tall and well made with an elegant but unassuming carriage. His great-coat and suit were tailored in a style that would allow him into any drawing room, the shirt crisp and white, the fabric finer than might be appropriate to the English climate. As he entered he looked approvingly at the fire that burned warmly in the room. The flames illuminated a face with the delicacy of a statue, emphasising the golden tone of his skin, and the fine cheekbones. His hair, smooth and very black, was thick and lustrous, the nose prominent and aquiline, the eyes as dark as French chocolate. He smiled and offered his hand to Frances, and she introduced Sarah as her trusted assistant.

'Miss Doughty, Miss Smith,' said their visitor courteously. He faltered a little under Sarah's penetrating stare before acknowledging her with a polite inclination of the head. Frances hoped that he did not think the look was on account of his being foreign; Sarah's glances of deep suspicion were aimed at all men. 'I am honoured to make your acquaintance and very grateful that you have agreed to see me with so little warning. I am the great-nephew of Mrs Caroline Wheelock who was married recently in such strange circumstances. Mr Rawsthorne advised me to come and see you as he said you have some information which might assist me.'

Frances indicated the chair that faced hers across the little table. 'I will do whatever I can to help you.'

He sat, and his posture fell for a brief moment before he recovered his composure and he straightened again. She sensed that he was attempting to conceal exhaustion following his long journey and the anxiety that must have been his companion on the way.

Frances and Sarah took their accustomed places. It was Sarah's usual habit not to sit facing the persons being interviewed, but to occupy an armchair behind them. There she busied herself with needlework, and said nothing unless spoken to, but all the time she was listening to the conversation with great attention. She was especially wary of male clients. The position enabled her to advance upon the visitor unseen should that seem to be necessary, but it also allowed her to communicate secretly with Frances. In the last months the two had been maintaining their study of sign language and Sarah used this to communicate her observations during interviews. The signs for 'liar' and other still less complimentary words which Frances thought owed more to the argot of Wapping docks where Sarah had been brought up, than the teaching of the Bayswater deaf, were frequently in use.

'I trust that I am not trespassing upon your time,' he continued apologetically. 'I seem to have arrived in Bayswater at a season of great fear and disturbance. Are there really deadly dangers on the streets? I have been told so, but it hardly seems possible. As I look about me it all appears so very peaceful, indeed to one born and brought up in Calcutta the district appears well-nigh deserted, and yet there are a great many anxious-looking men outside your door, all watching me very closely as I went in.'

'I regret to say that there have been three dreadfully savage murders in recent weeks,' Frances explained. 'It is thought that a madman is responsible, which makes it all the harder to find the culprit, as one cannot devise a motive for the murders, or look amongst the friends of the victims for a suspect. I am not engaged in those cases, although the press and gossips like to suggest that I am. The young men who you saw gathered outside my house were sent there by the west London newspapers hoping to speak to me and learn that I have solved the mystery. They are destined to stand in the cold for some while, I am afraid, and without result. As to my time, it is at your command.'

He looked relieved by this assurance. 'I fear that there is little time to lose – it may well be a matter of life and death, since I am concerned that my poor aunt might come to some harm at the hands of that criminal husband of hers. I understand that you have some information about the circumstances of my aunt's so unwise marriage. Mr Rawsthorne advised me of her intentions as soon as he learned of them, although unhappily neither of us was able to prevent it. I knew at once that she must have fallen into the hands of a fortune hunter, and felt sure that she had been duped by the flattery and charm of a younger man. I was also with some reluctance obliged to entertain the possibility that her brain has been affected by age, and she is not competent to make decisions, although there was no sign of any such incapacity in her correspondence. Immediately on my arrival in London I called upon her doctor to discuss the question, but would you believe the scoundrelly husband had forestalled me? He is a clever one, and I am only just beginning to discover how clever. I found that he had actually asked her doctor to come and treat her for some trifling ailment about a week before the wedding, and while not actually asking him to give a certificate that she was mentally competent it was obvious that Wheelock's intention was that during the visit the doctor would form the opinion that she was in her perfect mind. Dr Collin was naturally unwilling to provide me with any medical information regarding his patient but I did gain the impression that he believes my aunt to be very well indeed for a woman of her age, and mentally sound. I am happy for her sake, of course, but consequently that avenue of opposition to the wedding is closed to me. This morning I was able, however, to obtain an interview with my aunt, who seemed in good health, but having finally met her dreadful husband I can see that the situation is far worse than I had feared.'

Sarah gave Frances a quizzical look, and made a sign, which she understood. 'Prior to that visit, when did you last see your aunt?'

He understood her and smiled. 'Yes, of course, you must wonder against what standard I was able to judge her health. The answer is that I have no real comparison. I have only met my aunt once before. I came to London for a visit with my parents more than twenty years ago when I was just a child, and really I have few memories of it apart from the cold wet weather and grey buildings. We have corresponded occasionally since then, mainly on family matters. I think the last letter I received from her told me of Mr Outram's death.'

'Tell me about today's visit. I should mention that I have met Mr Wheelock many times, in his former professional capacity, but I have not seen him since the marriage.'

'Oh, I was received in a friendly enough manner,' Chandler admitted. 'There is nothing in his appearance to recommend him, as you know, but he can put on a show of kindness, even affection towards his wife; but it is all show, I am quite sure of that. And although he did not mention it I could see that he knew precisely what my business was. My aunt appeared to be calm and untroubled. I do not think her husband ill-treats her in any violent way, or she would have been nervous in his company. The house is a model of comfort, she has a maid to wait on her every need, and yet, I was sure that something was very wrong about the arrangement. It took me some time to realise the reason for my disquiet, and then it dawned upon me that my aunt was – well, there is really no other way to say it – she was under the influence of drink. While I was there I was offered a glass of sherry, which I declined, and Mr Wheelock did not partake, but the maidservant quite unbidden, poured a glass and gave it to my aunt, which she drank. She seemed perfectly content with her situation, and Wheelock referred to her in very pleasant terms, as one might an aged grandparent, but I could not help thinking that the fine house and servants are little more than an elegant prison.' He spent a few moments gathering his thoughts. 'Miss Doughty, I believe that my aunt is deliberately being kept in a state of befuddlement so that Wheelock may make free with her fortune to which I am sure he has no legal right.'

'There are many kinds of marriage,' observed Frances, who had often been responsible for dealing with the difficulties that emerged from the married state and understood how unpleasant it could be, 'but of course, however one might disapprove of a marriage, if the two parties are content then that is the end of the matter. In the case of your aunt, however, I do think it is probable that she was coerced into it. So you may be correct and the marriage is not a lawful one, although as yet I cannot prove it.'

He looked hopeful. 'Please tell me all.'

Frances revealed the theory that the former Mrs Outram had destroyed the will of her late husband rather than have a substantial portion of his fortune go to the Bayswater Vegetarian Society. 'I will write a letter of introduction so that you may meet the secretary of the society, Mr Lathwal, who can tell you about the circumstances in greater detail. He consulted me about his concerns, but was unwilling to make them public without some substantial evidence to maintain his allegations, for reasons that must be obvious. My difficulty was that not only is there no particle of proof of the destruction of a will, there is not even proof that it was ever actually drawn up. It is quite possible, for example, that the late Mr Outram simply changed his mind. He might even have had the will drawn up and signed and witnessed and then decided to destroy it himself, which he was of course entitled to do. If we assume, however, that you aunt did destroy a valid will, then Mr Wheelock could have found out something that has given him power over her, or even if he has not, he might have deluded her into thinking that he has.'

As Mr Chandler considered the position his optimism faded and his bronze features and dark eyes seemed to fall behind a cloud. 'It is very unfortunate,' he said at last, 'but if you are correct, then it does seem to me that the only way I can prove that my aunt was coerced into the marriage and so free her from this villain, is to prove that she is guilty of a very serious offence. If she did destroy the will then by so doing she defrauded the vegetarian society out of a substantial inheritance.'

'That may be the case, and it is a crime for which she might well be prosecuted, however we are a long way from facing that possibility and we may never do so. What I propose is this. I will look into the matter and see if I can discover any more about the events leading up to the wedding, and the wedding itself, and also if there is anything further to be learnt about the will. I will turn over everything I find to you, and then you will decide how to proceed. I cannot, however, agree to conceal anything I find which is proof positive of a serious crime.'

'Of course, I understand. That seems eminently sensible.'

'Do you know the date and location of your aunt's wedding?'

'I am afraid not. I suspected, of course, that it never took place or was conducted illegally, and so I did attempt to find that out, but Mr Wheelock, who took great care never to leave my aunt's side throughout the interview, made quite sure that I was never granted that information. I did go to my aunt's bank but of course they would not divulge anything other than that they were satisfied that there had been a genuine marriage and Mr Wheelock had become the lawful owner of his wife's property. He might have forged the papers, of course, and led my aunt to believe that she was married, but without seeing the documents I can do nothing.'

'If they were genuinely married it will be some time before the event appears in the registers of Somerset House. We really cannot wait that long.'

'I am given to understand by Mr Rawsthorne that there are very few barriers you cannot overcome.' He paused, and gave her a worried look. 'I can guess what you must think of me, Miss Doughty. If I am able to show that my aunt's marriage was invalid, then she once again becomes a single woman and the sole mistress of her fortune, of which I will stand to inherit a large portion. You may well believe, and I can scarcely blame you for this, that I am motivated only by love of money. Of course I do not deny that such an inheritance is something to be desired, nevertheless I can assure you that I have a secure administrative post in Calcutta, more than enough salary for my own needs, and no family of my own to support.'

Sarah signed 'watch this one' to Frances, but then she did this with most single male clients, it being her personal mission to ensure that Frances did not choose to marry the wrong man.

Frances appeared to be brushing a stray hair from her forehead but was actually telling Sarah that her message was understood.

'My main concern is my aunt's happiness,' continued Chandler, oblivious to the silent conversation, 'and foiling the actions of a criminal. If it came to it I would be more than happy to see that the vegetarian society is recompensed.'

The business was concluded, and before he departed Mr Chandler paid Frances an advance on her expenses and gave her the address of the lodging house where he could be contacted.

The plate of buns was extracted from the drawer. 'He's a smooth one,' said Sarah as they chewed thoughtfully. 'I don't know about him. Could be his foreign manners, could be something else.'

'He has posed a difficult problem, something I have never solved before; how to discover a marriage which if it happened was so recent that it cannot yet be in the Somerset House registers, when we don't know where it took place. I could put advertisements in the newspapers, of course, but I don't wish to alert Mr Wheelock to my actions. Even the most discreet enquiries will, I fear, come to his notice.'

'Was it a real wedding or a fake one?' That's the big question.'

Frances finished her bun and dabbed crumbs from her lips with a napkin. 'I think it was real. Wheelock knows the law all too well. Also, my observation has been that a man undertakes a false wedding when he only wishes to possess the woman's person. It makes it easier to discard her.' Sarah nodded sagely, since it fitted well with her general opinion of men, with the possible exception of Professor Pounder. 'When he wants the woman's money and land, especially if there is a great fortune involved, he proceeds differently. Wheelock will have a certificate hidden away somewhere that he can produce if he needs it. He must have shown it to his wife's bankers to make sure that he was able to take control of her property, but even if they retained the details they would not show them to me. All they would require is sight of a valid certificate and Mrs Wheelock's assurance that they were married.'

Sarah refreshed the teapot while Frances remained deep in thought and ate another bun. 'I can expect no information from either Mr or Mrs Wheelock. He is on his guard and she would not be friendly towards me in any case.' Frances mused.

The former Mrs Outram had once written to Frances offering what amounted to a bribe to change her testimony in some criminal proceedings against a young favourite of hers. The firm refusal had not been received well. 'It must have been hard to make her agree to marry him in such a way that would not at once arouse suspicion. They would have had to use their real names. He dared not do otherwise. What story might the witnesses have to tell? Who gave away the bride and stood as groomsman? Did the clergyman or registrar not have doubts? Mr Rawsthorne has already told me he has found no record of the wedding in London and I must proceed on that basis. I can certainly see why they did not marry in Bayswater. The bride is too well known here, by name at least. It would have been the gossip of the tea tables in minutes.'

'Unless he bribed or threatened those in the know.'

'I suppose he might have done so. Although bribery is always a risk. A person willing to be bribed is not the most honest associate. Such a one has no sense of loyalty and thinks only of money – he or she will always be happy to accept a larger counter bribe. I notice incidentally that Mr Wheelock made no attempt to bribe Mr Rawsthorne – he must have known that he would not succeed. His ploy there was to conceal his intentions for as long as possible.'

'Do you think Wheelock knew about Chandler before he married the old lady?'

'I think he would have made it his business to know about any relatives who might object. He must have hoped that there would be none, but if he had learned of a great-nephew, finding out that the only relative resided in India was almost as good. It gave him time to marry before Mr Chandler could arrive in England. It is far harder to upset an existing marriage than prevent one taking place. And Mr Chandler, as he has admitted, is no expert on his aunt's state of health and mind. Also any attempt he makes to invalidate the marriage will be countered by accusations that he does so only for financial motives.'

'That might be true.'

'It might, but that is not my concern. However avaricious he may prove to be, he is still entitled to inherit. You know my opinion of Mr Wheelock. If I can stop him swindling an elderly lady out of her fortune I will do so with great pleasure.'

Sarah grinned. 'The servants might know something. Of course we don't know if he dismissed the old ones and brought in new after the wedding, or just frightened them into doing as he says.'

'I suspect we will learn little from them if we make a direct enquiry, but I suggest that you find some way of befriending one of them when she goes out of the house. If she trusts you then she might be tempted to complain about her situation and her master, and then we may learn something. She might even know the date of the wedding, and if you can learn how long the couple were away from home that will at least suggest how far they travelled.'

CHAPTER FIFTEEN

It was ten days to the very hour of Jim Price's execution. Frances, unmoved by the sight of breakfast, gazed in despair at the letter she was writing to the *Chronicle* on his behalf. She was repeating old words, old pleas, and was bitterly aware that she had nothing more to say; yet she had to go on. There were no new clues, and she had no idea where to look for them or if they even existed. Frustratingly she had still received no message in response to the information she had already passed on about Mr Gundry, and did not know if it was being examined, or given any weight.

There was the usual litter of notes in the morning post, and it seemed that the rumour now pervading the neighbourhood was that the killer was a carpenter. Someone had even suggested that Jim Price committed all three murders, ignoring the fact that he had been in custody for two of them. Frances wondered if one of the letters came from the killer trying to divert attention from himself, and so wrapped them up and passed the bundle to the police.

She also reflected if she was beginning to detect a new feeling in the air. Ten days had passed since the Norfolk Square murder. Despite all of Mr Candy's efforts to ensure that Bayswater ladies had respectable escorts, Frances, as she peered out of the window, at what had so recently been a street almost deserted except for pressmen, was now starting to see a little of the normal traffic reassert itself. Once the morning fogs had cleared, the day promised fair and mild. It was dry underfoot, and ladies, often in pairs, but occasionally singly, strolled by. The fickle population was beginning to tire of the old excitement and was looking for something new, and, imagining that with the passage of time the danger was over, some were starting to relax their vigilance. Perhaps the murderer had moved away, perhaps, tormented by self-disgust, he had ended his life in some miserable place of filthy squalor, but in all probability, thought Frances, he was just biding his time, waiting for the next young woman to walk alone in the dark.

One of her morning letters was different; a plea for an early interview from Mr Digby, the father of Mr Candy's erstwhile betrothed. He was very insistent concerning the extreme urgency of the situation, and Frances responded with a note that he might call at his convenience. He arrived an hour later in a state of distraction.

'Miss Doughty I am so very grateful that you have spared some of your time to see me,' he gasped, 'I know that you must be engaged on other matters of great moment at the present time.'

Frances decided that it was useless to explain that she was not in hot pursuit of the Bayswater Face-slasher. She introduced Sarah, and offered her visitor a chair. He sat down quickly, eager to begin their conference. 'Tell me how I may help you. Am I correct in guessing that this concerns your daughter?'

'Oh who would be a father of a lovely yet wilful girl!' he moaned. 'Yes you are quite correct; it is Enid who troubles me. She is good and virtuous and the very best daughter a fond father could wish for, but she is susceptible in matters of the heart and will not be advised by me. If her dear mother were alive then perhaps it would be different, but that gentle guiding hand has been lost to us. You will recall, of course, that Enid is enamoured of that young dog Pargeter. No respectable family will admit him to court their daughters but I did not find out his true nature until it was too late. He means to secure her and then make me a beggar.'

Frances was not entirely sure if Mr Digby was more concerned about his daughter or his ducats, and from Sarah's gesture, neither was she. 'But you have already stipulated that they might not marry until Mr Pargeter has both paid off his gambling debts and provided proof that he could support a wife, neither of which event seems probable.'

'Yes, and Enid did appear to accept that, but she is nineteen and one of her bosom friends has just married at that age and she is starting to feel that it is time for her to do so too.' Frances, aged twenty-one and with no prospect of marriage or any anxiety concerning that situation, simply nodded. 'But the thing I am here to speak to you about is – well I received news this morning of a most dreadful tragedy. A cousin of Pargeter's, a young man of the best reputation and recently engaged to be married, only twenty-four years of age, has been killed in a riding accident.'

'That is a great tragedy indeed. And you are concerned that your daughter will fly to Pargeter's side to comfort him?'

'Oh, Pargeter cared nothing for his cousin, so he needs no comfort. No, it is far, far worse than that.'

'It is?'

'The cousin, being young and having no thought of death, had not made a will, and by some strange vagary in the family line, a substantial portion of his property goes to Pargeter. In fact if I had not known that Pargeter never rises from his bed before midday I would have suspected him of laming the horse, or laying a hidden rope to make it stumble. He is about to become very rich, although I doubt that the fortune will last long. Just long enough for him to persuade Enid that he is in a position to marry her and has overcome all my objections.' He ground a fist into his palm. 'What am I to do?' he wailed.

'Does Miss Digby know the news?'

'No, not yet, and I intend to keep it from her as best I can, but it cannot be long before she is informed of the position. She will want to marry at once, but I know that Pargeter will soon squander every penny of his inheritance and be in debt again, and they are both well aware that I cannot stand by and see my dear girl starve. If they were married I would have to support them both, not to mention any family they will have, and settle the new debts that Pargeter will undoubtedly incur. I will be ruined!' He thumped both elbows down on the table and pressed his fingers to his eyes.

Frances pushed the water carafe and glass closer to the distraught man, and spoke to him in a calming way. 'If, as you say, he gambles away what he has, then in six months he will be in debt again and under the agreement you have made with him he will once again be in no position to marry. Would your daughter be willing to wait six months for the wedding?'

Digby shook his head, and Frances poured water for him. He tried to drink it with trembling hands that could barely hold the glass. 'I hardly think she wants to wait six days! I suspect – I suspect very strongly that she has been meeting him in secret.

I think she does so when she goes from the house with her maid or in the company of a friend. I think they exchange letters – the maid has been carrying love notes and helping make the assignations. I have questioned her but she denies it. I can't very well lock Enid up, although it is tempting to do so, and if I try to impose a strict chaperone I am very afraid that she will simply up and run away with him, and then, of course, I shall have no choice but to agree to their marrying. She is very determined. It is hard for me, but I believe that if I appear to be lenient then I have the best chance of observing her.'

'That is very wise. Now this is my suggestion. I will have your daughter and the maid watched and followed. My agents are very discreet and should be able to overhear any conversations. I also have a number of messenger boys in my pay. If one of them can earn Mr Pargeter's trust, then he might be employed carrying messages and we would be able to examine them.'

'Oh, that would be a great weight off my mind,' said the overwrought father with an exhalation of relief, 'yes please arrange to do so at once.'

'Where can Mr Pargeter be found?'

Digby gave a little scowl of distaste. 'He lodges at the Piccadilly Club on Porchester Road. An ideal place for such a scoundrel. I assume he has been running up a bill on the strength of his family name. That is his usual way. I am only happy that they do not allow females in there. Gambling and pugilistic competitions yes, and a great deal of drink. Oh, don't mistake me, I have never been there and do not intend to, but when I learned that this was where he lodged I made enquiries about the place and learned its nature. How that did not open my daughter's eyes I simply do not know.'

'I take it you do not have a portrait of Mr Pargeter?'

'No, although I am sure if I was shameless enough to rifle though Enid's trinkets I would find one. He is tall, with blond hair very much curled. Females seem to think him handsome.'

'I am sure you have a portrait of your daughter.'

Digby put his hand in his pocket and brought out a little card, which he glanced at fondly before handing it to Frances. The subject of the photograph was seated by a small table on which rested a vase of flowers. Perhaps the flowers were intended to enhance the beauty of the sitter, and imply by association the youth and freshness of the young girl. Miss Digby, however, was no delicate fragile maiden inviting pure and honourable homage. She was broad of shoulder, and generously rounded in form, and the glance with which she favoured the camera was more defiant than demure. Her features were plain but not devoid of interest. If it was possible to read character from a face, which many believed one could do, then she was not a young woman to be trifled with, or from whom a father might expect unhesitating obedience. There was a determined curve to her mouth and a tilt to the tip of her nose as if everything she saw about her was beneath her notice. She looked like a young woman who would enjoy assisting Sarah apprehend a malefactor.

'If I may keep this, then I will show it to my agents who will see that she is observed.'

'That may save her for a while, but there is something else I would like done, because simply preventing the marriage will not end the matter. Could you find some means of making her change her opinion of Pargeter? She is dazzled by his handsome features and good manners. His foolish escapades she finds amusing. How I wish she had never met him! How I wish she had married Mr Candy, who is a dull fellow but honest and worthy. I fear, however, I very much fear, that having enjoyed the attentions of a fellow like Pargeter, even if she was to give him up she will never settle for Candy.

'But I do have a new hope for her. A young gentleman by the name of Berkeley, who is of very good family and would be an excellent match for Enid, has asked my permission to call on her. At present I doubt very much that she would receive him, but in time, she may. I think she might listen to you; I am sure you understand the female mind better than I.'

If Frances understood anything, she suspected that Miss Digby desired the kind of excitement that could only be gained by association with a handsome rogue, an enterprise which, while it offered temporary diversion to an adventurous female, was doomed not to last and was in danger of ending badly.

'Apart from his gambling is there anything else you know about Mr Pargeter which might change your daughter's mind about him? I could have him watched for you.'

'He has no brains to speak of and he flirts outrageously,' said her client with obvious disgust.

'Miss Digby may think she has brains enough for two and that the flirting will cease after marriage.'

'You are right about the brains, but she is not worldly wise. I approve her innocence, of course, but she will not look to me for advice as she ought to.'

'You mentioned Mr Pargeter's escapades?'

'Yes, he is a member of a club for young men with no sense. They call themselves the Bold Bloods. He may even be the founder. I think they meet at the Piccadilly Club, and dare each other to take risks, some of which are criminal. There have been shop windows broken by stones just lately which I am sure is their work. One of them actually jumped off a bridge!' Digby sighed heavily. 'I wish Pargeter would jump off a bridge! These japes are the subject of wagers. They have a secret sign which they chalk up on the wall beside their work if they have time, so they know it is one of their number who has committed the outrage.'

'What does this mark resemble?'

'Oh, I have never seen it. I think the police wash them off. Bayswater is in enough of a panic as it is.'

When Mr Digby had wended his miserable way Sarah took a look at the picture of his daughter and laughed. 'He'd best marry her off as soon as he can to the first halfway honest man who will have her. I've seen that one walking out with her maid and she fancies herself as a real attraction. Parades up and down the Grove in the latest fashions. Thinks all the young men are looking at her.'

'And they are not?'

'No, they're eyeing the maid, who has a saucy way, but the mistress thinks it's all for her.'

'Does Professor Pounder still give exhibitions of pugilism at the Piccadilly Club?'

'Sometimes. I'll ask him if he knows anything about this Pargeter and the Bold Bloods. They don't sound very bold to me. More like a rabble of boys who'd faint dead away at the first sight of real danger.'

'One of them jumped off a bridge. Wasn't that in the newspapers recently?'

Sarah gave another laugh, and went to get a copy of the *Illustrated Police News* from two weeks previously. One of the smaller pictures on the front cover was entitled 'Strange Prank of a Viscount's Son' and showed a youth making a leap from Blackfriars Bridge. Since the tide was out at the time, he had not been swept away by the river and drowned but had had a soft and unpleasantly sticky landing in the deep mud at the shoreline, from where he had been rescued unhurt by a policeman. He had explained that he had had no intention of destroying himself, such an attempt being a criminal offence, but had committed the act for a bet. He had later been bound over in court to keep the peace, and removed by his irate father.

Frances recalled that Chas and Barstie were members of the Piccadilly Club. They had joined it at her request, since she had wanted trusted agents in place to keep watch on suspicious residents, and the club would not admit youths under the age of sixteen to its membership, neither were women allowed through its doors. Chas and Barstie had found it a useful place for attracting business, but she wondered if they still frequented the club, since it had an undeniably shady reputation and nowadays they wished to be considered respectable. Barstie was aspiring to the hand of a lady whose father needed convincing of his spotless reputation and business acumen, and Chas was still casting about for an heiress or a widow of means. He liked to save time by courting them in triplicate, the essential part of his scheme being that each should never know of the other two. Frances decided to go and see them.

The office of the Bayswater Design and Advertising Co. Ltd was unusually tidy, and the directors were working quietly at their desks. They looked like men who were expecting to be visited by the police at any moment.

As Frances was ushered in Chas jumped to his feet and offered her a chair. 'We are very grateful to you for your warning, dear lady, since we are increasingly becoming valued agents for the police, who consider us to be model citizens. Regarding that unpleasant fellow with the knife, they have descriptions, they have drawings, they have information, and now it only wants to have the man himself behind bars.'

'Since you are both so very respectable nowadays I assume that you are no longer members of the Piccadilly Club?'

The directors glanced at each other.

'There was a time,' admitted Barstie reluctantly, after a long pause, 'when we were starting out in our endeavours and we had to look everywhere for custom and take what we could find. We could not afford to confine ourselves to the most salubrious places. Some of the associates we made at that time are men we still do business with, and many of them still prefer to manage their transactions at the Piccadilly Club.'

Chas nodded agreement. 'Clubs are places where men meet and talk about money. Sometimes they talk about other things, but it all comes down to money in the end. Everything always does.'

'They are the best places to find out who has the money and who needs it,' added Barstie.

'So you are still members? You still go there regularly?'

They glanced at each other again.

'I see that you do. Have you encountered a young man called Pargeter who lodges there? He is often in the company of other youths who call themselves the Bold Bloods.'

Both men gave a little snort of derision, and Chas grinned. 'Ah yes, they have made something of a name for themselves in certain quarters. Not a good name, in fact a very bad one, but a name nonetheless. Pargeter, if he is the one with the curled hair, and I think he is, is the biggest scapegrace of them all. He borrows money from any man foolish enough to lend it to him and boasts to everyone that he will soon marry a fortune.'

'There is a real danger that he will do so, and it is something I wish to prevent, since his motives are far from honourable. I am acting for a respectable gentleman whose daughter is enamoured of this Pargeter. I think she finds his discreditable behaviour more interesting than the honesty of other men. She probably knows all about his idle pranks but I need to find out something more, something that will make her see that he is not to be trusted.'

Chas looked thoughtful. 'And you say that the father has money?'

'He does.' Frances showed him the portrait of Miss Digby.

'Ah. A great deal of money, I assume.'

'I would like you to consider methods of opening this misguided lady's eyes to Mr Pargeter's faults.'

The two looked serious. 'It would be easy to entrap him in some scheme or other,' mused Chas, and Barstie nodded.

'I am sure you are right, as he is not considered intelligent. But if the lady suspects that he is the victim of a plot then it might make her all the more determined to have him. She will be his champion against adversity, and then it will be impossible to part them. Would you be willing for now simply to watch him and gather information? I can understand that you would not wish to become members of the Bold Blood fraternity, but you would be in a position to learn about their plans. They do not seem to be the most discreet individuals and might well talk about their exploits and what they intend to try next.'

This course of proceeding was agreed upon and Frances, declining an offer of refreshment, took her leave and mounted the stairs to see Tom Smith, who she found in conference with Ratty.

'What c'n we do fer you today, Miss Doughty?' asked Tom with a smile.

Frances recounted the tale of the unfortunate passion that existed between Enid Digby and young Mr Pargeter, and Mr Digby's fears that they might run away together. She handed over the portrait of Miss Digby and supplied her address. 'I would like someone to follow her when she goes out with her maid or a friend. See if they meet in secret with Pargeter and if possible overhear their conversation. If they do make plans to run away I will need to know at once. It is thought that the maid is carrying messages to arrange these meetings.'

'Right you are,' said Ratty, staring at the portrait. 'An' if she gives up on the marryin' idea she c'n always go in fer the pugilistics, 'cos from the look of 'er she'd be a champion.'

'I also wish you to collect as much information as you can concerning Mr Pargeter. Mr Digby is hoping to discover something that will make his daughter reject him.'

'I know the gent,' said Tom. 'All curls an' fancy clothes. Lives at the Piccadilly. We sometimes run messages for 'im. To a Mr Green, only that's not 'is real name; runs an off-course betting book. Don't the lady know 'e's a wrong 'un?'

'If she does, she probably imagines she can reform him. Tom, I hope you are not assisting Mr Pargeter in committing a crime.'

'I'm just the messenger. Might be anything in the notes. *I* don't read 'em.'

'Of course not. Well, if you should accidentally see what is in one of these notes, you must let me know.'

CHAPTER SIXTEEN

rances did not know how many people the meeting of
Mr Candy's Bayswater Vigilance Committee might attract
and had been wondering if he had been a little too optimistic
in hiring Westbourne Hall for the event when a far smaller room
suitable for perhaps two or three hundred persons would have been
better suited. She was astonished, therefore, to arrive at the venue
with Sarah and Professor Pounder to find the hall teeming with men
and women of all ages and levels of society, busily talking about the
terrible crimes and what could be done about them. A long table
had been furnished with tea urns and a team of ladies were handing
out steaming cups of tea as fast as they were able, while others were
putting printed leaflets on the chairs that had been set out in rows
for the audience. She was pleased to see that everyone who entered
the hall was being met at the door and asked to sign a petition.

At the far end of the hall, the musicians who had been perform-
ing on the platform were clearing away their instruments, the lady
and gentleman vocalists were descending the steps, and chairs
were being put in place for the guests of honour.

Frances wondered if Effie Price was there but it was hard to
see such a small slight figure in the great throng. She thought on
reflection that the girl was more likely to be at home looking after
her mother.

'Looks like half of Bayswater is here,' said Sarah.

'I expect we largely have Mr Candy to thank for that; and then
of course Miss Gilbert and Miss John have rallied their ladies.'

Mr Gillan of the *Bayswater Chronicle* approached, clutching a
notebook and pencil. 'Miss Doughty, will you be addressing the
meeting?' He had the bright enthusiastic look of a newsman surrounded by news.

'I will, and I shall expect to see a full report in the *Chronicle*.'

'Oh I can promise that, our readers are always interested in you.'

'To ensure accuracy I have my speech already written down, and I have brought a copy for you. That will save you a great deal of shorthand.' She handed him a sheet of paper, which he accepted with some surprise. 'Is Mr Ibbitson not with you tonight?'

'Oh he's off on another story. He has a sweetheart now, you know,' added Gillan teasingly. He looked carefully at Frances to see if he could spy any signs of jealousy and seeing none, went on, 'I suppose you have met Mr Pollaky?'

'No, we have never met, in fact I am not sure I have ever seen his portrait, so I would not recognise him.'

'Ah, well I have interviewed him and I can see that he is already here, so I could introduce you if you like. That would be a wonderful thing for our readers, the meeting of two great detectives. I am sure when the criminals of Bayswater see that you have compared notes and are working on the case together they will take fright and run away.'

'If that was true then you would have nothing to put in your paper.'

He laughed. 'Oh, there are always the romances and nasty accidents. We're never short of news.'

'I don't suppose,' said Frances impulsively, as her thoughts returned to the vexed problem of her own family mysteries, 'that you are acquainted with the names Vernon Salter and Lancelot Dobree?'

'Should I be?' asked Gillan.

'I really can't say.'

'Well I never heard of the first one, but the other one does sound familiar. Yes, that's it, Dobree, rich old gent, philanthropist. Gets listed in the papers with the subscribers to charities. Know anything against him?'

'Not at all.'

'Well let me know when you do. But come with me, I can see Mr Pollaky over there.'

Professor Pounder decided to take a stroll about the hall to take note of any potential trouble. There was something about his tall, calm, quiet muscularity that inspired confidence and respect, and wherever he walked, he created a little pool of order as everyone who fell under his gaze decided to behave themselves.

Frances and Sarah accompanied Mr Gillan to where a serious-looking man in his fifties with a fine moustache was standing alone sipping tea and surveying the scene. He had the carefully cultivated air of someone merely interested in the company, but there was shrewdness behind the casual demeanour, and he appeared to see and take note of everything.

'Mr Pollaky,' said Gillan, 'it is very good to see you here, sir. I am sure we will all benefit from your observations.'

'Thank you Mr Gillan,' said Pollaky. He did not, thought Frances, look quite the Englishman, although she had heard that he had lived in London for many years, and his accent too, though elegantly English, also had a hint of middle Europe.

'Allow me to introduce you to two excellent ladies. This is Miss Frances Doughty of whom I am sure you have heard, and this is her assistant the no less doughty Miss Smith. I expect you will have a great deal to talk about,' added Gillan hopefully, opening his notebook.

Mr Pollaky raised his eyebrows, and set aside his cup of tea. He extended his hand first to Frances and then Sarah, with great politeness, and made a little bow. 'Miss Doughty, Miss Smith, it is my very great honour to meet you. I have, of course, read about your exploits in the newspapers. But say – does Mr Gillan tell all?'

Frances smiled. 'I am delighted to make your acquaintance. Mr Gillan is under strict instructions from me to tell the truth, but I fear he does sometimes paint it with a very colourful brush. Of course he is only able to print what I feel I ought to tell him,' she added mischievously.

'And Miss Smith, I have heard much of your abilities to – ah – persuade criminals to give themselves up. Having now made your acquaintance I feel sure that nothing I have heard was an exaggeration.'

'You don't know the half of it,' muttered Gillan.

'Is it true that you are investigating the terrible murders that have taken place in Bayswater?' asked Pollaky of the lady detectives with a worried frown. 'I must say I would not ask any of my agents to do such a dangerous thing.'

Frances was quick to reassure him. 'That report was a misunderstanding. I am acting for the family of Jim Price who was recently convicted of the murder of Martha Miller; a murder that I feel was perpetrated not by him but the man who is currently reducing Bayswater to a state of terror. I have been looking for a witness who might exonerate him. Unfortunately a young inexperienced newspaperman thought that I was looking for the real killer and said so in the paper. It has drawn a great deal of attention to me that I could well have done without. There have been correspondents standing outside my front door waiting for an announcement ever since.'

'Well we have to do what we can to get the news,' said Gillan defensively. 'But I'm sure none of the men who annoyed you were from the *Chronicle*.'

'Did one of your men come back soaking wet and smelling of dishwater?' asked Sarah.

Gillan looked decidedly uncomfortable and Pollaky chuckled.

Frances was suddenly struck by a thought and decided to take the opportunity that presented itself. 'Mr Pollaky, if I might be so bold, I would like to ask your advice.'

He looked solemn. 'Ah well I do have a scale of charges for that. My experience has been gained over very many years and does not come cheap.'

'Whatever you think is appropriate.'

He laughed. 'Ask away Miss Doughty,' he said gallantly, 'meeting you is payment enough!'

She smiled at the compliment. 'You are very kind. I am currently trying to trace a marriage that has taken place very recently. The parties will not reveal where it took place and it does not appear to have been solemnised in Bayswater, which is where they both reside, or even in London.'

'Ah, I think I can guess what this is about!' exclaimed Gillan, scribbling rapidly in shorthand.

Frances turned to him. 'You will have the full story, I promise, when it is resolved, but I beg you, do not report it yet or there may be undesirable consequences.'

Gillan gave a little sigh of regret but assented.

'You think there was something suspicious about this marriage?' asked Pollaky.

'I do, and I believe that the location has been deliberately concealed to prevent enquiry. But I can hardly search every parish in the land.'

Pollaky gave this some thought. 'It is my experience that when a man wishes to vanish from sight he does not go to a place that he has never been before. He looks for a town or a village where he feels at home. It might be a place that he has not been to for many a year but still he is drawn to it, as it has a familiarity that makes him comfortable. If the couple married elsewhere than Bayswater then ask yourself if they have another place that would welcome one or both, a residential address in the area that they can enter on the certificate.'

Frances thanked him and he beamed and bowed, and took up his cup of tea once more.

Mr Candy had just leaped up on the stage, looked quite flushed with excitement at the success of his new venture. Usually neat and dapper in his dress, he had made an even greater effort that evening to be the epitome of smart young manhood as if he had arranged to be polished bright for the occasion. 'Ladies and gentlemen, please make your way to your seats. The meeting will begin very shortly.'

There was a last rush for the remaining tea and then everyone began to file into place. Mr Loveridge had just appeared and was standing by the side of the stage with a large sheaf of paper and his pockets stuffed with pencils, ready to sketch the participants.

Frances and Sarah greeted him. 'Is this a commission for the *Illustrated Police News*?' asked Frances, seeing that he had already with a few swift strokes of his pencil outlined the stage and its environs.

'It is, but also,' he glanced about him quickly and lowered his voice, 'more importantly the police have asked me to sketch as many people as I can as they think it very possible that the murderer might come here to gloat about his work and also to find out if he is close to discovery.'

'You think he might be here in this very room?' Frances cast a glance at the great assembly but could see no one suspicious. Everyone was very respectably dressed and well behaved, but she supposed that even the most depraved and maniacal killer could put on a good face and adopt pleasing manners and so fool everyone until he revealed his true self.

'At least that Filleter fellow isn't here,' said Loveridge. 'Judging from your description he would not be able to hide himself even in this throng.'

'I hope you will not be sketching me. Remember your promise.'

'I shall abide by your request, of course, and will not reveal your features to the press, but you must allow me to make a drawing of you one day, not for publication, but as a study of interest.'

'If you think it would be interesting then of course I would permit it,' said Frances, and she found herself blushing a little.

'And Miss Smith, also,' said Mr Loveridge, quickly. Sarah uttered a sound very like a growl. 'Incidentally, I did seek a commission to sketch Mr and Mrs Wheelock, and met with a very unfriendly reception at their door, but I will continue to try for an introduction.'

Inspector Swanson had arrived together with Sergeant Brown, and while Swanson made his way to the stage Brown remained at the back of the hall keeping a sharp eye on the company. Frances had expected to see Inspector Sharrock, who, although he was not in charge of the efforts to find the killer, was giving Swanson all the assistance he could, but of course, she reflected, he had all the other criminals of the district to attend to, who might well be taking advantage of the police being so heavily occupied to increase their activities.

Mr Loveridge indicated a poster on the wall advertising a forthcoming concert with a small orchestra and voices, at sixpence a ticket, the proceeds to go to a children's hospital. 'That is a very pleasing poster. Do you like music Miss Doughty?'

'Yes, very much.'

'Do you attend concerts?'

'Sometimes, yes.'

'I too enjoy music. I was wondering if you were intending to go to this concert?'

'I had not given it any thought but it does look very interesting. Sarah, would you and Professor Pounder like to go? I think we can spare ourselves one evening. I see that the money raised is going to a good cause.'

'Perhaps we might make up a little party and all go together?' suggested Loveridge.

Sarah said nothing, but she did so very loudly.

'That would be very pleasant indeed,' said Frances. The date advertised was two weeks hence, some days after the date set for

Jim Price's execution. If that went ahead she would not feel inclined to amuse herself, but might well need some activity to distract her. For a brief moment she pictured herself at the concert with the Price family, Mrs Price glowing with new health, Miss Price happily arm in arm with her brother, newly freed and earning the congratulations of all those around him. It was a scene from a fairy tale.

Mr Candy approached the front of the stage. Inspector Swanson and Mr Pollaky had already taken their seats and Candy beckoned Frances to ascend. Although it was not strictly necessary, Mr Loveridge gave Frances his hand and assisted her up the steps. There were now several other people seated on the stage, including Reverend Day of St Stephens, the rotund form of Mr William Whiteley, who took every opportunity to advertise his rapidly expanding drapery and clothing business that did not involve actual expenditure, and Mr Churchwarden Spencer of the Paddington Vestry. The fact that the vestry was currently in a bitter legal dispute with Mr Whiteley over his continuous flouting of building regulations in Queens Road, appeared to cause that gentleman not one whit of discomfiture.

Frances glanced back at Sarah and indicated that she should remain in the body of the hall and keep watch. Sarah folded her arms and nodded with a sideways glance at Loveridge who, she seemed to think, needed special watching. After a great deal of shifting of chairs and rattling of teacups in saucers as conversations were hurriedly brought to an end, Mr Candy's appeals for silence were finally heard and adhered to.

Frances took her seat and looked out across the hall over the sea of faces. There were a great many individuals she recognised, tradesmen who had served the needs of Bayswater for food and clothes, furniture and flowers for many a year. A manufacturer of umbrellas who had been handing out leaflets about their potential as a weapon of defence was busily demonstrating the sharpness of the ferrule of his own instrument to the gentlemen on either side of him. There were several clergymen, some prominent magistrates of the district, and Drs Collin and Neill. Mr Carter Freke was attending, presumably on behalf of Mr Rawsthorne, and there was a phalanx of the press as well as many members of the Bayswater Women's Suffrage Society. Miss Gilbert was positively bouncing with suppressed anticipation and Miss John had removed her bodkin from her reticule and was gripping it very tightly in her little fist and looking about suspiciously to see who she might plunge it into. Frances hoped she had not bought herself a gun. There were also several ladies amongst the throng who did not wish to be known as they were closely veiled.

A few attendees appeared to be there only out of boredom. One young man sauntered in late with two companions, pushed his way past a group of respectable gentlemen, and slid into a seat where he lounged in an insolent manner wearing his hat deliberately askew. His more timid associates sat with him and whatever he said to them clearly gave deep offence to those persons unfortunate enough to overhear his words, at which he uttered a burst of laughter. Much to the disgust of others, he drew a flask from his pocket and refreshed himself from it. Frances felt sure that the contents would not have been approved by the temperance society.

'Ladies and gentlemen,' began Mr Candy, 'it is my very great pleasure to see so many of you here today. We of the Bayswater Vigilance Committee are dedicated to ensuring that the streets are safe for our citizens to go about their lawful business. It is for this purpose that we have instituted the Guardians of Virtue to protect the lives of the ladies of Bayswater. At the end of the meeting our clerks will be taking the names of those gentlemen who wish to volunteer. All will have their names submitted to the Committee for approval, and they will without exception have to supply a letter of recommendation. Please see the leaflets on your seats for details of what is required. We will admit to our ranks only those gentlemen of the highest possible reputation. I am sure that in Bayswater there will be very many who will qualify. We will also be sending a petition to Parliament asking them to ensure the safety of honest citizens. Please do sign the petition before you depart. On the way out our clerks will also approach you with collection boxes and ask you to give generously to meet our expenses. The lives of our virtuous ladies are, I am sure you will agree, beyond price. There truly cannot be a better cause.'

The dissolute-looking young man made a loud comment of a highly irreverent nature concerning ladies who were not virtuous, much to the disgust of all right-minded persons who heard him.

'I would beg that gentlemen to moderate his language,' said Mr Candy, sharply. 'This is not a music hall or a common beer-house, and if you cannot show respectful behaviour then I suggest you leave and take your companions with you, who I believe are of the same ilk.'

There was a response of such a coarse nature that the room was shocked. Silently, Professor Pounder, who had been placing himself where he might best deal with the nuisance, approached the group of young men. 'I think you should leave,' he said. The bold youth jumped up, and swung a fist, but the professor caught it, neatly enclosed it in his own and applied just enough pressure to show that he meant what he said. The miscreant's surprise at this development was only increased when Sarah came up and dissuaded him from any further action by taking his other hand and moving it to a position between his shoulder blades that Frances would have thought impossible if she had not seen it.

There was a whimper, and an oath that was silenced by an infinitesimal motion from both Sarah and the Professor. 'Understand now?' Pounder asked, but it was obvious from the tears of pain that had appeared in the eyes of the immobilised youth that he understood his position completely. He nodded.

'Now go, and take your friends with you while you still have all your limbs,' said Sarah.

Swanson rose. 'Sergeant Brown, take those men's names and addresses and we will talk to them later.' Brown stepped forward, and in a few minutes the nuisance was dealt with and peace reigned again.

'I must thank our brave friends for their prompt and efficient action,' said Mr Candy, and the audience responded with applause. 'Do you think,' he asked hopefully, turning to Swanson who had sat down again, 'that we have caught the murderer?'

Swanson shook his head. 'I know that type. A lot of noise and not much else.'

Candy looked disappointed and continued his speech.

'How grateful we all are to those who guard us so well. In that case, it seems, youthful high spirits and not a little drink were the cause. But to return to my theme. Our committee accepts that the task of discovering the criminal who has dared to arouse such terror in our community is for those whose occupation it is to protect us with their courage and their expertise. I am delighted therefore to introduce to you today three of our most distinguished exponents of the art of capturing criminals. All three are working night and day to ensure your safety.

'First a gentleman whose many years of work as a detective has placed him at the very pinnacle of his profession, Mr Ignatius Pollaky of Paddington Green. I know he could tell you many an exciting story of his successes if, that is, they are not so secret that it would be dangerous to speak of them.' The audience gave little tremulous murmurs.

'We also welcome a famous inspector of Scotland Yard, who is in command of the police force's work on these terrible murders. Inspector Swanson, as I am sure you all know, recently apprehended the criminal Mapleton, the railway murderer, and I am sure he can be persuaded to tell you all about his adventures in that case.' The audience almost licked their collective lips in anticipation of such a delicious treat.

'And of course Bayswater's very own Miss Frances Doughty, a lady before whom all men tremble with fear. Does the man exist who can match her in a battle of wits? I have not yet met one. Miss Doughty has taken it upon herself to exert every particle of her wonderful brain to catch the criminal.'

Frances opened her mouth to protest and shut it again. The audience was by now very excited, which she supposed was not a bad thing as it would encourage them to join the cause, which was after all the point of the meeting. No one was asleep which was a very good sign.

'Our first speaker today,' announced Mr Candy, 'is Mr Pollaky.'

There was polite applause, and Mr Pollaky rose and extended his warm greetings to the assembly. Frances wondered how many of them were his clients.

'I am afraid that I have to disappoint you in one respect. Mr Candy is quite right that I cannot tell you all the secrets of my profession. If I was to say to you now, these are my methods, and this is how I find the men I seek, then the criminals would be sure to get to hear of it and know how to avoid me and my agents and then they would make their escape. Also my clients would not care to have their business put before the world. So I will not speak of those matters. This current business in Bayswater, however, I will speak of.

'Few men can be as dangerous as the man who has committed these crimes. His motive is mysterious. He most probably does not even know the women he has killed and can therefore have no grudge against them. He is undoubtedly insane. I am sure that Inspector Swanson will confirm this but there must have been enquiries made of all the asylums to discover if any inmate has recently escaped.' He glanced at Swanson who nodded. 'Doctors will be able to tell the police if they have any patients of distracted mind who might be suspect. It is also up to you, the citizens of Bayswater, to assist the police by being watchful, and concealing nothing that could be of importance. Is there a member of your family or a person you know who has been wandering in their mind, perhaps seeing visions or hearing sounds that are not there? Do they feel that they are being pursued by demons and have an urge to slay them? Do they utter threats? If so, you must tell the police at once. Do not hesitate! Your action may save the lives of innocent women.

'But it may be, of course, that the murderer, although insane, does not appear to be so. He is clever and can conceal his madness. All I can say is this: he may do so now, but he will not do it forever. In such a case it is only a matter of time before his brain finally gives way and he draws attention to himself. We will catch him, be assured of that.'

There was a hearty round of applause, and some cheering. Mr Pollaky went on to dispense sound advice concerning keeping safe in the streets, and ended with a small humorous anecdote after which he sat down to more applause.

Mr Candy addressed the hall once more. 'I am sure we are all very grateful to Mr Pollaky for his advice and assurances. And now if Inspector Swanson would like to enlighten us with his valuable experience? And maybe his account of the Mapleton case?' he added hopefully.

Swanson rose. 'I too must disappoint Mr Candy since Mr Mapleton has yet to come to trial. I will be giving evidence in court and I am sure that once all is completed there will be time enough to share what I have learned both with the public and the press.

I agree with Mr Pollaky that the man we seek is what is generally termed a homicidal maniac. But he is not so mad that he cannot be cunning. He knows the streets of Bayswater and how he might escape very swiftly from the scene of his crime without discovery. I would urge the public that if you have any suspicions even of a stranger passing in the street who is behaving in a peculiar manner, you should at once inform a policeman. Do not try to subdue or entrap this man yourself. Do not follow him. I have been told of the work he has done and it is not a sight for even a man of many years experience in police work. It is certainly no sight for a woman. But above all you must protect your own safety. Do all you can not to expose yourselves to danger. Ladies should travel by carriage if possible, or if obliged to walk, go in the company of respectable persons. If you have no male relative to walk with you, then apply to the Guardians of Virtue who will ensure that you need never be in danger, but will always have a strong male protector by your side. I hope and I trust that these precautions will not be necessary for long, and we will soon have this man behind bars.

That is all I have to say for now. Rest assured that as soon as this meeting is over I and my sergeant will be back at work guarding the safety of our streets. If anyone wishes to have a word with us in strict confidence then you may write to us at Paddington Green police station, which is where we are headquartered for the duration of this enquiry.'

He sat down.

'Thank you,' said Mr Candy, 'I think we all feel a little safer now, and I am very happy that my enterprise has the full approval of the police. I wish to make it very plain that the Guardians of Virtue are doing no more than act as any concerned gentlemen would do to protect the ladies. We are not the police, we are not the militia, we are not vigilantes, though of course, we should always be vigilant.

'And now I would like to ask Miss Frances Doughty to address the meeting.'

Frances rose and stepped forward. She realised that both Mr Pollaky and Inspector Swanson had already said all she might have wished to and more about public safety and she had nothing to add to that, so she decided to address herself directly to the position of the unhappy Jim Price.

As she opened her mouth to speak, however, the doors at the far end of the hall opened abruptly and were flung back with a crash that reverberated around the hushed space. Inspector Sharrock strode in, closely followed by Constable Mayberry. He wasn't inclined to linger but hurried towards the stage. As he approached and saw her standing in readiness to speak a curious look passed across his features that she was unable to interpret, then he ran up the steps. Frances and her talk were now forgotten and all eyes were on the Inspector. Mayberry stayed at the back of the hall, and had a quiet conversation with Sergeant Brown. Whatever it was he said Frances could see that the news was very bad.

Sharrock bounded on to the stage. 'A word,' he said, and drew Swanson aside. That one movement told Frances what had happened. She watched Swanson's face carefully, but all was now far too clear. There had been another murder.

CHAPTER SEVENTEEN

As the two Inspectors continued their close conversation everyone in the body of the hall began to talk at once. Mr Pollaky, who had been looking at his pocket watch, quickly put it away and paid earnest attention to the policemen whose faces revealed nothing other than that a very serious matter was afoot. Mr Candy looked about him for inspiration as to what to do, but seeing none, stood frozen in uncertainty.

After what seemed like a great deal of time, but was probably only a few moments, Swanson gave a swift nod. Frances was expecting him to leave the hall at once, but instead he glanced at her, and had further words with Sharrock. There was a brief hesitation, then Sharrock nodded assent, turned to Frances and beckoned her over to him. At first Frances wondered if it was indeed she who was required, but a sharper, more insistent motion of the hand convinced her and she crossed the stage to where the policemen stood.

The chatter from the floor of the hall intensified at this new development and ascended several tones up the scale.

Sharrock's face had the stony look of a man who had seen the worst and was facing it as a matter of duty. 'Miss Doughty? We can trust your discretion?'

'Yes, of course,' said Frances apprehensively.

'Come with me.' Both policemen retreated to the side of the stage, and Frances followed them to a spot where they were hidden from most of the audience by some draperies. Sharrock took something from his pocket. 'I was wondering if you can tell me who owns this?' It was a ladies reticule, handmade from an old piece of faded black velvet, decorated with a little coloured stitching and closed by a twisted cord.

Frances gave a little gasp of pained recognition, and took it from him. The last time she had seen it, it had been clean but now it was dabbled in mud and one corner was caked in what looked and smelled like dried blood. She was already suffused with the dread of what she feared and half-knew had happened, but seeing and touching and recognising this pathetic little object brought the tragedy close to her and made it heartbreakingly worse. Next moment Sarah was beside her, and Frances felt the firm shoulder touching hers, giving strength and support, doing nothing but being there and fiercely daring anyone to make her be anywhere else.

'There was one of your cards in it. I did think at first it might be yours but then …' There was an odd little waver in his voice, and he swallowed, noisily. Frances realised that he had actually thought for a moment that she had fallen victim to the killer. 'Well then I thought it might belong to one of your clients.'

Frances hardly trusted herself to speak, and when she made the effort it came out as a whisper. 'Where did you find it?'

'Celbridge Mews. And I'm very sorry to say,' Sharrock added with unusual gentleness, 'that it was lying beside the body of a young female.'

Until that moment Frances had clung to the faint hope that it was only the bloodied reticule that had been found – that the owner had somehow escaped, and might be lying wounded but could still be saved. What a cruel thing hope was, and how foolish she had been to entertain it.

Sarah laid a steadying hand on Frances' arm. 'Murdered?'

Swanson's deep-set eyes were as hard and dark as flint. 'Yes, and we think it was the same man as killed the last two, only she wasn't cut on the face. He must have been interrupted before he could do it, and ran away. Do you know whose bag this is?'

Frances nodded, almost too overcome with emotion to speak the words, as if the very act of saying them would make them permanently and unbearably true. Her voice seemed trapped in her throat but she knew that if she was to be of any use she must be strong. She took a deep breath. 'Yes. The owner is Effie Price, the sister of Jim Price. I gave her this card myself.' Her eyes suddenly filled with tears. 'Oh what a world this is! She was barely more than a child!'

Sharrock wrote in his notebook. 'Do you know her address?'

'Victoria Place. I have the number in my notebook.'

'Is there any family other than the brother and mother? Only I need someone to identify the body.'

'Oh please do not ask the mother to do this terrible thing,' Frances pleaded. 'It would surely kill her. The news will have to be broken to her very gently but even then I think she will be unable to endure it. I don't know of any other family. Let me spare the poor woman and go with you.'

Sharrock looked doubtful, but saw the sense of her offer. 'I wouldn't expect it, but if you feel strong enough …'

'I do,' said Frances, though she was far from sure that this was the case.

Sarah handed Frances a handkerchief. 'How was she killed?'

'Cut throat. Very quick, she wouldn't have known much before it was over. It's a bad enough sight, but not as bad as the others.'

Frances dabbed her eyes. 'That is some small mercy at least. I only wish I could have kept her safe.' She thought of the loving daughter and loyal sister, the small slight girl in a thin dress so patched and worn it could barely keep out the autumn chills; the slender fingers abraded by long hours of work with the needle; the shy blush when she saw the young reporter. A young life, a future, gone in a moment.

'Well if you are sure you want to do this we'd best go straightaway,' said Sharrock. 'I have a smelling bottle in my pocket if you feel you need it.'

'I can always get you a brandy on the way,' offered Sarah.

Frances pressed her companion's arm reassuringly. 'Thank you, but I think I had best keep a clear head. Celbridge Mews, you say? Just off Porchester Road near the railway. I wonder what her errand was there?'

Mr Candy approached them hesitantly. 'Er, Inspector I wondered if you might like to speak to the company and advise them if there is anything they should know? Miss Doughty, will you be making your speech?'

'Miss Doughty will not be making a speech,' snapped Sharrock before Frances could reply. 'She is coming with us on police business and everyone will know why I am here once I know all of the matter myself.' They prepared to leave and as they stepped down from the stage and filed past the wondering crowds the hall was abuzz with gossip and speculation. Mr Candy pleaded for quiet, and started to make an address to close the meeting and invite volunteers, donations and signatures on the petition. The little drama that had unexpectedly been played out before the eyes of the audience certainly stimulated all three.

There was a cab waiting outside and Frances, Sarah and the two Inspectors boarded it, while Sergeant Brown and Constable Mayberry, after a brief word with Swanson, followed on foot. Some of the audience had already left the hall and were milling about on the pavement waiting to see them depart. Mr Loveridge hurried out on to the street, his pencil moving across paper with fast deft strokes. As the cab drew away Frances saw Professor Pounder still maintaining his careful observation of the company, his glance alone persuading idlers to depart, while a heavily veiled lady, much bent and leaning on a stick stood still and watched intently as they moved past.

Frances felt a sudden pang, and could not help wondering if the mystery lady was her mother, who had come to see her, not daring to reveal herself. Had there been a chance to meet at last, one that might just have been snatched away and could be gone forever? Or was she hoping foolishly and seeing too much in what might have been no more than the natural curiosity of a stranger?

As they travelled north up Porchester Road, Frances saw an unfamiliar glow that resolved into the light of lanterns against which loomed the dark shadowy figures of policemen. Constable Stuckey was standing guard at the entrance of the arched passage that led into Celbridge Mews, while further down, past the glimmer of gas lamps, the space opened up into a small but rather better lit courtyard, where an officer was speaking to some of the residents. About halfway down the passageway, in the soft wash of light Frances saw something shapeless and crumpled lying on the ground. 'We've not moved anything like you said, sir,' Stuckey reported. 'Dr Collin is on his way.'

Sharrock gave Frances an anxious look. As Mayberry and Brown joined them, Swanson had a brief word with his sergeant, telling him to look sharply about for any footprints or blood-stains. Sharrock, with a quick nod and a gesture of the thumb, sent

Mayberry down the passage with his lantern then waited until Frances felt steady enough to continue. Sarah laid her hand on Frances' arm, just enough to show that she was there, and Frances patted her companion's hand, braced herself and followed Sharrock, Swanson and Mayberry into the mews. The body was half leaning against the wall where it had fallen, slumped forward so that the face could not be seen.

As Frances drew near she realised that something was not as she had expected. The dress, the coarse woollen shawl with its colourful darning and the cheap straw bonnet were not the clothes of Effie Price, but the ones she had last seen worn by the girl's mother. For a moment she thought that the body might be that of Mrs Price, but then saw that the figure was slender, and not the rounded shape of the older woman. So it must be Effie after all. Perhaps the girl's clothes were being laundered, and having no others she had been obliged to borrow her mother's, even though they were a poor fit. She had not tried to defend herself, and had probably never had the chance to do so, since the hands lay loosely on her lap uncut and undamaged, although the fingertips appeared to be smeared in blood.

'Is this Miss Price?' asked Sharrock.

'I *think* so,' said Frances, uncertainly. 'But it is her mother's gown. Constable, please bring the lantern nearer.'

Mayberry obliged, but as the light fell fully on the body, Frances saw to her surprise that the dark smudges on the fingertips were not blood at all, but ink, and the hands, while youthful and slim, were not as delicate as those of Miss Price.

'No,' she said, mystified. 'This is not Effie Price, nor is it her mother.'

'Then who is it?' demanded Sharrock.

Frances, with a new thought, just as horrible as the old one, knelt by the body and carefully untied the bonnet from under the chin, the ribbons already stiff with dried blood that had flowed from the throat leaving a dark bib on the chest. As she lifted the bonnet away she saw the bruise on the cheek, the imprint of the filigree-topped cane still visible.

She rose to her feet, the grief she had felt earlier renewed in a fresh surge of pain.

'It is George Ibbitson, a reporter for the *Bayswater Chronicle.*'

'What? Are you sure?' exclaimed Sharrock.

'Yes. I recognise him from the bruise on his face. He was injured a few days ago outside the *Chronicle* offices.'

Sarah stepped forward and after a quick glance turned to the Inspector and nodded. 'That's him, all right. I cleaned up that wound myself. Won't be two like it.'

Sharrock stared at the body in astonishment. 'Does he usually go about in women's clothes? Not a Boulton and Park type, was he?'

'I really don't know what you mean by that, Inspector,' said Frances with a sigh, 'and I would prefer it if you did not try to explain.'

Sarah gave Sharrock a fierce look. 'He wasn't what you're thinking at all. Very sweet on Miss Price he was.'

'Oh, I think I can guess what may have happened here,' groaned Frances in sudden realisation. 'Mr Ibbitson has been trying to help Miss Price – he wanted to exonerate her brother and must have hoped to do so by trapping the real killer. The foolish, foolish good-hearted boy – he thought to act as a decoy, and so he borrowed Mrs Price's garments and now it has led to his death.' Frances turned her head away, as she could feel fresh tears spill down her face. 'If you don't mind, Sarah, I think I could do with that brandy, now.'

Sarah took her firmly by the arms. 'I'll get you home. There's nothing else you can do here.' She was drawing Frances from the terrible scene towards the street when there was the sound of running footsteps and the panting of a man in a hurry. It was Constable Cross, and he stopped at the head of the mews and hung on to the corner for support. 'Inspector! If you could come quick! There's been another one! In Hereford Mews. And this one's all cut about, and there's a funny sort of chalk mark on the wall.'

'You get off home now, Miss Doughty,' ordered Sharrock. 'Leave this one to the police. Miss Smith, can I trust you to see her safe?'

'Always.'

Frances was allowing Sarah to lead her away when she suddenly stopped. 'Someone needs to go and tell Miss Price. She'll be waiting for Mr Ibbitson to come back and tell her what happened.

I don't want her to hear it from gossips or read about it in the newspapers.'

Sarah hesitated and eyed Frances warily. 'Please,' begged Frances. 'It is better from me than a policeman.'

'All right, but we go home straight afterwards.'

There was a flickering candle in the front window of the Price family cottage, and as they approached they saw the pale ghost-like face of Effie Price glancing out into the lane, hoping to see the sight that she would never see again.

The young girl knew that it was dreadful news as soon as the two women arrived. Thankfully Mrs Price had gone to her bed so it was only the daughter that Frances had to gently tell the worst, and Effie, weeping, confirmed what Frances had suspected; George Ibbitson, hoping to decoy the killer and put an end to the terror, had borrowed Mrs Price's gown as a disguise. Effie had placed the little reticule on his arm herself as a finishing touch. There were tears on both sides, and then Effie, gathering what little strength she had, wondered aloud what she could say to her mother.

'Keep it from her as long as you can.' Frances took a coin from her purse and pressed it into Effie's chilled hand. 'She will need a new dress.'

'I will repay you,' Effie murmured, although they both knew how many hours of work it would take her to do so.

'Please, there is no need. Think of it as a gift.'

Effie stared at the coin, and the tears started again. 'And is there no news about Jim?'

'I was at a meeting today with many hundreds of people present. I am hopeful that very soon all of Bayswater will come to the conclusion that your brother is innocent. I promise I will continue to do everything I can to see him reprieved.'

'Please help us! Only I couldn't bear it – especially now – to lose Jim in that cruel way, with everyone thinking him such a bad man, and I know that mother would sink and follow him.'

Frances looked into the face of a girl who was almost crushed with grief and only managing to live from day to day for the sake of two people she loved, both of whom she felt sure she would very soon lose.

'I will not abandon this cause,' she said steadily. 'And whatever happens I will be a friend to you.'

As they made their way home Sarah said, 'I thought for a minute you were going to promise to free her brother.'

'I very nearly did,' Frances admitted. 'But she has lived through so much false hope that I dared not give her more. If I can free Jim Price, I will, but if not then I will see that his family does not suffer for his loss.'

When they arrived home, they found Mr Loveridge waiting for them, and invited him into the parlour. 'Mr Gillan has gone to Paddington Green police station in search of news,' he said, anxiously. 'I hope it is not very bad, but I can see from your faces that it must be.'

'Yes, and far too close to home. The murderer has struck again, twice it seems.'

'Twice? While we were all at the meeting?'

'I can't be sure.'

'Because the police thought that the killer would be at the meeting.' There was a pause as they all considered this. 'After you left the rumour ran all about the hall that there had been another murder and you were being engaged to help the police. The collection boxes were filled almost to overflowing and there were long queues for men to sign up for the Guardians of Virtue. I applied myself, of course, but as I am not known in Bayswater I will have to obtain a letter from a clergyman who knows me and will vouch for my good character. Once I have that I will be available to protect the ladies of Bayswater, and it will be my great honour to do so.'

Sarah narrowed her eyes as if to say that she knew which lady he particularly had in mind.

'I will go to Paddington Green tomorrow and see if there is any news,' said Frances. 'Maybe the police will have gained some further clue as to the killer. And I will write more letters on behalf of Jim Price. I will ask for an interview at the Home Office to make my case in person. Surely if one good thing can come out of this terrible business it's that the authorities cannot now ignore the fact that there is a dangerous criminal at large in Bayswater and Jim Price's conviction must be overturned. One life at least can be saved.'

Loveridge could see that she was weary and grieved, and left her to the quiet of the late evening and Sarah's company. Frances was able to busy herself with letter writing, but once that was done there was nothing to prevent her thoughts dwelling on the loss of the young newspaperman. He had been a frequent visitor, and she almost expected him to suddenly appear at her door, his face glowing, his energy undiminished, saying that it had all been a ruse common to journalists and he was alive after all, and just about to go and see Effie. He did not come, and she wept again.

Early next morning, after a night of little sleep and what sleep there was disturbed by bad dreams, Frances peered out of her window and saw a larger group of pressmen than before, huddled in the cool misty rain. Some she recognised as employees of the *Chronicle*. She decided to address them, and so went downstairs, opened the front door and appeared on the doorstep. There was an immediate clamour of questioning but she held up her hands for silence.

'I have a statement to make. Please listen and take note. Last night I was present at the scene of a terrible crime. I identified the body of George Ibbitson who was cruelly murdered by the person who has been holding Bayswater in fear these last few weeks. Your colleague was a kind, brave and resourceful young man. You may have heard that when found he was costumed as a woman. This was a disguise he adopted in order to decoy the killer into making an appearance so that he might capture him. Sadly, this led to his death. He was a hero and I hope he will be remembered as such.

'I wish also to take this opportunity to appeal for the reprieve of Jim Price, who I think we can now agree in the light of the recent tragedies is an innocent man who has been blamed for the crime of another. Thank you. That is all I have to say. And now, since Mr Ibbitson was a friend of mine, I beg you to leave me in peace.'

The newsmen wrote copiously in their notebooks and rather sheepishly walked away.

'You need to rest,' Sarah told her, 'though I know you won't.'

'There is no time for that. I need to see Inspector Sharrock. I know why Mr Ibbitson was killed, he was simply mistaken for a female, but I want to find out as much as possible about the second murder. If I could put together all the facts I might see something apart from the obvious which is common to all these crimes and that might assist me.'

'Assist you in what?' Sarah demanded. 'Not chasing after a man with a knife I hope?'

'No, but if I can study what has occurred then I might be able to draw a picture of the type of individual we are looking for, a type that might exonerate Jim Price.'

'Got very interested in picture drawing just lately,' said Sarah, meaningfully.

'And what is wrong with that?'

Sarah did not reply.

They took a cab up to Paddington Green, and on the way Frances' weariness and the movement of the vehicle overcame her and on their arrival Sarah had to shake her gently awake. The area around the station house was busy with newsmen clustering on the pavement outside interviewing men and women, some of whom were there to report missing relatives and others to try to identify the second victim found the night before. As Frances stepped down from the cab a few of those present recognised her and eager reporters left the visitors they were interrogating to swarm around her, with a hailstorm of questions. Sarah did her best to keep the worst of the shoving and pushing away, some-times with a growl, sometimes with a shake of the fist, sometimes just by interposing her stout body between Frances and some of the more persistent offenders.

At last, Frances was able to assure the newsmen that she had no further information to give. They all wrote furiously in their notebooks and she only wished she understood the whirls and loops of their shorthand in order to know what fictions they were devising. It was time to turn the tables. 'But you may know more than I do. What can you tell me about the second body found last night?'

'Woman,' said one of the newsmen, clawing damp hair from his eyes.

'Young and good-looking,' said another. 'That's what I heard. Only not looking so good once he'd finished with her if you know what I mean.'

Frances and Sarah, since they did not resemble newspaper persons, were able to enter the station unimpeded, where they found a large crowd of men and women waiting for attention, and the desk sergeant, red in the face, employing a colleague to assist him with the crush. Inspector Swanson strode out of a side office accompanied by a doleful gentleman, shook hands with him and bid him farewell, then took a look at the record book on the desk, made some pencil notes in the margin, and called out a name. A woman bundled in dark shawls rose from a bench and went with him. Moments later Sergeant Brown emerged from another room bidding goodbye to his interview subject and beckoned to another. As each individual left the station, they were seized upon by the newsmen, demanding to know what questions they had been asked and what they had learned.

If the matter had been less urgent Frances would have left and returned later, but time was running out for Jim Price, only nine days from execution, and she remained. At length, Sharrock appeared, and on seeing Frances and Sarah, he gave them an almost sympathetic look before he beckoned them to his office. The normally crowded room now resembled a junkyard where the contents of every ash bin in the district was waiting to be sorted. Boxes and bundles were piled high in every available space, stowed on the floor, the desk, shelves and even on his chair.

'All right, but make it quick. I've got half Paddington out there looking for lost relatives.'

There was no point in Frances even looking for somewhere to sit. 'Is there any word on Jim Price?'

'No. Next question.'

'I was thinking —'

He puffed out his cheeks, but said nothing and gestured her to go on.

'Last night you said that whoever murdered Mr Ibbitson had been interrupted and ran away. So there ought to be a witness who saw him.'

Sharrock rolled his eyes. 'Any more ideas which the police have already thought of? There's men asking around everyone in the area right now. We've spoken to all the residents of the Mews; none of them saw or heard anything, and we don't suspect any of them either.'

'I assume the body of the second victim hasn't been identified yet.'

'That's right. Young female, might be a servant or shop girl or some such.'

'And was she cut in the same way as before?'

'Yes.'

'Constable Cross mentioned a chalk mark.'

'We find lots of those about the place. Might have something to do with the murder but I doubt it.'

'Only, I have heard mention of a club for young men with money but no sense who go around committing crimes and taking risks for a wager, and they show what they have done with a chalk mark. They call themselves the Bold Bloods and they have their headquarters at the Piccadilly Club. I would not be surprised if the three young men who were ejected from the meeting last night were of their number. Their leader appears to be a Mr Pargeter, although from his description I don't think he was amongst them.'

'Oh, really?' Sharrock sounded unimpressed. 'Well that won't solve the murders unless they have formed themselves into a murder club, which I rather doubt, but it might clear up some of the smaller crimes round here. I've questioned some of those sparks but when you ask them about it they keep quiet. Probably part of their code.'

'Have you had a report as to when the murders were committed last night?'

'Not yet. Of course we won't get an exact time, but we do know that Mr Ibbitson was last seen at seven o'clock and he was found at half past eight.'

'The blood on the bonnet ribbons was dry to the touch. He must have been killed soon after seven.'

Sharrock grunted. 'Well we'll leave that for Dr Collin to decide, shall we?'

'Inspector, I know you don't wish me to look into these murders, and I would not wish to do so myself, but I am thinking of the effect they will have on my attempt to gain a reprieve for Jim

Price. I would be grateful therefore if you could let me know as soon as the second victim is identified. I will ensure that I have messengers here to bring me the information. I cannot afford delay.'

'No, well neither can I.' He made to conduct her to the door, but as he did so there were loud hysterical screams from the public office. 'Looks like I might have the answer for you now.'

It was a while before some semblance of calm, or at least what passed for calm in the police station, was restored. A draper's assistant had arrived to make enquiries about her sister, a trimmer of hats, who had failed to attend a family gathering. She had not been permitted to see the body but after seeing her sister's best bonnet with the silk flowers she made by hand, was left in no doubt as to the identity of the dead woman. The victim had been twenty, and engaged to be married in the spring. Sharrock looked like a crushed man as he told Frances what he had learned. 'It's like we've got Old Nick himself walking about out there. Nothing more you can do here, Miss Doughty.'

'Do you know when the inquests will open?'

'Well with normal cases, the drownings and the drunks, I'd say Monday, but in this case – I wouldn't be surprised if the coroner sat this afternoon.'

Sharrock proved to be right. Frances and Sarah did not hope to learn anything at the opening of the inquest at Providence Hall, but somehow they both felt they ought to be there. The court was more than usually crowded with newsmen, many of whom must have known George Ibbitson personally, and they were very pale, quiet and strained. Mr Gillan sat in a corner, with a helpless look, like a man in a dream. When he saw Frances, it was the first time he had not hurried over to her, although she could see that he wanted to speak to her. She went and sat by him, and saw that his eyes, though dry, had a red rawness about them, as if much scoured. 'I didn't know,' he said. 'Honest. You've got to believe me. He never told me what he was planning. If he had, I would have told him not to, or at least had someone go with him.'

Frances would have done anything to spare George Ibbitson's family the pain of appearing to give evidence, and volunteered to do so, but in the end it was his father, who had seen the clean corpse, neatly shrouded in a sheet, who had made the formal identification at the mortuary and was called up to whisper out his words to the courtroom. A Miss Whitaker, her voice clouded with tears, confirmed that the deceased young woman was her sister. Both cases were adjourned until Monday, and the coroner urged very strongly that medical men should put all their other work aside and give their full attention to the Bayswater tragedies.

CHAPTER EIGHTEEN

It was the second of the three Sundays before Jim Price's execution. That morning at St Stephen's church, Reverend Day preached a sermon about guarding against the evils of the world, and the congregation joined him in prayers for the recent departed. Frances allowed herself some additional time to say a quiet prayer for the prisoner. He was not mentioned in the sermon and she suspected that she and Sarah were the only persons present to give him any thought. Sarah had put a pudding on to boil before they departed for church and later that day as they tackled the hearty assemblage of suet crust, beef and gravy, followed by fig jelly, Frances, with very little appetite for the feast before her, wondered what the condemned man was enjoying for his Sunday dinner.

Frances, in her continuing and so far fruitless efforts to acquire information about the Wheelock marriage, had asked Ratty and his men to watch the activities of the servants of Wheelock's new home. She had just settled down to an afternoon of letter writing when a small boy arrived with the news that the Wheelocks' parlourmaid, who had been away on her half day visiting her sister, was on her way back to attend to the household for the evening.

Sarah put on her cloak, picked up a basket of apples, and hurried away. The fruit was part of Sarah's plan to make the young woman's acquaintance, and there would follow a process of earning her trust to the point where she was willing to divulge information which she was supposed not to.

When Sarah returned it was with apples so bumped and bruised they looked as if they had been used for a game of skittles, although Frances had no doubt they would appear on her dinner table in some more tempting guise before long. Sarah said that after meeting the girl in the street following an apparent upset of the basket, she had represented herself as a cook working for a small family, and as servants did, they had compared notes on their situations. The parlourmaid, whose name was Hannah, was twenty-four and had been with the household for a year, having replaced a girl who had left to marry. The coachman, Mr Nettles, the cook/housekeeper and the scullery maid had all worked for Mrs Wheelock, the former Mrs Outram, for several years. Hannah remembered old Mr Outram, who had been a hale gentleman for his advanced age, and had died very peacefully several months ago. It had cost the cook some ingenuity to accede to his insistence that all meals be produced on strict vegetarian principles, something his wife had been able to tolerate only because there were secret supplies of roast beef and boiled ham in the larder. After his death she had regaled herself with meat dinners in plenty.

The lady's maid, Daisy, the one servant who was in constant attendance on her mistress, had been appointed by Mr Wheelock not long after the wedding, her predecessor having been summarily dismissed. Hannah did not know the reason for the dismissal. She did not like to say anything against Daisy, but then in a sudden rush revealed that she thought that Daisy was careless, and not respectful enough in her manner, and she was sometimes obliged to wonder if she had ever been a lady's maid before.

When Sarah ventured on the subject of Hannah's new master there was a difficulty, since the young woman was reluctant to say very much at all. 'I can tell when a servant has had her mouth stopped and this one has, good and proper,' Sarah reported.

'Would you learn more from Daisy?' asked Frances, not very hopefully.

'In Wheelock's pay, I'm sure of it. You'll get nothing from her. I don't know what he's promised her but we'd never match it. I could try talking to the others, but they're not close enough to the mistress to tell us much and if I approached them as well it makes it more likely that Wheelock will find out I've been asking questions. I did ask where the last lady's maid went, pretended I knew someone looking for one, but Hannah didn't know. The girl was called Mary Ann. No surname.'

Frances sighed. Without a surname she would be impossible to trace. 'Can you discover more from Hannah?'

'Give it time, yes.'

'When will you see her again?'

'Tomorrow. I mentioned a favourite recipe and now I have to make it so she can taste some. Nothing like a slice of cake to start a conversation. The cook is almost as old as the mistress and likes to put her feet up in the afternoon and let Hannah do most of the work, so I can go round then.' Sarah went to make the cake, and other rather more quickly assembled treats for teatime.

Tom called with a report on Miss Digby's romance, and seeing that there were scones in the oven, a pat of fresh butter in the larder and a new pot of jam, stayed a little longer than he had planned. ''Tisn't the maid carrying the notes, after all. It's Miss Digby's friend, a chattering type who she went to school with, an' knows all 'er secrets. Not that ladies' secrets are very excitin' but I bet 'er father thinks so. They went out to take a little turn in the park after church and she passed Miss Digby a message, an' then they whispered a lot. I did 'ope to get 'old of the note but she put it in 'er dress front, so that wasn't very advisable.'

'I don't believe ladies are careless with love notes,' said Frances, who had never received a love note but had read about such things in novels. 'I shall not tell her father about this just yet, or he might be tempted to challenge her with it. Let her imagine no one knows her secret, keep a close watch and see where she goes.'

The inquest into the death of George Ibbitson and the draper's assistant killed on the same night was due to resume on Monday morning. In the usual way of such things the first session had done little more than identify the bodies. Often a week elapsed between hearings, but given the urgency of the situation the medical men had agreed to give their examinations some priority. Frances was due to go to Somerset House to follow up her idea about tracing the Wheelock wedding, and Sarah agreed to attend the inquests and report back. There was a substantial amount of mail that morning, including quite a number of letters for Sarah from women denouncing their husbands as the Bayswater Face-slasher, and asking if she would come to their houses and take them away. 'Cheaper than divorce, less risky than arsenic,' was Sarah's comment.

When Frances had first visited Somerset House she had had
only a few pennies to spend and had gone there crushed inside
an omnibus that had heaved and creaked like an old sailing vessel,
and was as damp underfoot. On another occasion, having spent
the last of her funds on a certificate, she had walked all the way
home. Now, as a busy detective able to charge her clients the
expenses of travel, she adopted the relative comfort of a hansom
cab in which she could read through her notes and had the added
benefit of little low folding doors in front to protect her skirts
from mud splashes. The brief bout of fair weather had vanished
and all was now squally teasing winds and rain showers.

Her idea was to try and discover the home of Mr Wheelock's
parents, an address he might have used when planning his wedding. At first Frances feared that she might have to examine every
directory for London and the surrounding counties, but then
she thought of a better idea. Since she knew Mr Wheelock's age
to be about twenty-four, it was not hard to find his birth in the
registers and discover that it had taken place in Lambeth in 1857.
Hoping that his family had not removed from the area since then,
her next task was to examine the most recent Surrey directories,
thankful that the surname was an uncommon one. To her great
relief, she was successful. The name of the head of a Lambeth
household was Mrs Mary Wheelock. Frances might have gone
further, and obtained a birth certificate to confirm that Mrs Mary
Wheelock was Mr Timothy Wheelock's mother, but this would
have taken a week, and in view of Mr Chandler's great sense of
urgency in the matter, she felt pressed for time. She decided to
assume the connection, and go to the appropriate registry office,
the address of which was listed in the directory. Hopefully this
would supply the location of the wedding. It would be a long
journey and she could not get there that day before the office
closed, so it would have to be undertaken first thing next morning.

Much against her better judgment, she took the opportunity
to look into her own family mystery. In 1865 Alicia Dobree had
married Vernon Salter, who Frances believed to be her natural
father, when he was twenty-eight years of age. Frances expected
the bride to have been a young heiress but was unable to find
any trace of a birth of that name in the registers, which suggested

that she was either born abroad or before September 1837 when registration began. Old directories of Kensington listed Alicia's father Lancelot as resident from 1827 onwards, and showed that his fortune had been made in silk.

Frances was returning home, sitting alone in a cab with her thoughts, and was not far from her destination when the hansom, which had already been going barely more than walking pace in the growing weight of traffic, finally drew to a halt, impeded by a delivery cart which had paused for unloading. Through the vent above her head she heard the driver calling out to the carter to hurry up, and suspected that he was modifying the normally ripe language he would have used on such an occasion out of consideration for his lady passenger. She was craning her neck, trying to look ahead to see how far the obstruction went, but could detect nothing in the great crush of vehicles and horses. All about her was the rumble and creak of carriages, the panting of protesting animals, and the cries of coachmen and irate passengers, then the rain swept in with a mocking howl and attacked her face like needles. Frances was pulling her cloak more tightly about her when a lithe figure suddenly vaulted on to the cab, and managed by some acrobatic means to slither into the seat beside her. The sour stench told her at once who he was and she turned and stared in horror to see none other than the Filleter sitting beside her with an ugly sneer.

She tried to cry out but for a moment her throat was paralysed, then she gulped and called out 'Driver!' her voice sounding hoarse with fright.

'Moving on now, Miss!' said the driver and the cab jerked into motion. Frances gasped. Had he not noticed the weight of the extra passenger, or had he been distracted by the furore around them? She looked about, wondering if it was safe for her to demand that the driver stop and open the doors so she could jump from the cab, something he was unlikely to do without payment of his fare, or even whether in her long skirts it was possible for her to scramble over them herself, but then the Filleter's hand closed firmly about her upper arm.

'I wouldn't advise that,' he said quietly. 'Don't scream, do as you're told and you won't get hurt.'

She had never been so close to him before, and neither his smell nor his appearance improved with nearer acquaintance. He seemed to be dressed in the grave-clothes of a long buried corpse, which hung badly on his long thin frame. He did not look her in the eye but stared downwards, his body hunched like a predatory beast about to spring on its prey. His face was unshaven and grimed with dirt, the long dark hair thick with dried mud and dust.

Frances made an effort to remain calm. 'What do you want with me?' she demanded.

'Just a talk. I hear you've been spreading rumours about me. I don't like that,' he added in the curious soft voice that always made her shiver.

The cab was hurrying on now, weaving its way rapidly through traffic, and even if she could have somehow escaped she would have found herself trampled by horses and crushed by heavy carriages. 'Let go of me,' she demanded.

'I will, when we've had our little conversation.'

She paused, not sure what to say. His accusation, that she had been expressing the opinion that he might be responsible for the Bayswater murders, was quite correct, and it would be useless to deny it. 'I stand by what I have said. There have been knife murders in this vicinity, and you are known to carry a knife and to be willing to use it. Of course you are suspected. I suppose you will tell me now that you are no killer.'

'Oh, I've killed,' he said nonchalantly, 'I've done that all right, more than once; men who were best off dead. Men you would have wanted dead. And I'll probably kill again. Never killed a woman, though. Don't plan to. Not unless it has to be done.' His grip on her arm never faltered and she shuddered.

'Are you saying that you did not commit the recent murders?'

He looked up and grinned, revealing foul teeth and she turned her head from the horrid sight. 'Innocent as the new-born.'

'Do you know who did?'

'No, or I'd put a stop to him. Bad for my business having him about. Now you take my advice Miss Doughty. Don't dabble in things that don't concern you, or it could be you next, lying in an alley with your throat cut.'

'I suppose that would suit you,' she said, but he let go of her arm and in a trice he had manoeuvred nimbly over the folding doors and disappeared into the surge of traffic. Frances was left trembling and dry-mouthed with fear. When she was able to speak she ordered the driver straight to Paddington Green police station and reported what had occurred to the desk sergeant. It was rare that she was listened to with such keen and respectful attention, and once she had given her information an Inspector was summoned to hear her story, and three constables were swiftly dispatched. This was no comfort to Frances, since she knew that their quarry would be long gone.

While she was there Sharrock arrived and, seeing her, swiftly beckoned her into his office. 'Causing a stir again, Miss Doughty?' he said, moving some boxes from a chair so she could sit.

'It would seem so. Not by choice, I can assure you.'

'My sergeant tells me you have had a dangerous encounter.' He poked an angry finger at her. 'This is just the sort of thing I have been warning you about. It doesn't do for young women to be running about after criminals, that's men's work, I've told you often enough.' Frances decided not to reply. 'At least we might get that man behind bars and keep him there this time.'

'I hope so. I can't imagine what is keeping him in Bayswater since he knows he is wanted here. Some horrid business of his own, I suppose. He must have some secret lair where he can hide, perhaps with associates who are as bad as he is. And he keeps to the shadows or mingles in crowds where he cannot easily be seen.'

'I suppose it would be useless for me to warn you not to seek him out again?'

'I have never tried to seek him out, I can assure you, I hardly need to, he seems to be everywhere.' There were too many occasions in the past when she had encountered him unexpectedly; outside her own home, in Chas and Barstie's office, near Paddington Station, and times when he had been no more than a black shadow at the edge of her vision, a repellent shape that had filled her with dread, and she had turned to look and seen nothing. Had there been other times when he had been lurking nearby and she had not seen him at all? She began to tremble.

Sharrock looked at her sympathetically and sent a constable to fetch a glass of water. He watched warily as she sipped, in case she should suddenly feel faint. 'Thank you, Inspector, I feel very much refreshed,' she said gratefully. 'I was wondering if you have managed to find any witnesses who saw this man in the vicinity of Celbridge Mews on the night of the two murders.'

'Not as yet, unfortunately. The police have spoken to everyone residing and working in that area, as well as passers-by, carriers and coachmen, but no one saw anything suspicious. In fact no one seems to have entered or left Celbridge Mews at all between seven and half past eight o'clock. And we've got nothing on the other murder either.'

'You believe that the man who killed Mr Ibbitson was startled by someone and had to make his escape before he could continue his foul work. So if no one left or entered the mews then the only possible witness would have been a passer-by. But if the murderer was in the Mews, lurking unseen in the passageway and some-one walked past on Porchester Road, then he would simply have stayed hidden in the dark, and waited for them to go past. Could he have escaped from within the Mews?'

'No, the courtyard is enclosed, there's no way out. He didn't go that way.' Sharrock shook his head. 'Young Mr Ibbitson was playing a very dangerous game. I only hope other young men take note and don't try the same thing. I expect he strolled about the street hoping to catch the killer. The man was lying in wait, took him from behind and dragged him into the dark.'

'His poor family. And Miss Whitaker's also.'

'I know. At least Ibbitson's parents were able to see him made tidy and clean to say their goodbyes, and his mother gave him her last kiss. That's more than we can say of the others.'

'Do you know if Miss Whitaker was killed before or after Mr Ibbitson?'

'She was last seen alive at about half past seven. Dr Collin, judging from the freshness of the bloodstains, thinks she was killed afterwards.'

'And you are sure that she was killed by the man they call the Bayswater Face-slasher?'

'No doubt about it.' He gave her a hard stare. 'I know that look. You're thinking, and you know where that leads.'

'It leads to criminals being punished.' Frances handed the water glass to Sharrock. 'I shall go home and think further.'

'And you be careful. Celbridge Mews is hardly a stone's throw from where you live.'

She took a cab home, and all the way she looked about her very carefully, but if the Filleter was nearby he did not show himself. Two murders on the same night, she thought, and the police were assuming that both were committed by the same man, who having killed poor Ibbitson, was interrupted before he could take his time to make the cuts that were his signature, and, frustrated by this, had moved on to kill again. But no one had come forward to say they might have interrupted the killer. What if there was another reason why the boy's face was not cut? Supposing there had not been one murderer but two, and Ibbitson's killer was not the Face-slasher at all?

Frances would not dispute that Miss Whitaker was murdered by the Face-slasher, but began to wonder if Ibbitson had been killed by someone who had made him a deliberate target. Supposing, during Ibbitson's diligent enquiries in his efforts to help the Price family or perhaps in another of his endeavours, he had unsuspectingly made a dangerous enemy, who saw him as a threat. This enemy had followed him to the Price cottage, lain in wait, and then seen him emerge, perhaps overheard him speaking to Effie at the door, and realised from the conversation that the gowned figure was actually the young newsman in disguise. The recent murders provided the perfect cover for another crime. The killer had followed Ibbitson, and as soon as the opportunity arose, seized him from behind and dragged him into the mews. One swift cut with a sharp knife and the threat was gone. There was only one dangerous man whose name had been publicly mentioned in connection with the murders, and that was the Filleter. Only that very day he had told Frances that he had never killed a woman but he had killed men. One of those men, she now suspected, was George Ibbitson.

Chapter Nineteen

Sarah had not yet returned from the inquest and how Frances ached to have that solid and sympathetic presence home again. There was a caller to distract her, however, Tom Smith, to report on his observation of Miss Digby. Frances was glad of the company, and went down to the kitchen to make a pot of tea so he would remain there longer. He followed her, and went hunting around until he uncovered some scraps of bacon which he tossed into a hot pan with a lump of lard, an egg and crusts of bread. 'The friend called for 'er an' they went to a confectioner's an' would you believe it, they just 'appened to meet Mr Pargeter there, an' 'e bought 'er a little sweetmeat all tied up in a fancy ribbon, an' she went red in the face.' He looked thoughtful, as if assessing this as a suitable means of wooing a lady that he might undertake when the maiden he had been admiring from afar, Mr Jacobs' dainty niece, Pearl Montague, was of an age to have gentlemen admirers.

'What did they talk about?'

'Oh, the lady complained about 'er father and 'ow 'e was tryin' to keep them apart. But this Pargeter is very clever an' said 'ow 'e respected Mr Digby very much and would win 'im over. Then 'e said he 'ad just 'ad a stroke of good luck, an' would be comin' into some money very soon, and once 'e 'ad it in 'is 'ands they would announce the engagement. She were very 'appy about that. Then they made an appointment to meet again.' Frances poured the tea and Tom stirred the contents of the sizzling pan with a wooden spoon, inhaled the aroma and licked his lips in anticipation. 'An' there's another thing. This is the best bit.' He drew a slip of paper from his pocket and laid it on the table. 'This is the address of an 'ouse Pargeter visits. Young woman lives there. Very good-lookin', an' in the family way. Goes by the name of Mrs Jones, only I don't reckon she is a Jones nor a Mrs neither.'

The address was of a common lodging house in Porchester Road. Tom settled himself at the kitchen table and began to eat his supper from the frying pan, sopping up the grease with extra bread.

'I don't suppose you have seen any more of the Filleter?' asked Frances, sipping her tea.

Tom wiped a hand across his mouth. 'No. Slippery one, that. Can pop up an' then disappear quick as a wink.'

Frances took a deep breath and told Tom about her frightening encounter earlier that day. He listened to her quietly with a very serious expression, then polished off his meal and licked the spoon. 'So 'e didn't try an' 'urt you, it was more like a warning?'

'A warning and a threat.'

He leaned back thoughtfully in his chair. 'Bit strange weren't it, 'im just seein' you pass by. Like a lucky chance. Or was it? Sounds to me like 'e was lying in wait, just 'oping the cab would slow down enough for 'im to 'op on.'

Frances felt cold all over. 'You think he's been following me? Watching me?' She had almost persuaded herself that those dark indeterminate glimpses had been no more than imagination born of fear, a shadow assuming a form she dreaded like a mist becoming the shape of a ghost. Now she was not so sure.

'P'raps. But, now 'e's said what 'e 'as to say then maybe that's the end of it.'

'I hope so. Please do be very careful. I fear he will not hesitate to dispatch anyone he suspects of following him, even someone as young as yourself.'

Tom grinned. 'Don't you worry. My men know 'ow to go about an' not be seen.'

When Tom had departed Frances was left alone, and the house seemed strangely quiet. She tidied the kitchen and returned upstairs to her apartment, but found herself glancing behind doors and into corners, and starting at every shadow. It was an immense relief when Sarah arrived and she was able to tell her the whole story.

Frances realised that she was shaken in a way she had not been even after the terrible attack on her person earlier that year, when she had fought off an attempt to subdue her with chloroform. Then there had been an obvious and very physical assault but this was far more subtle, and in some ways worse. The Filleter's grasp on her arm had not been a violent one, and had left no mark, but it had prevented her from escaping him. He had not threatened her directly; in fact he had said he had no intention of killing a woman, although he revealed that it was not an action wholly against his nature; only insinuated that if she continued to pry into the murders then she might become a victim. More worrying was his casual admission of what she had always suspected, that he was a cold-blooded killer.

Sarah took in this news with a thunderous expression, her fists clenching and kneading as if she had the Filleter before her and was slowly and very determinedly strangling him. 'He didn't hurt you?' she asked, worried that Frances was hiding something in order to prevent her going out and committing a justifiable murder straightaway.

'No, it was just meant as a warning, I think.'

'I'll warn him alright!' said Sarah, promising that if she was ever to get hold of the Filleter then knife or no knife she would introduce him to all the tortures of the Tower of London and a few more besides that no one had ever thought of.

'At least leave him able to answer Inspector Swanson's questions,' advised Frances. 'Then we may get to the truth of the murders.'

'No going out on your own after dark!' ordered Sarah waving a stern finger.

'I wouldn't do so in any case.'

'No going out on your own at all, I'd say. Not any time of day.'

'That will make my work very hard, I fear. I need to go to Lambeth tomorrow morning, and I know you have a client coming then. Maybe I should hire one of Mr Candy's respectable gentlemen. Or perhaps Mr Garton might enjoy a drive.'

Sarah scowled because the woman visiting next day had lived for years in terror of her husband, and it had taken the unhappy creature all her courage and resolve just to make the appointment. She dared not put this client off. Fortunately the difficulty was settled when Cedric, on being sent a note, at once cancelled an urgent meeting he had arranged to discuss the engraving on a new cravat pin, and agreed to accompany Frances.

Sarah's report on the two inquests told Frances that the victims had probably died within half an hour of each other. The last person known to have seen George Ibbitson alive was Effie Price as he left her house in disguise, at about seven o'clock. They had paused on the doorstep to talk, and she had thanked him shyly for all he was doing for her and her mother, and then she had kissed him. She had not seen anyone lurking nearby, but then she hadn't been paying very much attention to anyone except George. Depending on how fast he had been walking, the journey from there to Celbridge Mews would have taken about ten minutes, and judging by the drying of the blood, it was thought that he had been killed not long afterwards. George Ibbitson's body had been found at about half past eight by a youth going into the Mews on his way home from a public house in order to answer a call of nature. Miss Whitaker had last been seen by her sweetheart between half past seven and eight o'clock, and her body had been found in Hereford Mews at about nine. In both cases the cause of death had been blood loss and shock due to severed arteries of the throat. Both had been attacked from behind by a right-handed assailant. While George Ibbitson's body had not suffered any additional injuries, Miss Whitaker's face had been cut in a manner very like that of the other victims of the Bayswater Face-slasher. The jurors had wanted to know how long it took to walk from the first murder site to the second, and traced a possible route that led past Frances' front door, then south down Hereford Road towards the Grove. It was certainly possible, based on the times and locations of the deaths, for the same person to have committed both murders. The murderer, who had taken both victims from behind, could have had little or no blood on his person, but in the dark he might not have noticed splashes on his sleeves or cuffs. The coroner asked all Bayswater citizens to report to the police anyone who had come home that night with blood on his clothing, however small the amount.

Sarah, with a surly look, revealed that Professor Pounder and some of his pugilistic friends had all volunteered for the Guardians of Virtue, but none of them being gentlemen, Mr Candy had rejected their applications. They had decided instead to make their own nightly patrols around Bayswater. Frances had a new task for Sarah. She was to befriend and gain the confidence of 'Mrs Jones', the young woman in the family way being visited by Mr Pargeter, and discover as much as she could about her.

When the early evening newspapers arrived, they showed that the panic over the murders was not only firmly established in Bayswater but was spreading east to cover the whole of London. What particularly exercised the populace was that such bloodthirsty savagery, previously thought to be confined to the slums and alleys of the ragged and drunken poor, where it might be deplored from a safe distance, could also exist in a respectable district, where even ladies of the carriage class could feel under threat.

There was a lengthy article about the fate of Mr Ibbitson, and tributes paid to his hard work, intelligence and bravery in trying to catch the killer. Crowds of the curious had been gathering about the sites of the murders, exchanging opinions on what should be done to the perpetrator, and spreading fresh rumours about his identity. Such was the interest that the police had been called out a number of times to disperse these assemblies, which were becoming large enough to impede traffic.

Reporters sent from all the major London newspapers had carefully recorded the popular theories, which they promised to hand over to the police. Three ideas were gaining considerable credence. According to some, the killer was a man who prided himself on being very moral and imagined that he was ridding Bayswater of bad women. It was thought that he particularly objected to female vanity which explained the cutting of faces, and a clergyman who had recently preached a sermon on that very subject had to his great bewilderment unexpectedly found his home surrounded by an accusing crowd. Others pointed out that there was a group of lawless young men who met at the Piccadilly Club, and egged each other on to commit ever fouler crimes. Now, it was suggested, they were committing murder for wagers. The police had recently paid a visit to the Piccadilly Club and arrested a number of youths, all of whom were drunk. The unruly reprobates had been closely interviewed and, as a result, several would soon appear before local magistrates on a variety of charges that ranged from obstructing a public highway all the way up to leaving a railway carriage while it was in motion.

Another popular theory was that the murderer was a medical student killing women for the sake of pieces of flesh he cut from their bodies, either for his studies or to sell. The whisperings as to what else he did with the flesh were, said the newspapers, too revolting to print. Frances feared that what the respectable daily papers refused to print would be in block capitals in the weeklies.

There had also been a number of violent incidents in the street when women approached by strangers had screamed 'Murder!' and the result had been the appearance of a mob followed by a hue and cry and a hail of missiles. Some very battered and unhappy men, claiming that they had only paused to ask directions, had had to be rescued by constables.

There were large advertisements for the Guardians of Virtue in all the papers, and an interview with Mr Candy, who explained the principles by which gentlemen would be selected. A few people were, inevitably, profiting by the situation. Locksmiths reported a substantial improvement in business, as did breeders of large dogs and manufacturers of leather neck-stocks. Some residents, thinking less of protection than the inconvenience of having a corpse deposited near their homes, suggested that gates should be erected blocking every mews and public garden, to be closed and locked after the hours of darkness, the keys to be held only by those with lawful business there, and it was thought that some had already been ordered.

There had been a number of angry exchanges in the *Chronicle* between two gentlemen, neither of whom had chosen to write under his real name, but judging from the tone and content of their letters, Frances recognised them both, and understood the reasons for their enmity. Writing to the newspaper under the pseudonym Idyllist was Arthur Miggs, better known as Augustus Mellifloe, minor poet and failed literary genius. Miggs had insinuated that the members of the Literati, the Bayswater Freemasons' Lodge, might have something to divulge about the murders, but that their loyalty to each other and code of secrecy required them to protect the guilty.

A founder of the Lodge, who had responded to Idyllist using the nom de plume Honesty, was devoted reader Mr Algernon Fiske, who with his wife Edith wrote reviews of new publications for the *Chronicle* under the name Aquila. It was Mrs Fiske, a rather more forthright commentator than her husband, who in the previous year had taken up the reviewer's pen and savaged

Mr Mellifloe's pretentious little volume of verses *Mes Petites Chansonettes*. The main thrust of her piece was that it would be better for the world at large if the author was to abandon all attempts at poetry and take up some other occupation. Unfortunately, Mr Miggs, who until then had been a prospective candidate for the Literati, had discovered the true identity of Aquila and a bitter and acrimonious squabble had ensued. Miggs had thereafter taken every opportunity to denigrate the members of the Literati, whom he represented as little more than a band of self-serving conspirators plotting the overthrow of society.

Honesty, through the medium of the *Chronicle*, had advised Idyllist that the Literati were a fine body of men in good standing in the community, noted for their generous support of educational charities. So far from wishing to conceal the wrongdoings of a brother Mason, they were duty bound if they knew of any such to report that member to the police. He added that the Literati's most pressing business at present was not, as Idyllist suggested, planning armed revolution but deciding on what to serve as pudding at the next festive board, a matter that had still not been determined to everyone's satisfaction.

Idyllist replied that he would not care to eat the Literati pudding as it would choke him, and retorted that it was well known that the brethren used secret signs to communicate with each other, and that chalk marks had been found on the walls near the murder sites which were undoubtedly of Masonic significance.

Frances cast the newspapers aside in despair.

Miss Gilbert and Miss John arrived, both greatly excited, with a new scheme in which Frances was, of course, to be included. Their visit was not expected, and Miss John beamed with approval at seeing her gift cushions still in pride of place.

'It will be a very great display!' said Miss Gilbert, almost breathless with enthusiasm, 'a march, of all the suffragists in Bayswater and their many supporters, with banners and drums and singing and music, and of course *you* my dear Miss Doughty, I can promise that you will be in the very front rank! We will demand –' she brandished her fists, each of which was clutching a bundle of leaflets 'yes – *demand* – that the street should be a place of safety for women to go about their lawful business. This dreadful criminal will know beyond any doubt that we will put an end to his evil ways. Oh, that poor young boy we met only the other day! What a terrible thing! If he had not been personating a woman he would be alive now!'

Miss John nodded emphatically. She was clutching her reticule very tightly, as if any moment the clasp might spring open and a large poisonous spider or venomous snake would emerge to wreak her revenge amongst the stubborn men of Bayswater. Frances feared, although she didn't like to ask, that there was a weapon there, something more substantial and potentially lethal than the bodkin that Miss John usually carried, and which was quite dangerous enough when she wielded it.

'When will the march take place?' Frances asked, politely. She did not feel a great enthusiasm to take part, but many of her commissions came from members of the Society and she always received a flood of applications for her services every time she made an appearance with them.

'Wednesday afternoon. We will assemble at Bishops Bridge near Paddington Station at four o'clock and go west along Bishops Road and then on down Westbourne Grove. We will finish in Ladbroke Gardens where one of our ladies has very kindly agreed to give us tea.'

Frances consulted her diary. 'I do not have any appointments for that afternoon.' She wondered if she had time to have some leaflets printed on behalf of Jim Price, which she could distribute as she went. 'Sarah? I hope you can be there, too.'

'I wouldn't miss it,' said Sarah, grimly.

'Oh, I am *so* glad to hear you say so!' exclaimed Miss Gilbert. 'I was quite concerned that with so much business at present, what with advising the police, you would not have time to spare.'

Frances saw that it would be pointless to reiterate that she was not advising the police. She gave the police her advice when it seemed to be required, but that was not at all the same thing.

Miss John gave a mischievous smile. 'I have a special plan. I mean to make a strong demonstration of our feelings on the way. I will throw a stone at one of Mr Whiteley's windows.'

'I really would not recommend that,' said Frances.

'Oh, but think of the all publicity when I am arrested! They might put me in chains! Wouldn't that be wonderful?'

'I thought suffragists wish to impress upon men that ladies are responsible intelligent individuals fitted to use the vote. Will your demonstration not give the opposite impression?' suggested Frances, cautiously.

'It would be quite a small window,' said Miss John, sweetly.

Frances did not believe that for a moment. 'Really, it would be better not to. And if you were to try I suspect Sarah might be obliged to prevent you.'

'Marianne,' sighed Miss Gilbert, regretfully, 'I do fear that Miss Doughty is correct.'

Miss John looked disappointed. 'I hope I may defend my life if I am attacked? I have a plan for that, too.'

'What is your plan?' asked Frances, but Miss John only clutched her reticule more tightly.

The ladies hurried away to make the final arrangements for the march and Frances had just completed composing the words of the leaflet she planned to distribute when Mr Candy arrived, all of a bustle. Frances complimented him on the speed and effectiveness of his advertising, which had clearly cost him a great deal of effort in addition to his regular work.

'I like to be busy. Idleness leads to dullness.' He took some papers from a document case. 'I have here a list of all the gentlemen who have thus far volunteered for the Guardians of Virtue. As you may imagine, recent events have resulted in a considerable flood of applicants. I have formed a little committee and we have been examining the names. All those we cannot vouch for ourselves from personal knowledge have been asked to provide a letter from a clergyman or justice. It would assist me if you were to glance at the list and let me know if there are any who you would vouch for or – on the other hand – not. This would all be in the strictest confidence, of course, and if any gentleman was not admitted we would simply say that we already have sufficient numbers so as not to offend anyone.'

'I will do my best.' Frances glanced down the list. Mr Candy had already examined the names in the manner of an auditor, ticking those applicants he approved and crossing out those who did not meet his exacting standards. Frances saw some names she knew amongst those who had not been approved. 'You have not accepted Mr Max Gillan?'

'Newspaper man,' said Candy, as if that was all the comment required.

'Neither have you accepted Mr Garton,' Frances added, seeing that Cedric's name had been crossed out twice.

'He has been questioned by the police, so they must regard him as suspicious. Also,' he hesitated, and lowered his voice to a whisper, 'he is a known invert.'

Frances decided not to argue with him. Mr Candy had, however, accepted with a bold tick Mr Hullbridge, the distinguished charitable patron who had paid off his pregnant servant girl with a twenty pound note. 'I think that this gentleman has business demands which may make him unable to give freely of his time.' She drew a line through the name. There was nothing else of note, and she handed the papers back. 'I do not see your name here.'

'No, my talents are for organisation, and in any case, ladies like a tall athletic gentlemen to protect them.'

'That is true. I would have appreciated the protection of one of your Guardians only this morning. Can you imagine, the man who is called the Filleter actually leaped into my cab and threatened me in broad daylight.'

Mr Candy gasped. 'The audacity! He did not hurt you?'

'No, but I was very alarmed. I went straight to the police, of course, but there was really nothing they could do.' Frances saw that Mr Candy had also brought the signed petition. 'May I see this?'

On examining the signatures she was soon in no doubt that the periodicals in the ladies reading room had been defaced by Mrs Hullbridge, who must know that something was very badly and painfully wrong with her marriage, and was unprepared to submit quietly to misery as so many wives were obliged to do. It was a situation in which there were few if any options. There were insufficient grounds for Mrs Hullbridge to divorce her husband, and while a separation might be agreed upon, all but the most desperate wife would shun the idea and prefer respectable unhappiness to scandal. Frances recalled Sarah mentioning the loss of the Hullbridges' youngest child last winter, and that suggested a way in which the distraught mother might find an occupation to ease her pain.

'Tell me, do you have many ladies employed in your charitable ventures?'

'Employed?' asked Candy, puzzled. 'We have lady patrons, of course, who make generous donations.'

'I meant ladies who actually gave their time. It struck me that the children's hospital might appreciate visits from ladies willing to give comfort to the little patients. The tenderness of a woman is of incalculable value.'

'I suppose that is so. Can you suggest any ladies who might be willing to make such visits?'

'There is a name I have in mind, and with your permission I will write to her. I will suggest she forms a ladies committee, which will explore the ways in which they can support this and other charitable endeavours.'

It was agreed, and once Mr Candy departed Frances wrote a carefully worded letter to Mrs Hullbridge.

CHAPTER TWENTY

Shortly after breakfast next morning, Cedric arrived in a cab, looking as he always did, elegant enough to sweep into a fashionable restaurant and order dinner with effortless aplomb. 'We must be very careful,' he advised Frances with great solemnity, as they made a start on their journey to Lambeth Registry Office. 'We make such a handsome couple, that if we linger there too long the registrar may decide to marry us on the spot, and not take no for an answer!'

As they proceeded on their way, they talked about the terrible events of the last weeks, Frances' fears and suspicions, her grief at the death of Mr Ibbitson, the plight of the man now only six days away from his doom, and the atmosphere of barely suppressed panic that was rife in Bayswater. Cedric was a good listener. He knew when to be flippant and amusing and when to be serious, and he never, as so many men did, tried to brush away her concerns as unimportant or offer facile solutions. To her regret, Frances found that it was almost a relief to leave the part of London that had once been so safe, and where she had felt so much at home.

Lambeth was a district of Surrey with which Frances was wholly unfamiliar. It was so near to London that it practically was London, and one day it would, in all probability, be swallowed up by the ever-hungry metropolis. Her father had rarely spoken of any place that lay south of the river, and when he did it was to suggest that everything north of the Thames had some pretensions to civilisation and all that lay south was a wilderness of thieves, smugglers and 'men whose heads do grow beneath their shoulders'. The cab deposited Frances and Cedric at Victoria from whence a train took them to Brixton Station. This was only a short cab ride to the registry office on Brixton Road; an attractive building whose portico, supported by classical columns, suggested that good taste had, after all, been able to cross the river.

They were obliged to wait to be seen by the clerk, a gentleman of middle years who had probably spent most of his life in this humble but essential profession, and had therefore seen everything there was to be seen of the happiness, hope and despair that could be brought to his door, and was unlikely to find anything very surprising.

'I am sure he thinks that we are here to be married,' confided Cedric, adding that the prospect was becoming so pleasing that the longer he waited, the more he felt he could be tempted to agree, but after much earnest thought decided that he would decline the honour as he felt he was not worthy. Frances was eventually permitted to explain her business to the clerk, and since the wedding had taken place very recently it was possible to discover that not only had Timothy Wheelock and Caroline Outram been married just two weeks previously but it had been a civil ceremony which had taken place in that very building. The clerk recalled the couple very well, since the lady, even though heavily veiled and gloved, was quite clearly considerably senior to the groom. The clerk had had his own suspicions about the wedding, that much was apparent from his expression and the care with which he chose his words, but he also knew that it was not his place to do any more than maintain the records. When Frances asked to see a copy of the certificate, he hesitated briefly, and then opened the books. She wondered if such an action was within the rules of his occupation, but his expression gave nothing away.

The witnesses to the wedding were the groom's mother, Mrs Mary Wheelock, and a Miss Daisy Atkins, who Frances suspected was the same Daisy who had been installed as the new Mrs Wheelock's personal maid. Both bride and groom had given their address as Mrs Mary Wheelock's residence in Lambeth, and there had been no banns. The marriage had been subject to an application for a license, and had taken place as soon as it was granted.

Frances completed her notes. 'I would like to speak to the registrar. When will he be available?'

The clerk consulted his watch and said that the registrar would be free to talk to her in an hour, so Frances and Cedric repaired to a nearby teashop to while away the time.

'Do you have no beau to occupy your mind with thoughts of marriage?' asked Cedric over a plate of fresh scones. His voice was light and a little teasing, but his concern for her was very plain.

'I do not think of marriage. At least, I do not think of it as something that I would ever undertake.'

'And what of Miss Smith and her handsome swain?'

'I am given to understand that they are no more than friends,' said Frances diplomatically. Sarah remained adamant that she would never marry, indeed never leave Frances' side, and Professor Pounder was too sensible a man to argue with her. In the last month, however, the two had made an ascent in a tethered hot-air balloon and returned to earth with more roses in their cheeks than seemed to be warranted. Neither had discussed the event except to say that it was 'very satisfactory'.

Frances suddenly found her vision misting over and she pressed a napkin to her eyes. 'Poor Mr Ibbitson was very fond of Miss Price.'

'There was nothing you could have done,' said Cedric quietly. They sat together in a companionable way until it was time to return for their meeting.

The registrar, a solid and assured gentleman in his forties who had been warned of their coming and given some indication as to their purpose, looked at them suspiciously as they were ushered into his office, nevertheless, he remained courteous. He began by ignoring Frances and addressing Cedric since he was the male and therefore presumably the senior individual present, but Cedric soon made it plain that he relinquished all authority to Frances, and thereafter remained content to sit silently by and examine his perfectly manicured fingernails.

Frances presented her card to the registrar who stared at it dubiously. 'I am a private detective and have come to investigate the circumstances of the marriage that was recently solemnised here between Mr Timothy Wheelock and Mrs Caroline Outram. I am acting on behalf of the bride's family.'

The registrar dropped the card on the desk in front of him. 'I remember the wedding, of course. I assume that the bride's family wish to contest the validity of the marriage?'

'That is correct.'

'On what grounds?' he asked frostily.

'That may become apparent when I have more information. You are aware that the groom is twenty-four and the bride is seventy-two?'

'They did not give their ages; it was unnecessary as both were of full age. But that does not invalidate the marriage. I should mention that I have been expecting a visit of this nature, though not from a young woman. If you are a detective as you claim to be, then you cannot be a very perceptive one.'

From the corner of her eye Frances saw Cedric's eyebrow ascend. 'Oh? Please enlighten me.'

The registrar permitted himself a superior smile. 'You are obviously unaware that the people who have sent you here do not have the best interests of the lady at heart. Mr Wheelock, when he applied for the licence, explained the unusual circumstances to me very fully.' He sat back and rested his clasped hands on the desktop.

Frances waited, but the registrar seemed to think that nothing more was required of him. 'I see that you wish me to desist from my enquiries but I really cannot do so without more information.'

The registrar gave a weary sigh and glanced at Cedric. 'Sir, could you explain to Miss Doughty that she is misguided, and there is no further information I am willing to divulge.'

Cedric buffed his nails. 'Since Miss Doughty speaks excellent English an interpreter hardly seems necessary. Ignore me, please, I am only of decorative significance.'

The registrar looked bewildered, and Frances seized her chance. 'I am here because a crime has been committed. It was committed in this office and you were a participant.'

'That is outrageous!'

'Is it? Then kindly convince me of that by letting me know what occurred.'

'Ridiculous!'

Cedric continued to buff his nails. Frances waited.

'Very well,' said the registrar at last. 'You clearly need to be informed of the correct facts. Once you appreciate them you will see the foolishness of your errand. These relations of Mrs Wheelock have treated her with great unkindness. Although a respectable widow and of their own blood, they did not wish to trouble themselves with having the charge and care of her in her old age, which is their duty. It seems that she enjoys the occasional glass of alcoholic beverage which is such a comfort to the aged, but of which they disapproved. The lady was a great friend of Mr Wheelock's late grandmother who shortly before she died made him promise always to look after her, and this he promised faithfully to do. It recently came to his notice that, despite the fact that she is of perfectly sound mind, her relations were planning to have the unfortunate lady declared insane and committed to an asylum at the public expense. The only way he could reasonably thwart their intentions and protect her was to become her husband, which he has done. That is the story behind the unusual marriage.'

'I see. Did Mr Wheelock name his wife's relations?'

'No, he did not, but they must surely be the very people who have directed you to come here.'

'I doubt it. I am acting for Mrs Wheelock's great-nephew, Mr James Chandler, who is a resident of India. He did not arrive in London until after the wedding took place, and I can assure you that he cares very much about his aunt's welfare and has no wish to place her in an asylum since he agrees that she is perfectly sane. Therefore he cannot be one of the relations to whom you refer.'

The registrar frowned. 'That is probable, I suppose,' he admitted grudgingly.

'And consider this. If these relations, whoever they may be, did not wish to trouble themselves to have the charge of a lady of advanced years, then her marriage to Mr Wheelock would place her under his care and achieve the same result. Why would they now wish to challenge the wedding since he does their work for them?'

The registrar was beginning to look uncomfortable, 'I believe that there is some small family property involved. If Mr Wheelock does a husband's duty and cares for his wife then he will make no profit out of the marriage, whereas if she is single and placed in the public asylum, the relatives would eventually inherit and not incur any expense.'

Frances provided the registrar with the card of Mr Rawsthorne. 'This is the lady's solicitor, who once employed Mr Wheelock as his clerk. He will confirm everything I am telling you, including the fact that Mr Chandler is the lady's only living relative. Prior to this marriage she was mistress of a very considerable fortune. Farmland, houses, bank stocks. She has never been a friend of Mr Wheelock's grandmother.'

The registrar, taken aback for a moment, stared at the card, then he rallied. 'How do I know you are being truthful?'

Frances had come prepared. She opened her reticule and extracted copies of the *Bayswater Chronicle*. Since becoming a detective she had learned the value of retaining her own library of local information, and she was therefore able to show the registrar a list of prominent wills showing the value of the late Mr Outram's fortune, and an obituary confirming that the former Caroline Outram was his relict.

The registrar paled visibly. 'I – will write to Mr Rawsthorne, of course.'

'And now, since I have had a long journey and do not wish to repeat it to conduct a second interview, I ask that we complete our business today by your describing to me exactly what transpired at the wedding.'

The registrar glanced at Cedric but it was a desperate, hopeless look.

'Better do as Miss Doughty asks,' Cedric advised. 'I find that people always do in the long run.'

Frances folded away the newspapers. 'The witnesses, I understand, were Mrs Mary Wheelock and Miss Daisy Atkins.'

'How do you know this?' It was the last defiance of a defeated man.

'I don't think that matters. Just describe them, please.' Frances waited patiently for the final capitulation.

'Oh, very well. Mrs Mary Wheelock was a female of about fifty and I was given to understand that she is the groom's mother. From observation, I am more than confident that that was the truth. Miss Atkins was a young person, not a relation I believe. Perhaps not the most respectable individual; her language was more colourful than I might have wished.'

'Was anyone else present? Was there a groomsman?'

'No.'

'Who gave the bride away?'

'A man; about the same age as Mrs Mary Wheelock. I regret to say that he was of somewhat uncouth appearance, and was overly familiar with the groom's mother. All the participants apart from the groom were in my opinion a little the worse for drink, something which in my experience generally happens after the wedding and not before.'

'Were you able to draw any conclusions about the state of mind and health of the bride? Was any violence used towards her?'

'Really, Miss Doughty, I would scarcely have permitted the wedding had there been anything of that sort! I thought she was a little tipsy too, and the man – I am afraid I didn't quite make out his name, held on to her very tightly – I thought it was to support her in her infirmity. She may have been pushed or pulled along, but again, I did not think at the time that it was coercion, but assistance.'

'Was anything said other than the words of the ceremony?'

Little fragments of doubt, things that had been buried under the explanations given at the time of events were, Frances saw, surfacing in the registrar's mind. 'I thought – it was hard to catch precisely what she was saying – but I had the impression that the bride was unhappy about the proceedings and did not want them to continue.'

'What was done or said to persuade her to go on?'

'No one spoke unkindly to her or used her in a rough manner. Had that occurred I would never have proceeded. Mr Wheelock said something like, "Come on, my dear, you know what will happen if we don't marry today. You don't want that, do you?" and she gave a little sob. I assumed – based on what I had been told, that if they did not marry then her relations would put her away, and that was what he was alluding to, and that was the reason for her distress.'

'The lady was distressed?'

He looked pained, but it was time to admit the truth. 'Yes.'

'Would you be willing to testify to that in a court?'

'If I receive the assurances you refer to from Mr Rawsthorne, yes. But I must make it quite plain, that at the time, given what I was led to believe – '

'Of course.'

Frances secured the registrar's card, and before they departed Cedric shook the worried man warmly by the hand. 'Well done, sir,' he said.

As Frances boarded a cab for the railway station her companion observed, 'You must remind me Miss Doughty, always to remain on the right side of the law, and if I was ever to transgress I must give myself up to the police at once rather than fall under your questioning.'

Once in Bayswater, Cedric departed for an urgent meeting with his tailor and Frances dispatched two letters, one to James Chandler to advise him of what she had discovered, and one to Mr Rawsthorne, in the hope that he had by now returned to the office.

Sarah had been far from idle. She had first delivered the text of the leaflet Frances had composed to a printer and extracted a promise to have the copies done by the end of the day, then returned home to await her new client. The fearful wife failed to arrive for her appointment and Sarah, dreading the worst, had gone to the house only to find the couple in a state of inebriation and boisterous reconciliation. There was nothing she could do but leave them to their marital activities and hope that she would not hear of the murder of one of them in due course.

Mr Pargeter's secret paramour, 'Mrs Jones' of Porchester Road, required more delicacy of approach. The lady lived very quietly, and rarely left the house. Sarah had obtained an introduction by bringing her some baby linen, saying it was being distributed by a charity and asking if she had any further requirements. It was agreed that she would call again.

Sarah had then had a long conversation with Hannah, the Wheelocks' parlourmaid, who was more confiding than previously. Under the influence of baked comforts, the maid gradually revealed further secrets about the household. She was unable to provide any information about the wedding itself, and only recalled that her master and mistress had departed early one morning by carriage and returned later in the day. She had seen them go and had gained the impression that her mistress was tipsy and not entirely willing to make the journey. She had assumed from what she had seen that the purpose of the journey was to sign some papers, or meet with a legal advisor, and was astonished to be told later that they were married. There had been no wedding breakfast or festivities of any kind.

It was a strange marriage, but Hannah said she had never seen Wheelock be cruel to his wife. He had never struck her or used her violently in any way, and in some respects he was very kind. Her mistress liked a drink of port or sherry of an evening, and he had given orders that she was to have as much as she pleased, so there was always a supply of both within her reach. He had also instructed the servants that since his wife was elderly and frail it was best and safest for her not to leave the house unaccompanied, not even with her trusted coachman, Nettles. He thought she would become confused, and wander away on her own, and might come to harm. Neither was his wife to send any letters unless he saw them first. It was for her own good, he explained, as she needed to be protected by his sound advice. If she did write a letter and asked one of the servants to post it for her, then they were not to do so, but must take the letter straight to him. Once, Mrs Wheelock had written a letter and given it to Daisy to post but Daisy had taken it straight to Wheelock. Hannah had not been able to see to whom the letter had been addressed and had been afraid to ask.

Sarah felt that there was still more to discover, and gave Hannah one of Frances' cards, writing the address on the back. 'Miss Doughty is a lady detective I know. Very kind and sympathetic. If you need help, go to her.'

CHAPTER TWENTY-ONE

The printed leaflets were delivered that afternoon and Frances thought them clear and convincing. Realising that she might not have the opportunity to distribute all of them as she proceeded along the walk with the lady suffragists, she and Sarah went out to the busy shopping promenade of Westbourne Grove and handed them to anyone in the street who they thought might be receptive to the sentiments expressed. A note came from Mr Carter Freke saying that Mr Rawsthorne was not yet back in his office but it was hoped that he would be there the following day. Frances wrote back at once saying that she would be there to see Mr Rawsthorne and would not accept any refusal.

At four o'clock, Frances and Sarah, wearing the purple sashes of the Bayswater Women's Suffrage Society, joined the assembled suffragists near Bishops Road Bridge by the railway offices where it crossed the multiple lines that snaked out of Paddington Station. Although the weather was cool and cloudy with rain showers threatening, it was impossible to dampen the sprits of Miss Gilbert, who was bouncing with enthusiasm like a young girl going to the fair for the first time. She had a large cloth bag stuffed with hundreds of leaflets, carried on a strap about her ample body to leave her hands free. Miss John had a smaller bag of leaflets, and was clutching her reticule with a strong gleam in her eye. Despite Miss Gilbert's promise of a very great throng there were only about thirty suffragists. Many were carrying mirlitons; unusual instruments that somehow translated the breath of the player into something like the musical buzzing of bees, so that no actual ability was required in order to create a melody. Three of the ladies had drums, and the two largest were bravely carrying the new banner on its heavy poles.

'Ladies, ladies,' exclaimed Miss Gilbert throwing up her arms, 'I am delighted to announce that Miss Doughty is joining us for the march and will walk at our head.' There was a polite cheer from the band.

'Oh, I don't think –' Frances protested.

Miss Gilbert squeezed her arm. 'But I insist! You are so modest, my dear Miss Doughty, but believe me, you will inspire us!'

'In that case, I cannot refuse. I hope you don't mind my mentioning it, but I am very concerned that Miss John is still intending to throw a stone through one of Mr Whiteley's windows. I beg of you, do try and dissuade her.'

Miss Gilbert uttered a trilling laugh. 'No, no, she has quite given up on that idea!'

'That is a relief, because from the way she is holding her reticule I thought it might contain a missile of some sort.' Frances glanced across at Miss John, and another far worse idea presented itself. 'Please reassure me that she is not carrying a gun.'

'But yes! A charming little pistol. She is very proud of it.'

'Do you think that is wise? She might cause an accident.'

'Oh, please don't worry yourself about that, she would never dare use it. It makes her feel safe, the dear thing.'

'Is it loaded?'

Miss Gilbert looked mystified. 'Do you know, I am not at all sure.'

A cold wind swept across them, rippling banners, and fluttering the purple sashes. There was a loud rumbling sound that was nothing to do with either the drums or the traffic or even passing trains, but produced by the vibration of the large advertising hoardings that flanked the bridge creating their own unearthly music.

Miss Gilbert tied her bonnet more securely and took her place at the head of the throng. 'Let us start, now, ladies, and before we know it we will be done and there will be tea and cake for all!'

There was another even louder cheer. Frances and Sarah were ushered to the front where they were to walk alongside Miss Gilbert and Miss John, then the two large ladies followed carrying the purple banner. Behind them were the drummers and finally the massed mirlitons.

'Onward!' shouted Miss Gilbert, waving an arm, and the drums began to thud and the buzzing began. As they proceeded along the road, a few faces looked out of windows at the unaccustomed din, and passers-by stopped and stared. One or two men waved

their hats and not a few made unkind comments. Miss Gilbert and
Miss John marched cheerily unabashed and offered their leaflets.
'Save our women!' cried Miss Gilbert, to which one wag asked if
she could save one for him as he needed his laundry doing. A few
men jeered but there were also some who wished them well.

Frances kept a careful watch on Miss John. She was not especially worried as they marched along Bishops Road past some
respectable houses and Holy Trinity church, but decided to keep
her in view as they neared Westbourne Grove, with its rows of
shop windows. There was a small school on the north side of the
Grove, and Frances hoped that if Miss John was planning anything
violent she would not do it there.

Having passed by the Royal Oak public house where a constable was always stationed in the hours of darkness, a thought
occurred to Frances. 'Miss Gilbert, have you advised the police of
your intention to carry out this march?'

'Why no, why should it concern them?'

'They would have appreciated a warning and might have
helped make the roads clearer for you.'

'They would have banned us altogether!' declared Miss John.
'They are all men, you know, and everything that that entails.'

Frances looked about her with growing anxiety. 'I fear we may
be in danger of arrest for obstructing the highway.'

Miss John uttered a little sigh. 'Oh I do hope so!'

As they entered the Grove women shoppers paused to wave
and cheer, and some even ran up to Miss Gilbert and took hand-
fuls of leaflets and helped to distribute them. Frances was able to
pass on her remaining leaflets too, which saved her some effort.
The walk was not without danger, since the Grove was busy with
carriage traffic, and horses unused to the strange sound of the
mirlitons became restless and hard to control. A few coachmen
became annoyed with the obstruction and waved their whips,
shouting at the marchers to get of the way.

They were walking past the school near which there was a narrow
cut, Westbourne Grove Terrace, that led up to the school playground
and a Presbyterian church, when Frances saw something out of the
corner of her eye. It was a dark flicker and she knew at once what it
was. He ducked back quickly into the terrace, but she had seen him.

She tried to stay calm and put her hand on Miss Gilbert's shoulder. 'It's him – up there – the wanted man the police have been looking for! I've just seen him! We must summon a policeman at once!'

Miss Gilbert stared quickly about, but he was out of sight. 'Where?'

'Hiding around that corner.' Frances looked around for a messenger she could send.

Miss Gilbert stopped, faced the throng and held up her arms. The little band came to a halt. 'Ladies! Miss Doughty has found the criminal! Our quarry is in sight! Let us all go and secure him! Follow me!'

Before Frances could say another word, and to her great horror, Miss Gilbert rushed into the alley crying 'Tally ho!' and all the other ladies apart from the two with the heavy banner, swarmed after her.

'No! Stop! Come back!' Frances exclaimed, but for once the lady suffragists ignored her. Sarah and Frances looked at each other and there was nothing they could do except follow. Frances once more exhorted someone to send for a policeman, but her words continued to go unheeded. As she ran, gaining on the others with her long stride, she was comforted by the fact that the Filleter was easily able to outrun any of them. At the top of the alley he could make a turn into Westbourne Park Mews, and after that he would be able to make his escape across a small green, or between some houses. She could only hope that there were no schoolchildren about, as the day's lessons were by now over.

At the top of the terrace, the ladies stopped and looked around, unsure where to go next. There was no one in the vicinity of the church and the school playground was thankfully deserted.

'We've lost him,' said Frances, and for once she felt relieved. She faced the suffragists, many of whom were out of breath, and clutching at heavily corseted abdomens. 'Now, please, everyone, what we should do is go back and get a policeman.' Miss Gilbert pouted with frustration but did not object.

The ladies were just about to comply when one of them, peering into the little mews, let out a piercing scream. Frances and Sarah, fearing that another murder had been done, hurried up, and there, at the end of the narrow walled passage, was the Filleter, his way barred by a tall, shiny and very new set of gates. He turned to face them and he was dark and sweating and surly as a beaten dog.

Frances seized hold of the woman who had screamed and pushed her away. 'Get a policeman! Now!' The woman nodded, and ran back to the main road, her voice, high as a whistle, shrieking 'Murder!'

The remaining women had gathered at the head of the mews, and there they stopped and stared at their trapped quarry. His eyes flickered about. The crowd had effectively blocked his way, and while they stood there, he had no avenue of escape. 'I'll deal with this,' said Sarah stepping to the fore, and rolling up her sleeves, her lip curling in anticipation, but in an instant he had pulled out the thin sharp knife that was his calling card.

'Now then, ladies,' he said softly, his voice like the purr of a wild beast, 'I don't want to cut any of you up unless I have to, so here's what will happen. All you have to do is stand aside, and let me though. Just make it quick and do it now, and I promise that no one will get hurt.'

Sarah made to move forward again but Frances seized her arm. 'Please. Don't.' She had seen Sarah disarm a nervous man with a knife, but the Filleter was a hardened killer and he could move fast. 'I don't want you hurt. Please.' Sarah paused, unwillingly, and gradually the women, mesmerised by the cruel knife, began to shrink back. As he saw them step aside, and open a path to freedom, he moved forward.

'We can't just let him go like that,' hissed Sarah.

'If we wish to avoid bloodshed we may have to, unless ...' Frances glanced at Miss John, who was clutching her reticule convulsively, her hands like claws, her eyes staring almost out of her head. Frances reached out and pulled the reticule open, and there, nestled amongst the fabric scraps and sewing threads, and a little clutch of bodkins, was a small pistol. She took it out and strode forward, pointing it at the Filleter. It at least had the effect of surprising him.

The little gun was heavier than it looked, but her fingers were strong and she managed to hold it steady and find the trigger. 'Now then. *This* is what is going to happen. You are to put the knife down, and then we will all wait here for the police to come.'

He stared at her, but made no move.

'Put the knife down!' she rapped.

He sneered. 'I bet that isn't even loaded!'

She hoped he didn't see her hesitate. She bit down on the inside of her lip, took a deep breath and gathered all her courage. 'A betting man, are you? And what would you like to wager that this gun is not loaded? Your life, perhaps? Are you lucky in games of chance?'

He wavered. 'You wouldn't dare.'

'Wouldn't I?' Frances suddenly began to shake and tears started in her eyes, not from fear but anger. She clasped her other hand to the gun to hold it level. 'You murdered a friend of mine! A boy, just seventeen, with all his life in front of him! You butchered him without a thought, as if he was an animal! And you really think I wouldn't dare? Because at this very moment nothing would give me greater pleasure than to shoot you dead.'

There was a short silence. Tears were running hotly down her cheeks, but she managed to keep the gun aimed at him. 'Now put. The knife. Down.'

The expression on his face was unreadable, and then suddenly his arms dropped by his sides and he gave a strange sour laugh. 'All right, Miss Doughty, you win. I surrender.' He leaned forward and laid the knife on the ground in front of him, then he straightened up. 'What now?'

'Now step back – move away from it, so it's out of your reach.'

He backed away and she moved forward, still keeping the pistol pointing towards him, and maintaining a safe distance. As she reached the knife she kicked it still further from him.

Sarah marched forward, pulling off her purple sash. 'On the ground! Lie down! Hands behind you!'

With some trepidation, he obeyed, and Sarah stood astride his prone body. As the weight of her knee descended hard into the small of his back, he cried out and gasped for breath. She pulled his arms firmly together, and trussed his wrists tightly, tying the stout silk into knots. At last, the watching suffragists burst out into cheers of approbation.

'Ladies, stand aside please!' said a familiar voice, as Inspector Sharrock pushed his way through the crowd, followed by Mayberry. 'Just stand back as calm as you can, police officers coming though.'

'You are too late,' cried Miss Gilbert triumphantly, as Sharrock stopped and stared in amazement at the Filleter lying face down on the muddy path, his wrists tied in a purple silk band embroidered with a demand for women's suffrage, Sarah kneeling crushingly on his back and Frances pointing the gun at his head. 'We ladies have forestalled you and caught the murderer ourselves.'

'Oh my blessed aunt!' Sharrock bellowed. He turned to Mayberry, who was spluttering and red in the face. 'What are you laughing at? Go and whistle up some more constables, we're not letting this one get away!' At first Frances thought he might come forward and take charge of the prisoner, but instead, after surveying the scene, he scratched his head, and made a helpless gesture. 'Go on, I hardly like to interrupt.'

Frances and Sarah continued to act as guards until more police arrived, and the Filleter, who appeared considerably relieved when Sarah's weight was no longer pressing on him, was dragged to his feet and handcuffed. As he was marched away he turned and gave Frances a curious look. 'We'll meet again, Miss Doughty! And it won't be so pleasant for you next time!' One of the policemen pushed him on and he disappeared around the corner of the mews.

The lady suffragists, with more cheering, gathered about Frances and Sarah, and there was a babble of congratulations. It was with some difficulty that Sharrock managed to make his way through the crowd and confront Frances. 'I'm not sure what to say to you.'

'It is not necessary to say anything. I am just glad that it is over.'

'Where did you get that?' he demanded pointing to the gun.

'Oh that is mine, Inspector,' claimed Miss Gilbert, quickly. 'A charming little trinket don't you think? For ornamental purposes only, of course. I just chanced to be showing it to Miss Doughty when we encountered that nasty man, and she used it to save us all!'

'Really?' said Sharrock, cynically. He reached out for the pistol and Frances handed it to him.

After a quick glance, he pulled back what looked like a small lever, and rotated the central portion. Five shiny brass cylinders with grey tips fell into the palm of his hand. Then he closed the lever and returned the gun to Miss Gilbert. 'If I were you, Madam,

I would not walk about with a loaded pistol unless you know how to use it. It might go off and kill someone.'

'Dear me, I had no idea!' said Miss Gilbert, innocently and uttered a merry laugh.

Frances did not share the amusement. 'I am very grateful that the police came so quickly.'

'You can thank young Tom Smith for that,' Sharrock told her. 'Bright lad. He's been keeping his eyes open and helping us out for some days now. Regular little Pinkerton, he is.'

'He knew where the Filleter was?'

'No, Miss Doughty, it wasn't him he was watching – it was you. I think the villain has been following you, perhaps looking for a chance to make good on his threat.'

'I am very glad to have him locked up at last. And I will not claim any glory for myself; you may have it all. The last thing I want is to be on the front page of the *Illustrated Police News*.'

'Ah, but *we* will know the truth!' crowed Miss Gilbert. 'Why, what a wonderful policeman you would make, Miss Doughty, and you too Miss Smith!'

'Oh yes, I can just imagine you both in uniform,' enthused Miss John. 'What a sight that would be!'

Sharrock turned to the assembled drummers and mirliton players. 'Now then, all you ladies, the best thing to do would be for you to go on quietly to your homes, and see about some nice dinner. I'm sure you all have homes, and some of you might even have husbands waiting for you. My job,' he rubbed his hands together, 'is to ask some very pointed questions of the man I have just arrested, and also inform Inspector Swanson of Scotland Yard that the Bayswater Police have made the collar.' He was grinning broadly as he strode away.

CHAPTER TWENTY-TWO

rances did not think she would enjoy the tributes that would inevitably be hers were she to accompany the suffragists as they dispersed in the direction of the promised tea and cake, and after making a number of increasingly desperate excuses she was permitted with many expressions of regret to go home. There, Frances and Sarah contemplated what the momentous event of that day might lead to. Frances was not entirely sure that the Filleter had committed all the murders, although she was certain that he was responsible for the death of George Ibbitson. While she had always felt uncomfortable about the barbaric and irreversible finality of the death penalty, there were times when she condoned it, and also times when, as now, she might have been willing to pull the fatal lever herself.

And there was still the murder of Martha Miller, which was so different from the others. With only five days before the execution of Jim Price, Frances once again took up her pen and wrote a plea to the Home Office saying that now this dangerous man was in police hands they should explore the possibility that he had committed the murder for which Jim Price was about to suffer. There was nothing more she could do.

She had very little appetite but Sarah persuaded her to partake of a light supper and then they settled to reading while the light was good enough, assisted in that activity by a jug of hot cocoa. It was comforting to be indoors where one could forget the oppressive gloom of dark grey clouds and bursts of showery rain.

They were intending to retire as soon as the cocoa was finished but then there was the sound that Frances always knew heralded some urgent matter, a loud thudding at the front door and a clanging of the bell, as if the caller could not risk that one such clamour would go unnoticed and had to make two alternately. Frances looked out of the window and through the gathering mist saw a small boy, very wet and shivering standing on the doorstep. 'I think that's Dunnock,' she said. The lad, who was probably about ten, was a valued member of Ratty's team of runners and watchers.

Sarah went to fetch the child before he roused the entire street, and once he had been brought into the parlour a blanket was laid out for him to sit on and more blankets brought to wrap him in. He looked not merely cold but terrified, his lank hair stuck to his face like a coat of paint, his eyes glassy in the firelight. He was panting like an animal that had escaped a huntsman.

'What is it, Dunnock?' asked Frances gently as Sarah poured a cup of cocoa, stirred in extra sugar and handed it to the boy.

'More murder,' he whimpered. 'An' I saw it. It was like somethin' not real.' He clutched the cup and stared into its dark depths as if he hardly recognised what he was seeing.

Frances, facing this fresh horror and hoping desperately that there had been a mistake, tried for the sake of the child to stay calm and not show her emotions. 'Take your time and tell me what happened. Start from the beginning.'

The scent of the cocoa seemed to comfort him a little. He gulped at it and wiped his mouth.

'I was takin' a message to Mr Rawsthorne's office. You asked us to keep an eye on what goes on. It's been funny roun' there, lots of back and forth and you never see the boss man 'imself, 'e's always out. It's that Mr Freke who seems to do it all now.' He finished the cocoa and held the cup out to Sarah who refilled it. 'I was just comin' out when I saw a carriage pull up outside. Very fancy it was. Coachman jumps down, and goes to open the door, but then 'e gives a yell and jumps back, and 'e's shakin' like 'e's in a fit an' all of a fright. It's like 'e's seen the Divil 'imself. Then 'e crosses 'imself and I think 'e says a prayer an' then 'e jumps back up and whips up the 'orses as fast as they'll go. So I jumps up behind, don't I, 'cos I wanter know what's up.'

He put the cup down. Sarah proffered a plate of bread and jam and he looked at it. Pinched and thin as he was, he shook his head. 'The carriage went straight up to Paddington Green p'lice, and the man, 'e jumps down and runs inter the station as if he was bein' chased by somethin'. An' then –' Dunnock sniffed. 'I got down an' I thought I'd see for myself, an' it was like nothin' in the world I'd ever seen before. It was a woman – only not a woman – I mean she had a dress an' that, and I 'spect she must've been a woman once, but it was more like one of those big dolls you see at the fair, all with fancy paint, what people throw things at. Only the paint was all red, and then I knew it wasn't paint, but blood – blood all over, an' down the dress, an' the face – but there weren't a face at all. It was all one colour – blood!'

He began to cry and Sarah put the bread and jam away then sat beside him and hugged him in a motherly way, and gave him a handkerchief.

'So then I went inside, an' stayed at the back so I could 'ear what the coachman was sayin' to the sergeant. They was all tryin' to calm 'im down, and 'e was telling' them 'ow 'e had taken 'is mistress to see 'er s'licitor and she were all right when they started out an' 'e found 'er killed when they got there.'

'Did you hear any names?'

'Yes, the coachman was called Nettles, an' 'e said 'is mistress was Mrs Wheelock. An' 'e said he saw a man climbin' in the coach an' then jumpin' down an' runnin' off later. Only 'e didn't think anythin' of it at the time as 'e thought it must be 'er 'usband and they'd p'raps 'ad an argyment. An' all the police run out and looked inter the carriage an' one of 'em was sick there and then. So I thought you oughter know an' I jumped on a carrier's cart an' come 'ere.'

'You are sure that it was Mrs Wheelock who was killed?' exclaimed Frances. 'The elderly lady?'

'Yes, the one what used to be Mrs Outram. I know the carriage, it 'ad a big letter O painted on the side with a sort of wheat sheaf in it.'

Sarah brought a rough warm towel and began to rub the lad's face and hair. 'You'll need dry clothes. Wait a bit and I'll go and get Tom to send some.'

'Do take care!' Frances exclaimed.

'Oh, if I meet that Face-slasher I'll take care of him, all right!' Sarah snorted. She wrapped another blanket around the boy and hurried away to get her cloak.

'Stay here by the fire Mr Dunnock,' said Frances. 'You have been a brave man today and you will have a reward.'

He nodded but with only faint enthusiasm, as if to say that a reward was all very welcome but he would gladly have foregone it not to have seen the sight of Mrs Wheelock's mutilated corpse. Frances, realising that Mr Chandler would need to be informed and that the police would not have his address, quickly penned a note telling him to go to the police station as a matter of urgency, and handed it to Sarah to deliver on her way.

'Did you hear the coachman say anything about the man who got into the coach and ran away? Why did he think it was her husband?'

''E dint say. Jus' said that a man came up an' there was a bit of talk through the window which 'e dint 'ear an' then 'e got in.'

Frances reflected on this. The lady was well known for her philanthropy and might have responded to an appeal for help, but would she have permitted a stranger in the carriage? 'It was a closed carriage – not open at the front like a hansom?' Dunnock nodded. 'If the coachman thought it was her husband then even if he did not see the man's face, which he would not have done from his perch, it must have been a man of similar build, and one agile enough to run away.'

'Could've been that Filleter cove, the one with the sharp knife,' Dunnock suggested.

'If so, he will not kill again, for he was arrested today.' A thought crossed her mind. 'What time did you arrive at Mr Rawsthorne's office?'

'Dunno.' Dunnock thought for a moment. 'Yes I do. The gent I was takin' the message for said 'e wanted it to be at Rawsthorne's by six o'clock, and 'e took out 'is watch an' said I could get it there in time if I ran very fast. An' I did run fast so it must've been six or jus' before.'

'Then it was not the Filleter. He has the perfect alibi; he was in police custody at the time. But the killer almost certainly did not know that. I think Mrs Wheelock *was* killed by her husband, thinking that her death would be put down as one of the ones perpetrated here recently by the same man. I wouldn't be at all surprised if the police came to the same conclusion.'

'Yes, well, if a married woman gets killed it's short odds the 'usband did it,' said Dunnock with all the wisdom of his ten years.

When Sarah returned she took the boy in hand, rubbed him down well to dry him out, and gave him fresh clothes. He slept by the fireside that night, and was gone by morning.

According to Mr Carter Freke's information Mr Rawsthorne was due to be back in his office that morning. Frances had heard nothing more on that subject but whether or not she was granted an appointment she determined to go and see her solicitor and wait for his attention. Even with the Filleter safely in the police cells, Sarah, before she left to see 'Mrs Jones' again, warned Frances only to travel in closed carriages. She was thankful to do so, since a sharp wintry autumn had now descended and a bitter wind scoured cold streets where fallen leaves were strewn still damp from yesterday's rain. The newspapers predicted stiffer breezes, even moderate gales to come.

She was just about to depart when James Chandler was announced, and she postponed her journey to see him. He looked weary and shocked and she gestured him to a chair, where he sat, his body tense with the effort of retaining his equilibrium in a crisis. 'I must thank you for the note you sent me last night. How did you know of it so quickly?'

'I was brought a message by a boy who saw the carriage outside the police station.'

'Had you not informed me I might not have heard until it became a matter of common gossip. As it was, I was able to speak to the police and let them have all the information in my possession. I am thankful, given what I have learned, that the coachman, Nettles, was able to identify the body of my poor aunt, and I was not asked to do so. The greatest mercy is that although the killer did terrible things to her body I have been reassured that she would have known nothing about it.' He shook his head, the strain tightening his fine features. 'It is a sad end to a noble woman whose only wish was to do good.'

'Do the police have a theory as to who committed the murder?'

'They do indeed, and I believe that a formal arrest will be made very soon. When I learned of my aunt's death and the dreadful manner of it, my first thought was that the man who has been killing in Bayswater recently was responsible, but at the police station I was informed that this dreadful monster could not have carried out the crime, as they already had him in custody, something for which we must all be grateful. I went to the house and found enquiries being made there under the command of an Inspector Swanson. The husband, however, was not there and had not been for some time. I naturally told Swanson of the action I have been taking to invalidate my aunt's marriage and he saw at once that her death would hinder my case, since she would not be able to give witness to her foul husband's coercion and cruelty. I took the opportunity to look about the place and see if there were any papers secreted that might assist me but there was nothing. The servants all seemed afraid and unwilling to speak out, but one of them, the parlourmaid, said that my aunt had gone out for a drive, even though her husband had given orders that she was not to do so unaccompanied, and when he discovered this he became very angry and rushed out to look for her.'

'Has he reappeared?'

'Yes, he returned to the house while the police were in the process of interviewing the servants, and pretended to be very upset at the news of my aunt's death, which he claimed to know nothing about. He said he had been trying to find her, as he did not know where she might have gone. There was no blood on him, but he had had more than enough time to find somewhere to put that right. Of course he said my aunt must have been killed by the man who has murdered so many in this district of late, and there is no denying that it came as a shock to him when he learned that this could not be so.' Chandler appeared grimly satisfied at the discomfiture this news must have created. 'The police decided to take Wheelock to the station for more questions. They think they have their man, and don't want him to run away before they have made their case. I believe it is only a matter of time before he is charged.' His story done, Chandler looked suddenly bereft of energy. 'When I came to London I knew there would be much to do, and thought I was prepared for it, but this ugly business, I could never have anticipated.' He quickly gathered himself again. 'And there is more still to do and I must go on.' He rose to his feet.

'Thank you Miss Doughty for everything you have achieved. Your work will see that villain hanged, I am sure.'

He left and Frances was just putting on her gloves when an unexpected letter arrived, the envelope printed with the address of Marsden and Co. solicitors. Mr Marsden was Mr Rawsthorne's most prominent rival for Bayswater business, and an impudent person who lost no opportunity to belittle Frances' achievements and insinuate that she would be better occupied looking for a husband, if that is, she had any ability to attract one, which in his opinion was doubtful. He had even suggested that it was Frances herself who wrote the Miss Dauntless stories under the nom de plume W. Grove in order to increase her fame and attract clients.

Miss Doughty

The letter began curtly.

You might be aware that my client Mr Timothy Wheelock has been arrested on suspicion of the murder of his wife and is currently being held at Paddington Green police station where he is being questioned. For reasons which I am unable to fathom, he wishes to see you. Please comply with his request, and advise me of the outcome of your visit without delay,
H^y Marsden

Frances had one thing in common with the unpleasant Mr Marsden; she too could not imagine what Mr Wheelock might want with her. It was a situation not without interest, however, and gave her the ideal excuse to visit the police station and discover more about the murder. She hired a cab and departed, intending to visit Mr Rawsthorne immediately afterwards.

She found Sharrock sitting in his office looking miserably at the great mountain of material that surrounded him. He was in a poor mood since Inspector Swanson had assumed control both of the Filleter and Mr Wheelock, relegating the Bayswater police to more commonplace crimes.

'And now you're wanted,' he grumbled. 'I'll just retire now and have you put up for Inspector, shall I? Not that that means much round here nowadays. I've got a serious case in hand of throwing paint at a shop window, if you'd like to look into it.'

'I really don't know why Mr Wheelock wishes to see me. I have no desire at all to see him. Is he in the cells?'

'Interview room with Swanson and Brown. They'll make a music hall act yet.'

Frances hoped that Sharrock's irritation with Scotland Yard might make him more informative. She took some boxes from a chair and sat down. 'Am I right in supposing that the murder of Mrs Wheelock happened after the Filleter was taken into custody?'

'Right as usual, Miss Doughty.'

'And before the arrest could be generally known in the neighbourhood?'

'I would say so.'

'I understand, of course, that the police do not wish to reveal the details of the cuts that were made by the man known as the Bayswater Face-slasher,' as she spoke the words they inevitably brought back to her the memory of George Ibbitson noting down that very phrase, 'but do you think Mrs Wheelock was killed by the same man or someone simply hoping it might look like the work of the same man?'

Sharrock squeezed his eyes shut and thought. 'This one was different alright, but then the circumstances were different. I would say that, with the others, since he was out in the open, he didn't want to hang about and risk being caught so he did what he wanted in a minute or less. But this killer was in the carriage with his victim for a good ten minutes, so it's hard to tell. Could have been another man, or the same one with more time. I'll know better when the surgeon reports.'

'She had gone out alone? I was told her intention was to visit her solicitor.'

'Well you know all about it, then.'

'Not all. I assume you have interviewed Mr Nettles the coachman?'

'Oh yes I was trusted to do that!' he said sarcastically. 'Very generous of them!'

'I have been told that Mr Wheelock did not permit his wife to leave the house without him.'

'So Mr Nettles confirmed, but he had his suspicions of Wheelock and thought his wife wanted to escape him. Not surprising really.'

'He must have risked dismissal for that.'

'He was going to hand in his notice as soon as the lady was safely away. He wouldn't have been blamed for leaving that employment.'

'What else did he tell you?'

Sharrock hesitated and drummed his fingers on the desk. 'Well it'll all come out at the inquest. Nettles liked to look after his mistress so he made sure that the door was secure before he drove off. Rich folk don't like to have their carriages invaded by thieves so they bar the door if they feel inclined. Only the coachman can open it from the outside. They'd not gone far when a man knocked on the door and she signalled Nettles to stop. He thought it was Wheelock and did as he was told. They had a talk, then she opened the door, and the man got in and she told Nettles to drive on. Just before they got to Mr Rawsthorne's, the door opened and the man ran out. It was too dark to see who it was but he just assumed it was Wheelock. When they got to Rawsthorne's Nettles got down to assist Mrs Wheelock from the cab and had the fright of his life. So he jumped back on to the cab and drove straight to the police station.'

Frances had just made a note of this information when Inspector Swanson appeared, having completed his questioning of the new prisoner who had been returned to the cells. He had already been told that Wheelock had asked to see Frances, but was surprised to see her there so promptly and in conference with Sharrock. 'Miss Doughty has called to offer us some helpful advice on the catching of murderers,' Sharrock explained.

Frances rose. 'I will see Mr Wheelock now.'

'Not a nice place for a lady,' observed Swanson, with narrowed eyes.

'Do you mean the cells or the company of Mr Wheelock? I am familiar with both and have no intention of remaining very long.'

Chapter Twenty-Three

Timothy Wheelock seemed quite at home in his cell. He was like a burrowing insect that preferred to crawl into small spaces he could call his own. She found him sitting on a bench, oblivious to the cold and the unwholesome smell, reading a law book. His legs were stretched out comfortably in front of him, and by way of a footstool he was resting his heels on a Bible.

He looked up as she arrived, and grinned. It was never a pleasant sight as his habit of chewing pens and pencils had left him with permanent stains on his teeth and gums.

Frances gave him a cold look. 'I can't imagine why you have sent for me.'

He snapped the book shut. 'Well I have, so there!'

Swanson entered the cell, but the prisoner scowled at him. 'You'd better go or I'm saying nothing!'

Frances was inclined to turn and leave at once, as she felt unwilling due to Wheelock's many previous insults to see him at all, but curiosity made her stay. 'It will be perfectly in order to leave me here,' she told Swanson.

Swanson looked reluctant. 'If you insist, but I won't be far. Shout out if you need help.' He gave Wheelock a warning stare before he departed.

Frances sat down on the wooden bench as far from the prisoner as possible. There seemed little point in any delicacy of approach, which would only lengthen the proceedings. 'Did you murder your wife?'

He was both unfazed and unsurprised by the boldness of the question. 'Why would I do that? I already had her money!'

'You know why. Her great-nephew Mr Chandler is intending to have the marriage declared invalid on the grounds of coercion. By murdering her you eliminated her as a witness and have made his case far harder to establish.'

Wheelock laughed derisively. 'If he really is her great-nephew, or any sort of a relation!'

'What do you mean?'

'He turns up out of the blue all the way from India. If he ever was in India. All she has is a picture of him and his parents taken who knows how long ago, and a few letters.'

'He was clearly able to satisfy Mr Rawsthorne of his identity,' Frances pointed out.

'Oh, documents can be bought, or stolen or forged,' said Wheelock airily, as if this was an everyday occurrence, which in the world he inhabited it might well have been. 'And Rawsthorne would like nothing better than to cheat me out of my wife's money, so he'd want to believe Chandler.' He wiped the back of his hand across his mouth, inspected the result for traces of ink, and licked up the residue. 'It could be worse than that. Rawsthorne could be in on the cheat himself, and is being paid by Chandler. Perhaps Rawsthorne is the brains behind it. The real nephew might be dead. Perhaps the impostor killed him.'

'Oh this is ridiculous!' exclaimed Frances. 'Is that what you brought me here for? Wishful thinking and wild allegations?'

'So you'd like to think. But it could be true. You see, after this Chandler's visit to my house, my poor darling wife was very troubled in her mind. There had been some chat about family and the like, all very sociable and nice, but when he had gone, she got to thinking, and next day she asked to see the old pictures, and she looked at a box of family correspondence. I didn't mind, it kept her quiet and happy, so why not? But she thought about it, and after a glass or two, which she was very fond of and I couldn't deny her, she said that the man who had called on us wasn't her great-nephew after all.'

Frances remained unconvinced. 'How could she be sure? Did she say why?'

'No, more's the pity. Went off to the land of sweet dreams and when she woke up couldn't remember what she had said.'

This was a wholly new concern. Frances could not believe that Rawsthorne was involved in any cheat, but it was certainly possible that Chandler was carrying out a lucrative imposture, deceiving the solicitor with false papers. It worried her that this was something to which she had not previously given any thought. Had she been taken in by her client's charming manners and undeniably pleasing looks? She resolved to put the question before Mr Rawsthorne as soon as possible since he might have better information.

'If my wife could prove that he was an impostor then I would want her alive, now, wouldn't I?' argued Wheelock.

Frances had to admit that there was some sense in this. 'But it might be hard, even impossible to prove it. Her words might have been based on nothing more than an old memory and no one would be able to show that she wasn't simply mistaken. You would have to go to law to prove the allegation, which would be costly and might take years, and if you failed, that would still leave Mr Chandler with a sound claim on your wife's fortune and a case against you for slander.'

'Well I'm not a murderer,' said Wheelock doggedly. 'I never killed anyone. Ruined a good many, but never killed. And if I was going to don't you think I'd have got myself a proper alibi? They don't cost much.'

Frances could only agree with his reasoning. 'Can you suggest who did murder her?'

'That's not hard, is it? Not round here. Not lately.'

'That is where the killer miscalculated. He hoped that your wife's death would be blamed on the man suspected of carrying out the recent murders in Bayswater. But that man has been caught. He was arrested by Inspector Sharrock before your wife was killed.'

'Might have got the wrong man. Like your friend Mr Price.'

'What do you know about that?'

'Nothing, or I'd have sold you the information.' Wheelock sucked his lips and thought hard, then his eyes narrowed and he grinned. 'I know who has a very good motive to kill my wife. That Chandler. He must have realised he had given himself away and decided to do the old girl in. You'd better go after him.'

'It really isn't my business to look into murders.'

'No? Well how come you keep on doing it?'

Frances had no answer to give. 'You still have not said why you sent for me.'

He chewed his fingernails like a man who relied on their contents for sustenance. 'I want to employ you, that's why.'

'A strange choice.'

'I don't think so.'

'Why me? I am not the only detective in Bayswater.'

'No, but you're the only honest one.'

It was a compliment, but Frances could hardly imagine a less desirable client. 'I will need to know exactly what it is you wish me to do and why, or I shall leave now. I also wish to make it clear that I will not under any circumstances act against the interests of anyone who is already a client of mine.'

'That's up to you. But it's easy enough, I just need some documents. My own property. You're to go and get them and bring them to me, that's all. I'm not asking you to do anything against the law.'

'What documents are they? Why do you need them? I don't usually ask such details of my clients but in your case I think I need the whole story.'

'You won't like it.'

'I never like anything I hear from you.'

There was a long pause. Frances rose to depart.

'All right, sit down.' Reluctantly, she sat. 'Marsden hates Rawsthorne; well you know that. He'd do anything to see him go to the wall, and gobble up all his business, including getting me off of a murder charge. So we did a deal. That's where the papers come in.'

Frances reflected on this, and the realisation when it came, appalled her. 'Do I understand you correctly? Are you saying that in return for Mr Marsden's services, to ensure that you are cleared of the murder of your wife, you will provide him with some means by which he might ruin Mr Rawsthorne?'

Wheelock sucked his teeth noisily.

Angrily, Frances rose to her feet again. 'I knew there was something wicked and underhand happening here! You know very well that not only is Mr Rawsthorne my solicitor, but he has been a friend of my family and in particular of my late father, for many years. Yet you ask me to assist in a scheme to ruin him? It is quite extraordinary and I can have no part in it. In fact, I shall go to him at once and warn him of what you have just said. Good day.'

He gazed at her through slitted eyes, like a snake. 'Don't you want to learn more? Because there is more. A lot more.'

Frances was at the cell door when she hesitated. Everyone has their price, she reflected, and for most people it was reckoned in money but for her, it was information. She turned and looked at him sternly but he only smirked. With great reluctance she returned to the bench and sat down again. 'You have told me nothing of any interest or value so far.'

He leaned forward. 'This is between us. Just you and me. I need your promise.'

'If you are about to tell me of a crime and give me the power to bring it home to the perpetrator I cannot remain silent.'

'Oh the perpetrator will suffer, you need have no doubt of that. And you will be a part of it.'

Frances had a dreadful sense of foreboding. 'Very well,' she said against all her better judgment, 'I promise.'

'To begin with, Mr Rawsthorne was not best pleased with me when he found I was going to marry Mrs Outram. He felt cheated, because he wanted a dip in that pot himself.'

'I don't believe you. Mr Rawsthorne cannot have had ambitions there, he is a married man.'

'But his brother is a widower. Rawsthorne was going to introduce him to Mrs Outram and engineer a marriage. In return for that service he would get a share of the bounty. That is why he worked so hard to try and stop my marriage and when he couldn't do that, have it declared invalid. While my wife was alive she could be made single again, all ripe for his little scheme. Now she isn't I wouldn't mind betting that Rawsthorne has a profitable agreement with Chandler. For all I know Chandler was his puppet right from the start. How do you even know he came here all the way from India? You only have his word for it.'

'Your late wife may have been a susceptible woman but she was fully able when sober to make her own decisions. If she had married Mr Rawsthorne's brother that would have been her choice. It might have been an unwise choice but if all such choices invalidated a marriage there would scarcely be a married couple left. And there are marriage brokers who charge introduction fees. I see nothing blameworthy in that. Her marriage to you, however,

I believe was the product of blackmail. I think that you were able to prove that she destroyed her first husband's most recent will, and threatened her with exposure.'

He looked impressed. 'Nice theory. You're almost there. I couldn't prove it but I had my suspicions. Surprising how gossip gets about amongst legal men. Things you can't say out loud, things you can only whisper. Juicy things.'

'But you were able to convince her that you had proof?'

'Your words, not mine.'

'Do you think there was a new will?'

'Oh, I'm sure of it. And I'm also sure that there isn't one now, because if I can't find it no one can. But I couldn't prove if it was my wife who destroyed it or her first husband. One's a crime the other isn't. Judging by her reaction when I tackled her, she did it.'

'But you have no proof of any wrongdoing on Mr Rawsthorne's part, only fanciful allegations, which I am disinclined to believe. I doubt that his brother would support your story. You still haven't told me what documents you require.'

Wheelock descended into his own thoughts for a while. 'I'll tell you all about it,' he said at last. 'And if you think what I just said was bad, well this is worse. Much worse. You know, of course, that Rawsthorne lost a lot of money when the Bayswater Bank crashed, but I happen to know that he was in trouble well before that. Tried to make a fortune on the stock market. A few men succeed that way, but he wasn't one of them. So when things were tight and bills needed paying he used to draw on his clients' accounts. When he was able to, he put the money back. I suppose he wasn't exactly a thief as he never meant to keep it, but it's not the kind of thing a solicitor ought to do. He's still in debt now, house mortgaged twice over, but marrying his brother to Mrs Outram would have solved all his troubles.'

'If this is true, and I am not saying that I believe you, then I am sorry to hear it. I wonder how many other men in his position would have been tempted to borrow from funds entrusted to them. But you say he put the money back?'

'When he was able to,' Wheelock repeated meaningfully. 'Don't you see it? When the bank crashed – something you played a part in I seem to remember – there were immediate demands from every creditor in Bayswater and no money to be had anywhere. And that was more or less the same day your father died. Died leaving you nothing but debts. All his savings gone in bad investments. So Rawsthorne told you. Now then, think of your dear old father and ask yourself this question, was he the kind of man to take risks with his money? Because I don't think he was.'

Frances was speechless as all the elements of the story suddenly fell into place. Tears sprang to her eyes and she pressed her hand to her face so he would not see them. When she had recovered a little she said, 'Are you telling me that Mr Rawsthorne took my father's money – his savings – what would have been my inheritance?'

'Yes. All of it. He needed it for an urgent debt, but thought he could pay it back. He had an investment with the Bayswater Bank that was due to mature in the next few weeks. Thanks to you, it never did.'

'And when my father passed away Mr Rawsthorne had no means of putting his account to rights, but he was in a position to conceal what he had done.' Frances tried to collect her thoughts. 'If true – and you have not yet supplied me with any proof – then the thing that grieves me most is not the loss of the money my father would have left me, it is the fact that he was betrayed by a friend and then branded a fool. Can you prove what you say? Because I refuse to accept it until you do.'

Wheelock scratched his scrawny neck pensively. 'No, not with ink and paper. Rawsthorne was too careful, he kept all that to himself. But he tripped up over Mr Agathedes. Now *that* I can prove.'

'Mr Marios Agathedes? The man who was once suspected of murdering Annie Faydon?'

'The very same. Rawsthorne thought he had burnt all the evidence, but I have fireproof fingers where those sorts of things are concerned. He knows I suspect, but he thinks I can't prove anything against him, and all he has to do is stop my mouth. Nothing would make him happier than to see me in prison, or better still, hanged.'

'Mr Agathedes has been judged insane – delusional.'

'Easy enough to do if you know the right people. Rawsthorne acted for him in a few small matters, but he soon found that Agathedes, while not himself a rich man, had come to England with a nice parcel of family money to invest. So Rawsthorne

kindly offered to look after it for him. Agathedes had told him
that the money would not be wanted for another five years so
Rawsthorne felt safe in using it for his own purposes. But after a
year Agathedes was offered a business opportunity and decided to
draw on the funds. When he went to the bank where Rawsthorne
told him the investment had been made, he found that the
account didn't exist. He went straight to Rawsthorne to demand
an explanation. Agathedes needed the money at once, or the
opportunity would lapse, so there was no time for Rawsthorne to
put him off. Agathedes couldn't prove he had handed the money
to Rawsthorne, who had kept all the important papers. Agathedes
could show that he had once had the money but there was nothing to prove that he had not squandered it himself. So Rawsthorne
simply denied that the transaction had ever happened. Agathedes
made a fuss, as you might imagine, and Rawsthorne accused him
of slander and had him removed. Then he burned the papers – or
so he thought.'

'Then Mr Agathedes is not mad after all?'

'No madder than I am,' said Wheelock.

'I would like a better assurance than that.'

'He went down with a brain fever, ranting about how he had
brought disgrace and ruin to his family, and when it was thought
that he might lay violent hands on himself, he was taken to the
asylum. Rawsthorne was very sympathetic and offered at his own
expense to write to Agathedes' family in Greece to advise them
of his condition and implore them to come at once. Strangely
enough they did not reply.'

'Because he did not write to them.'

'Very sharp, Miss Doughty.'

'And you have these papers well hidden I suppose. I imagine
Mr Marsden would dearly like to have them.'

'Oh he would indeed!'

'Then why do you not give them to him – or tell him where
they may be found?'

'Because if I did, I would not trust him or any agent of his
to pass the packet of papers to me unopened. There are things
in that packet that Mr Marsden does not currently know
I have, and would not wish to have made public. If he saw them,

he would destroy them, and then he would destroy me.' Wheelock sucked ink off the heel of his hand, pensively. 'Mr Marsden doesn't care for me much.'

Frances could have replied that no one cared for Mr Wheelock at all, but said, more diplomatically, 'Mr Marsden does not care for anyone. He particularly dislikes me.'

'That's because he thinks you have no business being cleverer than him. I don't like you either, but I like your brain. It's like a man's brain only better, because women are more enquiring than men, they know people, and their faults.' He grinned. His teeth were stained red and black with ink. 'We would make a good partnership. I'm a rich widower, I'm very eligible. Once I get off this murder charge we should get married.'

A shudder of distaste ran through Frances' body and she made no attempt to conceal it. 'Never say such a thing to me again.'

He shrugged. 'I didn't mean it in any case.'

'I assume that you wish me to retrieve the packet of papers and bring it to you.'

'Yes. I will then remove the papers relating to Mr Rawsthorne and you will pass them to Mr Marsden. The others I will ask you to seal and deliver to another agent who will keep them safe for me. And it must be done quickly. Before Marsden finds them.'

Frances gave this suggestion serious thought. She knew, of course, that she should have nothing to do with any of this man's dealings, and yet the opportunity of confirming what had happened to her own inheritance was impossible to resist. 'I make one condition. That before any papers concerning Mr Rawsthorne are sent to Mr Marsden, you must agree that I may examine them. That is the only proof I will accept that what you have told me is true. If I find you have not been truthful then I cannot act for you.'

Wheelock thought for a moment and nodded.

'And the other papers, the ones Mr Marsden does not want made public?'

'They will be, when the time is ripe, you can be sure of that.' Wheelock pushed a hand into an inner pocket and removed a small key on a thin chain. He unfastened it and handed it to Frances, then reached out for her notebook and pencil and wrote an address and some numbers. 'We haven't talked about your fee yet.'

'I am really not sure what it is worth,' she replied, reluctant to ask for anything from him.

'My life; my freedom. You might think they are worth nothing to you, but I put a value on them. Shall we say that it is a good turn you are doing for me, that you can put in your bank and draw upon whenever you like?'

Frances hardly cared. 'If you wish. But this business remains between us, and nothing of the like will ever be transacted again. What about Mr Chandler? I am sure you must know I am acting for him in the question of your marriage.'

'Oh these things get about. Can't hide much in Bayswater. You leave him to Marsden.'

When Frances left the station she felt that what she most urgently needed was a cleansing bath. It was a strange situation she found herself in, representing both Chandler and Wheelock. She would not under any other circumstances have agreed to it, but tried to reassure herself that assisting Wheelock to secure the services of a prominent solicitor to deal with the murder charge while simultaneously collecting evidence to contest the validity of his marriage were not incompatible or contradictory. A nagging voice in the depths of her conscience told her that she was wrong.

The distasteful task required her to travel out of Bayswater, which she did in a closed cab that took her to a select banking house in the City. There she presented the key and the details she had been given, and recovered a small package from a safety deposit box. The papers revealed – and she was familiar enough with Mr Rawsthorne's handwriting not to doubt it – that the solicitor had indeed received money from Mr Agathedes for the purposes of investing it in his client's name. She had wanted so much to find that the material did not exist or that Wheelock had somehow got a clever forger to write the notes, but there was no mistaking Rawsthorne's orderly hand, and the characteristic little flick of the pen at the end of each word was carried out with a fluidity and freedom that a copyist could not easily reproduce.

There were other fragments of correspondence too, items in which no names were mentioned, but which Frances, with her knowledge of the affairs of her own family, realised referred to her father. With mounting grief she saw the full extent of

Rawsthorne's betrayal. Frances reflected that she had only made promises to Wheelock about the Agathedes papers and the material that related to Marsden. He was probably unaware that material he might have imagined was part of the Agathedes papers actually referred to her family. Had she felt any trust at all in Marsden then she would have been content to pass this on together with the Agathedes papers, but she could not even be sure that he would recognise the documents for what they were. She therefore removed them to her own safekeeping.

Returning to Mr Wheelock with the horrid parcel lying like a toad in her reticule, the business was transacted. The remaining papers were separated into two bundles; the one relating to Mr Rawsthorne's dealings with Mr Agathedes were placed into an envelope for delivery to Mr Marsden, the other was parcelled for delivery to a solicitor in Regent's Park. With a heavy heart, and thankful that she could do so almost without words, or she thought she would have broken down, Frances assigned these errands to a trusted messenger, and was greatly relieved when she was told that both deliveries had been made.

CHAPTER TWENTY-FOUR

It was only once her tasks were completed that Frances finally allowed herself to consider the implications of what she had learned and what she had done. The one professional gentleman she had trusted all her life, she now knew to be a thief, a thief, moreover, who had stolen from an old friend, been content to see her left almost destitute, and had sent a man he had ruined to the asylum. She had seen the evidence with her own eyes and could not doubt it. That evidence would even now be in the hands of Mr Rawsthorne's bitterest enemy who would put it to use without delay. The effect of the collapse of Rawsthorne's long-running business could scarcely be imagined, but her only consolation was that he would no longer be free to ruin anyone else. The more she thought about it, the more her distress gave way to a blazing fury and when that had subsided there remained only a cold pitiless anger.

But what of her own client, James Chandler – was he what he appeared and claimed to be or was he the paid associate in a fraud operated by Rawsthorne? She had no idea. If she was to warn Chandler that Rawsthorne was in trouble and it transpired that the two were in league, then Chandler would take flight and a guilty man would evade justice. If he was innocent, however, he did not stand to lose either his fortune or his life by Rawsthorne's ruin. She decided to test the water on Mr Chandler by sending him a note asking if he had received any news from Mr Rawsthorne regarding the information she had supplied regarding the Wheelock marriage.

There was, however, another and far deeper concern. With Wheelock's defection, Rawsthorne must have started to feel the nets of justice closing in on him. He had been largely unavailable in the last few weeks and she began to wonder if he was not troubling himself to act for his clients at all, but preparing to flee London, or even England. Had he even been out of town at all as Mr Freke had claimed? While keeping up a pretence of normal business Rawsthorne would have been attending only to his own interests and those clients from whom he could extract large fees. He had probably only agreed to see Frances on that one occasion to prevent the suspicions of someone he knew was naturally suspicious. He certainly would not have been exerting himself for clients like Mrs and Miss Price. What, thought Frances, had become of the information about Jim Price that she had so trustingly handed over? She dedicated her afternoon to assembling copies of every fact in her possession regarding Jim Price and his alibi Mr Gundry and ensuring that urgent reports were sent by hand to the police, Mr Gladstone and the Home Office.

Then there were Rawsthorne's other clients, some of whom she knew. They had to be warned. Frances took a cab and had a brief private word with her Uncle Cornelius, who was able to confirm to her relief that he had no current business in hand with Rawsthorne, then she hurried down to the Grove for a quick call on Chas and Barstie. They told her that Mr Rawsthorne acted for them but there had been some unaccountable delays of late that he had said were due to pressure of work. She needed to say nothing more; they understood at once what news she had brought. She left them busily going through every item of paperwork in the office.

Frances then made a brief call on Tom who confirmed that in the last few weeks Mr Freke had dealt with most of Rawsthorne's minor cases, although one of his agents thought he had seen the man himself recently, sneaking about at a time when it was being given out that he was unavailable.

When Frances returned home she found a note from Chandler saying that there was no news from Mr Rawsthorne who, he understood, was back at his office, but he had been granted an appointment to see him the following morning.

She was reminded that Mr Marsden had asked her to report on her visit to Wheelock, and wrote him a short note.

Sir
I have received your letter of today's date and visited your client as requested. I have carried out a small service for him and will not act for him further.
F. Doughty

By the time this was done Frances felt more than just physically exhausted. It was only four days before the execution of Jim Price and she did not know if she had done enough.

Mr Loveridge called to show her some of his recent sketches, but he could see that she was weary and disinclined to talk. He asked if he might read to her instead, and she agreed as long as it was not concerned with the news, which she did not feel able to contemplate. He found Sarah's copy of Mr W. Grove's latest story *Miss Dauntless Goes to the Ball*, in which the intrepid heroine, partnered during an evening of glamour and excitement by a devoted swain wearing a long swirling black cloak and a Venetian mask, and who whispered words of romance into her willing ear, managed to thwart an assassination plot without so much as missing a dance.

By the time Sarah returned Frances was drowsy and Mr Loveridge quietly slipped away.

Frances was awoken in the night by a howling screaming noise that intruded into her dreams and which, she only gradually realised, was all too real. She rose from her bed and looked out of the window. A thrumming as if from a thousand drums mystified her until she realised it was produced by every pane of glass in the house rattling in its frame. It was the gale, but a hundred times worse than promised, sweeping along the street, bending trees, some of which had lost their branches, driving showers of leaves and dust before it, overturning handcarts, making high wild eddies in the areas in front of the houses, and battering the ash bins. Lights were going on in the houses opposite as sleepers awoke, and there was the occasional sound of glass or slates shattering. Frances quickly checked her bedroom window and satisfied herself that it was in no danger of breaking, then hurried to the parlour, where she was joined by Sarah, and they busied themselves pushing strips of paper into any crevices where window glass was vibrating dangerously.

'It's six o'clock,' said Sarah when they had done all they could, 'I'll make some tea.' They spent the hours before daylight watching the street. As the heavy storm raged it seemed to Frances to be a sign of the end of things, of the end of the world. It was, she thought miserably, the end of part of her world, an end she had brought about. She had liked Rawsthorne and, more to the point, she had trusted him. That was over now. As she sipped her tea she consulted the current Bayswater directory and read without enthusiasm the list of available solicitors.

As the morning wore on, the wind died until it was no more than a stiff cold breeze. With the immediate danger past, some of the residents of Westbourne Park Road sent their servants out with brooms to sweep up the litter of broken branches, collect the fragments of fallen roofing slates and restore order to the ash bins. Frances hoped that the damage was no worse elsewhere.

It was three days before Jim Price was to be hanged. Frances, anxiously awaiting the post, was relieved at the arrival of notes showing that her urgent letters of the day before had been received by the proper authorities and were being examined. She wrote to Miss Price to assure her that everything possible was being done. Should she be offering hope of success? Miss Price and her mother wanted hope, they dined off it, it sustained them. Even if Frances had not offered it they would have made their own out of nothing. Without hope they would collapse. Yet hope was a double-edged sword, since it could only last so long and once hope was dashed then their misery would be crueller than if there had never been any hope at all. Frances decided to communicate only the plain facts and not anticipate any result.

After the previous day's events Frances could, had she wished to, have secured the services of one of Ratty's men to keep a constant watch on Mr Rawsthorne's office and advise her of any developments, but she decided not to. She did not want to reveal her involvement by showing any curiosity about events that she would not have been expected to predict. She had carried out her task, a task for which she would not ask payment, and now she wanted to take a step back and entirely forget her role in that affair, sweep it from her memory as if it had never taken place.

Over breakfast, Sarah, eyeing her almost silent companion, demanded to know what had happened the day before and Frances realised that the friend who knew her better than anyone saw that something was the matter and probably suspected that some tender event had taken place between herself and the young artist. Frances was quick to reassure Sarah that Mr Loveridge had been a model of decorum, and then not without expressions of emotion, described her visit to Mr Wheelock and its results.

'Never liked that Rawsthorne,' growled Sarah. 'These professional gents get above themselves. You pay them to do what you want done and then they think they can do what they please. No better than a plain thief who robs you in the street. So what happens now?'

'I am not sure. I will wait and see. It was all so strange that now I think of it, it almost feels as if it happened to another person, or was quite imaginary, like something I have read in a novel or seen done on a stage. When I learn of the outcome I think it will be as much a surprise to me as anyone in Bayswater.'

'You've got two new clients coming this morning. Do you want me to see them, or make new appointments?'

'No. If they are able to make their way here to see me I shall conduct business as usual. And I would welcome something to occupy my mind.'

The newspapers arrived, and with them the claim that the Bayswater Face-slasher had been caught, a circumstance wholly attributed to the intervention of Scotland Yard.

The first visitor of the day was Dunnock. Frances was surprised to see that the boy appeared to have recovered from his ordeal two days before. She wondered how he had managed to put from his mind the horrible sight of Mrs Wheelock's disfigured body. Perhaps, she thought, he had not, and the damage was still lurking within, waiting to emerge in night terrors.

'It's like the last trumpet out there,' Dunnock panted, scrubbing hair from his eyes. 'The trees in 'yde Park are all torn up by the roots. One of the big 'oardings on the Bishop's Road got picked up and blown away like a leaf an' almost broke the canal bridge, an' there's more shops without windows than with. P'lice are all over the place.'

'I hope no one has been hurt.'

'Broken 'eads an' cuts an' that, yeh, I seen lots. P'lice are round Rawsthorne's, too. Dunno why. I went up there with a message this mornin' an' was tole 'e weren't there. An' then the p'lice took that clerk of 'is, Mr Freke, an' 'e were very upset, an' they 'ad to cuff 'im 'cos they thought 'e'd run off.'

Frances almost regretted her deliberate lack of curiosity and wished she could have found some reason to go there to witness that particular sight. 'Let me know if you learn any more,' she said, giving the boy sixpence. Dunnock pocketed the coin and ran off.

The first client of the morning, the wife of a tailor who had written to complain about a neighbour who threw rubbish into her garden, did not appear. Given the weather that had ravaged Bayswater, Frances was unsurprised; a little rubbish was currently the least of anyone's concerns. A Mrs Berkeley, a lady of the carriage class, did, however, meet her appointment, arriving half an hour late, complaining bitterly that the streets were full of broken chimney pots and that there were policemen everywhere warning drivers away from buildings in a dangerous condition, which was making travelling extremely inconvenient. She declared herself to be very annoyed and wished she had not come, and had only done so because her business was urgent. Frances supplied her with a glass of water and when her client felt sufficiently recovered, she said that she had come on account of her darling son Adolphus, who while the very best of young men, was keeping unsuitable company at the Piccadilly Club. He had already been questioned by the police for some small indiscretion, and his father had managed to deal with the matter before it came to court, and given him a good talking to, but she was concerned that he would be led astray by bad companions once more. She described him as a sensitive youth easily influenced by others, but on providing his portrait Frances felt sure she had seen him once before, only on that occasion he had been wearing his hat defiantly askew and was being ejected from Westbourne Hall by Sarah and Professor Pounder. She promised that the matter would be attended to. If young Mr Berkeley was in the company of the Bold Bloods then she would soon discover it.

The name Berkeley was familiar, and Frances recalled that this was the surname of the young gentleman Mr Digby had mentioned who had asked permission to call on his daughter. Was this the same young man or another? She wrote a note to Chas and Barstie.

A little later, Sarah, once Frances had reassured her that she would be perfectly content to stay at home with her correspondence, left to take one of her ladies' classes, and thus Frances was alone when there was a knock on the front door. Her visitor was Mr Chandler, who arrived with a desperately troubled expression and the demeanour of a man who had enjoyed little refreshing sleep of late.

'Have you seen Mr Rawsthorne recently?' he asked.

'I have not spoken to him for more than a week,' replied Frances, cautiously, 'why do you ask?'

'Do you happen to know where he is?'

'I am afraid not. I learned from one of my agents just moments ago that he was not in his office as usual this morning. I thought you had an appointment to see him?'

Chandler flung himself distractedly into a chair, and rubbed his eyes. 'I did. At ten o'clock. I went to see him as arranged, and I have just come from there. I know he resides above the office so I did not see any difficulty in his being able to see me despite the dreadful weather. To my surprise not only was Rawsthorne absent from the office but so was his confidential clerk, Mr Freke. And there were any number of policemen swarming all over the premises who appeared to be searching for something. A few junior staff were present and I tried to discover what was happening but they knew nothing about it and appeared to be very upset. No one would tell me anything. Is Mr Rawsthorne dead? I have heard rumours that there have been people killed this day, what with walls and trees being blown down.'

'I don't believe so.'

'This is very awkward. If I am to pursue my claim on my aunt's will I will be obliged to stay in London for some little time, and I need to make financial arrangements, since most of my funds are in India. What am I to do?'

'Have you given Mr Rawsthorne any of your funds to invest?' Frances asked, trying to make the question sound no more than idle curiosity.

'Not yet. That was to be the subject of the interview. Under the circumstances I think I had best seek another solicitor.'

'That would be my advice.'

Something in her tone must have alerted him, and he started and stared at her, suspiciously. 'You know something, don't you?'

Frances felt very uncomfortable. 'I can only speculate on what might have occurred, but whatever the truth is behind the situation you encountered today I think neither of us will know the full story for several days.'

'And you definitely don't know where Rawsthorne is?'

He was clearly dissatisfied with her replies, and Frances thought she ought to learn to dissemble better. 'I do not, but based on what you have just told me, if I was to hazard a guess, I would say he is most probably at Paddington Green police station answering questions.'

'But I entrusted some of my papers to him! When will I get them back? Are you saying that he is a charlatan?'

'I can't comment on that. If you speak to the police I am sure that when they have completed their work you will be able to recover your papers. In the meantime, there are several other solicitors in the area, smaller firms than Mr Rawsthorne's. You would be advised, however, not to employ Mr Marsden since he is acting for Mr Wheelock. Not that he would be averse to acting for both sides of the same dispute.'

'Who is your solicitor?'

'I am sorry to say, Mr Rawsthorne, so I am in much the same position as yourself. He has acted for my family for as long as I can remember, and I have never heard a word against him.' Frances took the Bayswater directory from the shelf and handed it to her increasingly agitated client. 'Does Mr Rawsthorne have the documents that you brought with you to establish your identity?'

'No, I still have those. Why do you ask?'

'Because your priorities and therefore your requirements have changed. When you arrived in Bayswater your main intention was to prove that your aunt's marriage to Mr Wheelock was invalid. Now that she is deceased you will want to make a claim under her will, and you will be expected to prove that you are her relative.'

'I don't see any difficulty about that, at least.' He studied the list of Bayswater solicitors. 'Is there a man here you can recommend?'

'They are all unknown to me by reputation.' She gave him a sheet of notepaper and a pencil. 'I can only tell you which are the longer established firms.'

'The ones who have got away with their villainy for many years, as distinct from those who are just starting out on that path,' he said, dispiritedly, 'I might just as well go to the nearest.' He began to write.

There was another knock at the front door, followed a minute later by the sound of heavy feet on the stairs, a familiar tread which Frances knew could only herald one person.

CHAPTER TWENTY-FIVE

A h, Mr Chandler,' said Sharrock throwing the door open, 'I thought I might find you here. I was told that you had been to Mr Rawsthorne's office this morning.' Sharrock was not the most smartly attired man in Bayswater at the best of times, but that morning his clothes looked crumpled and dishevelled as if he had not been to bed all night, and there was brick dust on his shoulders.

'Yes, for a business appointment which never took place,' said Chandler, bitterly, folding the paper and putting in his pocket. 'Where is Mr Rawsthorne?'

'Well, I suppose you'll know soon enough, he's under arrest. His big rival Mr Marsden has a face on him like a Cheshire cat – not a pretty sight. Under the circumstances we are currently interviewing all of Mr Rawsthorne's clients.'

'What offences has he been charged with?'

'That is being determined as we speak, but based on the evidence to hand, I'm expecting a nice long list.'

'This is very unfortunate, but of course I will assist you in any way I can. Perhaps if I was to come to the police station this afternoon?'

'You're to come now, Mr Chandler,' said Sharrock, mildly.

'But I have important business to attend to!' Chandler protested.

'Not as important as mine.'

Chandler rose, looking both annoyed and disheartened. 'And, of course, now I have no man to advise me. This is really too bad!'

'This must be a busy time for you today, Inspector,' ventured Frances, hoping to provoke him into revealing some useful titbit of information.

'Oh, you don't know the half of it! The station chimneys came down a few hours ago, fell right into the cells. I've got men hauling out the rubble now.'

'Is anyone injured?'

'I hope not, there's questions need asking. Still, we have to get on and do our best. Come on, Mr Chandler.'

'I assume you will want me also, Inspector,' said Frances, rising to her feet and going to fetch her cloak.

'And why would that be?' demanded Sharrock with a frown.

'Because I too am a client of Mr Rawsthorne.'

Sharrock looked awkward and Frances saw that this was something he had not taken into account. But there was more to it than that, she suddenly realised. If Wheelock had accused Chandler of being not only a fraud but a potential suspect in the murder of his wife, the true purpose of Sharrock's arrival was not to find a witness he could question about Rawsthorne's affairs, but to take a possible savage knife-murderer into custody. The motive he had provided was simply a ploy to get the man to the police station quietly and without arousing his suspicions. Sharrock had left her door slightly open and this belief was confirmed when she saw a constable on the landing outside.

'Very well, both of you then,' said Sharrock grudgingly.

Chandler glanced at Frances, thoughtfully. 'In any case, I would like Miss Doughty to be present at my questioning since I now have no solicitor and require a competent witness who has some familiarity with my affairs.'

Frances found her natural curiosity reasserting itself with full force. This was the perfect excuse to accompany Sharrock and Chandler to the police station and learn more about Mr Rawsthorne's downfall without revealing her part in it. Chandler, drowned in his own feelings of vexation, headed for the door where he was taken aback on being unexpectedly confronted by the constable who looked disinclined to step aside for him.

'Oh, just one little formality,' added Sharrock, casually. Sharrock was no expert in appearing casual, and a polite request from him always sounded as if it would be followed by force if not complied with. 'It's a quirk of our English police stations. We always take care to check that civilians are not carrying any weapons before we allow them in.'

Chandler submitted to a search with increasing bad grace. This revealed the presence on his person of a folding pocketknife. Sharrock took immediate charge of the find, disappointingly affording Frances no opportunity for a close look. Chandler was faultlessly neat about his person, but she knew that even the most careful of men could miss a spot of blood trapped in a crevice between blade and handle. They boarded a waiting cab in which Sharrock made sure that Frances was as far from Chandler as possible with the constable placed solidly between them.

On the way, Frances saw that Westbourne Park Road had been fortunate indeed in escaping with some slight damage to trees and roofs. The stout houses had stood up well, but further on, the commercial heart of Bayswater had suffered badly. Several of the shops which not been protected by shutters had had their windows blown in. Planks had already been hammered across open frontages, fringed with splinters like savage teeth, and carts were taking away shovelled heaps of broken brick, slate, glass and terra cotta. Everywhere was a misery of drifting debris, and unhappy people creeping on their way to important business, looking about them at their changed world with expressions of fear and wonder. Some humourist had chalked on a wall 'The Bold Bloods are to blame'.

Both policemen remained uncommunicative during the journey. Sharrock stared at Frances as if expecting her to pepper him with questions, but faced with the risk of exciting his suspicions by saying the wrong thing, she decided to remain silent.

The front of the police station showed no obvious external sign of damage, but inside there was a great deal of activity, and constables darted back and forth with worried faces. Inspector Swanson, who had been commanding operations in the manner of a military gentleman, took Sharrock aside as soon as he appeared, and there was a rapid discussion. Whatever Swanson had to impart, the news was met with a serious frown and at last Sharrock puffed out his cheeks and nodded. Swanson hurried away.

Sharrock had a word with the desk sergeant, then he conducted Chandler and Frances to the interview room, the constable accompanying them and standing at the door. They sat down, facing the Inspector across the table.

'I don't suppose I will have the opportunity of speaking to Mr Rawsthorne,' said Chandler.

Sharrock leaned back in his chair, looking as though he was waiting for something before he began the interview. 'He isn't here.'

'Can anyone tell me where he is?' asked Chandler with mounting irritation.

'At this very moment?' Sharrock consulted his watch. 'On his way to the cells of Marylebone police court, where he is to appear later this morning. I have just been informed that he has been charged with theft, fraud, embezzlement, and misappropriation of funds. That's just the first few we could think of and others might follow.'

Chandler sighed and pinched the bridge of his nose. 'I must say this is all very distressing.' He glanced at Frances. 'You seem to have very little to say for yourself. What am I to do?'

'Like you, I am awaiting the Inspector's questions.'

The door opened and a second constable arrived. To Frances' consternation, he was accompanied by Wheelock and Marsden. Both were seated, and the constable departed. Marsden was making no attempt to conceal his pleasure at the situation and Wheelock appeared unusually jaunty for a man who had just spent a night in the cells under suspicion of murder and then had the roof fall in on him. There was a scratch on his cheek but he seemed otherwise uninjured.

'What is this?' exclaimed Chandler, leaping to his feet. 'Inspector I am more than happy to assist you in your enquiries regarding Mr Rawsthorne, but I really cannot see why these – gentlemen – are present.'

'Mr Wheelock, of course, you are already acquainted with, and this is Mr Marsden his solicitor,' said Sharrock evenly. 'Now then Mr Chandler, you must sit down and the questioning will begin.' Chandler complied, but with great reluctance.

'I would like you to tell me where you were at six o'clock on Wednesday night?'

'I don't see the relevance of that question.'

'Just answer it please.'

Chandler looked at Frances.

'Just tell the Inspector the truth,' she advised.

'I am always truthful. But I cannot see why I am being questioned as if I was a criminal. Very well, if I must. Wednesday – that was the night before last. In fact –' realisation dawned. 'That was the night my aunt was killed, and as I have been informed, the time of her death.'

Sharrock was silent.

'Well, if you expect me to supply Mr Wheelock with an alibi, or provide any evidence concerning the tragedy, I cannot. I have already told you where I was at that time. I was in my lodgings, alone. I knew nothing of what had occurred until I received a message from Miss Doughty and took a cab to the police station. You have my address. What more do you need?'

Mr Chandler's lodgings were, Frances knew, barely five or ten minutes walk from any part of the route between Mrs Wheelock's home and Mr Rawsthorne's office, at some point on which the killer had entered her carriage. If Chandler had carried out the murder he had had ample opportunity to return to his lodgings and remove or destroy all traces of his dreadful work.

Wheelock chuckled gently to himself and Chandler flashed him a look of astonishment. 'I fail to find any amusement in this situation. It only confirms my opinion that even if you are not a murderer you had no regard at all for my aunt.'

'If she was your aunt,' sneered Wheelock.

'What in the name of heaven do you mean by that?'

'Just to make this clear,' interrupted Sharrock, 'Mr Wheelock here has informed us that after your visit to his home his wife revealed that she believed you were not her great-nephew at all but an impostor. If that is the case and you realised during your visit that you had given yourself away then it would provide you with a motive for murder.'

Chandler could only stare at him in speechless amazement. He glanced at Frances.

'You will receive no assistance or comfort from Miss Doughty,' said Marsden. 'She is in any case acting for my client.'

And there it was, thought Frances, the punishment for her sins. She had made a terrible error and now she was going to suffer for it.

'What?' Chandler cried out, aghast, 'But that is outrageous! Miss Doughty, tell me this is untrue!'

Marsden turned to Frances with an expression of supreme satisfaction. 'Do you deny that I wrote to you saying that my client had asked to see you, and that you complied with that request? Do you deny that you had a long interview with him and further, that as a consequence of that interview, you carried out a commission on his behalf?'

Frances was unable to meet Chandler's look. 'I do not deny it –'

'Because you dare not!' trumpeted Marsden with a smirk, 'I have here the very letter you wrote to me confirming the fact.'

'– but I wish to point out that the commission was in no way connected with my representation of Mr Chandler, which I believe he has found satisfactory,' she added weakly. It was not enough to rescue her from the appalling embarrassment.

Chandler groaned and buried his face in his hands.

Sharrock appeared unmoved. 'Mr Chandler, I suggest that you now hand over to me all proof of identity on your person. If there are any additional papers we require then we will send a constable to your lodgings to obtain them. In the meantime you will have to remain here.'

Marsden looked entirely satisfied with his morning's work. 'Thank you Inspector. I trust that our business here is now complete and my client will be released?'

'Not a bit of it. He stays put. One of these two men killed Mrs Wheelock and they both stay locked up until I find out which one did it.' Sharrock signalled the constable. 'Let's get them in the cells. I think we still have two that are habitable. You're not planning to give us any trouble are you, Mr Chandler?'

That gentleman appeared too dazed to contemplate such a thing. Unable even to look at Frances, he allowed himself to be led away. Wheelock, who appeared unconcerned, was also removed.

'You will hear more of this, Inspector,' said Marsden, gathering his papers. 'I trust and hope, however, that this sordid little incident marks the end of Miss Doughty's disreputable career as a so-called detective. In fact, I happen to have a client who is in need of a washerwoman, which I am sure would suit her far better.' He gave an acid snort of triumph and departed.

Frances was left feeling desperately ashamed of herself. She knew she could and should have refused to act for Mr Wheelock in any capacity, but had been lured into doing so with revelations concerning her own family, and the promise of proof. The information had brought her neither pleasure not profit, yet she could not help thinking that despite everything, knowledge was preferable to ignorance. Her only small fragment of comfort was knowing that there were papers in the possession of Wheelock's agent that would one day spell the end of Mr Marsden. It was a moment she would savour when it came.

Sharrock gazed at her sympathetically. 'Well Miss Doughty, here's a nice little tangle, and no mistake! Would you care to tell me what it was you did for Mr Wheelock?'

'No, Inspector, but I can assure you it was within the law and did not concern Mr Chandler's claim on his aunt's property.'

'Is he a right one or a wrong one, do you think?'

'I really couldn't say.'

'I do have one piece of advice for you.'

'Oh?'

'This might be one of those cases where you would be advised not to send your client an invoice.'

Frances had already reached that conclusion. 'Will you need a statement from me about my business dealings with Mr Rawsthorne?'

'I will. And any documents you may have which might assist us. Our evidence is sound, so any sympathy you may feel for the man will be wasted.'

'I have no sympathy for him and will help you in any way I can. I have only recently discovered some papers concerning my late father, which suggested to me that he did not after all die penniless, as I was informed, but that Mr Rawsthorne made use of my family investments for his own purposes. This arrest has merely forestalled any action I might have taken, although I have no hope of recovering what I am due.'

'He'll be made bankrupt, I shouldn't wonder. At least he won't want for accommodation though it won't be as spacious as he was used to. He should even have Mr Carter Freke for company.' Sharrock gave her a questioning look. 'And Mr Rawsthorne's downfall was not down to you? Come on, Miss Doughty, every other big upset round here has your fingermarks on it.'

'I have nothing further to say on the matter. I will tell my story in court if need be. But on another more pressing subject, can you advise me if there has been any news of Jim Price? The authorities are examining all the information I gathered, and I do hope that they will see sense and issue a reprieve, especially in view of the subsequent murders, all of which were committed when he was in custody.'

'No news, and to be blunt, I doubt there will be.'

'What of the man people call the Filleter? Has he confessed?'

'Funny cove that, no name, no address, no nothing. Swanson said he just sat there without a care in the world and denied everything.'

'But surely he'll be questioned again? We only have three days. You must make the man talk by whatever means necessary.'

'Thumbscrews? The rack? What would you suggest?'

'I really don't know, Inspector, I leave that to you.'

'Well that's all out of my hands in any case. Sergeant Brown has just dug him out of the roof fall and taken him to hospital to have him checked over for broken bones.'

'Is he fit to be questioned?'

'I've not been informed of that. Apparently he wasn't saying much when they carried him off. But Brown will stay with him until he talks.'

It seemed to Frances that every circumstance that might have saved her client was weighted against him, and through no fault of his or anyone else. 'Well you must not let the man escape.'

'Don't you worry about that. From what I was told, he won't be going anywhere for quite some time.'

CHAPTER TWENTY-SIX

rances arrived home to discover that the two elderly ladies who occupied the ground-floor apartments had decided that if they remained in Bayswater another day they would be murdered in their beds, or blown to pieces. They had accordingly paid their month's rent and quit the premises. Mrs Embleton, though understandably anxious about finding a respectable new tenant, did not ask Frances if she knew of any, presumably on the grounds that most of the people she was acquainted with were criminals.

There was a note waiting from Chas and Barstie. Mr Adolphus Berkeley, they revealed, a jaunty young fellow with an impudent nature who liked to wear his hat askew, was one of the leading lights of the Bold Bloods, and a particular friend and rival of Mr Pargeter. The two of them often engaged in wagers on every subject under the sun. Recently they had been meeting in private and it was rumoured in the club that a substantial speculation was afoot, the nature of which had been kept secret. Chas and Barstie promised to do their best to uncover the facts.

It was a commission that would no doubt lead to success but Frances thought she had little with which to congratulate herself. Her client, who might be both an impostor and a murderer, had been arrested, and Jim Price would almost inevitably go to the gallows. She could not decide if the Filleter was guilty of all the murders although she felt sure he had killed George Ibbitson. The other murders did not bear his stamp, but he was more than capable of carrying them out, and she wondered if they had been done at the behest of another person. Now he was lying in hospital with Sergeant Brown waiting at his bedside, and all she could do was wait and hope that very soon he would be able to provide the answers she so urgently needed.

Next day, the morning newspapers both local and national gave extensive coverage to the murder of Mrs Wheelock and the arrest of her husband. They had not yet been alerted to the arrest of Mr Chandler, although some correspondents who had come to Bayswater to report on the gale had found out about the remarkable events at the office of one of the district's leading solicitors, and had been busy questioning some of the junior staff. Frances had no wish to see Mr Wheelock again, and felt sure that Chandler would have the same reservations about her, and was therefore surprised to receive a summons to attend Paddington Green police station to speak to Inspector Sharrock.

She was conducted to his office, where there was now hardly room for two people, and he greeted her in a friendlier manner than he had done of late.

'The reason I have called you in here for a little talk is because I have some news for you. It's not in the papers yet but I thought you would want to know as soon as possible. In the light of recent events the Home Secretary has agreed to a stay of execution of two weeks for Jim Price.'

Frances gave a little gasp of delight.

'That is not to say, of course, that he will not be hanged when the two weeks are up, but it shows that it is recognised that there is new evidence that should be examined.'

'Has the family been told?'

'I've just come from speaking to them now, and they have gone straight to see him.'

Frances wondered if there was enough evidence to exonerate her client, and reluctantly admitted to herself that there was probably not. The best hope at present was for the sentence to be commuted to imprisonment for life, and she wondered how a young man such as he might face this prospect. There was, in her estimation, only one way of freeing him and that was proving that he had not murdered Martha Miller. She would, of course, write to the Price family to say how glad she was to hear the news and that she would continue to do all in her power to ensure that Jim was finally freed. How she might achieve this she did not know.

'Oh and Mr Chandler asked me to give you this.' Sharrock handed Frances a card. 'It is the name of his London banker. If you would present your invoice to him he will deal with it.'

'I didn't think –'

'No, neither did I, but it looks like he is now, due to your efforts, able to take steps to have the marriage of Mrs Outram and Mr Wheelock declared void, for which he is grateful. He doesn't, however, feel inclined to deal with you directly.'

Before she left, Sharrock suddenly said, 'That young lad who works for you – calls himself Ratty.'

'Yes,' said Frances, hoping her assistant was not in any trouble.

'I've been seeing him about, and I'm pleased to say he's smartened himself up. Quite the young gent.'

Frances smiled, recalling the time not so long ago when Ratty had been a small boy with a grubby face bundled in an assortment of ill-favoured rags. 'Yes, he has grown up fast.'

'You're sure he doesn't know his real name?'

'So he tells me.'

'Because he reminds me of someone. Can't put my finger on it, but there's something about him looks familiar.'

When Frances left Sharrock was shaking his head with the puzzled look of someone trying to extract an old memory.

It was the third Sunday since Jim Price had been condemned to die, but not now the last Sunday in his life. That morning in church, Frances gave silent thanks for the gift of more time and prayed for some inspiration that would finally set him free. Strange as it seemed to her, she also prayed for the recovery of the Filleter but only so that he could finally submit to questioning by the police, and confess to his crimes. He wouldn't be the first murderer to be carefully nursed back to health only to be hanged.

Sarah made them a hearty dinner, which Frances was too worried to enjoy. Had the weather been more pleasant they might have gone for a walk in Hyde Park, but it was cold and very windy and there was still some danger from broken branches. They stayed indoors and kept warm by the fire.

To their surprise there was a knock at the door and Sarah glanced out of the window. 'It's Hannah,' she announced, 'the maid at Wheelock's.'

Hannah arrived very chilly and windswept. 'I come to see Miss Doughty. I didn't know what else to do.'

'You have come to the right place,' Frances reassured her. 'Come and sit by the fire, and we will warm ourselves with some tea.'

Hannah cheered up at the welcome. If she was surprised to find Sarah there, she made no comment, but seemed relieved to see a familiar face. 'I expect you know that I am parlourmaid to Mrs Outram as was, and now poor Mrs Wheelock who was killed.'

'I do.' Frances said, 'Sarah has told me about your conversations.'

'I couldn't say all what I knew then. I was too afraid. We were all afraid, some of us more than others, except Daisy, and she was not a good girl, I could tell. She knew what was going on, and she didn't care. Only now master is locked up I come here to say what I couldn't before.' She cradled her teacup in her hands and shivered, but not with cold. 'Master – Mr Wheelock – before they were married he used to come and go, calling on Mistress with papers and things, and then one day they went away together in a cab – not the carriage with Mr Nettles but a hired cab, and no one knew where they were going. They came back quite a lot later and Mr Wheelock brought us all together and told us that he and Mistress were married and he was now master of the house. Daisy came back with them. That night Mary Ann packed her box and left and Daisy was lady's maid after that. We all had our orders. Mr Wheelock said that Mistress was old and unwell and he was going to look after her and do everything for her. He said she was wandering in her mind and got confused. Well she never wandered in her mind, but it wasn't my place to say so. Everything he did, it was all a pretence that it was for her good, but it wasn't. She was like an animal in the zoo. Kept in a cage and fed but never let out.' Hannah gulped her tea. 'And Mistress never used to drink much before. A sherry or a port, just the one, but then he started giving her more to drink, and she always seem to be a bit – well – under the influence. There was this decanter full of sherry and it was kept beside her all the time and Daisy used to give her glasses of it. Master said it was medicine and would do her good. But it wasn't and it didn't. So – I started to water it down. I had to be careful, because sometimes Daisy took a swig. But it meant that Mistress had a clearer head. The day before she was killed she wrote a letter.

It was to Mr Rawsthorne. She asked me to post it for her and I didn't know what to do. I didn't want to give it to Master and I couldn't get out of the house to post it, and I didn't trust anyone else to do it. So I put it in my pocket and waited my chance. Then that morning — the day she was killed, she asked me to take a note to Nettles, so I did. Nettles read it and told me that Mistress wanted to go and see Mr Rawsthorne, but he had been ordered not to take her out. He knew something was wrong though, and I said I thought Master was being cruel to her and she wanted to get away. And he thought so too. Then he said he was inclined to take her out, and not tell Master. I said he should. So that was what he did. Master was working in his study at the time. He didn't know anything about it until he came downstairs and found she'd gone. Daisy had been at the sherry so he blamed it on her and slapped her face. I never saw anything like it. Then he ran out.'

'And the letter?' asked Frances.

Hannah delved into her pocket and took it out. 'What with all the business when poor Mistress was killed I forgot about it. Then I thought I'd run up to Mr Rawsthorne's and give it to him but he wasn't there. I heard later as he'd been took off by the police. So I didn't know what to do, and then I remembered I had that card with your address on.' She handed the letter to Frances.

The envelope was addressed to Mr Rawsthorne in a shaky hand, and so imperfectly sealed that when Frances tried to peer inside the flap gave way. 'Well, I suppose that is a sign that I should read it.' She slipped the pages from the envelope.

The unhappy woman had written that she had never wanted to marry Mr Wheelock but had been forced to do so when he had threatened her. She did not know how to extricate herself from the marriage, but then her nephew James had come from India and he had grown up into such a kind clever young man. She knew he would help her. She asked Mr Rawsthorne to see if the marriage could be annulled. She also said that once she was free she wished to make some changes to her will, as she wanted to make a bequest to the Bayswater Vegetarian Society in her first husband's name. There was no suggestion that she thought Chandler was a fraud, and every indication that she had believed him genuine. Wheelock, Frances realised, not realising that this letter existed, had simply lied in order to suggest that Chandler had a motive for murder.

'She wrote this on the day before she died?' Frances examined the letter carefully and there was a scrawl that might well have been the date.

'Yes.'

'Hannah, I am very grateful that you have come to me. This letter is of vital importance, and I need to take it to the police. They will know what to do with it. In time, you will probably have to answer some questions, but if that means bringing Mr Wheelock to justice, I know you will be brave enough to do it.'

'If it means putting that awful man in prison, then I promise I will be.'

Sarah had a gleam in her eye. 'The police will want to talk to Daisy. I think I'll go round there and see she gets delivered to the right place.'

'She's run off,' said Hannah despondently, 'I don't know where to.'

Frances smiled comfortingly. 'Oh, I think I can guess where she might be found. With her former employer, Mrs Mary Wheelock of Lambeth. I'll make sure the police know where to go.' She poured more tea. 'Do you remember Mrs Outram's first husband?'

'Oh yes, very nice old gent, he was. She was very sorry when he died, though he was quite ancient.'

'You don't happen to know if he made a will just before he died?'

'I never saw any will. Not that I'd know what such a thing looked like.'

'You weren't asked to sign anything?'

'There was a paper I signed. Cook and me, we both did, but we didn't see what was on it. There was a gentleman – I don't know his name – very portly gent, he was, but he put a piece of paper over the writing and we signed at the bottom.'

'And you didn't see the paper again?' asked Frances, feeling sure that the portly man was the late Mr Thomas Whibley.

'No.'

'Did Mrs Outram ever burn papers? Especially after her husband's death.'

'Oh yes, she burned quite a lot. Mainly to do with vegetables. There were some books she had us bundle up and send to the vegetarian society, but everything else of that sort she just burned. And then she ordered a roast dinner.'

Frances decided to deliver the murdered woman's letter to Paddington Green police station in person. An idea had formed in her mind. Thus far the Filleter had confessed to nothing, but she wondered if the reason for this was the kind of harsh questioning he had been facing from the Scotland Yard men. Perhaps with her quieter less policeman-like ways she might be able to persuade him to make a confession. She decided to offer her services. The police might laugh at her, or doubt her, but she thought that she could win them over.

As soon as she walked into the station she knew that something was different. The interior was quieter than it had been of late, and while Sharrock was not there, she could see through his office window that the debris of papers that had accumulated over the last weeks had been stacked high against one wall clearing sufficient space to move about.

After a brief wait she was interviewed by a sergeant she had not seen before, but who knew her by name and reputation. She learned that Mr Chandler had appointed a new solicitor, a Mr Bramley, who had been gathering evidence to prove that his client was exactly who he said he was. Bramley was confident that this would be achieved with little further delay and there would soon be no reason to detain Mr Chandler any longer. Frances handed over the letter, which was both evidence against Mr Wheelock and in favour of Mr Chandler.

'Is Sergeant Brown here?' she asked hopefully.

'No, both he and Inspector Swanson have returned to their duties at Scotland Yard. There's the Mapleton trial coming on soon at Maidstone so they'll be fully occupied with that.'

'But I thought they would remain here until they were able to establish that their suspect should be charged. Or have they already charged him?'

'No, there won't be any charges for a while, Miss Doughty. The suspect hasn't confessed but they are as sure as anyone can be that they have their man. Inspector Swanson thinks that in his condition it could be several days, perhaps even weeks before they can question him again.'

'Weeks? I hope not. How serious are his injuries? I was going to suggest that I try questioning him. He might talk more openly to me.'

'He can't talk to anyone. Cracked skull, smashed ribs, punctured lungs. To be honest with you, it's very doubtful he'll recover.'

Frances stared at the sergeant, hardly knowing how to react. At last she said, 'And the murder of Martha Miller? What of that?'

'Solved and closed. We don't think that man had anything to do with it.'

It was a very foolish thought, but Frances realised that had she not effected the arrest of the Filleter when she did, he would not be in his current position, and unable, due to his injuries, to save the life of Jim Price.

Later that day, Chas and Barstie called with good news. They had succeeded in gaining the trust of young Mr Berkeley, and found him to be susceptible to alcohol, cigars and gambling. He was also less close-mouthed than his friend Pargeter and when plied with his favourite pleasures, and allowed to win some trivial wagers, he had admitted paying court to Enid Digby. He had done so, Berkeley revealed, not because he cared anything for her, as there were other girls he far preferred; indeed he had not the slightest desire to marry Miss Digby, not even for money, but because he had undertaken a substantial bet with Pargeter that he could win the maiden's affections. Chas had suggested that they make a bet on the subject too, and Berkeley had readily agreed, taking a notebook from his pocket and entering the details. Copious quantities of champagne were then consumed, after which Chas extracted Mr Berkeley's betting book from his pocket, and brought it to Frances. It was in the hands of Mr Digby within the hour.

Throughout the next day the news that the dreaded Face-slasher was in hospital and likely to die filtered through Bayswater. It was not as satisfying as a hanging, but all the same, there was a very tangible sense of relief, although a few nervous souls still felt unwilling to venture out. For some, however, the damage had been done and the streets would never feel safe again.

Mrs Embleton had let the ground-floor apartments very quickly and without the need to advertise. The rooms had been taken by Professor Pounder. It had formerly been the policy of the house to accommodate only ladies, but since the threat of violent crime had thrown the district into a state of terror, having a champion pugilist on the premises was not without its appeal. The Professor was gentlemanly and respectful and said he would move into the accommodation in one week's time.

Frances paid a visit to the Price family. Greatly cheered by the respite, they had visited Jim, whose execution day that should have been, and found him in good spirits. All were clinging to the hope that the full truth would come out in time to save him and he would be free, and were confidently expecting that the agent of his salvation would be Frances.

That evening Frances was at home alone. Sarah had gone to visit 'Mrs Jones', the young woman who was being maintained by the faithless Mr Pargeter, and had intended to be home in time for supper, but instead Frances received a note from her assistant saying that Mrs Jones had been taken very ill and she was staying to look after her. Depending on how the patient did, she might not be back until the following morning.

Frances was therefore left idle with her thoughts, and the more she thought about it the more she found herself unable to agree with the official view of the murders. The Filleter, whatever one might like to say about him, and there was a great deal to be said, was the kind of individual who killed for a reason, albeit that reason was usually money, and not from some senseless love of slaughter for its own sake. He had killed George Ibbitson to avoid capture. If he had killed Martha Miller then there had been a motive for it, a motive that had yet to be discovered. It could hardly be a coincidence, she told herself, that these were the only two murders where the victim's face had not been mutilated. Wheelock, she thought, had either killed his wife or paid a man to do it for him, but on re-examining all the details she held of the young female victims, Frances could see no reason why anyone would pay an assassin to remove any of them. The cutting of the faces spoke of some dreadful mania, a sickness in the mind of the killer. If she was right then the Bayswater Face-slasher was still at large.

CHAPTER TWENTY-SEVEN

rances could do nothing but start another round of letter-writing on behalf of Jim Price. She was feeling somewhat dull, and it was a welcome relief when there was a knock at the door and Mr Loveridge arrived. He was a little shy, but asked if he might make a sketch of her for a portrait. Frances agreed, and they sat quietly by the flickering fire as he studied her features, and there was the gentle whisper of his pencil on paper. It was a simple companionship, and she wondered again what his origins were. He had told her almost nothing about himself, and she had begun to think that this was a deliberate omission. At last he put the pencil down.

'Is it complete?' she asked.

'No, not yet. It's just that – I had something I wished to say to you. I hope you won't be offended, as we have only known each other for a very short time.'

Was it a trick of the firelight, wondered Frances, or was he blushing? 'Please, tell me what it is.'

'I suppose it's – in the nature of a confession.' There was a knock at the front door that startled him. 'Oh, are you expecting a visitor?'

'No. It might be for Mrs Embleton,' she said hopefully. 'Go on with what you were saying.'

He was about to, but they heard footsteps coming up the stairs, and the maid appeared to announce Mr Candy.

That gentleman seemed surprised and a trifle disappointed to see that Frances already had company, nevertheless he greeted them both. 'Miss Doughty, I have come on behalf of the Bayswater Vigilance Committee to thank you for all you have done in apprehending the criminal. Miss Gilbert and Miss John have apprised me of the circumstances, which are quite astonishing. You are a very courageous lady, and we are all extremely grateful to you.'

'That is most kind, but I am sure I do not deserve such gratitude. I am only relieved to have played some small part in the capture of such a dangerous man. I do hope, however, that you will not be disbanding the Committee or the Guardians. Their work is still necessary.'

'Oh, but surely the danger is over, now,' said Loveridge, innocently.

'I suspect that in the usual way of these things both those organisations will fall into obscurity,' Candy advised them. 'But they served their purpose when they were needed, and I am proud to have been a part of them. I know there were other murders while they existed, but who knows how many more there might have been which were avoided.'

Frances could not hide her concern. 'But I think they are still needed, and urgently. Please promise me you will keep them alive for a while at least.'

'Why is that?' Loveridge asked. 'Is there some new danger? I have not heard of any.'

'I am sorry to say it but I feel that there is still the old one.'

Candy looked bemused. 'I am afraid I don't understand.'

'It is my belief that the man who has recently been captured only committed two of the murders, those of Martha Miller and Mr Ibbitson. The rest were the work of at least one other person.'

The men were both silent and thoughtful for a time. 'People are saying that Mrs Wheelock was murdered either by her husband or her nephew,' said Loveridge, at last. 'They are both under arrest. Poor lady, she was said to be a great friend to charity. I called at the house once to offer to make a sketch and left my card, but I was never able to see her.'

Candy shook his head. 'I still think that ruffian was responsible.'

'Mrs Wheelock was killed in a closed cab,' Frances pointed out. 'She allowed her killer to enter. She would never have admitted someone of that man's unpleasant appearance. He was, in any case, in police custody at the time she was killed. But if any such ruffian had tried to get in she would simply have ordered her driver to move off.'

'In that case,' said Candy, 'one of the men the police already have in custody is her killer. Probably the husband. I have heard no good of him. As to the other murders, I and my friends on the Vigilance Committee are all of the opinion that the culprit has been caught.' He looked about him. 'Is Miss Smith here? I may have some business for her.'

'No, she is caring for a sick friend. You will be able to see her tomorrow.'

'Then I shall return. But the main reason I am here tonight is that the Committee has arranged a small reception for you. We have prepared a memorial to show our appreciation and hope that after the presentation you will join us for dinner.'

'That is very kind, but I am not sure I can accept that honour.'

'But it is all arranged. We are even now awaiting you. You need not worry that you have to make a speech, I will do all that.'

Frances had no great wish to go out that evening and much preferred to sit by the fireside with Mr Loveridge and listen to what he had to say. She wondered how she might politely refuse, but it seemed churlish to do so.

'I will quite understand if you do not wish to disappoint the Committee,' said Loveridge. 'Would you permit me to accompany you?'

'Mr Loveridge, you are not a member of the Committee,' Candy reminded him, sternly. 'You are not even one of the Guardians.'

'I would like to make a sketch. You are conferring an honour on Miss Doughty and it will be my very great privilege to record the event.'

Frances made a decision. She rose to her feet. 'And it will be mine to attend.' With that, Mr Loveridge went to procure a cab.

Mr Candy ordered the driver to take them to Leinster Square, where he resided and where the Committee met.

'I do hope,' said Loveridge, as the cab drew away, 'that for once, Miss Doughty, your concerns are misplaced and all the guilty men are under lock and key. Do you really think the scoundrel with the knife killed Miss Miller?'

'I can't prove it, of course, in fact I believe I never will, and I am very much afraid that Jim Price will still go to the gallows for a crime he did not commit. But I am sure about Mr Ibbitson, who I think was killed because he was trying to bring the man's crimes home to him. The police theory is that he was killed by the same man who cut his victims' faces but was interrupted before he could do so. I don't agree. The police did everything they could to find a witness who might have interrupted the murderer but no one has come forward.'

'It is said that the murderer wanted to kill women,' mused Loveridge. 'Why, I cannot imagine. Was it only because they are weaker and therefore easier to overcome? Or was there some other motive? The papers say that Mr Ibbitson was killed by mistake because of his disguise, and the murderer didn't go on with the face slashing when he realised that his victim was a man.'

'But how would he have known Mr Ibbitson was a man in the dark?' reasoned Frances. 'He had a very smooth youthful face, and even in the light, to someone who didn't know him, disguised as he was, he would have looked very like a young woman.'

At this point in the conversation a suggestion might have been put forward that the killer had committed other actions that would have alerted him to the sex of his victim. Frances knew that this was not the case, since the clothing had not been disarranged, and fortunately neither of the men was willing to air that particular subject.

'But you identified him at the scene of the crime,' said Loveridge. 'Was there much light?'

'Very little, but I identified him because I knew who he was. I recognised him from a bruise on his face.'

Loveridge was thoughtful. 'I am still wondering if this Face-slasher person did kill Mrs Wheelock. Perhaps there was a mistake about the time. I know some of the police think that. In fact I was able to find out something today. Now that the case is regarded as closed the police are being more talkative about it. I was told that Mrs Wheelock was disfigured in the same way as the others, although the murderer had more time to do it, and did it more thoroughly. But it was the same method. All the victims apart from Mr Ibbitson and Miss Miller were cut in exactly the same way.'

'Did your informant describe it?' asked Frances.

'He did, but it is very unpleasant.'

'You are right to hold back,' interrupted Mr Candy. 'I am sure that Miss Doughty has no wish to hear about it. It is not for the ears of a lady.'

'But I want to know,' Frances insisted. 'I have been trying to discover this information for weeks. Please don't think to spare me, I am sure I have heard far worse.'

'Are you sure?' said Loveridge cautiously.

'Sarah has been reading me the tales of old Newgate. After those, there can be very few horrors I am unacquainted with.'

The cab reached its destination, and drew to a halt.

Candy turned to Loveridge with a hard frown. 'Sir, I beg you not to upset Miss Doughty, whatever she might say. In fact I wish you to take the cab onwards and leave us now. I cannot approve of your attendance at this meeting if this is the way you behave.'

Frances made for the door. 'Help me down, Mr Loveridge, and then tell me what you know.'

She stepped out into the cool quiet. Leinster Square boasted a select terrace of tall houses with handsome pillared porticoes opposite some gated gardens. It lay between Hereford Road and Garway Road, just far enough from the bustle of Westbourne Grove to afford the fortunate resident an elegant retreat. The lamp-lit street was almost deserted apart from a cloaked figure clinging on to some railings, a masked reveller obviously very much under the influence of drink. He waved in friendly fashion at the arrivals, an action that almost caused him to fall, since he needed both hands to keep him upright, then cracked the silence with an attempt to sing a popular ditty in a high tuneless voice. They winced at the noise, but it was reassuring that the inebriate appeared to be of no danger to anyone but himself.

The cab drew away, and Frances looked expectantly at Mr Loveridge.

'I was told that the cuts were made as if the killer wished to obliterate the women, cancel them, cross them out. Large crosses like letter Xs. And then – and this is the thing I really cannot understand – he cut their noses off.'

No wonder, thought Frances, that the police had concealed that extraordinary detail. 'How remarkable! I wonder what it can mean?'

'It is fortunate that you stopped him in time, or he would have gone on killing, I am sure.'

Frances wondered why a man would hate women so. Why would he be impelled to kill them one by one? Why cut off their noses? Did he think that women were prying and poking their noses into areas they should not and wanted to stop them? There were many men who said women were doing just that – she had often been accused of it herself – but from disapproval to murder was a very long step. The killer was undoubtedly insane, but she could now see that there was a pattern to his insanity although it was something she could not fathom, a kind of – what was the word – monomania.

Monomania. She had read about it in one of her father's medical books. A passion, a frenzy concerning a single subject in someone who otherwise appeared sane. Perhaps, therefore, he did not want to kill all women, but only one woman; one who had aroused his anger and frustration and he was, by using the same method, killing her over and over again.

There was a pattern forming in her mind. A killer who was known and trusted by Mrs Wheelock. A killer who would have recognised Mr Ibbitson by his bruised face. And then there was the portrait of Miss Digby, the supercilious glance, the upturned nose that seemed to be tilted in scorn, how Mr Candy had once said that his betrothed had turned her nose up at him; the large crisscross markings he had made on the list of candidates for the Guardians of Virtue. She had not seen him arrive at the hall for the meeting, and had assumed that he had been there from the start, but there had been such a great crush of people. There had been time, she realised, ample time for him to carry out the murders, go to his home or his office, both of which were within a minute's walk of the hall, check himself for bloodstains, put on clean cuffs if necessary, and then arrive at the meeting as if nothing had happened.

Frances spoke very cautiously. 'I fear that I should not have asked for those details after all. I confess that thinking about it has made me feel very faint.'

'There, what did I say?' exclaimed Mr Candy. 'Mr Loveridge you should not have complied with Miss Doughty's request, she is more delicate than she might like to admit. Please leave us now before you upset her further.'

Loveridge was suitably contrite. 'Oh, please accept my apologies! I did not want to distress you, but you were so very sure you were equal to it.'

'Then it is my fault alone,' Frances reassured him. 'And now, I think that I would like to return home. Perhaps Mr Candy we will have the meeting of the Vigilance Committee on another occasion.'

'Of course,' said Candy. 'Really, Mr Loveridge, you have done quite enough for one evening. Now please go. I will conduct Miss Doughty safely home myself.'

Frances felt a prickling sensation like ants crawling through the roots of her hair. 'Would it not be best if you were to go and advise the members of the Committee that I will not be there tonight? Mr Loveridge can accompany me home.'

'Oh, but I insist on taking you to your home,' retorted Candy, and there was a steely note in his voice that Frances had not heard before. 'I do not trust you to be alone with Mr Loveridge. Why he did not even qualify as a Guardian of Virtue.'

'I had letters from a clergyman and a judge, but the man was caught before I could send them to you,' Loveridge protested.

'So you say, but am I to believe it? Now then, Miss Doughty, if you will permit me –' Candy went to take hold of her arm, but she flinched away from him. It was a horrible mistake, but she could not help it. She saw a sudden flash of anger in his eyes.

'It is very obvious that Miss Doughty does not wish to accompany you,' said Loveridge, placing himself between them. 'Really, I might almost think –'

It happened too fast to see. Candy struck Loveridge hard in the chest, and the young artist gasped as if the breath had been knocked out of his body and to Frances' horror he crumpled silently to the ground.

Candy turned to Frances. 'Oh you are far too clever for your own good. I am very sorry, Miss Doughty, I had grown to like and admire you.' He moved towards her and she saw that he had drawn a knife. There was no help to hand. Loveridge lay winded on the ground. The only other figure in the street was too drunk to assist. She screamed as loud as she could, turned and ran.

So many things passed through her mind as she raced along the street. Would help come in time? Who would hear her screams? Could she run faster than the man who wanted to kill her? Frances was young and strong, with long legs, but hampered by her heavy skirts she knew that she could not outrun a man for long. Should she dare to turn and confront him and take her chances with the knife, or should she just run and run? How she wished Sarah was with her. She felt her heart thudding in her chest, so hard that it was starting to hurt, and she had no more breath left for another scream, only running. She prayed that she would not stumble and fall. Behind her she heard the harsh panting and pounding steps of Mr Candy, and the sound was gradually getting closer. Soon he would be able to reach out and grasp her, perhaps by the hair, and then he would pull her head back and expose her throat to his knife. She would fight him, she was determined on that, she would fight with fists and feet, she would claw and bite like a wild beast, using every ounce of her strength, but she would not submit to the knife.

The figure when it came seemed to appear from nowhere. She was aware only of a tall man, his dark cloak swirling about him like a whirlwind, and the stark white shape of a Venetian mask. Frances staggered and fell against a railing panting with exhaustion, her legs trembling and weak, almost unable to support her. She hoped her saviour would not suffer for his intervention, all too strongly aware that the drunken reveller was all that lay between her and a horrible death. But the reveller was not drunk. He had never been drunk. He was swift and strong. There was a calm, ruthless and practiced efficiency with which he disarmed the murderer, and then with a single movement smacked Mr Candy's head against a gatepost. Candy slid to the ground unconscious.

For a moment, Frances thought she would join her attacker on the pavement. Then the masked man turned to her, holding out his hands. She managed to stumble forward, and somehow, she was never able to decide just how it had happened, she found herself enclosed in his arms, and pressed against his chest. She flung her arms about his neck, and felt the smooth line of his jaw lie against her forehead, and for a few intoxicating moments they clung together like lovers. 'You're safe now,' he said, 'you're safe.' And she was safe. If she knew nothing else, she knew that.

A police whistle sounded from the direction of Garway Road, and running footsteps approached them. Her rescuer drew back, and held her gently at arm's length. 'I think we can let the police deal with this fellow,' he said.

Wordlessly, she nodded.

He released her – she sensed that it was with some reluctance – and began to move away.

With an effort, Frances found her voice. 'Please! I don't know your name!'

He paused and turned back to face her. How she wished he would remove the mask. 'The name is Grove,' he said, 'W. Grove. Good night, Miss Doughty.' Then he was gone.

Her ordeal seemed to have taken minutes but in reality it must only have been seconds before her screams had alerted both the patrolling police and the residents of the square. Windows were going up and frightened faces were peering out at the scene below.

She looked around and saw Constable Mayberry and another constable hurrying up behind him.

'Miss Doughty!' Mayberry gasped, as he reached her. 'Was that you screaming? Are you hurt?'

'Thankfully, I am unhurt, but you must arrest this man at once. It is Mr Candy. He has just tried to murder me, and I believe that he is the Bayswater Face-slasher.'

'Oh, but I thought – well never mind, I know you are always right about these things.'

Candy began to groan and Mayberry quickly secured him with handcuffs, dragged him to his feet, and took the fallen knife in charge.

'Where is Mr Loveridge?' asked Frances, peering up the long terrace. 'He was with us but I fear he may be injured.'

'I don't know. I didn't see him on my beat.'

Constable Cross arrived, out of breath.

'Right,' said Mayberry, 'we have a dangerous man here so we need to get him back to the station to be charged with attempted murder and that's just for a start.'

'There's a body up there,' Cross told him. 'Stuckey is with it.'

Frances felt suddenly very cold. 'Who is it?'

'I don't know. A man.'

Exhausted as she was, Frances began to run again, retracing the path of her flight from Mr Candy to where she had last seen Mr Loveridge crumple to the ground.

He still lay there, stretched upon the pavement, his position unchanged. Stuckey was standing beside him but making no attempt to assist, he just wrote in his notebook. 'Help him!' Frances begged, but Stuckey only looked at her pityingly as she fell on her knees beside the young artist, and saw the spreading stain of blood on his shirtfront, directly over his heart.

CHAPTER TWENTY-EIGHT

After the inevitable interview at the police station, an event that passed with the torment of a waking nightmare, a note was sent at Frances' request and Cedric arrived. Waving aside all Sharrock's objections he put her in a cab, and took her back to his apartments where he and his manservant Joseph coddled and fussed over her. When she was finally able to sleep from a combination of brandy and sheer exhaustion, they wrapped her in a warm quilt, and laid her on Cedric's handsome wide bed while Cedric slipped away to sleep elsewhere.

Next morning, Sarah came to take Frances home and she did not stir from the house or see any visitors for several days. Prospective clients were firmly turned away, letters remained unopened, and newspapers unread. Sarah gave her the kind of quiet companionship that demanded nothing, and supplied a watchful and reassuring presence. From time to time little gifts would arrive from friends; hothouse flowers, little cakes and baskets of fruit. The flowers Frances admired, but she had very little appetite even for her favourite treats. One day Sarah went out and bought two picture frames for the sketches made by Mr Loveridge, which were placed on display.

One matter had at least been resolved. On Sarah's visit to 'Mrs Jones' she had discovered the young woman in the throes of a fit, and had at once summoned a surgeon. It had taken the vigorous efforts of both, but they had managed to save the life of the unfortunate woman and also preserve that of the child she carried. When the patient was finally able to speak she said that she had been given something to drink by her betrothed, Mr Pargeter. It had smelt of almonds and tasted strange but he had told her it was a medicine that would do good to herself and the child and she had trusted him. There was no doubt in the mind of the surgeon that she had been given a deadly poison and Pargeter, who had clearly hoped that his mistress would be thought to have taken her own life, had been arrested and charged with attempted murder. This revelation was too much for the Bold Blood fraternity who promptly disowned their leader and disbanded.

Following the removal of her beloved suitor into the hands of the police, Miss Digby had managed to swallow her disappointment and was about to consider the offer from his rival Mr Berkeley, but had then been shown the evidence that he had only wooed her for a wager. Since her last remaining beau was now known to be a dangerous lunatic, her father had decided to send his unfortunate daughter abroad for a long holiday.

The arrest of Mr Candy had naturally created considerable disarray in the three charities he had managed, but all was soon settled when Mrs Hullbridge and a committee of ladies arrived to take charge with an energy and determination that was gratefully received by all concerned.

If Frances reflected on Mr Candy at all, it was to berate herself for not realising that he was a killer. The charity work, which had given him a false front of benevolence, his lack of any proper feeling which had appeared to be no more than the natural reticence of a shy young man, and his quiet ordinariness had fooled everyone. Despite this, Frances still felt that she should have been able to see him for what he was. She began to doubt if she was fit to be a detective.

A week after the tragedy of Leinster Square a note arrived, addressed to Frances, hand delivered by a constable from Paddington Green. Sarah said she thought it should be opened, and Frances, after some hesitation, was reluctantly obliged to agree. It was an invitation for them both to take tea with Inspector and Mrs Sharrock.

Frances had little stomach for anything, but she knew she ought to go. 'It is unusually thoughtful of the Inspector not to demand my presence at the police station. I assume that this is not primarily a social event, and he wishes to ask me some questions, yet he has taken care that I should feel comfortable.'

An affirmative reply was sent and later that afternoon a cab delivered them to the Inspector's cottage. The parlour was warm and light, and a tea table was amply furnished with everything that Frances might have wanted to eat had she had any appetite.

Mrs Sharrock was pouring boiling water from a giant kettle into a large brown teapot, and looked at Frances with some sympathy, not liking to mention how pale and thin she appeared. The older Sharrock children, all scrubbed and brushed for the visitors, sat around the table, gazing hopefully at an array of large tea plates the heaping contents of which were covered in snowy napkins, while the youngest and most impatient sat on her father's lap, squeezing bread and butter tightly in her fists so it emerged like pastry between her fingers.

'I'm so glad you could come to tea with us, Miss Doughty,' said Mrs Sharrock. 'Bill talks so much about you, and I have asked him that many times to introduce us.'

'It is my pleasure to meet you and your family,' replied Frances. The plates were uncovered and she accepted a cup of tea and a sliver of sponge cake. 'There is something I should tell you. As a result of recent events I have come to a decision. Inspector, you will I am sure be very pleased to hear it. From now on, I will no longer be following the profession of private detective. I have given this a great deal of consideration, and I believe it is for the best. Other detectives I am sure are able to dismiss their errors and failures without giving them any thought. I cannot.'

Sharrock managed to steer a cup of tea to his mouth, while his infant daughter smeared butter into his hair. 'There's many a criminal in Bayswater will rejoice at the news, but I think it is a wise decision.'

'But you didn't fail, Miss Doughty,' protested his wife. 'You caught a very dangerous man.'

Frances shook her head. 'Not soon enough. I feel I ought to have seen all the signs earlier, and been better at what I did. If I had been then poor Mr Loveridge would still be alive. I cannot help but blame myself for what happened.' Frances had recently had the unhappy experience of a meeting with the young artist's parents, who wanted to hear about his last moments. His father, she had discovered, was a judge of the assize courts, who had hoped that his son would follow him into the legal profession. On discovering that the youth was determined to become an artist he had allowed him the space of two years to make a success of his preferred occupation, after which, if he failed to do so, he should agree to study for the law. He had been under strict orders not to reveal his family connections but to succeed solely on his own merits. Quiet pride was a salve to their pain as Frances told them of their son's bravery in defending her against a dangerous killer, and tears were shed by all.

'If it's any comfort the police don't hold you responsible for that,' said Sharrock. 'No one does.' His infant daughter almost knocked the hot cup of tea from his hand, and with Mrs Sharrock occupied Sarah very firmly took charge of the child, who stared at her with large round eyes. 'I do have some good news for you, though,' he went on, brushing crumbs from his lap and rubbing a napkin over his buttered hair. 'You know, I suppose, that Mr Candy has confessed to all the killings?'

'No, I did not know that. Mrs Wheelock's as well?' Frances suddenly recalled that she had told Mr Candy of how the Filleter had leaped into her hansom cab and feared that this had given him the idea of committing murder in a carriage. Was she to blame for everything? It seemed so.

'Yes, well, once we had him for one murder we couldn't have stopped him confessing if we had wanted to. It's my theory he is aiming to be thought a maniac, and escape the noose. Not that spending the rest of his natural life in Broadmoor will be any easier on him. The thing is – one of the murders he confessed to was Martha Miller's.'

'Oh!' said Frances, in great surprise. 'And – do you believe him?'

Sharrock piled a plate with cake and sandwiches. 'I have to admit I wasn't so sure, at first, I thought it was just another one he had added to the tally to make it certain he would be judged insane, and when I questioned him he didn't seem to know any more about it than was in the papers. But he doesn't have an alibi for that night, and then more importantly there is all the work that you did, finding the witness to support Mr Price's story. I think that was the clincher. I saw a note from the Home Office this morning, and putting all the facts together, it's been decided to accept Mr Candy's confession, and Mr Price is about to get a Royal pardon and be freed.'

In all her misery, Frances at last felt some healing joy. 'But that is wonderful! I hope the family have been told.'

'They have learned of it today, and I am sure you will get a visit from them very soon. There's no doubt in my mind that if it hadn't been for you, he would still be a condemned man. Not that that's any reason for you to take up detective work again. I just thought you ought to know.'

'That is the best news I have heard in a very long time.'

'Of course the slight damper on the proceedings is that we had to release Mr Wheelock. He's been charged on the forced marriage, but he's out on bail. I would have liked to see that slippery customer behind bars permanently. Mind you, he's young, so I might get to do that yet. Oh, and Mr Chandler's in the clear, and not only for the murder of Mrs Wheelock. We had word from some friends of his family in India. He was able to answer some questions they put to him, and it's now understood that he is the genuine article.'

Frances felt somewhat ashamed of herself, both for believing Mr Wheelock's lies and causing the harmless Mr Chandler such pain. 'I feel sorry now that I doubted him, although I have met so many frauds it is beginning to come naturally to me. I am sure he will succeed in getting his aunt's marriage invalidated.'

'Oh, you may trust to that, although I suspect that Marsden will manage to find some way of keeping Wheelock out of prison. In fact I wouldn't be surprised if Wheelock ended up working for Marsden. They seem to suit each other.' Sharrock gulped his tea noisily, and his wife bustled about the table keeping plates and cups well filled. In the face of six hungry children the heaps of food seemed to melt away like snow in the sun.

'What of the Filleter? Is he still alive?'

'Alive, if you call it living. If he does recover he won't be the man he was.'

'Even if he can't be charged with the murders there must be a catalogue of crimes that can be laid at his door.'

'They won't be making any charges. Swanson says there's not a lot of point, since he isn't fit to plead. He's in the workhouse infirmary now, and likely to stay there, and that's worse than any prison if you ask me.'

Frances finished her sponge cake, which was excellent, and accepted a second cup of tea. A buttered scone appeared on her plate. 'I have been told that Mr Rawsthorne has been committed for trial at the Old Bailey.'

'He has, and Mr Agathedes who lost his mind has found it again and will be giving evidence against him.'

'I hope I won't have to appear in court. As far as I am concerned the money is gone and there is an end of it. What about Mr Carter Freke? Has he been charged?'

'He'll be in court, but as witness, not defendant, and singing like a bird. Sometimes you have to let the sparrows go free if you want to catch the hawks.'

'The thing I regret most is losing an advisor who I thought was also a friend.'

'Speaking of friends, this man you mentioned in your statement, the one who came and saved you from Mr Candy. Just between the two of us, did you really not know who he was?'

'I have told you, Inspector, he did not show me his face, his voice was muffled by the mask he wore and he gave an obviously false name.'

'Hmmm, well you were lucky he was about.'

Frances agreed with him, though secretly she thought that there had been no actual luck involved. She often thought about Mr Grove; the commanding power with which he had immobilised her attacker, and the tenderness of his arms around her. There had been a scent, too, a delicate aroma of spice and citrus, like a gentleman's soap. She was not familiar with it, but she thought that she would know it again.

The next day Frances was pleased to receive a visit from Mrs and Miss Price, accompanied by Jim, a free man at last. He looked deadly pale, and prison had aged him a little, but Frances thought that with the care of his loving family he would recover both his looks and health. What effect his ordeal had had on his mind she could not say. He expressed his warm and grateful thanks but was almost too exhausted to speak, and Mrs Price held tightly on to his arm as if he would vanish if she let go. Effie was the most talkative, and gushed with praise for Frances. It seemed wrong to speak of payment and Frances waved away any suggestion that she might submit an invoice, but Effie said that if she liked, Jim could make a handsome piece of furniture for her, and it seemed impolite to refuse.

'We have decided to leave Bayswater,' said Effie. 'We think it for the best. Even though the world now knows Jim to be innocent there are always those who don't like to be proved wrong. We worry that if we stay here the police will be constantly watching him and trying to catch him out. Also, his old employer had put another man in his place and doesn't want to discharge him, and we find that there is no other work to be had for him here. Luckily we have an uncle with a carpentry shop in Whitechapel, who is happy to employ him. We mean to live very quietly and Jim has promised to be a model of good behaviour.' As they departed for a new and better life, Frances enjoyed a brief moment of contentment. At least one thing she had done had had a good result.

Frances' determination to no longer work as a detective remained unchanged. She would continue to carry out her occasional missions for the government, which required little more than delicacy and careful observation. She would undertake research for clients in Somerset House and newspaper offices where no crime was involved. Sarah would still deal with her own cases and teach callisthenics to ladies at Professor Pounder's academy. They would manage.

The quiet time gave Frances the opportunity to think about her own family. Since obtaining the certificate showing that Vernon Salter, the man she believed to be her natural father, had married Lancelot Dobree's daughter Alicia, she had been studying the newspapers with even greater care for any reports that might add to her knowledge. Thus far she had found only one item. Lancelot Dobree had recently been the distinguished guest of a school in Kensington to distribute the annual prizes in connection with his membership of the Worshipful Company of Mercers, which made grants to the school. She had also located his address in a Kensington directory, the same entered as Alicia's address on the marriage certificate.

Her mother's old schoolfellow, Vernon Salter's sister, Louise, had proved impossible to find. Frances had given some thought to trying to find Miss Edith White, the other witness to the wedding, but with no further information, the common surname was an obstacle. It was as she studied the certificate that she had a new inspiration. Many of her father's papers had included fragments of old copies of the *Chronicle*. She had never been certain if they were there purely as wrapping or if they carried any relevant material, but had retained them. With a new spark of determination Frances went through all her family papers once more, and this time discovered amongst them a yellowed page cut from the *Chronicle* dated April 1865.

It was reported that Alicia Dobree, only daughter and sole heir of Lancelot Dobree, silk mercer, had married Vernon Salter, gentleman. There were descriptions of the bride's and bridesmaids dresses, and the best man was Mr James Felter, silversmith. An examination of the Bayswater directories did not reveal any resident of that name. So William Doughty had known for certain the identity of the man for whom his wife, Frances' mother, had deserted him. The newspaper gave no details of the groom's family other than that he was the son of Bernard Salter, silversmith, which Frances already knew. There was, however, a paragraph about Lancelot Dobree. The son of a silk weaver, he had married his childhood sweetheart in 1827 but she had died only a year later. He had never remarried, but devoted his life to good works. Alicia must, therefore, have been thirty-seven at the time of her wedding, an extraordinarily advanced age for the first marriage of an heiress.

The thing that most puzzled Frances, however, was how Vernon Salter, son of a former bankrupt who had died in 1864 with barely a few pounds to his name, had just months later made such a glittering marriage. She put the papers aside.

Letters from applicants for her services as a detective continued to arrive and received polite replies regretting that Miss Doughty was no longer undertaking enquiries. Anxious visitors offering

large sums of money were turned away, sometimes more than
once. Ultimately she was obliged to place a notice in the *Chronicle*,
but some would-be clients were unable to believe what they read,
and still came to her door hoping that she would make an exception for them.

'Is it really true?' exclaimed Mr Fiske, who arrived with a rolled up
copy of the *Chronicle*. 'Oh please say it is not!'

'It is true. If you wish me to draw up your family tree I will
gladly do so, but I cannot become involved in anything that might
lead to criminal charges.'

He groaned, and sank into a chair. She poured him a glass of
water. 'There are other detectives in Bayswater,' she reminded him.

'Doubtless, but none with your discretion and perception.'

'Sarah does undertake her own cases, but she generally acts for
wronged wives.'

'Oh, it is nothing like that! No no, not at all, in fact it is the
most unusual and intriguing mystery. I could scarcely credit it, but
a man has actually vanished into thin air from within a locked
room.'

'Is that possible?'

'I assure you it is. I was present at the time. Please, at least let
me describe the incident. Any comment you might have to make
would be appreciated. And I promise that you will hear a remarkable story.'

She smiled. Mr Fiske was not a fanciful man, and she decided
to hear him out. 'Very well, you may have my observations gratis.'

He breathed a sigh of relief. 'You know, of course, that I am a
Founder and Past Master and currently Charity Steward of the
Bayswater Literati Freemasons' Lodge.'

'I do,' said Frances who was well aware that there were several Bayswater schools that had good reason to be grateful to the
Literati.

'Two nights ago at our regular meeting we were very pleased to
welcome a distinguished visitor from another Lodge. Our meetings are held in a room above a tavern in Kensington, which we

share with a number of other Lodges. During one part of the ceremony it is customary to extinguish the lights, which were out for a number of minutes, and when the lights were re-lit we found that our visitor was no longer there.'

'And you say that the room was locked?'

'Yes. One door secured and guarded by one of the brethren. The other locked.'

'I assume you have checked to see if your guest arrived home?'

'We waited to receive a note of explanation but when nothing came we made discreet enquiries at his home. His servants told us that he had left word before going to our meeting that he planned to be from home on business for a day or two so he was not yet expected back. The man is missing and it seems that only we know about it. Of course he may have gone missing for his own reasons and I would hesitate to inform the police, since we don't even know if a crime has been committed. But all the same it is most peculiar.'

'That is curious,' Frances admitted. 'I understand your concern. I assume that such behaviour is quite out of character with this gentleman. Of course, he may have sent you a letter, which has been lost or delayed. If he does not return home his servants will in due course report the matter to the police, however, it might be as well for you to inform them now of what has occurred. You will have done your duty and they will keep a look-out for him.'

Fiske sighed. 'I do hope he has come to no harm. He is a well-respected man, and I am certain that he would not have become involved in anything disreputable. Are you sure you cannot help?' he pleaded.

'Let me know his name. All I can promise you is that if I hear any news of him I will tell you at once.'

'Very well,' said Fiske. 'His name is Dobree. Lancelot Dobree.'

✳ END ✳

AUTHOR'S NOTE

On the morning of 14 October 1881 Britain was lashed by severe gales, and there was considerable damage in Bayswater, where shop windows were blown in and trees torn up. At Paddington Green police station some chimneys fell into the cells, which were unoccupied at the time.

Norfolk Square and its gardens may be visited today, but All Saints church is no longer there. Originally constructed in eleventh-century Gothic style, it was consecrated in 1847, burnt down in 1894 and rebuilt. Closed in 1919 it was later demolished.

Victoria Place is still there but was renamed Bridstow Place in 1938. Richmond Road has been renamed Chepstow Road.

The Newgate Prison of Frances' day was completed in 1782 and public executions were performed outside its walls from 1783 to 1868. It was closed in 1902 and demolished two years later.

The Cooper's Arms is fictional, though Bott's Mews and Celbridge Mews are real, as was the Shakespeare public house at No. 65 Westbourne Grove, whose landlord in 1881 was Mr Charles Bonsall.

Donald Sutherland Swanson, born in Truro in 1848, was an Inspector with the CID in 1881. He first came to public notice in July of that year when he arrested Percy Lefroy Mapleton, the Brighton Railway murderer. That autumn he was busy with enquiries into the Lefroy case, but in this work of fiction I have allowed him a little time at his disposal to apply his energies to the case of the Bayswater Face-slasher. In 1888, as Chief Inspector of the CID, he was in charge of investigating the Whitechapel murders. For more information see *Swanson: The Life and Times of a Victorian Detective* by Adam Wood (Mango Books, 2015).

Ignatius 'Paddington' Pollaky was a private detective known for his keen questioning and mastery of many languages. He retired in 1882. For more information see *'Paddington' Pollaky, Private Detective: The Mysterious Life and Times of the Real Sherlock Holmes*, by Bryan Kesselman (The History Press, 2015).

Thomas Ernest Boulton and Frederick William Park were cross-dressers and defendants at a notorious trial in 1871 accused of conspiring to commit an unnatural offence. They were acquitted. For a detailed biography see *Fanny and Stella* by Neil McKenna (Faber & Faber, 2014).

Angela Burdett-Coutts was an extremely wealthy philanthropist. In February 1881, at the age of sixty-seven, she married her twenty-nine-year-old secretary who was also very active in trading and philanthropic ventures.

'Men whose heads do grow beneath their shoulders' are mythical creatures referred to in Shakespeare's *Othello*.

Mr Barkis, a character in Charles Dickens' *David Copperfield*, indicates with the words 'Barkis is willin'' that he wants to marry Clara Peggoty.

The British Bull Dog introduced by Philip Webley & Son of Birmingham, England, in 1872, was a small, double-action five-shot revolver, suitable for carrying in a coat pocket.

ABOUT THE AUTHOR

Linda Stratmann is a former chemist's dispenser and civil servant who now writes full time. As well as the Frances Doughty mystery series, she is also the author of the Mina Scarletti mysteries, set in Brighton. She lives in London.

ALSO BY THE AUTHOR

IN THE
FRANCES DOUGHTY
MYSTERY SERIES

The Poisonous Seed: A Frances Doughty Mystery

The Daughters of Gentlemen: A Frances Doughty Mystery

A Case of Doubtful Death: A Frances Doughty Mystery

An Appetite for Murder: A Frances Doughty Mystery

The Children of Silence: A Frances Doughty Mystery

IN THE
MINA SCARLETTI
MYSTERY SERIES

Mr Scarletti's Ghost: A Mina Scarletti Mystery

The Royal Ghost: A Mina Scarletti Mystery

PRAISE FOR THE FRANCES DOUGHTY MYSTERY SERIES

'If Jane Austen had lived a few decades longer,
and spent her twilight years writing detective stories,
they might have read something like this one.'

Sharon Bolton, bestselling author of the Lacey Flint series

'A gripping and intriguing mystery with
an atmosphere Dickens would be proud of.'

Leigh Russell, bestselling author of the Geraldine Steel novels

'I feel that I am walking down the street in
Frances' company and seeing the people
and houses around me with clarity.'

Jennifer S. Palmer, Mystery Women

'Every novelist needs her USP: Stratmann's
is her intimate knowledge of both pharmacy
and true-life Victorian crime.'

Shots Magazine

'The atmosphere and picture of Victorian
London is vivid and beautifully portrayed.'

www.crimesquad.com